DEATH AT THE HIGH-END

A Brad Stephens Novel

Hole #2

J.A. MALONEY

1

HE AWOKE EARLY, AROUND SIX A.M.—A DISTASTEFUL JOB AND, IRONICALLY, PROFES-
SIONAL BASEBALL ON HIS MIND.

After doing his customary hundred push ups and two hundred crunches, he turned on the television just in time to catch the local weather report. The announcer, a geeky looking guy in a polka-dot bow tie and cheap gray suit with a flower in the lapel, announced that San Diegans would experience another summer day of early morning low clouds giving way to sunshine around eleven thirty along the coast.

How boring.

He didn't like predictability. The nature of his business required him to plan his movements meticulously but do so without establishing a repetitive pattern. Today, for instance, he would visit the pool and Jacuzzi early. He would take a good book with him and order breakfast by the pool. Yesterday, he ate in the café. The day before, he ventured out.

Unpredictable.

If the hired help was asked questions about the man in room 227, they would confirm that he acted like any other normal tourist.

Nothing special.

No unusual characteristics.

Just another ordinary guy.

Tonight, he hoped the fog would stay offshore until late evening. He was going to the ballgame and wanted to dress light.

As he ventured poolside, he took great pains to ask the front desk and bell men for directions to the ballpark. It was important they know he intended to go to the game downtown. It started at five p.m. and would take him at least an hour to get there from the coastal hotel. The time line should provide adequate coverage for his afternoon activities.

He wondered if he'd really ever need a true alibi. After all, he had been performing his duties on this specific assignment for several weeks. Neither the local police from San Francisco to San Diego to Palm Springs, nor the FBI—or whatever special Federal task force they used these days— appeared close to catching him.

Hell, they hadn't even discovered a plausible motivation behind his crimes.

The 'experts' seemed fully content labeling him a "Serial Killer" with a pent up grudge against people in a certain profession. In this case, real estate agents. Obviously, they concluded, the killer either had 'mommy issues' or had been burned by the recession and was now acting out.

He was sure that law enforcement spent hours—if not days—researching local real estate transactions that had gone awry, death threats that had been made to local realtors, or digging for any violent connection to the local real estate communities in which the murders had occurred.

What idiots.

As long as those bozos continued barking up the wrong tree, he wouldn't need an alibi. They'd never question him. However, since he was a professional and since he prided himself on his preparation as well as his performance, it was imperative that he continue to back-fill his actions and make certain that the hotel staff see him daily. If some smart cop expanded the search criteria to suspicious visitors or persons of interest he would be prepared. His alibi—if needed—would be airtight.

He finished his morning swim, Jacuzzi, breakfast and reading session around eight thirty in the morning. After showering and shaving, he packed a few items in a day bag and announced to the front desk and the valet that he was going sightseeing in the North County. Did they have any suggestions?

After exchanging ideas about his proposed itinerary, he hopped into his non-descript gray Chevy Nova, waved goodbye, and told the parking attendant he'd see him in a few hours. He headed towards the freeway. Ever the stickler for details, he entered the I-5 going north. He continued for a few miles and then, abruptly, took the next off ramp, doubled back and headed south.

———

THE DAY WAS unfolding just as the geeky weather guy had predicted. By the time he reached his destination, Coronado Island, the sun was clearly burning through the clouds. Driving around the island, he noticed several 'For Sale' signs in front of various styles of homes.

There were Spanish homes for sale. There were older Tudors, older Craftsman, and one unique Victorian. Coronado had originally been established as an Air and Naval support area. Sections were still filled with military housing, condos and apartments.

Along the water, however, the real estate averaged well over a million dollars in value. Base commanders and other political dignitaries had built and established their homes on the island. These were of higher quality and larger size than the homes occupied by average military families.

His target—his soon to be latest victim—that warm afternoon, would be found in the older, 'unique' Victorian.

He drove slowly around the neighborhood, casing the house while acquainting himself with the various driveways, alleyways and walkways adjacent to the property.

Satisfied with his early reconnaissance, he allowed himself a quick trip over to the famous Coronado Hotel. His favorite movie of all time, *Some Like it Hot*, with Tony Curtis and Marilyn Monroe, had shot many memorable scenes at the elegant hotel.

He laughed at the irony. The gangster in the movie, George Raft, would be proud of his current role—the hired professional killer. The Raft character would understand and appreciate the killer's main motivation: money. The stately hotel looked smaller in person. And really, really old.

Disappointed, he exited the island via the bridge and found the nearest on-ramp for I-5 North. Time to actually visit a site or two in the North County, grab some lunch and make the return to his hotel obvious to all.

Along the way, he opened the disposable cell phone he had purchased while driving through Los Angeles. Searching for the number on the newspaper ad, he quickly found it and made the call.

"This is Anna Marie Gustapo," the female voice on the other end said.

"Hello, Anna Marie. Do you mind if I call you Anna Marie?" he asked confidently, knowing full well she preferred the two name moniker. Her advertisements—which could be found in any local real estate rag, the local newspaper, and on shopping carts all around upper-end communities in San Diego—declared, "There's only ONE Anna Marie!"

Now here he was, speaking to her.

"That's fine, Mr. . ."

"Feinstein. John Feinstein," he said. "Please call me John."

"Well John, what can I do for you?"

"I'd like to preview the listing you have in Coronado. 14752 Island View Way."

"The older Victorian? It's a lovely house. Good bones. Well worth the $1.8 million the owner is asking. It was recently remodeled and the views are to die for!"

"That's exactly what I'm looking for, Anna Marie," he said with a grin, recognizing the irony of her last statement. "Can you meet me there at oh, say, four p.m.?"

"I'm not sure I can make it, but I can have one of my assistants open it for you and your agent."

"Well, that's the thing. I don't have an agent. I was hoping to see the house, meet you and discuss *you* representing me," he said in a calm yet assertive manner. "After all, there's only ONE Anna Marie," he added.

Motivated by the notion of double ending the commission—making money from both the seller and buyer—Anna Marie Gustapo quickly agreed to meet Mr. Feinstein at 4:00 p.m. sharp.

She had one final question, "Have you been prequalified for an appropriate loan?"

"Won't need one I'm an all cash buyer. See you at 4:00." He said goodbye and hung up.

Oh Anna Marie, he thought. 'How quickly the moth does come to the flame'.

He opened his glove compartment and caressed the butcher knife wrapped tightly inside a San Francisco street map. Lying next to the knife was a ticket for the Padres game that evening.

Anna Marie had better be prompt, he thought, caressing the knife. If the bitch made him miss the first pitch, he'd be pissed.

Right now this was a professional hit. A cold, calculated murder. Done properly—although this one would be the bloodiest yet—she wouldn't feel much pain. The first thrust of the knife would be directly to her heart. His training in this matter had been precise. She'd be dead before she hit the floor. Once dead, he'd cut her up, make it look like a crime of passion.

But, if he missed part of the ball game due to her tardiness or some other unforeseen delay it would become personal.

"Believe me, Anna Marie, my ONE and only," he mumbled quietly, "You do *not* want me to make this personal."

2

"I REALIZE YOU'RE UPSET AT THE BANK, MRS. GONZALES," BRAD STEPHENS SAID CALMLY INTO THE PHONE WHILE SITTING BEHIND HIS DESK IN SANTA BARBARA, CALIFORNIA, SOME TWO HUNDRED MILES NORTH OF SAN DIEGO.

When the woman on the other end didn't respond, he took a deep breath and continued. "We all feel that the institutions should be doing more to help those in danger of foreclosure. But it is very important that you listen to me. You're not going to like what I have to say. Are you listening?"

The line was quiet and then Brad heard a soft, "*Si*."

"Good. I was in a similar situation to yours. I have had hundreds of homeowners call me with the same concerns you have. Neither I nor any of the people I've spoken to received relief from the bank. Do you understand, Mrs. Gonzales? *Comprendes*?

Again, "*Si*."

"They're not going to modify you. They *will* foreclose. You will lose your house. Your best bet is to contact a local realtor and attempt a short- sale on your property." He paused and took a cleansing breath. These conversations were never easy. "Do you know what a short-sale is?"

"No."

He knew. He knew all too well. He had seen way too many of them since the recession began. "It is the bank allowing you to sell the house for less than you owe. I think it is your only realistic option."

On the other end, only sobs.

"Mrs. Gonzales, please stop crying. I'm just telling you the truth. I don't want you to waste money on one of those fake legal services who swear they can save your house."

Again, sobs.

She's not going to listen.

He just knew.

———

BRAD FELT AWFUL. The process of capitulation was always very difficult. In the case of a woman losing her home—her nest—it was downright, heart-wrenchingly painful.

Obviously, Mrs. Gonzales felt very strongly about keeping her house. But, like so many millions of homeowners during the crazy recession, she was unable to make her payments. Could be she lost her job. Could be her husband had a stroke or heart attack. Could be she got talked into a subprime loan and the rate had adjusted so high that she couldn't afford it.

Could be a combination of all those things.

Bottom line: She was six months delinquent on her payments, the bank or servicer had given her the run around on loan modification and had requested hundreds of pages of paperwork from her three times now. One representative from the lender actually recommended she miss payments. "It's the only way they're going to listen to you," the operator had said.

Six months later, they were hearing, but the bank wasn't listening.

Mrs. Gonzales obviously wasn't a sophisticated woman. Brad doubted she had access to photocopiers and fax machines. The 'system' was going to win. The lender was going to foreclose. It was just a matter of time.

Would she take his advice? Probably not. Not only is capitulation painful, it tends to meet very firm resistance from those who are about to lose. She would probably hang up with him and immediately call one of the lawyers he just told her to avoid because a friend of a friend of a friend had told her they had success with the guy. She'd waste a thousand bucks.

It was bullshit but Brad couldn't stop her. He had done what he could.

The ball was in her court.

She wasn't going to listen.

IT WAS A SUNNY day in Santa Barbara. Most are. The area only gets an average of sixteen inches of rain per year and golfers could play—if they wanted to—year round. Brad knew; he had done just that many times. He had opted to wear khaki shorts, blue golf shirt and sandals. Definitely not as impressive as the 'buttoned-down' businessman look he often sported but infinitely more comfortable. At 53, he was still in good shape, sported a full head of hair, and somehow, miraculously, had maintained his sense of humor.

Mrs. Gonzales wasn't the only one who had hit a rough patch. Brad could give her a run for her money.

Thank God it wasn't a competition.

He glanced at the leather-bound appointment book lying on the corner of his desk. Nothing scheduled for the rest of the day.

It was only noon. The sun didn't set until 7:30. He could still get in eighteen holes of golf, maybe twenty seven. The forecast called for heavy fog this evening, but it was beautiful currently—seventy degrees with just a wisp of wind.

Standard for Santa Barbara this time of year.

He pushed the intercom button and connected with his assistant, Stefanie Ramirez. "Hey Stef," he began, "looks like I've got a clear schedule for the rest of the day. What's my favorite client doing this afternoon?"

"Your favorite client is supposed to be cleaning the gutters and mowing the lawn," she replied. "And if you pull him away to go play golf, he better either be done with those chores or be prepared to finally pay a gardener to do them."

Brad's 'favorite client' was his buddy, professional golfer and former U.S. Open Champ, John Linden. Linden had recently moved to the area.

Brad had represented him in buying a nice, modest home near where Brad lived in Montecito, California. The process had been interrupted by a dispute with Linden's former management firm, the death of his personal manager and the breakup with his former fiancée, Fabiola.

And, of course, it didn't help when a right-wing fanatic tried to kill Brad and his 'favorite client' while they played in an exhibition match at Harbour Town in South Carolina.

When the dust settled, Linden made Brad his new manager—a task Brad was unfamiliar with but was anxious to perform. The challenges were many, and so far, he was having fun learning the ropes.

"I'll call him and find out how much progress he's made," Brad assured her. "You know, he's a wealthy man. He can afford a gardener. What's his problem?"

"He's cheap. Besides, he feels that by doing the gardening and fixing the small problems, the house will become a 'home'." She said this while making small quote marks in the air with her fingers. "He's tired of treating places he's lived in as if they were temporary quarters. I think he really wants to make this his home for a long time," she added.

"Yeah, makes sense I guess. He grew up in the Midwest watching his father do things around the house. Think that has anything to do with it?"

"I'm not his shrink, but I'd bet good money on it."

Brad chuckled. "That's why you make the big money. I'll let you know what he says."

3

"I hear you're doing manual labor," Brad began.

"Yep. Real man's work. Want to come over and help?"

"Nope. As a matter of fact, as your new agent, I insist you stop working with dangerous ladders and sharp lawnmowers immediately! You could chop off a finger or a foot. Then where would you be? Hell, where would I be?"

"You're just trying to protect your pocketbook. This outdoor work is good for the soul. I'm almost done, anyway. What's up?"

"I've got a clear calendar this afternoon and I thought we could sneak in a quick round."

"Great. Your timing, like always, is perfect. Where do you want to play?"

"I'll call my old club, I'm sure they'll accommodate us as long as they don't have a special event going on."

"Sounds good, give them a call and then confirm with me. I can be ready in twenty minutes."

Brad called the club and was told that the course was wide open for the U.S. Open Champ and his *guest*.

Ouch.

Being referred to as a 'guest' stung. He had been a member of this club for twenty years. An unfortunate series of economic events coincided with the recession and Brad had given up his long-held, beloved membership.

You don't lose the amount of money Brad had and still belong to a fancy private country club.

At least Brad Stephens didn't.

His cell phone rang as he approached his car. His first reaction was to ignore the call. However, upon further inspection, a familiar name popped up on the display: Raoul Espinoza.

"Raoul, what's up, buddy? Is this an official or unofficial call?"

"Every call I make is ooooh-fficial amigo. I'm the 'man'."

Raoul Espinoza was a local police sergeant and good buddy of Brad's. He had also saved Brad's life recently.

"It's a nice afternoon" Espinoza began, "I've got the day off. You want to go grab a few beers and play 18 at the municipal golf course?"

"Funny you should ask. I just cleared my schedule and called John. We're going to play in thirty minutes at my old club. Come join us."

"That would be great," Espinoza said. And then, suddenly, he turned more serious. "And Brad, there are some official things I *do* want to discuss with you if we get a chance."

"Can't we talk about them over the phone?"

"Nope. This is something I need to brainstorm with you about in person. I want to pick your brain about the real estate profession."

"Thinking about quitting law enforcement after twenty years?

"No, nothing as stupid as that. I'd rather stick needles in my eyes than sell houses. But here's the thing, there's been a rash of real estate agent murders lately. I'm sure you've seen some of the stories. San Francisco, Palm Springs, Newport Beach and, the day before yesterday, San Diego. The Brass wants us to do some background research. I want to kick some ideas around with you."

"Hey, man, before this goes any farther, I want to be on the record. Sometimes I get angry with real estate agents—hell, we all do—but I didn't kill any of them."

"Duly noted. I'll see you in twenty minutes. And Brad, bring your wallet. I plan on cleaning your *Gringo* clock!"

4

The killer had stayed in San Diego an extra day to gauge local coverage of the murder. Surprisingly, the media hadn't given it much play.

No love for realtors?

He gathered his things and then left the area mid-morning. If all went right, he'd be home by 3:00.

It was a hazy, summer afternoon with light fog just beginning to burn off. Above the mountains to the northeast, it looked like a rare summer rainstorm might be forming. Flowers didn't care. He knew that the predominantly Mediterranean climate of Southern California needed rain. It needed a lot of rain. He traveled north on the I-5 at 65 miles per hour. Traffic was light.

Things had gone smoothly for the killer in Coronado. The Padres had beaten the Giants 2-1 and fortunately for the real estate lady, Anna Marie

Gustapo, he had made it to the ballpark on time for the first pitch.

He had one stop to make before heading home; the most important person in the world deserved a visit. It would be brief and then he would continue on to Malibu.

As he passed the Pico St. turnoff in West L.A., he shook his head slowly. Pico ran all the way through Los Angeles—from west to east. He had been raised on the streets of East L.A. and the Pico St. gang had played an important role in his young life. He grimaced at the thought.

Born Eduardo Rodrigo Flores to illegal immigrant parents, the killer had anglicized his name while in the military. He had entered Eduardo Flores and emerged Ted Flowers. His comrades had convinced him that in time of crisis it would be easier for them to yell 'Ted' than 'Eduardo'.

Apparently, 'Ed' was not an option.

The false name given Anna Marie Gustapo the day before, John Feinstein, was especially ironic given the fact that Flowers was clearly of Hispanic descent. The real estate agent must've been very confused when the six foot, two hundred pound, dark Latino with wavy black hair and cold, brown eyes appeared at the front door. Her surprise had probably multiplied by a factor of one million when he pulled the knife from his back pocket.

He smiled at the irony.

DRIVING NORTH ON the I-5, he drifted out his lane slightly. Day-dreaming, he supposed, could cause that to happen. He corrected his course and accelerated.

A black Mercedes with shiny, spinning rims and fully tinted windows honked its horn and began to pass. The passenger window lowered and

Flowers could see the driver flip him off while the passenger yelled, "Hey, Beaner, get off the road. You almost hit us." Both driver and passenger wore white wife-beater tee shirts and dew rags on their heads.

Flowers smiled, made a pistol out of his thumb and forefinger and pointed it at the passenger. He mouthed, "Bang, bang, you're dead," and then spit out his window. He had had many confrontations with punks like these. If they wanted to start something, he would surely finish it.

The Mercedes slowed and again the tinted window lowered. This time a gun appeared. Responding quickly, Flowers hit his brakes and swerved to the right just as the first bullet was fired. Accelerating, he fell in line behind the Mercedes and watched as the shooter contemplated firing backwards out the side window.

No further shots were fired, but the episode was not over. Flowers followed the Mercedes as the driver took the Wilshire exit. He kept his distance but made it obvious he was not backing down.

The Mercedes took a right and then two quick lefts and then came to an abrupt stop in the back of a small restaurant. The place had seen better days. Weeds grew along the outside of the building and the parking lot looked like a mine field.

Flowers inched forward slowly.

All four doors opened on the Mercedes. Four bodies emerged. "So, it's not just a driver and one passenger," Flowers said quietly to himself. He breathed deeply and then exhaled. "Hell, maybe they've got the whole gang in that car."

The thought brought a strange smile to his face.

Stopping twenty feet short of the Mercedes, Flowers pulled a pistol from under his front seat, found the silencer he kept in the glove compartment and screwed it tightly on the barrel.

No need to wake the neighbors.

He surveyed the back of the building. No security cameras. This was indeed his lucky day.

For the passengers of the car—homeboys from South Central—it would be their worst.

"HEY, AMIGO," THE driver, a scraggly looking black guy who couldn't be older than twenty and couldn't weigh more than a hundred and forty pounds said. "My boys and me don't want no trouble." He walked towards Flowers with his arms open, his hands free of any weapons.

Flowers got out of the car, leaving the engine idling. "You've got a strange way of showing it punk."

"Who you calling a punk?"

"You're all punks. I'll tell you what, you all come over here, apologize to me and kiss the hood of my car and I'll let bygones be bygones."

"Kiss your car? Fuck that. You come over here and kiss my ass," the skinny driver said, chuckling nervously, pulling his drooping pants up and glancing at his homeboys for validation.

The other three gangbangers stood side by side, various pistols and assault weapons clearly on display. Flowers smiled. This would be like shooting ducks in a barrel. The dumb shits didn't even have enough sense to spread out.

He gave them the same smile he had given the real estate agent the day before.

He moved closer.

"I was a member of a gang once," he began, holding his left arm out as if to make a dramatic point, his right hand lightly caressing the silenced pistol behind his back. "I got lucky. My grandmother saved me. She convinced me to quit the gang and get a real life."

"Why you smiling?" the driver asked.

"Fuck your grandmother," the passenger who fired the shot on the freeway added.

Flowers shook his head slowly. "Now you disrespect my Grandmother?" Before the Crips or Bloods or I-210's or whatever stupid name they called themselves could respond, Flowers raised his weapon and fired three times.

The three passengers hit the pavement like sacks of potatoes, small red dots on each forehead. The driver watched in horror as his homeboys fell. He glanced at their lifeless bodies and then back at Flowers. "Hey man, you crazy. I ain't carrying no weapon, see?" He spread his arms wide.

"You, my young friend, are carrying the worst weapons of all: bigotry and the false notion that you are a leader."

"You talkin' crazy talk. Leader? I ain't no leader. My brother, Felix, he the head of our gang."

"Your fallen comrades appointed you the leader by making you the driver and then you assumed that role by confronting me unarmed."

"So?" the skinny kid said, sniffling.

Flowers pointed the gun at the driver's head. "Let me ask you something. Do you know how to kill a rattle snake?"

The young man looked perplexed. "I from the city; I never seen no snake."

"Too bad, I might have let you live had you shown any interest in my question or any knowledge beyond your gang." Flowers pulled the trigger.

Flowers removed the silencer, put it back in the glove compartment and stashed the pistol under the seat. He took a deep breath, glanced at the fallen bodies and shook his head. "The correct answer, my little coked-up deviant is: You cut the head off."

He put the car in gear, merged with traffic and continued on to his original destination. He hoped to make it before traffic picked up.

5

The game was decided and the bet set: a five dollar Nassau with the group stroking off of John Linden's plus six handicap. Tees were tossed to determine partners. Brad would team with the local pro, Marc Greenfeld. Espinoza, with Linden.

Well played Raoul. Advantage Espinoza.

A bit of a walking paradox, the heavyset Espinoza was graceful and athletic on the golf course. And, contrary to his daily business uniform consisting of rumpled gray suits combined with various semi-ironed black and white shirts and old beaten-up shoes, he wore freshly pressed slacks, a perfectly clean golf shirt, and spit polished shoes on the course.

Remarkable transformation actually.

Since neither Espinoza nor Brad had warmed up, they were both granted a breakfast ball by Linden.

23

Good thing. Both hooked their first tee shots out of bounds. Their second shots both found the fairway.

Game on.

Surprisingly, the match was tied at the turn. Brad was playing well and his partner, Greenfeld, was putting lights-out. Good thing. Linden was knocking the crap out of the ball and making putts like... well, like a touring pro who had recently won the U.S. Open.

ESPINOZA CAUGHT UP with Brad and slapped him on the shoulder as the group walked down the tenth fairway.

"So, Bradley ol' boy, how's life in the mortgage and management worlds? Is the lending market getting any better?" Espinoza asked with true concern. "Please tell me it is," he added quickly.

"Raoul, it's only getting better, because it's not getting worse. Does that make sense?"

"Yeah. I know what you mean. Sometimes when you're real sick and you know you're going to throw up, it freaks you out. Once you get to the stage where you're still sick but you don't have to puke every thirty minutes, it feels much better. But you're still sick. You're not out of the woods for a few days."

"You got it. Gross analogy by the way, but basically that, in my opinion, is our current economy. And, I fear, my personal future economy as well. We're not out of the woods yet."

"Damn! I feel it too. I got a furlough coming up. I was hoping, though, that you had a more professional analysis and were going to tell me that everything was A-Okay."

"Wish I could. See me this time next year."

The big cop shook his head sadly, frowned and slowed his pace. After a moment, he faced Brad again and said, "Anyway, the thing I wanted to talk to you about is this recent killing of real estate agents."

"Can we talk about it in the bar after the round?" Brad asked. "I seem to remember some stubborn, burned-out jock, telling me he was going to, and I quote, 'clean my Gringo clock'. I need to focus right now. *Amigo*."

"Yeah, let's talk then. Start thinking though about who might want to kill all these agents. I want your insight into the real estate business."

"Fair enough. Now hit your ball. Don't shank it!" Brad said. He laughed at his own joke and watched as Espinoza set-up for his next shot.

"Hey, that's a word we never use on the course," Espinoza said.

Brad just smiled and winked.

TWO HOURS LATER and twenty bucks to the victors (Linden and Espinoza) later, the four players entered the club bar. Save for a few old guys playing backgammon at a table in the back, the bar was empty. Brad's group chose the table closest to the television and settled in.

The country club's bar reeked of class...and money. The walls were covered with rich walnut paneling, the tables made from the finest wood and the chairs were covered with burgundy-colored leather. This was how a country club bar was supposed to look, Brad thought.

He missed being a member.

"Nice round, boys," Linden said. "I wasn't sure I could keep up with you studs. Lucky for me Raoul showed up those last few holes." He raised his draft beer in a celebratory 'cheers' and clinked glasses with Espinoza.

Good winners.

Contrary to his typical nature, Brad had become a decent loser. He couldn't afford to get angry any longer. After losing most of his savings and ruining his credit, anger had given way to humility.

"Yeah, yeah, yeah. Nice round," Brad said sarcastically. "Marc and I want a rematch. Same time next week?"

They agreed on the rematch and Greenfeld, claiming he had to close the golf shop, shook hands and bid farewell.

"He's a good player," Linden remarked as the club pro disappeared around the corner. "He'd be better if he came over to the dark side and used the 'claw' grip when he putts, however. And I'm going to talk to him about calling you a guest. I think he should have more respect for the twenty years you put in at this club."

"Don't make a big issue out of it," Brad replied. "As long as I can play here from time to time, I'm a happy 'guest' camper."

The group laughed, sipped their drinks and, when the waiter came around, ordered one more round.

Espinoza turned to Brad. "Can we talk about those murders? Have you given them any thought?"

"What murders?" Linden said.

"Raoul has been asked to brainstorm with people in the real estate business about some recent killings of real estate agents statewide?"

"How many?" Linden asked.

Thinking about it and counting on his fingertips, Espinoza told them that there had been seven killings so far. The last one, committed the day before yesterday by far the most brutal.

"I'm wondering if the guy is escalating or is just changing the way he kills to try and throw us off," Espinoza said.

Linden whistled softly. "Seven fucking murders of real estate agents! Sounds like when that guy was killing taxi drivers in Vegas a few years back. Let me ask this, were all the agents female?"

"No. That's the thing. There've been four male and three female so far," Espinoza answered. "No real pattern. No rape. No robbery. Very little forensic evidence left at the scenes. And, most importantly, no witnesses."

"So, you're telling us that there's a very gifted serial killer out there whacking real estate agents throughout the state?" Brad asked.

"That or a professional," Espinoza said. "I just don't know why a professional would go after unarmed real estate agents. It just don't add up." He took a sip of his drink, shook his head slowly and shrugged his big shoulders.

"No pattern at all?" Brad asked.

"So far the only thing the FBI is saying is that all the real estate agents worked in wealthy communities."

Brad hesitated for a moment and then seemed to catch a second wind. "Okay. So they're all high-end realtors."

Espinoza flashed him a big smile. "You are a master of the obvious."

Brad gave his buddy a flat stare before continuing. "And you want my input into the real estate business?"

"That's what the Feds asked. They told my boss to have us talk to guys in your business for some insight. You know, because we live in a wealthy community."

"How can I help? I'm a mortgage broker not a real estate agent," Brad said.

"We don't know shit about real estate. I figured you've been doing loans for so long, you could bring some fresh perspective."

"Okay, I buy that. Let me ask this: Did these agents all work for the same office? Maybe someone out there has a hard-on against Century 21?"

"Nope. All came from different offices."

"Did they, as a group, piss somebody off during a transaction?"

"Again, there is no evidence of any connection between the dead. The guy in San Francisco had been an agent for twenty years. The gal killed in San Diego had only been selling for the past ten years. No common clients. No competitive link as far as statewide authorities can tell."

"Were these agents big advertisers?"

"Don't know," Espinoza said. He hesitated and then asked, "What do you mean by *big*?"

"Well, in real estate there is your basic advertising. Spots in the newspaper and local real estate rags.

Then there are those people who go way beyond. Names on bus benches, pictures on shopping carts, that kind of thing. Hell, in Las Vegas, they even take out billboard ads."

"Billboards. Really? We'll have to look into that. What if they were?"

"Your killer might be keying on agents he's seen advertising in some specific publication or at some specific spot in each community."

"You know what? That's a new twist," Espinoza said, a satisfied smile spreading across his face. "I knew you'd add something to the dialogue. Anything else you can think of?"

Before Brad could respond, Linden interrupted. "Yeah, I got something."

"Go ahead, I'm all ears," Espinoza said.

Linden smiled and then said, "When are you going to investigate the murder that took place here today? You and I killed Brad and Marc! And I plead guilty." He held his wrists out as if to allow the sergeant to cuff him.

"Very funny. You're about as funny as a rubber crutch."

"Hey, don't hate me because I'm beautiful. I'm just speaking the truth," Linden shot back and then added, "Sometimes the truth hurts. What can I say?"

Brad laughed quietly, told Raoul he had nothing further to add although he reserved the right to contact him if he thought of anything new.

Espinoza told him that he'd bring over a few of the working files the next day. Maybe Brad would see a real estate angle if it were in print.

With that they finished their drinks and adjourned for the evening –Linden proud of his victory, Espinoza happy to have a new angle to propose to his superiors, and Brad happy to have spent a great afternoon with wonderful friends.

Driving home Brad thought about his conversation with Raoul. Something Espinoza had said nagged at him. What did the victims have in common other than selling real estate?

Well, whatever it was, he had never been happier to be the 'mortgage guy' and not a real estate agent. Last thing he needed after all the recent drama he had experienced was more violence in his life.

6

THE DAY HAD BEEN A PERFECT BLEND OF CAMARADERIE AND COMPETITION.

Days like this were rare in Brad Stephens' life lately. He hoped his good luck would continue when he arrived home later in the afternoon.

Sadly, it was not to be.

"Hey Mel," he called to his wife of thirty years, "What's up?"

"Hi honey. I've got a great recipe to try tonight. I've been watching the Food Channel all day," she said.

Mel stood five foot six with long blonde hair, deep tan and almost translucent green eyes. Her smile brightened any room she entered.

She possessed many fine traits.

Cooking was not one of them.

She didn't mean to be an awful cook. It wasn't like she woke up and said, "Gee, I'd like to poison my family today." No, Mel's problem was that she didn't know how to combine various ingredients. She could watch it on television, think she had it wired and then butcher the recipe.

"You sure you don't want to rent a movie and pick up a pizza?" Brad asked.

"No way. Pizza is fattening and I really don't feel like committing to a movie tonight."

Damn. The 'old movie and pizza' strategy was in jeopardy.

Brad had explained to Mel dozens of times that movies could not be delivered via satellite to their home. This wasn't true, of course, but Mel bought it. So, when Mel cooked something exceptionally adventurous, Brad offered to rent a movie for the night and secretly visited the pizza place or the Taco Bell next door.

It had worked for years.

Apparently, as is the case of many fine con-men, his master plan was beginning to fade.

Hoping to change the subject—and somehow convince her to reconsider—Brad discussed his day with her.

"Business was awfully quiet and you know what happens when I get this type of break in the day, don't you?"

"Let me guess, you played golf."

"You got it. Linden, Espinoza and Marc Greenfeld played with me."

"That's a good group. Where did you play?"

"The old club. Linden got special privileges and Raoul and I were his 'guests'." He made little quote marks in the air.

Her expression softened. "Are you okay with that?"

"I wasn't before, but I am now. It is what it is."

"You think we'll ever rejoin that club?"

"Never say never, but I doubt it. We've got a lot of debt to pay off. I think we will be 'guests' for quite some time."

"No worries. As long as I get to keep my house and as long as you get to play golf at other courses, that's all that matters." She approached him and gave him a quick peck on the cheek.

Wonderful woman, he thought for the millionth time.

"Besides my decent golf game—which I know you don't care about—an interesting thing did happen today."

"Do tell."

"Raoul is working with a statewide task force looking into the recent deaths of high-end real estate agents."

"I think I read about that the other day. The writer was comparing it to the Taxi Driver murders in Las Vegas a few years ago."

"Really? I don't remember those killings. Linden brought them up too. Who did them?"

"Turned out it was a disgruntled union member. The guy was denied benefits and he decided to take it out on the drivers rather than the union reps."

"Isn't that always the way?"

"It is."

Brad turned his body and stared out a nearby window. The fog was slowly rolling in from the ocean, covering the valley below. It would be a cool night. The weather report said rain in Los Angeles. He smiled as he reflected on the local climate.

Perfect. This is why we pay the big bucks to live here.

He took one last look and then turned back towards Mel. "Well, this one isn't going to be so easy. Raoul says that there aren't any connections between the dead agents. They worked for different companies. They were located in different parts of the state. There were no notes or evidence left linking the killings—just the fact that all the victims were real estate agents."

"I've been married to you for thirty years. I've seen many times when you'd like to kill the agent on a deal. Think it might be an irate mortgage loan officer?"

"There's a thought." He chuckled and then caught himself. "No, seriously, it could be. You might be on to something." He rubbed his chin as if deep in thought.

"I was just kidding."

"I know, but hey, it's a theory. Don't discount it. The police have nothing. So asking questions like this tends to lead them—eventually—in the right direction."

"What exactly did Raoul want you to do?"

"He asked me to review the case files because I understand the real estate business better than most. He says that the other cops have no clue about what goes on in my world."

"What did you tell him?"

"I said I'd be glad to look at the files. Maybe there's a connection between the victims' advertising methods. I don't know. It is intriguing, though. Don't you think?"

"I do," she said and then hesitated.

"But?"

"But not as intriguing to me as the chicken cacciatore I'm going to make tonight."

"What's so intriguing about your cacciatore?"

"You'll see. It's unlike any you've ever had before."

Uh, huh.

Brad poured a Jack Daniels and surveyed the room, searching for the family dog. If worse came to worse, Brad could play the 'old fake trip and drop the food in front of the dog' trick. Rufus was a Rottweiler, he'd eat anything. After a minute, he found the dog lying on a couch in the back room.

"You chicken," Brad said quietly, taking a sip of his Jack. He sat next to the dog and rubbed his ears. "Mel's made one of her concoctions again. Get up and come with me, you might have to eat it." Rufus looked up, gave Brad a quick lick and then put his head back down.

Oh man, I got problems. Even he's not excited about this cacciatore.

He rose and strolled back towards the kitchen. He snapped his fingers for the dog to follow. Rufus rose reluctantly and sauntered down the hall.

Brad raised his drink towards the dining room. "We who are about to die, salute you," he said as he and Rufus made the slow walk towards Mel's cacciatore.

7

THE RAIN BEGAN TO FALL. HARD.

JOHNNY RIVERS HAD sung *It Never Rains in California.* For the most part he was correct. But on the rare occasions when precipitation did fall, Southern Californians went crazy. Drains clogged; gutters overflowed; and worst of all, cars hydro-planed. Drivers routinely slid into each other like ducks running on a frozen pond.

Pleased to get off the crazy road, Flowers pulled into the driveway of his rented Malibu bungalow early that evening. Covering his head with an old newspaper, and stepping carefully around puddles that had formed, he went to the back of the car and grabbed a black suitcase from the trunk.

He paused for a moment and reflected on his last stop of the day.

The visit to his grandmother's grave had gone well. Maria Flores had raised him; had been his savior.

Now she was dead, the victim of gang violence and an unfair, unjust, cold world.

Well, fuck'em; fuck'em all.

As he always did when visiting her grave, Flowers had lain a freshly cut bouquet of flowers on the grass and spoke directly down to her gravesite. "Please forgive me mama," he had said. "I have sinned again. I know this is not the life you wanted for me but it has been thrust upon me and I must continue. Please understand."

He had paused, wiped a small speck of mud off her headstone, and then continued. "I know you are in Heaven and at peace. It should be obvious to you by now that when it is time for me to leave this mortal life, I will not be joining you up there." Inadvertently, he had raised his eyes towards the sky and then he blew a kiss towards the ground and departed.

He had thought about her numerous times on the drive back to Malibu. He knew she would be horrified by his chosen profession. He also knew, he couldn't go back, couldn't become her little Niño, Eduardo. As he approached his beach house, his thoughts returned to the present.

THE BUNGALOW WAS framed by vibrant red and purple bougainvillea. It had been painted beige with blue trim. It looked nice. It looked very unassuming. Compared to the beach houses around it, it looked very bland. Perfect for a movie star trying to hide from the media or... a trained assassin lying low. The house rested squarely on the beach. It cost ten thousand dollars a month to rent—a bargain by Los Angeles standards. He would miss this place when it was time to move on.

As he approached the front door, his cell phone vibrated. The blinking blue icon in the corner indicated that he had received a new text message. When he scrolled for Caller I.D., the screen read "Unavailable".

New instructions?

He pressed the text message button and information appeared. He read it twice, pushed delete and pursed his lips. "Why so many?" he said under his breath.

He settled down on a cheap brown leather couch the owner had left behind, twisted the top off a cold beer, took one long pull and then turned on the local news.

Three stories into the broadcast, the platinum-haired female reporter on the screen announced that four male bodies had been found in the back parking lot of a restaurant off Wilshire Blvd. The shooting looked 'gang related' she concluded and then quickly moved on to the next story.

Flowers smiled to himself. "Would've only been three dead bodies if the little idiot had ever watched Animal Planet." He took another pull of beer, turned off the television and stared out the window towards the choppy Pacific Ocean.

His thoughts turned to the new instructions he had been sent.

WHEN HE TOOK the original contract, it had been explained to him that time was always of the essence to his employer. Apparently, executions for this guy had to be done dramatically and quickly. Flowers wondered if things weren't moving too fast though.

He had snuffed two wise guys in Vegas and had terminated seven real estate agents so far in less than thirty days, had done these jobs in Nevada and California. Had put over fifteen hundred miles on the aging Nova.

The travel alone was a bitch.

Did his employer think murder was easy? These things had to be planned. Timing and conditions had to be precise. Rushing almost always led to mistakes.

He silently wished he could contact the guy who had hired him. He would ask for more time between hits.

Unfortunately, he had been instructed to not contact his employer. Communication would travel one way. He would abide by his contract but he didn't have to like it. He drained the remaining beer from the bottle, grabbed another one from the refrigerator and stepped outside.

The rain had subsided and the wind had picked up as the sun began its low descent into the swirling ocean. White capped waves crashed on the shore while seemingly tireless seagulls flew against the southern wind—barely making progress. He wondered, not for the first time, if he were like the persistent seagull—exuding tremendous energy in life, but often getting nowhere.

He shrugged it off and returned inside. The contract he was working on would pay handsomely. The money would get him somewhere. Fast.

Flowers finished his beer, made a tuna fish sandwich and settled in for what he hoped would be a comfortable evening.

Sleep should come easily. The nightmares had stopped long ago.

8

"STEF TELLS ME I NEED TO GET OUT OF HER WAY AROUND THE HOUSE," JOHN LINDEN TOLD HIS LONG TIME CADDIE, HENRY 'HANK' BLOOM THE NEXT DAY WHEN THEY MET AT A LOCAL DRIVING RANGE IN SANTA BARBARA.

Bloom, a huge man in his mid-sixties, stared down at Linden and chuckled. "Well boss you need to start making us more money too. That means we need to enter more tournaments. It's been a few months since you played."

Linden nodded and grinned. "Or get more endorsements."

"Yeah, you could do that," Hank agreed. "But to get endorsements, they got to see you play."

"I hear you."

Life had become more complicated since he was dumped by his former fiancée, Fabiola, and then subsequently hooked up with Brad's assistant, Stefanie. Truth be told, Linden had been enjoying his new role as domestic partner, but he knew all good things must come to an end.

"We'll fly to Ponte Vedra Beach in a few weeks. We'll play a few practice rounds with Phil and Freddie. That TPC course at Sawgrass is one tough son-of-a-bitch—especially that fucking17[th] hole. I'll need as much practice as I can get to be competitive," Linden said

"Good idea," Hank agreed, and then added, "You better bring a few thousand bucks in cash. Those guys like to bet big during the practice rounds."

"No problem, big man. You do your job, hand me the right clubs and help me read the putts. We'll do okay."

"We always do, boss."

BLOOM HAD BECOME Linden's caddie fifteen years earlier. Known for possessing a hot temper, Linden had fired his previous caddie in the middle of an important round. Bloom came from behind the ropes and grabbed John's bag. He had been on it ever since.

Hank had never doubted Linden's playing ability, just his work ethic.

"We signed up for the Players Championship several months ago," Hank said. "Since then, you haven't played in any tournaments and we've only had four or five practice sessions. You sure your game is up to it?"

"I know I've been a bit pre-occupied with the new house and my new relationship but my back feels good, I'm in my prime, and I've played a few rounds with Brad lately," Linden said. "We'll be okay as long as we can get past that damn 17th hole each day."

"I didn't want to bring it up," Hank began. "But are you sure you can deal with facing the 17th again? You know, after what happened before and after Hilton Head and all."

Linden grimaced remembering how he was almost killed by a few crazy assholes at Harbour Town. And then, of course, there was the 'meltdown' on the 17th at Sawgrass. After a moment, he tilted his head slightly, spread his arms wide and said, "There's only one way to find out, isn't there?"

THE 17h AT TPC Sawgrass is a hundred and thirty yard shot to an island green. Some call it 'stupid'. Most call it insidious.

In 2001, Tiger had made a forty foot twisting, diving putt on the green to, essentially, win the tournament. The announcer had infamously declared early in the roll, "better than most" and as the ball dropped into the hole he repeated the phrase more assertively. It was a hall of fame putt. The announcer's statement had become common golf language. And don't ask Sergio Garcia about the hole. . . Enough said.

A par three—perhaps the hardest par three other than number twelve at Augusta—on the tour, the green juts out into a lake like a serpent's round tongue. There's nowhere to bail out. Hit the green, or hit the water. Those are your only choices.

Known by most golf enthusiasts for being a U.S. Open champ, John Linden was also famous in the golfing world for 'the other meltdown' at 17. (Again, don't ask Sergio about it. Just let it be).

It was several years earlier. The final round of that year's Players Tournament. Linden came to seventeen with a two shot lead. The wind blew strongly from left to right. The pin, as was the Sunday custom, was tucked in the bottom right hand corner.

A former girlfriend broke through the ropes and screamed at Linden as she grabbed his bag from Hank and threw it in the water. She was immediately apprehended but Linden was obviously shaken.

After Hank dried his clubs and grips, Linden hit the next four balls in the water.

He took a thirteen on the hole.

He had never come close to winning the tournament again. He had, however, birdied the 17th several times since then. The former girlfriend committed suicide several years later.

Linden did not mourn.

"Let's get out there and practice. I'm still nervous about 17," Hank said.

"*You're* nervous. Hell, Hank, *I've* got to hit the shot!" Linden smiled, patted his caddie on the back, let out a deep breath and then in a moment of absolute honesty added, "I'm fucking terrified."

9

HE WOKE UP TO THE SOUND OF WAVES BREAKING LAZILY ON THE SHORE. WHEN HE TOOK A LOOK OUTSIDE, HE SAW THAT A LIGHT FOG HAD FILLED THE MORNING AIR.

This is paradise. Why am I leaving?

But Flowers knew it was time to leave his Malibu bungalow—perhaps for the final time. He knew it was time to perform his next duties.

This was all happening too fast, he thought again, while showering. Mistakes happen when you rush. Got to slow down. But the client wanted the job done quickly.

He was trapped and he knew it.

He had to press forward. No choice. He was fully committed.

For a moment, he felt a wave of guilt for killing seemingly innocent victims. Just as quickly as it came, the feeling disappeared.

It was too late for a bout of conscience.

When he was young, his entire family had been murdered. And then, as a teenager, he had watched as first his grandfather was gunned down by a drive-by shooter and then his grandmother—his beloved grandmother—had been raped and tortured by gang bangers.

Ted Flowers had seen violence.

And now, violence was his world.

HE PULLED ON a pair of blue jeans and a grey sweatshirt and stepped outside. He sat down in an old, wicker chair. It was a brisk morning. He was glad he had put the coffee on before his shower. The rich, brown liquid would warm him as he took in the scene before him.

The storm had completely cleared overnight and the ocean was now fairly calm. The fog was burning off and neighbors or tourists—or both—filled the beach.

He watched as an older woman struggled with an impossibly large Great Dane. He smiled as a thin blonde woman with large breasts jogged in the thick sand, her perfectly matched outfit clinging tightly to her perfectly shaped rump. He actually chuckled when an older guy in Gucci loafers, brown socks and board shorts strolled by.

Southern Californians after a rainstorm.

He took another sip of coffee and then went back into the house and poured the remains down the drain. He walked into the bedroom, grabbed his still unpacked travel bag and headed out the door.

Time to travel again.

His employer had him going north to Ventura, Santa Barbara and then on to Pebble Beach and, finally, Atherton.

It would be a long, bloody week.

10

THEY SAY IT'S EASY TO BECOME A JACK OF ALL TRADES, WHILE REMAINING AN ACE AT NONE. BRAD STEPHENS WAS BEGINNING TO UNDERSTAND WHAT THE INFAMOUS "THEY" MEANT.

Since taking on the task of representing John, in all things Linden, he hadn't been putting full effort into his day job: Mortgage lending. The result was several recent loan denials and overall sloppy processing. Fortunately, the denials could be reversed. It would take time and energy, but he could do it.

Processing was Stef's area of expertise. Apparently, her recent romantic involvement with Linden had affected her eye for detail.

Loan applications had been submitted unsigned. Income information had been missing. Title reports on the wrong properties had been submitted. All correctable stuff, but sloppy.

The straw that broke the camel's back however had occurred the previous week. A credit report on a borrower had been submitted in the wrong file. Not only was this time consuming to correct, but in a highly technical sense, it probably violated several federal privacy laws.

Stef and Brad needed a good, old-fashioned 'sit down'. Time to right the ship. He made arrangements to meet with her later that morning.

Linden's scheduling, his endorsements, and his promotional appearances were going well. No complaints from the reigning U.S. Open Champ. Brad wondered, however, if things in the mortgage world—a world he knew everything about—were going so poorly, might there be something amiss in his new role as Linden's manager?

After all, he knew nothing about managing a professional athlete. Sure he had seen Tom Cruise play *Jerry McGuire* and had been a devoted fan of HBO's *Arli$$,* but what did those Hollywood renditions really teach him about managing the daily schedule—and controlling the ego—of a world famous athlete?

Nothing.

The easiest part of the job, so far, had been 'showing John the money'. Brad had taken over the management of Linden's substantial portfolio and it was growing nicely. Linden's endorsements had doubled since the events at Harbour Town.

Overall, the task was still daunting, however. Linden spent money like a drunken sailor. He tended to travel first-class at the last moment—costing ten times more and creating scheduling difficulties. And his romance with Stefanie Ramirez posed unique problems.

Advertisers and other representatives flooded *her* with calls requesting time with the great and handsome John Linden.

Apparently, word had spread that John Linden could be influenced by the advances of sexy, young women. Stef was not happy with this turn of events. Brad had made that item #2 to discuss with his assistant that morning.

THEY MET IN his office just before lunch. "Stef, we need to tighten up processing," he began.

"You think?"

"Okay, okay. It's obvious that I haven't been giving enough attention to the files. But, apparently, neither have you. What are we going to do about it?"

"I think we need to get an assistant," she replied without missing a beat.

So, she's been thinking about this too.

"An assistant! We don't have that much volume and, besides, an assistant will cost, what, another forty thousand a year?"

"I know we've handled much greater loan volume in the past. But managing John is a full time job for you and me," she exclaimed. "And combine that with all the new regulations..." She shook her head and looked at him, her brown eyes focusing directly on his, her expression, serious.

Stef was a beautiful, intelligent woman. She had been his partner through thick and thin. Through the birth of his children and hers. They had remarkable history together. And he knew the look she was giving him usually made him melt like jelly. But not today. Today, Brad would be strong.

She crossed her arms and finished her thought. "I have my hands full just dealing with the new compliance issues."

"Damn! I was afraid of this," he said, providing minor capitulation. "Linden's got us running around like chickens with our heads cut off and the Feds have created ten times more paperwork."

"And, don't forget, we live in Santa Barbara. The loans we do are complicated. Nobody works just one job. Most of the borrowers have partnerships, trusts, corporations. It isn't like processing loans in Des Moines," she pointed out.

"Okay. I don't know if I can afford another processor. I'm still in debt up to my eyeballs over that fucking Truckee fiasco...but if we *did* venture forward, who would we get?"

"I've got an idea but you may not like it."

"Don't worry, I won't shoot the messenger."

"Okay. How about Mel?"

"My Mel?"

"Yes. Your Mel."

"Stef! She's never worked in an office before. She's never processed a loan. She doesn't even know how to turn on a computer for Christ sakes!" He said all of this quickly, defensively.

"She could do set-up and quality control. I can teach her the basics. The computer is always on. She doesn't need to be computer literate. She's got a college education," Stef said looking amused and irritated at the same time. "You know, Brad, she's no dummy. Don't sell her short. And don't forget, this would keep the money in your immediate household."

"Okay. I'll think about it," he lied. "Any other suggestions?"

"We could work until midnight, seven days a week, I guess."

"Oh, sure. That would work." Brad sighed and rolled his eyes. He loved his wife dearly, but he knew for an absolute fact that it would be catastrophic to hire her. Thoughts of Lucy and Ethel working in the candy factory filled his head.

There must be another option.

"How about Blake or Scott?" he suggested. "My sons know how to type and I think they're fairly computer savvy. It wouldn't keep the money in my immediate household, but it would keep it in the family."

"Okay, I'll buy that. Let's get them both in here soon and see who has more aptitude for the job," Stef said.

"I'll have them come in tomorrow," Brad said quickly, feeling as if he had dodged a bullet. "Now let's move on to item #2."

Clearly surprised that there was even an item #2, Stef adjusted her red blouse, picked up her pen and prepared to write notes on a yellow legal pad. After a brief interval, her eyes returned to Brad's and she nodded her head and said, "Okay. Fire away boss."

"Item #2 is kind of sensitive. Let me know if I'm trespassing on sacred ground."

"You're not going to pick on my religion again, are you?" she joked.

"No. Worse than that, I think. I'm going to discuss your relationship with John."

"Mister Stephens..." she said in a tone suggesting he was, indeed, walking a slippery slope. She only called him 'Mister Stephens' when she was perturbed.

Stefanie Ramirez had been Brad's personal assistant for more than 25 years. They had fought many battles together. They had had formed a bond second to none. She had never butted in on *his* personal business.

It probably wasn't appropriate for him to butt in on hers.

This was different, however. This involved their client—and her current live-in lover—John Linden. This was business as much as it was personal. She would just have to understand.

"Here's the thing," he began, "ever since you moved in with John I've noticed a certain, let's say, passivity." He cleared his throat and continued. "As you know, in the mortgage business we have to remain lean and hungry. Otherwise we don't see the possibilities on a loan request and we don't get motivated to work the crap out of the file. Follow me so far?"

She sat rigid. Stone faced. This wasn't going well. Might as well get right to it, he thought.

"I think the comfort he's brought into your life has made you soft," he said.

"Made me soft! That's bull, Brad. I work just as hard as ever. I'm in here an hour before you and sometimes several hours after you've left. It's not my fault this stupid Dodd, Franks regulation has made the business ten times more difficult."

He waited a beat. Stared at his hands for a while. Chose his next words carefully. "Maybe it *is* the over-regulation but I get the sense that fighting to get the file done right the first time is not as important to you as it was before. Maybe it's your divorce? I don't know. But we can't be submitting files with the wrong credit reports in them."

"The credit report issue only happened once. And the other data omissions will be resolved when we put another processor into the mix," Stef said.

Hoping that his words would appear conciliatory, Brad continued. "Okay. I buy the additional processor. Hopefully that will cure the problem. I just wanted to put you on notice that we have to watch these things more closely. I rely on you heavily, you know that. I'm still feeling my way around the issue of managing John's professional life."

"And you think because I'm sleeping with the man, it has made me Loco? Like he's the greatest lover in the world and I, the weak female, have been smitten by his prowess! Give me a break."

"No, no, no. That's not what I meant," Brad said. He raised his hands to stop her as if she were mounting a charge—which in a way, she was. "Do *not* turn this around on me. I knew it wasn't a good idea to talk about personal stuff. Why do you think I've avoided it for twenty five years?"

She said nothing.

Disappointed?
Mad?
Confused?
Probably all three.
Damn! Damn! Damn!

"Okay. Listen, you're getting too defensive about all this," he said pushing his hands gently towards his desk as if saying, 'slow down'. He took a cleansing breath and continued. "What I meant to convey is that obviously you and I have been distracted lately. Me because I'm basically broke and just barely hanging on, and I'm trying to figure out what an 'agent' does for a professional athlete, and I was almost killed a few months ago, and I'm attempting to help Espinoza with thoughts about these recent killings." He rattled his list off quickly, much too quickly.

Stef just continued to stare.

What the hell, in for a penny, in for a pound he thought. "Add to it that I'm dealing with all of the changes in the mortgage industry and maybe you can understand my frustrations."

She put her pen down, adjusted her skirt, crossed and then uncrossed her legs, sat up straighter and prodded him to continue. "What's your point?" She gave him that look again.

He sighed. "Well, with you, the only thing I could think of was your recent lifestyle change. You know, divorce from Tommy and hooking up with John."

"Because I don't have other things going on in my life too? You've really insulted me this time, Brad. I don't know if I can get over this. My suggestion is that you consider looking for *two* new processors." And with that, she picked up her legal pad and stomped out of the room.

Damn! Damn! Damn!

That didn't go well.

But, hey, he was the boss.

The burden of authority could weigh on a guy.

Some days, you just stepped in dog poop.

The self-talk and positive reinforcement was all well and good, but Brad knew that he and Stef had just experienced a seminal moment. In twenty five years, this was their first real confrontation; the first time the employer/employee card had been played. The seeds of their new working relationship had been sown. It might flourish. She might calm down. She might understand the underlying truth in what he had said. Then again...

Would she really quit? After 25 years? And if she did, the reality was...he'd be up shit creek without a paddle.

He knew it and, unfortunately, she knew it too. He had no leverage. His only hope was that logic and reason would prevail.

Doesn't it always when dealing with human emotions?

HE RUBBED HIS forehead, contemplated his naval for a few moments and then picked up the phone. He called Espinoza. It was time for a little target-practice with his new pistol.

Maybe spending the afternoon with his friend would lighten the mood. Provide him better perspective. Raise his level of optimism. Enhance his understanding of the human race in general, women, in particular.

After all, hope *does* spring eternal.

11

SOMETHING ABOUT THE SHORT MESSAGE HE HAD RECEIVED THE DAY BEFORE MADE FLOWERS THINK THE CONTRACT WOULD EXPIRE AFTER THE NEXT FEW MURDERS.

He certainly hoped so. The kills were coming too quickly. The risk of being caught would increase.

The instructions from his employer had outlined his new targets and had expressed the desire for one of them to be killed with 'maximum prejudice'.

Maximum prejudice? What the hell?

Dead is dead.

As he drove north on the 101 towards Ventura, Flowers' mind wandered back to his first and only meeting with the man who was to make him rich.

HE HAD MET his employer on a sunny afternoon several months previously. Using intermediaries, the man had summoned Flowers to a sprawling estate outside of Las Vegas.

"Mr. Flowers, let me introduce myself," the conversation had begun. "I am Gino Falicello," the man said as he extended a pudgy right hand.

"Gino Falicello? From Chicago?"

"Yeah. That's me. Do you like my West Coast White House?" the old man chuckled.

"It's fantastic," Flowers said, staring at the front of the mansion. "I didn't realize you lived in Las Vegas."

"I have for the past ten years. Life in Chicago got too...complicated," he said with a wave of his hand. "Out here, things are free and easy."

Gino 'The Fridge' Falicello stood five foot eight and weighed at least three hundred pounds. His deeply tanned skin spoke to his Italian ancestry and, lately, to the many hours he obviously spent in the harsh, desert sun. At first blush, Falicello looked harmless—a heavy-set businessman who had gotten too much sun.

A closer look into his eyes, however, revealed another side of the man. Flowers could see pain and anguish in the deeply furrowed brow. The half-closed eyes used to be called 'smokey' by overly romantic beat-writers in the sixties. Today, they looked cold and calculating. They looked like a man who could take your life as if swatting a fly. Flowers had seen the look before.

Hell, he personally tried to strike that look himself.

Rumor was that Falicello had been bestowed his nickname not only because he looked like a 1956 one door Amana refrigerator, but because, in his youth, he had put so many competitors "on ice".

Wise guy humor.

"Not so free if you gamble," Flowers said. He returned his attention to his host. "And most things in life only look easy but turn out to be very hard."

The old man laughed. "Yes, that is true. I try to stay away from the tables. It seems to me that I have gambled enough in my life. Why would I want to compound it?"

Flowers had no response. He was still in awe of his surroundings and quite impressed that a 'made' man of Falicello's standing and pedigree would contact him about a job.

"I suppose you are wondering why I summoned you here."

"I assume you have a job for me."

"You are correct," Falicello said while reaching into his breast pocket and pulling out a neatly folded piece of paper. "I hear from my friends that you are very gifted."

Flowers smiled. "What can I say?"

Falicello pursed his lips and nodded. After a brief pause, he handed Flowers the piece of paper. "I would like you to take care of a few problems for me."

Flowers stared at the paper, said nothing.

"What you have in front of you is a list of several of my enemies," Falicello said. "They have insulted me and insulted my family. Do you understand?"

"Yes sir. I do. Is there a protocol you would like me to follow?

"Not really. Use your best judgment. Just make sure they never dis-respect me again. Got it?"

"Got it."

There was a long pause and then Flowers asked, "How much?"

"I had heard you were direct," Falicello said.

"And good," Flowers added.

"And good." The Fridge smiled for the first time.

The two discussed various details of the operation, settled on a price—one hundred thousand U.S. Dollars per target—and were about to have lunch when a beautiful, petite, young woman entered the room.

"Mercedes, my dear, what an unexpected pleasure" the gangster sang out as the young woman approached. "I didn't realize you were home."

"Hello, Papa. I just now returned."

Looking a little embarrassed, Falicello turned to his new employee and said, "Mr. Flowers, let me introduce my granddaughter, Mercedes."

Flowers smiled and gave the girl a nod. "My pleasure," he said.

Extending her hand, Mercedes Falicello walked towards Flowers and looked him directly in the eye. He noticed first her tan skin, then her shapely figure, then her beautiful face and finally, her deep blue eyes. His new employer's granddaughter was absolutely stunning.

"So good to meet you, Mr. Flowers," the girl said. "Will you be staying for lunch?"

"We were just about to sit down," Falicello interjected. "Just let us finish a few details and we will join you shortly."

A FEW MINUTES later, business concluded, Falicello and Flowers sat down at the table for lunch. Mercedes was already seated. She looked as if she was enjoying a glass of champagne and a small bowl of strawberries.

After they were seated, Falicello added one final business thought. "You will receive your instructions for the operation shortly. Do not question these instructions. They will arrive anonymously. Follow them and you will be quite well compensated. Do not contact me. Communication will be one way. Deviate and I shall be very, very angry," the old man said. And then, as if touched by an angel, his face grew softer, more benevolent. "Come, let us enjoy lunch with this beautiful young woman. She is only twenty-three years old and is just now venturing out into the business world."

"Not your business, I hope," Flowers said softly.

"No, no, no. I would not have that. Ours is a man's business. Wouldn't you agree, Mr. Flowers?"

Flowers said nothing.

"She has studied hard and wishes to be very successful. Look at the way she shakes your hand. Very professional, eh?" Falicello said proudly.

"Very impressive," Flowers agreed. "What field?"

Before the girl could answer, Falicello said, "She doesn't know yet, but it will be a professional business."

"During this awful recession? Will it be a business out here in Vegas?" Flowers asked, turning his head from grandfather to granddaughter.

The girl did not answer.

Shy?

Again, Falicello did the talking. "No, she has her heart set on living in California. She attended the University of California, Santa Barbara and she fell in love with Southern California."

He shot his granddaughter a proud grin and then continued. "I have raised her since she was seven. Her parents, my son and his wife Angela, died in a tragic auto accident." His eyes wandered towards the sky. "My son was in the family business," he added with a wry smile and a slight raise of his eyebrows. "He would be very proud of the beautiful young lady his daughter has become."

Flowers wanted to tell the old man that his own parents had died when he was young and that he was raised by his grandparents as well, but sensing his comments were not welcome, he wisely bit his tongue.

He was sure Falicello would scoff at any notion of similarities between the two. Flowers was a mechanic; Mercedes, a princess.

The three of them enjoyed a wonderful lunch of lobster, salad and chardonnay.

But for the contract to kill several unsuspecting people, the day might've been just a nice lunch between old friends. The table talk had been interesting and lively. The group discussed politics, the economy, and the Royal wedding. Flowers found himself impressed by the beautiful twenty-three year old.

She had given him her card: he hoped to meet her again once the job for her grandfather had been successfully completed. Their hands touched in a gentle, yet firm handshake and their eyes stayed fixed for a moment longer than normal.

Had there been a special 'spark' between them?

———•———

RETURNING TO THE present, eyes fixed on the road, Flowers grinned as he flashed back to the meeting. He felt a slight tightness in his chest when he thought of the beautiful, granddaughter. Would he ever see her again?

He shrugged, picked up his speed. Ventura was still forty minutes away. He had to get a move on. There were things to do before dark.

12

REAL ESTATE SALES HAD RECENTLY DROPPED DRAMATICALLY FOR JOHN PORTER.

As far as he knew, he was still Ventura's highest volume agent, but his listings were sitting and prices were falling. During the 'go-go' days of the early 2000's, he averaged three sales a month. Now, he was lucky to make one every other month. Despite the economic recession, he was determined to stay number one.

He'd just have to work harder; be better organized—or so he convinced himself with daily affirmations.

Five foot nine, one hundred and sixty pounds, with short brown hair, the forty-five year old agent was known as the 'little bulldog' by his peers. Never married, he seldom dated. His work was his mistress, his fleet of expensive cars, his reward for success.

Flowers, wearing a crisp gray suit, sun glasses and dark beard entered Porter's real estate office walking with a pronounced limp. He found the 'little bulldog' working behind his desk.

"Mr. Sanchez, so good to meet you," Porter said as he greeted his new client, Mr. 'Alvaro Sanchez'. Flowers nodded, limped forward and sat down, avoiding the outstretched hand being offered him.

The assassin had called Porter from the road. He had told the real estate agent that he was a wealthy industrialist from San Salvador. He desired a professional agent who would exercise discretion in a transaction. He wished to buy a luxurious home in Ventura for his mistress, Maricella. Porter understood immediately. "Discretion is my middle name," the agent had assured him.

They agreed to meet in a few hours.

Now, two hours later, Flowers sat in Porter's office and asked him about available properties. "I want something in the hills. Away from the rank and file. Maricella loves her privacy, and it may be necessary for me to provide her with, let us say, some minor protection," he said with a conspirator's wink.

Porter smiled. "I completely understand Mr. Sanchez. I've got several properties in mind for you. Let's take a look at the property profiles and if any of them interest you, I can make arrangements for a viewing tomorrow or the next day."

"No, no, no Mr. Porter. I have come on a mission to buy. I have heard from one of my associates that you are quite aggressive," Flowers said. "I don't need to visit the property. Viewing the profile will be good enough. As soon as we find one that suits my needs, I want you to seal the deal. Preferably today."

. This was Porter's kind of guy. Knew what he wanted, had the money and wanted to get it done. Fast.

"Understood, Mr. Sanchez. Let's view the properties. Would you like a drink?"

Wanting to avoid leaving fingerprints or, more importantly, DNA samples, Flowers declined. The two went to a nearby computer and Porter called up several properties on his computer.

"Stop!" Flowers declared, pointing at the screen. "This one will do. How much will they take?"

"They're asking one point seven, but I think they'll take one point three."

"Offer them one point five, ten day close. All cash," Flowers said.

Porter smiled and said, "Yes sir. I'll be right back."

This was definitely his kind of guy.

FLOWERS WAITED FOR Porter to leave the room. Once he was sure the real estate agent was gone, he pulled a small ball of putty from his right coat pocket. From the left he produced some wires and a motion-activated unit. He placed the device under Porter's large, red leather chair and turned the sensor on and set a small timer. The chair would explode exactly one minute after the motion sensor was tripped. It would deactivate and reset if Porter got up from the chair.

Special Ops had used this type of explosive recently in Pakistan. Very neat; very limited blowback. Flowers had purchased it on the black market. Once again, police would be thrown off. They might figure out the killer was former military, but they would never connect it to him personally.

Fifteen minutes later, Porter returned with a huge smile on his face. "Mr. Sanchez, it is my pleasure to inform you that the sellers have accepted your offer," the agent said, looking indeed like a bulldog in heat. "I need to get some signatures and then I will open escrow tomorrow. Closing is set for ten days."

"That is wonderful news, Mr. Porter. My friends were right about you." He paused, smiled broadly— displaying a large silver cap on his left front tooth. If his visit was captured by security cameras, the full effect of the disguise would throw off any viewers. He continued, "Let me check in at my hotel first. I can meet with you this evening. I will sign the papers then."

Wishing to conclude as much of the transaction as possible at his office—he knew buyers have a funny way of changing their minds when not bound by con-tract—Porter suggested they, at least, pen the offer before Sanchez left.

Alvaro Sanchez shook his head no. "Tonight, my friend. I will call you and give you the name of my hotel. We can meet for cocktails. Bring the papers." Flowers rose, avoided shaking the man's hand again, and left.

Porter called after him, "See you tonight. Be sure to bring your checkbook." He smiled at his own joke.

Porter walked outside, rubbed the decal on his Porsche Boxer and said quietly, "Maybe I can buy you a little brother now. How about a new Cayenne?" He laughed and returned to his office.

Three minutes later, as he viewed the office from two blocks away, Flowers witnessed the substantial explosion.

"Goodbye, Mr. Porter. I'm afraid I won't be buying the house after all. It seems I forgot my checkbook," he said with a slight chuckle. It was the way he liked his kills; efficient and clean. He put the Nova in gear, tossed the beard on the back seat and veered on to the freeway heading north.

One down, two to go.

He'd make sure the next one went just as well. He accelerated.

Next stop, Santa Barbara.

13

THE PREVIOUS GUNSHOT STILL ECHOED THROUGH THE CANYON AS BRAD PULLED THE TRIGGER ON THE NEXT ROUND. TO THE WEST, THE SUN HUNG ABOVE THE OCEAN, THINKING ABOUT BEGINNING ITS LONG DESCENT BELOW THE HORIZON.

The firing range was located in a small valley several miles outside of town. Bulls eye targets and criminal composite cut-outs had been placed at various intervals along an open field. The targets were backed with large bales of hay and the hillside sloped gradually behind the bales. Raoul Espinoza had suggested to Brad that they meet to practice their shooting. Brad suspected the police sergeant had ulterior motives as well.

"Damn. High and right again. Is it my sights or is it something else?" Brad asked as he prepared to fire another round from the .45 caliber handgun he had purchased after the IFPG incident.

"Brad, mi amigo, I think the answer is simple...It's your Loft," Espinoza replied.

"Loft? I didn't realize guns had loft on them. Like loft on a golf club?"

"No like L.O.F.T. as in Lack of Fucking Talent!" Espinoza busted up as he emphasized the 'talent' portion of his witty acronym.

Brad did his best imitation of abject disappointment and then added sarcastically, "That hurts, Raoul. That really hurts. I think you've damaged my self-esteem. That remark is going to cost you a beer when we get done here."

"Gladly. I've been saving that little gem for weeks. Didn't know if I'd use it on the golf course or the shooting range, just knew I was going to use it."

"Job well done. Now come on, you need to teach me to shoot straight. I'm missing a self-defense class with Mel to do this."

"Self-defense?"

Brad shrugged, looked a little embarrassed. "Mel thought it would be a good idea after all the excitement lately."

"Who's teaching it?"

"Some guy who was on Letterman a few weeks ago. He seems pretty good, although his main advice is: Run," Brad said.

"Good advice. How many classes have you attended?"

"Mel signed us up for ten, but I've only gone to five. Now let's get back to the matter at hand, why am I missing high and right?"

"It's the recoil. You're not adjusting for the kick. Let's try stiffening your grip on your right wrist with your left hand and anticipating more snap when you shoot."

Brad took a few shots with the tighter grip. "Hey, that really works. It's just the opposite of holding a golf club. Sam Sneed used to say that he gripped his four-iron as gently as he would a little bird."

"Sam who?"

"Sneed. He won more tournaments than Tiger. Don't tell me you've never heard of him."

"Before my time. Now take a few more shots and let's wrap it up."

Brad stared at his buddy in disbelief. Hadn't every serious golfer heard of Sam Sneed? He rattled off three more shots at the target. All hit the mark. He breathed a sigh of relief. They continued working on Brad's aim for another twenty minutes and then decided to call it quits. It was getting dark. And they were thirsty.

"See you at the bottom of the hill. If you get there before me, order me a Jack," Brad called over to his friend. Espinoza gave a 'thumbs up', hopped into his truck and sped away, gravel and dust shooting towards Brad's newly washed BMW.

"Dammit," Brad mumbled under his breath. "Okay, let's see who's got LOFT at the dart board." He pulled the BMW onto the country road and set off down the hill.

14

THE BEER WAS COLD, THE JACK DANIELS SMOOTH.

Espinoza and Brad sat at an old wooden table which was placed in the middle of a raw concrete floor covered with large clumps of saw dust and abundant levels of peanut shells. Old Western pictures lined the wall—testaments to a simpler time. The place wasn't going to win any modern design awards, but it was comfortable. Despite the decor, the Wagon Wheel Saloon was Brad's favorite bar in the northern part of the town.

Although smoking was no longer allowed indoors, the air contained a heavy, lingering scent of cigarettes and stale cigars from years past. The lighting was dim. Then again, inebriated patrons really weren't there to look each other in the eyes. By the end of the night, in a bar like the Wagon Wheel, most eyes were bloodshot anyway.

As they began nursing their first drinks of the evening, Raoul's phone rang. He excused himself from the table and walked outside.

"No worries," Brad said. "Just be ready to throw darts when you get back."

When Espinoza returned, his expression was grim.

"What's up?" Brad asked.

"There's been another real estate related murder. An agent in Ventura was blown up this afternoon."

Brad said nothing for a moment just shook his head and stared at his friend with an expression half-filled with shock and the other half, dismay. Finally, he broke the silence. "So now this guy is blowing people up? What's going on Raoul?"

"Wish I knew. Whatever it is, he seems to be escalating. Explosives are not easy to obtain and are even more difficult to control." He paused for a second, took a swig of beer, rubbed his ample jaw and then continued, "If we had any doubts before, we don't now, the guy's a pro."

"And he's killing upscale real estate agents exclusively. Will wonders never cease," Brad said, staring at his drink.

"We've got to figure out why this guy is doing this," Espinoza said.

"Did they look into the advertising angle?"

"Yep. No common thread."

"Damn! I hoped that would be it."

"Would've made it simple."

"How about additional trade associations?"

"Same thing. No link."

They both sat quietly for a few minutes sipping their drinks, deep in thought.

"Still feel like throwing a few darts?" Brad asked.

Espinoza shrugged. "I don't know..."

"Raoul, what's up? I don't think I've ever seen you this intense before. This isn't even your case. The killings all occurred outside your jurisdiction. The Feds are just asking you for ideas. Aren't they? They don't expect you to solve the crime do they?"

"I guess I *am* taking it seriously. I got this way when the Night Stalker was killing people in the San Fernando Valley. I dislike criminals in general, but I fucking hate serial killers," he admitted after thinking about it a moment.

"So you want to prove it isn't a serial killer? You want to discover the pattern and then you'll feel better?"

"Yeah, I think that's it. Serial killing is so random. The victims are totally helpless and totally unaware. It pisses me off. Such innocent people..." he said, his voice drifting.

He took another pull from his beer and stared at a floating shadow roaming across the ceiling.

Across the room, two cowgirls dressed in leather and tassels, danced a two-step to some old Billy-Bob song. Brad thought he recognized it, but when the words suddenly referenced a tiger, he realized it wasn't as 'achey-breaky' as he originally thought.

Brad took another sip of his whiskey and then suddenly remembered something Espinoza had told him a few years earlier. "Your niece was killed by a serial killer, wasn't she?"

Espinoza hadn't talked about it much. Just said she had been killed, but somewhere in the back of his mind, Brad knew that Raoul's niece had been going to school at Chico State. She was brutally murdered by an insane serial rapist and killer.

"Yep. My little niece, Maria. She was murdered by this asshole, Randy Setus. Happened almost twenty years ago. She was an angel. Setus stalked innocent young women, raped them and then did unspeakable things to them." His eyes began to swell. "My brother and his wife have never been the same."

Brad nodded. "Ain't fair, buddy."

What else could he say?

"These animals, they don't deserve to live with civilized human beings," Espinoza said, slamming his empty beer on the table.

"That's why you're in law enforcement. You deter this type of activity every day—whether you know it or not. You can't take it so personally, though. It'll eat you up, Raoul."

"That's what my shrink says, too. What you gotta understand is that I *have* to take this stuff personally. It's what drives me. It's the reason I go to work each day. Once I lose that drive, I will retire. And if we don't catch this latest serial killer—or whatever he is—I will feel irrelevant. Does that make sense?"

"Yep," Brad conceded. He too, knew that he would shrivel up and die if he didn't have purpose in his life. It wasn't about making a fortune, although that would be nice. It wasn't even about being the top dog. It was about getting up each morning and knowing that you might make a positive difference in somebody's life. And, of course, if things really went well, you might get paid for it.

"Some people obtain purpose through religion," Brad began. "You and I experience it through performance and dedication. I get it. I'll help however I can. Maybe, if you were a better teacher, I could shoot this guy before he attacks someone else."

"Brad, my friend, your shooting technique needs more than a good coach. You need divine intervention," Espinoza said with a slight chuckle.

"Okay, that's it. I can take no more of your insults. To the line we go."

They ordered another round, grabbed some darts from behind the bar and headed towards the dart throwing area.

Brad patted his big friend on the back. "Seriously, Raoul, the fact you care so much separates you from the rank and file. You're a good man and a good cop. But despite that, I am going to kick your ass."

A smile came across the sergeant's face. "Fair enough, bring it on."

Good to see him relax again.

At least for one night.

15

CARPINTERIA, CALIFORNIA, A SLEEPY LITTLE BEACH TOWN, LOCATED FIFTEEN MILES SOUTH OF DOWNTOWN SANTA BARBARA WAS TED FLOWER'S NEXT DESTINATION.

Known for its orchid greenhouses and miles of sandy-bottom beaches, Carpinteria, in a move that was surely motivated by an over-reaching and statistically ignorant city council had been dubbed, 'The World's Safest Beach'.

It *was* true that very few people were seriously injured while swimming in its waters. And it *was* equally true that the area, in general, hadn't suffered from the ever increasing crime wave that seemed to envelope Southern California. But 'Safest'? In the world?

Maybe it is. Who knows?

If it helped tourism—especially during the crappy economy—then let the accolade stand. Someone could study the true statistics later. Might make a good thesis for a marine biology student at U.C.S.B.?

TED FLOWERS PULLED the gray Nova into the hotel parking lot exactly thirty minutes after departing Ventura.

He checked-in under his real name. Just as there was no need for an alibi, there was no need for an alias. The Keystone cops would never catch him. Hell, they would never even catch a whiff of him. After all, it was unlikely that they'd check all of the guest registries for a common name in all of the areas he had traveled. Not even the FBI was that smart nor did they have those types of resources these days, what with budget restrictions and funding delays. The search area was just too big.

He immediately made himself known to the staff, joking that he planned to visit several of the orchid growers in the area because his last name was 'Flowers'. It was six p.m. when he checked in, too late to visit anything tonight. Best to get a good dinner and a full night's rest.

In reality, he would use the time to scope-out the area and begin planning how and when to contact his next target. He had decided how to kill with 'maximum prejudice'. It would involve torture.

He was excited by the proposition. Hopefully, his employer would be satisfied with his decision.

If not, fuck 'em. The real estate agent would be dead. Flowers would've done his job. He'd move on.

He would wake early and make sure the staff knew he was going to enjoy the 'world's safest' beach and then would head into Santa Barbara proper.

Flowers entered his room. It was standard fare: Queen sized bed, cheap dresser drawers, small bathroom with sink and mirror, faint scent of bleach and Lysol. He opened the window, unpacked his clothes and lay down on the bed. Time for a catnap before dinner. As he dosed off, he dreamed the dream of a hit man. Faces, names, locations and particulars from previous 'kills' popped into his head.

The woman in Coronado had been messy. The others, however, had been very clean. He knew it was important to vary the way he killed. Because of this, he had used explosives in Ventura, the knife in Coronado and various types of guns in San Francisco, Palm Springs, Corona Del Mar and Pacific Palisades.

Police and Federal investigators prided themselves on finding patterns to murders. From patterns, they developed clues. From clues they often found the perpetrator. There was no pattern to his kills; they'd never find him.

HIS THOUGHTS TURNED to the guy in San Francisco, John Finglebaum. Flowers had called him on a cold, foggy morning. They had decided to meet in Finglebaum's personal office located in the Castro section of town.

That was the killer's first clue about how he was going to handle Mr. Finglebaum.

San Francisco is famous for its gay population. The Castro District is known as the epicenter of gay activity. Finglebaum, therefore, was gay. Flowers was, tall, Latin, buff, and handsome.

It didn't take a genius to put two and two together.

Arriving on time for his 'interview' (as the arrogant Finglebaum called it) to discuss local real estate, Flowers did his best impersonation of a rugged, gay male, even going as far as adopting a slight lisp, and expressing a flamboyant appreciation for Finglebaum's 'magnificent' office. He even had commented on his 'extraordinary' taste in décor—the place was totally modern, like something out of an *Austin Powers* movie.

Flowers had used the false name, Bruce Sandoval. Finglebaum was duly impressed and suggested that he and 'Bruce' meet for drinks that evening. 'Sandoval' quickly agreed, confident he would catch the unsuspecting real estate agent alone at some point in the evening.

It was easier than Flowers had imagined. Feigning interest in an intimate relationship, he was able to convince the awestruck agent to take his big 'hunk of Latin love' back to his place for an evening of adult frivolity.

Finglebaum even hinted at showing Bruce his exotic 'toy' collection. Flowers had giggled outwardly, while thinking to himself, "I've got a few toys to show you as well, John. I think you'll find them quite interesting."

Twenty minutes later, the real estate agent lay in a pool of his own blood—Flowers having shot him twice in the chest. He had toyed with the idea of making the scene look even more obviously like a gay tryst gone awry but decided that there was no need to overdue it. The authorities would most likely conclude it was one anyway.

AS HE LAY on the verge of sleep in Carpinteria, Flowers couldn't help but wonder what 'toys' Finglebaum had intended to show him that evening and what he had planned to do with them. He smiled internally as he thought of the 'toys' he would use on his next victim.

Content and amused, his thoughts shifting to memories from his childhood, he slowly drifted to sleep.

16

PAULA SMITH-NEWHALL HAD HYPHENATED HER NAME AT MARRIAGE.

It was all the rage back in the eighties. Besides making Gloria Steinham proud, the name had actually helped her in her chosen field of real estate sales. To her, the name sounded regal and professional and, in a business full of schlock's and unprofessional amateurs, anything that separated her from the pack—made her appear more professional—was prized.

Her career had been fairly successful up to this point: One of the top sales agents in her office nine years running. Top 1% in the nation for her parent company the past five. Everybody knew it, she made sure of that. It was printed right there on her business card—and on every shopping cart at two of Montecito's three grocery stores.

Despite the economic downturn, real estate was still selling in Montecito, California. Although beautiful and pricey, the area wasn't entirely immune to the destructive forces of the recession—prices *had* dropped 30% from their peak in 2006—but since most upper-end buyers used cash or sold assets in order to purchase, the credit freeze hadn't completely deterred the wealthy. They knew they were stealing a piece of paradise at the current prices. Still, the buyers *were* picky and they *did enjoy* playing games.

Paula had adjusted along with the market. She knew the rules and she played the game very well. Real estate transactions with the wealthy were complicated to say the least and, while no rocket-scientist, Paula Smith-Newhall welcomed the challenge.

A PETITE WOMAN, Paula stood five foot three, one hundred and ten pounds dripping wet. At 53, her blonde hair was beginning to gray. To combat this, she had it styled weekly. She assumed she appeared responsible, yet friendly.

Despite her conservative appearance, she did have a 'racy' side. She went out with the girls quite often, had a few drinks, flirted constantly and engaged in her share of enthusiastic 'whoops' as the night progressed.

And then there were the substantial breast implants.

Her former husband had convinced her to get them. "The only good decision that sorry son-of-a-bitch ever made during our marriage," she often said. "They look great on me and I feel better about myself, but he only wanted me to get them so that he could play with them. He called them 'the girls'. He made *me* pay for them. Well, he's gone now, but I still got these beauties," she would say while thrusting her chest forward and wiggling her hips.

Paula sold real estate exclusively in Montecito. Although she had come from humble roots, and was a divorced mother of two, she had disassociated herself from the 'common' people, choosing rather to fully embrace the lifestyle of the rich and famous. "How else will I know my client's temperament?" she would reply when asked why she only ate, shopped, socialized, and lived in the rather small—and exclusive—enclave.

In real estate circles, she was known as a tough listing agent who treated her assistants rudely.

"Cold-ass bitch with big tits!" was how one former member of 'Team-Paula' described her when complaining to management about her boss.

Despite her antics in the office, she was considered a good person by her social circle—which included Melanie Stephens and Stefanie Ramirez.

And, unknown to her, Paula Smith-Newhall, star realtor to the rich and famous, was next on the killer's list.

With 'maximum prejudice'.

17

THE PAST YEAR HAD BEEN FINANCIALLY LUCRATIVE FOR BRAD—AT LEAST WHEN COM-PARED TO THE PREVIOUS SEVERAL YEARS. HE STILL HAD A LONG WAY TO GO TO GET BACK TO WHERE HE WAS BEFORE THE RECESSION—HELL, THE WHOLE COUNTRY DID—BUT, LIKE THE COUNTRY, HE WAS ON THE ROAD TO RECOVERY.

Unfortunately, it was a very slow road.

Interest rates had been low. People who could qualify—and there weren't many of them—were borrowing again. The commissions were significantly lower, but, hey, it was a job.

And, thankfully, the day job was once again paying the bills.

On the golf management side, John Linden wasn't playing much golf. Brad was sure Linden would eventually win more golf tournaments and income would begin to flow from representing him but it wasn't happening yet.

Good thing he was a patient man.

On the mortgage side, things were beginning to slow down. Rates had risen and, surprisingly, more and more buyers were paying all cash. Financially, he understood the decision of the wealthy: loans were a bitch to get and they had cash sitting in the bank getting zero percent interest. Why not pay cash? If asked, he'd tell them why: At four percent, the money was free since it was in theory trading below the rate of inflation and, furthermore, he, Brad Stephens, made no money when buyers didn't borrow. That's why.

Clearly, it was time to push some buttons.

Since he was now working both as an independent mortgage broker and as John Linden's personal manager, he had two options: Advertise more and try to generate commission income from the loan business or try to find revenue opportunities for John Linden.

He chose option two.

No-brainer, really. Much more fun and potentially, more lucrative.

John Linden was a former U.S. Open Champion. He was tall, good- looking, well-spoken and talented. Women loved him. Men strove to be like him. For all Brad knew, Linden probably rated well with young children and non-English speaking immigrants as well.

Lack of financial motivation was Linden's biggest problem. He played golf for fun—not money. It was common knowledge that between promotional golfing events held during the 'silly season' in professional golf—the time between the end of the official tour events of one year and the beginning of the next—and endorsement opportunities there was literally hundreds of millions of dollars out there for the taking.

He called John Linden.

Time to pick some of that fruit.

"I think it's time we approached Nike for a major sponsorship. What do you think?"

"Brad buddy, you know as well as I do that if I sell my soul to Nike, I'll never get it back. Why don't we wait until after the Masters? I think we'll get offers from all of the big boys then."

"Could be, but your stock is pretty high right now and still they're not calling. Nike has expressed an interest from day one. I really think you should consider hooking up with them."

"Okay, buddy. I'll think about it." Changing subjects quickly, Linden asked, "Are you and Mel coming over for dinner tonight?"

"I'm not sure," Brad said uneasily. "Did you hear about my meeting with Stef? I got a feeling she doesn't want to socialize with me right now."

"Bullshit. She loves you. Every family has spats from time to time. You two have history. She'll get over it. What did you say anyway?"

"I told her—in a diplomatic way—that her relationship with you *might* be getting in the way of her normally efficient work. It was no big deal."

"No big deal! You might as well have told her she's got body odor for Christ's sake. I don't know if you've noticed, but women don't take suggestive criticism the same as men."

"Oh, and you're the expert?"

"Apparently more than you."

Brad blushed at the obvious. "Point taken."

"What motivated you to do something so stupid?" Linden asked.

"I knew she wasn't going to like it, but the fact is work hasn't been going as smoothly as it should. She suggested we get an assistant. I'm not *totally* against it, but things have slowed down quite a bit in mortgage land."

"What about my shit?"

"You're not playing often enough to make me money, if you hadn't noticed."

On the other end, Linden sighed audibly. "It seems everyone wants to remind me about that."

"Who else said it?"

"Hank mentioned it the other day. And Stef has hinted recently that I'm not very good around the house."

"She's right."

"I know, but you're changing the subject. What's wrong with her suggestion?"

"She's talking at least forty thousand a year. She also said that while I was at it I should look for somebody to replace *her*."

"Again, I say bullshit. She's not going anywhere. She loves you. You love her. You two just need to work it out. Let's begin that process tonight. Okay?"

"You got it. In the meantime, I want you to think about this offer from Nike. You'll be set for life. It won't put major constraints on you. Give me one good reason you don't want to consider it," Brad demanded, hoping he wasn't over-selling his hand.

"Okay, here it is. I don't like their golf balls. They come off my clubs hard. I don't expect you to understand, but I need crisp, soft feel with every shot. I don't get that with their golf balls."

"That's it? That's the reason you would turn down millions?"

"Gotta get the ball in the hole, pards. I'm not sure I can feel comfortable playing their ball."

"Can't you fake it? Pretend you're playing the brand you like?"

Keep your cool, don't plead, he reminded himself.

"It doesn't work that way. I tell you what, next week, let's set up a meeting with the company whose ball I *do* like. Let's see what they'll offer."

"They're no Nike."

"Nope, but their ball is softer. Do we got a deal?"

"All right, it's a start."

"Good. Now what's for dinner?"

Brad and Linden discussed options for dinner and settled on a simple salmon dish, salad, and baked potato. Brad felt compelled to ask the fatal question.

"Do you want Mel to make or bring anything?"

Without missing a beat, Linden quickly replied, "Nope. Stef has it covered. You guys just bring some wine, a witty story or two, an apology for Stef and a healthy appetite."

Brad knew what Linden was saying: *'We can't trust Mel's concoctions. Love to socialize with you guys, but don't let her cook something creative. The Food Channel is great, but it's not for Mel'.*

Linden got it.

He knew.

Rather than disputing the point—there was really nothing to dispute—Brad said he'd see them at seven and hung up.

"THAT DIDN'T GO well," Brad muttered under his breath. "Not only didn't I change John's mind about the Nike endorsement, I now have to explain to Mel that Stef needs no additional food for tonight's meal."

0 for 2.

He was sure Mel had been watching the cooking shows all day. She would have a new recipe she'd want to make. If she didn't do it tonight, then *he'd* be forced to eat it by himself the following night.

It was a no win situation.

He sighed, swiveled his chair around to face his desk and stared at all of his recent bills.

Still manageable?

Barely.

Hope things pick up.

The thought made him very, very uncomfortable.

18

TO SAY HE WAS SURPRISED BY THE CALL HE HAD JUST RECEIVED WOULD BE A MAJOR UNDERSTATEMENT.

Flabbergasted was more like it.

But there it was, Mercedes Falicello, the granddaughter of his employer, Gino Falicello, was waiting for Flowers to respond.

"Ted, are you still there?" she asked.

He cleared his throat and said, "Yes I am. How did you get my number?"

"Oh, Papa thinks he hides his business from me, but I hear things and I have access to all sorts of information."

He thought about this for a moment and then concluded that it made sense. The Vegas house was like a mausoleum; secrets would be hard to keep in such an environment.

"I'm in the middle of something. I can't talk now," he said softly.

Now it was her turn to pause. As if she just found the right words, Mercedes finally spoke. "Listen, Ted, I realize you are working for my grandfather. I'm calling to tell you I like you. I noticed that look in your eyes when we met."

So there was a spark.

He didn't respond.

After a brief, awkward silence, she continued. "Listen, I know you're a complicated man. I am a simple woman. But I want to see you when you are done with my grandfather's business."

Again, the killer said nothing.

A few moments later she added, "So finish up the work. Do it quickly and come see me. Okay?"

What was it with this family?

Did they want everything done quickly?

"Ted, are you still there? Why don't you answer me?"

How long had it been since a woman had expressed true interest in him? Sure there had been some girls when he was young and then a string of prostitutes when he was in the military, but never a true girlfriend. Maybe this could work? After all, she knew what he was, didn't she?

She really *was* lovely. He pictured her tan skin, her beautiful mouth and her perfect breasts. For a moment he fantasized about making love to her.

Maybe, just maybe...

When this contract is finished, maybe. . .

He snapped back to the present and reminded himself about the task at hand.

No time for this foolishness. Besides, he was a peasant; she a queen.

He cleared his throat and said more to himself than to Mercedes, "We'll see."

"Okay, I'll accept that for the time being. Can I ask just one question?"

He reluctantly said, "All right, go ahead."

"What's it like to kill someone?"

Startled by the question, he quickly and assertively replied, "You don't want to know."

He hung up without saying goodbye.

19

THE NEXT MORNING, THE HOUSE HE FOUND HIMSELF VIEWING DIDN'T LOOK LIKE A TEN MILLION DOLLAR MANSION. LOOKED MORE LIKE A MILLION. MAYBE TWO. BUT WHAT DID HE KNOW?

The flyer he held in his hand was written by his next target—a local realtor named Paula Smith-Newhall. It contained a well written and descriptive narrative:

This lovely four bedroom, three bath home with upgraded kitchen, Jacuzzi hot tub,

study and detached guest house can be yours for the remarkably low price of $9,995,000. This 1946 Cape Cod bungalow boasts panoramic ocean and mountain views, direct access to the beach, privacy established by the large eucalyptus trees on either side and a relaxing 'crow's nest' patio equipped with fireplace, barbeque and dumbwaiter. Perfect for entertaining or just relaxing.

The flyer ended with:

This unique property will be shown by appointment only. Beginning dates have
not yet been set. Offers will be entertained, however, in advance. Please contact Paula Smith-Newhall.

Flowers shook his head and looked at the house again. Not much there. He still didn't get it. The style was California beach bungalow with a slight 'Cape Cod' twist. The color was standard blue/gray with white trim. A crow's nest rested atop the northwest section of the house.

Scaffolding erected along the north wall indicated that the house was in the process of being painted. He had watched the house for more than two hours. He'd only seen one painter. The owners must not be in a hurry, or were incredibly cheap, he thought.

Perhaps he should take a look at the home from the beachside. Maybe he was missing something?

MEMORIES OF THE phone call from Mercedes filled his head as he made his way back to the Nova. Should he call her back? Apologize for being abrupt? Was there really the possibility of a future with such a woman?

And, what was up with her fascination with death?

Truth be told, he looked forward to finding out.

He shook his head as if removing cobwebs and focused on the job at hand. Maybe the reason this realtor could price the property so obscenely high would become obvious when viewed from the sand. Maybe he'd see a full work crew painting and sanding the front of the house? It was 10:00 a.m. If there was, in fact, more than one painter employed, they'd be fully involved in the task by now.

Wishing to avoid the attention of nosy neighbors, Flowers pulled the car from its parking spot and proceeded back down the coastal frontage road for nearly a mile. He parked the car, got out and worked his way through scrub and ice plant down to the sand.

The hike took nearly ten minutes but was well worth it. His descent to the beach seemed to go unnoticed by the late morning dog walkers and local fly fishermen who worked the shallows, hoping to snag a decent-sized perch or sand shark.

Flowers took off his sweater, tied it around his waist and rolled up his sleeves. Then, knowing it would look odd if he strolled along the shoreline in expensive leather loafers, he took off his shoes.

The sand was still cold from the evening frost. The air was crisp. Small waves broke peacefully along the shore. Out beyond the waves maybe three hundred feet, a pod of dolphins played joyfully and effortlessly in the calm waters.

All in all, a beautiful California beach morning.

Too bad there was so much work to be done.

The house was nestled amongst several dozen other beach homes—some truly spectacular, some very plain. It would take him a few minutes to back-track the mile or so. The walk wasn't a problem. The problem, as he found out, a few minutes later, was that the house was protected by a tidal pool. In order to get the beachside view, he'd have to wade through three feet of water. He cursed himself for not wearing shorts.

He rolled up his pant legs and held his shoes high above his head as he entered the water. He began a slow shuffle towards his destination. After fifty feet, he made it around the point and walked onto dry sand.

Inconvenient as the move was, it gave him a more legitimate beachcomber look. He decided it was a nice touch.

The house immediately came into view. No work crew, only the scaffolding that could be seen from the street and the one lonely painter sanding and scraping some exposed wood.

The killer quickly formed his plan of attack. He would not lure Paula Smith-Newhall to her death by demanding a private showing as he had done in Coronado with Anna Gustapo, rather he would position himself on the premises and wait for the appropriate time to act. He now knew enough about the property, the painter, and the limited access points. He just had to be patient. His time would come. It always did.

He inhaled the crisp salt air, turned to watch the dorsal fins of the dolphins cut through the water and smiled. He glanced back at the house, shook his head and still wondered how the sellers could justify such a hefty price? Ten million bucks! Incredible!

He was still shaking his head when he returned to his car. The next morning he'd show up early and wait for Ms. Paula Smith-Newhall. If she didn't appear tomorrow, surely she would come by the following day; high-end realtors always visit their vacant listings. He'd just have to be patient.

He was actually getting kind of excited. It was getting closer to the time for him to exercise 'maximum prejudice'.

And he was ready.

20

LAS VEGAS, NEVADA.

JIM STACK AWOKE GROGGY, LIGHT HEADED, AND SLIGHTLY NAUSEOUS.
Slowly rolling his head to the left, he saw a well-endowed blonde lying by his side, her face covered by a goose-down pillow save for a small sculpted bridge for her nose to breathe. He couldn't remember her name. Names weren't important. He *did* remember they had hooked up during the cocktail party the night before. Most of what happened after that was a blur, however.

Based on the looks of the room—bra and pant-ies were strewn across a nearby chair with his pants, shirt and boxers next to them—it appeared that they had had tremendous fun. He smiled and then silently prayed she'd leave without incident.

Stack, a tall man with neatly trimmed blonde— almost white— hair, dark tan and deep-set blue eyes wasn't used to feeling hung over. He kept himself fit with a daily regimen of stretching and weight train-ing. He usually avoided alcohol.

The events of the previous day, however, had caused him to slip.

THE CONFERENCE HE headlined in Las Vegas had started out well. Over two thousand anxious real es-tate agents from all around the country had paid five hundred dollars each to listen to him 'coach' them on his now famous, and surprisingly non-controversial, 'Stacking Method of Positivity'. It was 'guaranteed' to bring the true believers personal wealth, success and happiness.

In reality, the 'Stacking Method' was nothing more than an organized goal-setting program based on purging—or temporarily denying—negative thoughts. Realtors loved this stuff—ate it up, actually.

Stack loved the money and prestige.

The fringe benefits of meeting lovely young ladies like the one sleeping next to him weren't too bad either.

He had begun his conference like he had dozens before. "This room is filled with negativity," he had admonished the star-struck group. "You are lazy and you are liars. You say you want to make money, but you don't really work at it. You don't mean it. You say you want joy, success and happiness but you allow your minds to be cluttered with junk! It's time we took all of those negative thoughts out of your head and replaced them with positive, produc-tive and optimistic ones!"

The room had exploded with thunderous applause. A few of the people he had strategically planted throughout the audience added a few "Whoop, Whoops".

And the guru, Jim Stack, was off and running.

Looking very serious and very professorial he addressed the group. "I want you to take the notebook and pen I've provided you and write down the five main reasons you are not now a millionaire."

The audience did as instructed, seemingly mesmerized by the larger than life personality on the stage. Serious looks of concentration filled each participant's face as they carefully chose their personal five reasons.

Of course, none of the two thousand attendees referenced the Great Recession of 2008.

That would be too easy.

Only losers would blame the recession.

After ten minutes, and now with an overhead projector at his disposal, Stack started up again. "Okay. Now we're going to circle that list." He circled a few nonsensical words he had written on the screen. "And then we're going to take that pen and put a big X across that circle," he said as he made a grand sweeping gesture with his own grease pencil.

"That's it. Cross out those negative ideas. Wipe out the reasons you've failed. Destroy evil, self-defeating thoughts!" he screamed to his audience.

Wiping his brow and taking a minute to collect his thoughts, he swept the audience with his eyes. After a moment, he settled his gaze on a beautiful redhead in the front row.

"You, darling," he said pointing at her. "Yes, you. Please come up here. Bring your notebook and pen."

The startled girl hesitated for a moment and then jumped to her feet and ran up onto the stage.

"What's your name?" he asked.

"Tammy. Tammy Mae Linstrom," she squealed.

"Where are you from, dear?"

"Seattle, Washington."

"Well Tammy Mae Linstrom from Seattle, do you know what we're going to do next?" Stack asked, just as he had a hundred times before, while sizing up this scrumptious flaxen haired beauty standing in front of him. He wondered if red was her 'true' hair color. Maybe he'd have a chance to explore that issue later.

Before the girl could answer, hundreds of voices shouted in unison—like ten year olds screaming that it was 'Howdie Doodie Time'—"We're going to start stacking up our positive thoughts!" they screamed.

"Yeah. What they said," the girl said in a high-pitched giggle, pointing towards the audience, her ample bosom jiggling as she jumped up and down.

"That's right, Tammy Mae. It's time for you to release the negativity. It's time for you to focus on the positive. It's time for you to be true to yourself." Stack let the last words hang in the air and then finished with a flurry, "It's time for you to start packing up the negative and 'stacking' up the positive!"

Again, the crowd erupted. An eminently sat-isfied Jim Stack then proceeded to break down Tammy Mae's list, basically call her stupid, implore her to think positive thoughts about herself and her

profession and insisted that she begin making lists of
realistic goals to accomplish daily.

These lists, he told her, would build upon themselves. And in so doing, she would be 'stacking' up the
positive.

Real heady stuff.
Who would've thunk it?
Goal-setting.
Lists.
Organized thoughts.
Wow, what a break through!

Certainly worth the hundred thousand dollars the
group had collectively paid to listen to their anointed
guru. If his system didn't turn their lives around,
he claimed, nothing would. It was certainly turning
around his.

WITH STACK LAPPING up the attention, the conference continued as planned for several hours. Things
turned bad, however, during the first thirty minute break.

"What do you think of all the realtors being killed
in California, Mr. Stack?" a gawky woman with bad
teeth and a pale complexion asked. She was wearing a plaid dress with a white top covered by a yellow
jacket. (Apparently, one of the national companies
still thought this attire was an appropriate uniform
for its salespeople). "Do you think it's a disgruntled
client or something?" she asked.

"I don't know anything about it. I haven't read
a national newspaper in a few days," he grudgingly

admitted. He didn't want his minions to think he was uninformed, but sometimes the truth just slipped out.

"I suppose you must be pretty busy before one of these seminars," she deduced.

"Yes, you're right," he quickly responded, happy for the excuse she had provided him. Truth was he hated reading; hadn't picked up a paper in years. The only written word—other than his own—he respected was that of a bank statement.

He looked directly in her eyes and put on a sincere smile. "It takes quite a bit of time and energy to pull this conference together. I usually shut out the modern world for a few days while I prepare. I have to stack my positive energy you know."

Where was the perky redhead? I need to get her phone number.

"Well, they've been going on for a while now," the girl said.

"What have?" he asked.

"The murders."

"Oh yes, the murders. What about them?"

"The police just in the past few days acknowledged to the public that there was a pattern. I've got a copy of the story in my backpack," she said as she reached in the bag hanging from her shoulder.

Oh, great. Shit! There goes the redhead.

He waved at Tammy Mae. She waved back but kept walking.

Got to get rid of this woman, she's cramping my style.

Pulling the newspaper out of her backpack and holding it so Stack could clearly see the headline, the girl continued. "The police have no idea why someone would want to kill real estate agents, but it's obvious that someone is. Do you think it's because these agents stored up their negative energy and didn't focus on positive thoughts?"

Stack was about to respond to the ridiculous question when something in the article caught his eye. A large box containing the names and locations of each of the victims had been inset within the main story. Photographs of each victim had been placed above their names and a brief description of how they had been killed had been added.

A sick, sinking feeling came over the guru of positive thinking.

He snatched the paper from the woman's hand and began scouring the story:

Police Admit Real Estate Agent Killings Related

SAN DIEGO – California. Federal agents and local task force officers today admitted for the first time that seven recent murders in the state of California are related.

Federal agent, Jim Krnich, confirmed during an afternoon press conference that law enforcement is now working on the theory that all seven murders were done by the same group or individual. "We believe the killer is targeting currently working real estate agents in certain markets," he said.

The article went on to caution active real estate agents about going on appointments alone, encouraged them to report any strange activity and discussed the fact that the task force had no idea what the motive behind the killings was.

Jim Stack, he of the positive energy, suddenly felt like the wind had been knocked out of his sails.

The redhead would have to wait.

21

"WE KNOW THAT EACH OF THE AGENTS KILLED SO FAR DEALT EXCLUSIVELY IN HIGH-END PROPERTIES," SPECIAL AGENT JIM KRNICH SAID AS HE BEGAN THE MEETING WITH HIS NEWLY FORMED TASK FORCE.

"What we need is an expert on real estate," special agent Zach Curlander said. "You know a guy don't you chief?"

"Yeah, I think so. His name's Brad Stephens. I've already been in touch with a mutual friend, a police sergeant in Santa Barbara named Raoul Espinoza." Krnich rose from his seat to get another cup of coffee. He continued speaking as he walked towards the coffee pot. "Espinoza's a good guy. We worked together on that... *trouble* back in Hilton Head." The group of several men and a few women shook their heads in joint understanding.

'Trouble'. Hell, I should be dead, Krnich thought.

Got lucky that time.

At least it led to this new job.

He looked around the room and then continued. "I have to admit, we don't get it. The world of real estate is a mystery to us. Wouldn't you all agree?" Without hesitation, all nodded or grunted.

Forty-seven years old, six feet tall, with short cropped hair that was slightly graying, Krnich was a former Secret Service Agent. His last assignment had been to guard the Speaker of the House, Thorngood Wilson.

It was during this stint that agent Krnich had saved the lives of the Speaker, John Linden and Brad Stephens. The three were playing in a competition at the links at Harbour Town when Linden's former management company tried to kill them.

Still too young for retirement, recently divorced and totally bored with the political scene in Washington D.C., Krnich had asked for—and had been granted—a transfer to the FBI special task force unit.

He had hoped to see Stephens and Espinoza again sometime in a social setting—maybe play some golf. This case, unfortunately, was anything but.

"Okay, so Stephens is your expert. When can we talk to him?" Curlander asked.

"Soon."

Satisfied, Curlander smiled. "Good," he said. He took another sip of his coffee and sat back as if the matter had been resolved.

"We gotta figure a motive, chief," came a chirpy voice from the back of the room.

"No shit Anderson! Of course, we have to figure out the motive. But these killings are all over the state. The only thing we know so far is that all of these agents sold expensive properties. From what we can tell, they didn't know each other, they didn't belong to the same trade groups, they didn't go to the same church goddammit." Krnich was frustrated and growing more so by the minute. He sat back down at the head of the table.

"It'll be good to talk to someone who seems to have a handle on this real estate crap," Anderson interjected.

Krnich nodded. "You make a good point. What the hell do we know about real estate? Hell, all I know is that my brother was foreclosed on last month and my mom is two months behind on her payments."

"Mine too," Anderson added.

"Yours too, what?"

"My mother is two months behind and my sister was foreclosed on last year."

"Holy Shit! Is this a national epidemic or what?"

The room went silent.

The fact was, yes, this was a national epidemic. Although they didn't all understand it, almost everyone was in some type of real estate distress.

Maybe this killer was too? Krnich wondered. Was that his motivation? Foreclosure. Loss of material possessions. Did he blame high-end realtors for his losses? Lots of questions. No answers.

"Okay, anyway, you guys get ready for Stephens. Begin making a list of pertinent questions." He went silent for a moment and then added almost as an after-thought, "It'll be good seeing those guys again."

"Will do, chief," Anderson responded. "And chief," he added, "I'm sorry about your mom. Maybe yours and mine can rent a small apartment and live together?"

Krnich said nothing; just stared at his task force agent.

So, this is what my world has come to, he thought.

22

SANTA BARBARA, CALIFORNIA.

MEL HUNG UP *the phone and yelled to* **Brad** *who was reading the newspaper out on the patio.*

"Paula just called," she said. "I'm meeting her and Stef for breakfast tomorrow at *Jeromes*."

"*Jeromes*? He doesn't serve breakfast. Just coffee. You better reconsider."

"Oh, I think you missed it while dealing with John and all the changes in your business. Jerome remodeled and added a kitchen. He still emphasizes coffee and muffins, and, God help me, he still plays that awful reggae music, but he now serves breakfast," Mel said.

"Really? Good for him. You don't see many business people expanding during this recession. I wonder where he got the money."

"Probably inherited it. I seem to remember hearing something about his father dying."

"Ah, the old fashioned way."

Mel smiled.

"Well, it sounds good," said Brad. "John and I will have to try it out. What else is Paula up to?"

"She has a nice ten million dollar listing on the beach. It's her biggest yet. She wants to have breakfast and then cruise over to the house. It's being painted but shows pretty well. She wants to get our input."

"Or more likely," Brad added, "she wants to show off."

"Maybe," Mel said with a quick shrug. "But I think this time she really wants to know what we think. This is such a screwy market and this sale means a lot to her."

"I'm glad she values your opinion, but what are you going to tell her? I mean you can't say the price is too high, can you?"

"No, but we can discuss if the kitchen should be painted or the furniture should be repositioned. Things like that. I'm sure I'll just confirm what she already knows: Everybody wants to live on the beach."

Brad nodded, acknowledging the truth of her statement. Make it comfortable, convenient and put it on the sand and some east coast hedge fund guy or Hollywood bigwig will buy it.

"I hope she knows it's a recession for rich people, too," Brad said, returning his gaze to the morning newspaper.

"I'm not sure she does. She's such a Pollyanna. It bugs me sometimes."

"I've learned in business that it's good to be optimistic, but you still have to be realistic. You can't just *wish* a problem away. I know she's been slow lately, I hope she doesn't spend too much money supporting this listing," Brad said, genuinely concerned.

It was common knowledge in the real estate community that when times went bad, it was easy for an agent to get too many listings and spend too much money promoting them.

Many an agent had gone broke during times of recession not because of lack of business, but because of too much business. Paula was recently divorced. She should be careful, Brad thought.

Hell, who was he to give advice? Look at how he'd been Madoffed.

"I'm sure she's spending her money wisely," Mel replied. "She's much better organized these days. You should see the lists she keeps and the goals she sets. It's amazing."

"You can never be too organized," Brad agreed. "Say hello for me and be sure to invite her over for dinner soon. I'll barbeque some salmon."

"Sounds good, I'll be sure to tell her."

Over the top of his reading glasses and down the bridge of his nose, Brad stared at his wife. Her long hair was bunched back into a ponytail and she wore jeans and a white blouse. She looked much younger than her age. He liked that. And, not for the first time, he was impressed by her seemingly endless energy and desire to socialize with friends. He vowed to share some of that energy.

Changing the subject, Mel asked, "Have you talked to the boys lately?"

"I saw Blake the other day. He was doing well. Now that you mention it, I haven't seen Scott for a few weeks. I wonder what he's up to. Why do you ask?"

"No reason, just wondering," Mel said quickly. "I've got to run. See you later." She closed the door and prepared to head to the market.

Brad returned his attention to the sports page. No golf stories. He made a mental note to call the sports editor of the local newspaper later that day. He'd plant some information about Linden's upcoming schedule.

An agent's work was never done.

———

AS SHE SETTLED into the driver's seat of her SUV, Mel picked up her cell phone and made a call. It rang five times and then went to voicemail.

"Scott, I just talked to your father, he has no idea how you secured the funding for your food truck," she began. "I think he assumes you got a loan from the bank. You should tell him the truth soon. He might have some good ideas and he really should know that John and Steve invested in it. He *is* John's manager, after all, and he *should* know where the money is going. Anyway, give me a call when you get a chance. Love ya." She pushed 'end'.

Scott Stephens, her youngest son, had recently aspired to opening a restaurant. A popular guy with an outgoing personality, Scott had been convinced to begin his food career with a mobile—rather than fixed—location.

Gourmet or niche food trucks had become popular in California over the past few years. The up-front costs were less and the flexibility was incredible. One day Scott could serve hundreds of hungry government workers downtown, the next provide food for hungry beach-goers.

His truck featured burgers, dogs, sandwiches, pizza, salads, and what was quickly becoming his signature dish: Scott's sizzling chili. It had only been operating for two weeks, but already things were going well.

People seemed to love his chili.

As she put the car into gear and began her descent down the driveway, Mel smiled and began thinking of all the recipes she had seen on the Food Channel. It didn't matter that Stef hadn't wanted her to cook the night before, one way or another, she was sure she would contribute to Scott's new food truck.

Now all she had to do was convince her son.

23

AFTER FINISHING HIS COFFEE, BRAD SHOWERED, SHAVED AND SET-OFF FOR THE OFFICE.

He usually enjoyed the morning drive but today's was extra special. Brilliant light shown through scattered fluffy clouds, marking a potential change in the weather. The ocean was calm. Small waves barely caressed the shore. And, fortunately, traffic was light.

Arriving at his office a bit past ten, Brad parked his car, entered the building and said good morning to Marge.

"Good morning! More like good afternoon, if you ask me," Marge barked.

"Yes I know it's late, but I don't have any meetings scheduled today and it was such a nice morning I decided to stay at home and read the newspaper outside."

"Must be nice; I've been here since eight."

"And thank you for that. It's absolutely essential someone be here early. I never know when calls might come in. You're doing a fine job I'm going to talk to Donna about giving you a raise," he said.

Surprised and suddenly pleasant again, Marge puffed her hair with her right hand and smiled brightly. "You are. Really? Don't mess with me. I could use an extra dollar an hour. Things have been tight around the house what with Oscar's gout and all."

"I'm serious. I'll talk to Donna today. Now do me a favor and bring me a cup of decaf when you get a chance." He began ascending the stairs when Marge spoke again.

"Thank you, Brad, it would mean the world to me."

"You're welcome. Now how about that coffee?"

———

"MORNING ANDREW. MORNING, Peter," Brad said to the two interns. "Stef still not in?"

"Don't you remember, Mr. Stephens, she's not coming in today or tomorrow," Peter, a slightly built, twenty-three year old with long brown hair and still active acne said.

"I thought she might be kidding. She rarely misses a day."

"She's pretty pissed at you, Mr. Stephens," Andrew said.

"Stefanie Ramirez does not get pissed. She might get even. She might get flustered, but she doesn't get pissed. She'll be back soon. In the meantime, you two need to carry the load." He looked from Peter to Andrew for validation. They both nodded looking like more like deer's in headlights than semi-trained professionals.

God help me, he thought.

With that, Brad entered his office, sat down in his chair and turned on his computer. Fifteen minutes later, he pressed the intercom button.

"Peter, could you come in here please and bring the Fitzpatrick, the Culbert, the Reyes, and the Freelander files."

"I'm not sure where Ms. Ramirez keeps the files," the young man admitted.

"I'm sure she keeps them in the filing cabinet."

"Yes she does, but I'm not familiar with her filing system."

"What do you mean?"

"She has a unique system. It will take me a few minutes to find those files. They're not filed alphabetically. I think she files them based on their status."

"Well, whatever. Find them and meet with me in ten minutes." Brad said.

In all the years he and Stef had worked together, this was, by far, the most strained the relationship had ever been.

If there was any doubt about it, it had been confirmed the night before at dinner.

Linden had greeted him and Mel at the door, handshakes and hugs all around. Stef had appeared in the doorway and threw her arms around Mel. For

Brad, she nodded her head and pointed towards the bar.

The rest of the evening with Stef went downhill from there.

Now he was in the midst of work and, apparently, nobody knew how to find the tools of his trade. It was frustrating, but it also put things into proper perspective. He needed Stef more than she needed him.

Damn!

A LONG FIFTEEN minutes later, Peter found the files. He had just placed them on Brad's desk when a voice from the street filtered through Brad's half-opened window.

"Brad Stephens! *Ju com* out here," the voice bellowed. "I *wanna* talk to *ju.*"

Brad approached the window and opened it fully. Standing—almost swaying—in the middle of the street was a middle-aged Hispanic man. In one hand he held a bottle, in the other, a piece of paper.

Brad yelled to the man below, "Hold on, I'm coming." And then mumbled to himself, "Ah shit, what now?"

24

"MY LUPE: TAKE A GOOD LOOK AT HER, JU PUTO!" THE MAN SHOUTED AS BRAD MADE HIS WAY THROUGH THE FRONT DOOR.

Brad walked towards the man, his hands held high in a conciliatory gesture, his eyes fixed on the photo the man held in his left hand. The late morning sun shined directly in his eyes. He wished he had grabbed his sunglasses.

"Hey, now let's just calm down," Brad said. "I don't know what this is all about, but why don't you come inside and we can talk about it."

The man swayed some more, chugged a shot from the bottle he was holding. Brad could see it was Tequila.

Of course.

The Devils' Juice.

He had seen many men go loco from too much Tequila.

121

"I not *gonna com* in *jur* office. *Ju gonna* face me right here," the drunk man said. "Look at *tis* picture. Look at my Lupe. *Mi amor. Mira!*" he slurred.

"She's a lovely woman," Brad acknowledged. "I'm not sure I ever met her."

"*Ju* talk to her on *tee* phone. *Ju* tell her she *gonna* lose her house—our *casa. Ju* remember now?"

Brad didn't but played along. "I've spoken to hundreds of people in foreclosure since this recession began. I don't remember all of them."

"She call *ju*. She ask for help. *Ju* tell her she *gonna* lose her house. *Ju* say, 'Lupe give up. The man gonna win.' She blame me for getting *tee* shitty loan and signing *tee* papers," his voice began drifting as his eyelids drooped.

Suddenly, Brad remembered.

Mrs. Gonzales. The one who wasn't going to listen.

"Oh, yeah, Lupe. I remember now," Brad said, grabbing two folding chairs from the reception area and walking towards the man. "I never met her, but she sounded like a nice lady. How's she doing?"

The man's eyes focused and a sudden calm came over him. And then, like Dr. Jekyl and Mr. Hyde, the drunken man's eyes turned steely with rage. "How she doing? How she doing? She dead. *Muerto. Ju* gave her the final advice. *Ju* killed her. *Ju* killed my Lupe!"

"I killed her? Now hold on Mr. ...I don't even know your name?"

"Jose. Jose Gonzales," he slurred.

Brad approached the man slowly, hands still raised. "Well Jose, I'm so sorry to hear about Lupe. Come on over here and sit down," he said unfolding the chairs on the sidewalk. "Let's talk about it."

Mr. Gonzales heaved a huge sigh, and walked over next to Brad. "What did *ju* say to my Lupe?"

"All I said, I think, was don't waste your money. The bank is going to win."

"*Tas eet?*"

"Yes," Brad said, helping Jose into a chair and then sitting down next to him. He turned and looked Jose Gonzales directly in the eye. This man was in desperate pain. How could he possibly know the grief the guy must be feeling? But, was Brad responsible for Lupe's death? No way.

"After she talk to *ju*, she call two lawyers my brother recommend and then she *com* into *tee* room and say, 'Jose, *ju* lying, cheating piece *ub sheet*. *Ju loss* all our money and now *ju loss* our home!' How *ju tink* that make me feel?"

"Like crap, I'm sure. I'm so sorry. When did this happen?"

"Two days ago," Gonzales said, raising the bottle to his lips and taking a big swig. "She hop in *tee* car and she drive up to *tee* bridge and she jump off!" He began crying, his eyes filled with anguish and loss.

Brad sat frozen. He looked at the pathetic figure in front of him. He felt the man's loss. He felt the pure suffering. It was gut-wrenching but he was powerless. He couldn't bring Lupe back. What did Jose Gonzales want? Brad decided to ask.

"What can I do to help?"

The man said nothing. Just sat stone-faced, staring at his shoes.

After a brief pause, Brad said, "Jose. I've been married a long time. I love my wife too. I'm so sorry for your loss. It must be a real shock to you and your family."

Still no reaction.

"Listen, I see the police across the street. They're concerned about the situation." Brad waved to two uniformed officers who had come out of their cruiser and were headed towards the two sitting men. "Maybe these guys can arrange grief counseling?"

"Grief counseling? I don't need no grief counseling, I need Lupe. What am I gonna do?" He took another swig from the bottle.

"I don't know Jose, I really don't, but I know it begins with talking. You need to tell somebody how much you loved Lupe and how much you needed her. You've begun that process, now let me get you help and you can finish it." Brad looked down at his hands for a moment. They were trembling slightly. Did he feel guilty? No that wasn't it. He had nothing to feel guilty about. He took a deep breath and suddenly realized what was bothering him: There, but for the grace of God went Mel.

Brad had considered suicide for a brief moment back in the dark days of the Truckee fiasco and since then there had been several attempts on his life. Mel could easily be the grieving widow right now—just like Jose Gonzales. He shook the notion from his head and raised his eyes to face Gonzales. "Do you have any immediate family I can call?"

Gonzales nodded. "My *seester*," he said, putting the Tequila bottle down on the sidewalk and staring straight ahead. Brad rose and took him gently by the arm. "It's all right, he's just had a little too much to drink," he said to the approaching policemen.

"Are you sure there's no threat?" a tall, young-looking officer asked.

"I'm sure," Brad said.

"Okay, he's your responsibility."

"Got it. Have a good day. Come on Jose, let's get you some coffee and then we'll call your sister."

Gonzales rose and slowly moved with Brad towards the office door. "How I *gonna* pay for a shrink?" he asked, his brown eyes looking sadder by the minute, his voice growing fainter.

"Don't worry about it Jose, I'll take care of it... somehow," Brad said, not knowing how in the hell he would be able to afford the care.

I guess we can cutback some more.

Wait until I tell Mel.

Brad turned the inebriated man over to Marge, asked her to call Gonzales' sister and began to head upstairs. He was stopped abruptly when a guy dressed in khaki shorts, Hawaiian shirt, and sandals, slapped his chest with a manila envelope.

"You've been served, dude," the guy said and strolled away smiling.

Served?

What the fuck?

Surprised and upset, Brad ripped open the envelope and inspected the documents. Nevada County, California was suing him for un-collected supplemental property taxes.

The paperwork said he owed twenty thousand dollars on that house he built up in Truckee. The damn thing had cost several million to build and when it was done, sold for $875,000.

How could he owe taxes?

Damn!

"Oh great," he said under his breath, continuing his ascent up the stairs. "What's next, a federal indictment for writing EZ-Qualifier loans?"

25

"*WHAT DID THE GUY WANT?*" ESPINOZA ASKED WHEN HE CALLED LATER THAT DAY.

"Which one?" Brad asked.

"You mean there was more than one drunk yelling at you?"

"No, there was only one of them. But while I was resolving that issue, I was served a lawsuit over supplemental taxes."

"Suppla... what?"

"Supplementals. It's the difference between the old tax base on a property and the new tax base. Nevada County claims the house I short-sold for $875,000 was worth $2,000,000."

"And they want the difference in taxes?"

"Yep."

"Damn. Why don't they just tax all the medical marijuana being grown in the backyards of Nevada County?"

"That would be too easy, I guess."

"Yeah, you're probably right. Well, anyway, I hope you can fight it."

"I'm not sure. I'll give them a call later today." Silently, Brad thought about all the other borrowers out there who were about to be screwed and didn't know it yet. Like he, there were many good people caught in bad situations. And like he, those who had experienced temporary relief could at any time have the process come back to bite them in the ass. Banks were hanging in the wings, waiting for the right time to exercise full recourse.

For many, it would be a shock that would lead to bankruptcy. Brad was determined to avoid that fate. This most recent bill from Truckee wasn't making it any easier though.

"Good luck," Espinoza said and then added, "But anyway, I was asking about the drunk. What did he want?"

"He claims I drove his wife to commit suicide."

"Did you?"

"What kind of question is that?"

"Hey, I'm a cop. I get paid to ask stupid questions."

"That's true. I've seen you in action. And, by the way, you're good at it."

"What?"

"Asking stupid questions."

Espinoza paused for a moment and then prodded Brad on. "Well...?"

"No, Sergeant Espinoza, I did not motivate Mrs. Lupe Gonzales to jump off the bridge."

"Oh, man! She was a jumper, eh? You know they're going to put a barrier up on that bridge so people can't jump. The state still has to fund it. Might not happen for a year or two."

"Sounds like she was distraught and that she would've found a way to kill herself—pills, gun, drowning, whatever—the bridge was just convenient," Brad said.

"Personally, I think that's the way it is with most suicides. A barrier might discourage jumping, but it won't stop suicide. What's the old saying: 'A lock just keeps an otherwise honest man honest'."

"I agree," Brad said. "But, still, it's a real tragedy. The lady called me earlier in the week and asked for advice in dealing with her bank. She wanted to get her loan modified and they had denied her several times." Brad paused for a moment. He thought about all the distress he had heard in people's voices lately. Didn't seem fair. After a beat, he continued. "I've received hundreds of similar calls since the recession hit. I can't remember all of them. I usually recommend the same thing: short-sell or declare bankruptcy."

"Why didn't she just give the house back to the bank?"

"I think it goes back to the definition of a 'home'. Obviously, her house was more than just sticks and mortar. It was a home. It was her nest. It was where she planned on raising grandkids and serving Christmas dinner. It sounds like she panicked when she finally figured out that there would be no government relief."

"Yes, Lupe, there is no Santa Claus," the sergeant said regretfully.

Brad said nothing. Unfortunately, he knew how Lupe must have felt. He'd been there.

It wasn't fun.

ESPINOZA GAVE IT a few moments and then changed topics. "We still on for going to L.A. tomorrow?"

"I don't see why not. See you at eight fifteen."

Before Espinoza could respond, Brad joked, "The way things are going in my life these days, you might want to drive an armored vehicle"

"Don't laugh. I was planning on commissioning a standard police car with bullet proof glass, battering ram, roll bar, and extensive weaponry. You got some bad juju following you."

Brad laughed at the joke, said good bye and hung up.

Maybe there really was a dark cloud hanging over his head? He'd ponder it that evening over a stiff Jack Daniels.

26

THE NEXT MORNING, ESPINOZA—AS USUAL—WAS RUNNING LATE.

Brad was waiting for him in the kitchen nook when Mel came down the hall, hair wet and towel wrapped around her otherwise naked body.

"You're up early," Brad commented.

"I'm glad I caught you before you left," she said. "Do you have some extra cash? I've got a feeling the girls will split the check and I want to pay my fair share."

"That's right. You've got a breakfast meeting with Paula and Stef."

"Yep, we're going to *Jeromes*."

"Here I thought you might want to seduce me before my big interview with the cops."

"The thought crossed my mind, but like so many things as we get older, it vanished quickly."

"Maybe later?"

"Maybe. Let's see how our day goes. I got a feeling yours is going to be much more stressful than mine," she said.

"Okay. Say no more. At least I've got a goal. Here's forty bucks. It's all I've got. I'll make Raoul buy coffee," Brad said. He reached into his pocket and pulled out his money clip.

"Make sure you tell Paula that I'm still in the mortgage business. If she gets a buyer who needs a loan, send them my way," he added.

"I'm sure she knows. I just don't think they see many loans on these expensive properties. Buyers tend to pay cash."

"Well, remind her anyway. And I'll see you tonight. Don't bother changing your clothes." A horn sounded from the front of the house. Brad rose, gave Mel a kiss and strode through the front door.

"YOU'RE TEN MINUTES late. What's up?" Brad asked when Espinoza parked his car in Brad's driveway.

"I told you I was going to requisition a patrol car," Espinoza said, getting out of the vehicle and walking around the exterior. "Does this look like a patrol car to you?"

The car Espinoza had pulled up in was bright red with gold stripes along the sides. It looked to be a 08 or 09 Mustang. In the back it had USC TROJANS painted prominently between the trunk lid and the bumper.

"Now that you mention it, no, this is not a patrol car," Brad said as he joined Espinoza's exploration of the vehicle. "From what I can see this is either the worst stakeout car in the world or the work of a demented USC graduate who now works in the car pool."

"Almost right on both counts; it's a car we impounded during a long drug stakeout a few months ago. The dealer was a crazy Trojan and Raider fan. His other car is a van painted black and silver and has a huge Oakland Raiders logo across the front grill."

"No shit?"

Espinoza just shrugged.

"How did you get stuck with this beauty?" Brad asked.

"No other cars were available. I didn't take into consideration that today is annual 'Police Appreciation Day' in Santa Barbara. All the patrol cars are in the parade and the normal fleet has been reserved by the detectives."

"So how did you get this...?"

Before Brad could finish the question, the tinted rear passenger window began to roll down. Ten seconds later the smiling face of Brad's quirky, wealthy friend, Steve Zindo, appeared.

"Hey Brado, what's up, dawg?" Zindo had taken to calling everyone 'dawg' recently. And then followed it with a fist bump rather than a handshake.

It was a phase and, fortunately for everyone concerned, it had replaced his former greeting of: 'how's it hanging cross-dresser'.

Startled, Brad bumped fists with his friend and looked to Espinoza for an explanation.

"Zindo bought this vehicle at auction a few weeks ago. What can I say," he said as if that would explain it all.

"It's my mid-life crisis toy," Zindo interjected. "I always wanted a cool car and what can be cooler than this baby? It glorifies USC, my alma mater, and it has all sorts of neat gizmos." Zindo grinned like a proud father talking about his kids.

Espinoza grimaced slightly and then continued. "The car is specially equipped with armored panels, bullet proof glass, and re-inflatable tires. The engine has been souped-up and it actually gets decent mileage."

"Yeah, it only cost me twenty grand," Zindo said.

"Okay, I get it," Brad said, now grinning too. "There were no other cars available and you felt it was better to impose on Steve than to drive one of our own cars?"

"It's no imposition," Zindo quickly said. "Raoul called me about borrowing the mighty 'Trojan Mobile' and I said yes. I wasn't using it today anyway. All my friends in Montecito have already seen it and ridden in it."

"Did Raoul tell you why we're going to L.A.?"

"He did. That's when I said I'd come along. I've been watching cop shows my whole life. I bet I saw every episode of *Dragnet*. I've been watching *Criminal Minds* lately and I'm a fan of various famous murder shows on the cable channels. My favorite is the one about women who kill."

"They're not going to let you in Parker Center, you know," Brad said.

Espinoza cleared his throat and said, "Actually, I already checked with them. I explained who Steve is and that he is a savant when it comes to putting patterns together. They balked at first and then said, 'what the hell', the more the merrier. The case is already baffling them."

"See, Brad? They want my input," Zindo said proudly.

Brad shook his head slowly. "Man, the Feds must really be desperate to solicit input from a mortgage broker and a retired weirdo."

"Hey, I'm not weird. You've even said it yourself, I'm...quirky. My mom always said I was 'special'. Other kids called me weird. I think it hurt my self-esteem."

He had gotten the last laugh though –about a billion laughs, actually.

"The other thing he brings to the table," Raoul said, "is a keen understanding of real estate. I brought to their attention that he owns hundreds of residential, multi-residential, and commercial properties. He might see a pattern from an ownership perspective."

Zindo bobbed up and down in his seat like a kid on Christmas morning. "See, Brad? It's not just morbid curiosity. It's my expertise they're after. Besides, if they boot me, I've got a hot tip on a horse in the fifth at Santa Anita. I can always drive over there and come back and get you guys when you're finished. Now get in and let's get this show on the road."

Brad got in the car and Espinoza began backing out slowly. The sergeant's hand slipped when he hit the bottom of the hill and a loud noise came from the rear of the car.

"What the hell?" Brad exclaimed.

"Oooh, oooh, listen carefully," Zindo said excitedly from the back seat. "I swear I didn't even know the song had been programmed in. It was a bonus I discovered one day when playing with the knobs."

Of course, Brad thought, the USC Fight Song.
Perfect.

"Oh, what the hell...High, Hoe, Silver, away," Brad joked as he stuck his hand out the window and made a Trojan victory 'V' with his fingers and bent them up and down as the song continued.

Espinoza put the Mustang in gear and the three began the two hour journey to downtown Los Angeles.

27

PAULA SMITH-NEWHALL SIPPED HER COFFEE AND THEN LOOKED UP AS MEL WALKED THRU JEROME'S FRONT DOOR.

"Morning," Paula said, returning tired eyes to her coffee.

"Good morning, how you doing today?" Mel said.

Smith-Newhall said nothing.

Reggae music filled the air. It was either Bob Marley or Jimmy Cliff, Mel wasn't sure. Didn't matter. Whichever one it was, he was singing about retribution and fairness.

Mel liked the song.

Stef joined them a few minutes later.

"Hi girls, what a beautiful day," Stef sang out as she entered the restaurant.

"Made all the better by Paula's premiere listing," Mel added, raising her cup of coffee in a toast to her friend.

"I hope you like the house. It's absolutely beautiful, but I can see some room for improvement," Paula admitted, perking up some.

"I'm sure it's wonderful," Mel said. "For God's sake, it's on the beach."

"Well, it *is* older and it *could* use some upgrades, but, yes, the location should sell. It's just hard to know these days. Three years ago it would be sold before it hit the market." She sighed as if reminiscing about a long lost love. After a moment, she picked up the menu, studied it for a minute and then asked the girls, "Now what does everyone want for breakfast? I'm starving."

Mel ordered a Denver omelet, Stef a bagel with tomato slices. Paula, two scrambled eggs, bacon and toast.

"I notice you're eating lighter, Stef," Mel observed.

"Just trying to maintain my figure. John likes my boobs but I can tell he would prefer me thinner. Fabiola had a twenty two inch waste and his previous wives all had flat stomachs. Look at me. I've got 'birthing hips'," she said while placing both hands on her hips and making a pouting face. "I don't think I can get six pack abs, but I'm going to try."

"Your figure is outstanding! Don't let him tell you otherwise," Paula said.

"Sounds like things are working out with you and John?" Mel interjected more as a statement than a question.

Crossing her fingers and knocking wood first, Stef said, "I'm cautiously optimistic. He seems happy and I think he's wonderful. No wedding bells yet, but we're...comfortable."

"And, I'll tell you another thing," Stef said while sipping on her coffee, "He's insatiable in bed! I swear that man could make porno movies."

"You mean he's that big?" Paula asked.

"No, oh God no, I didn't mean that. He's no John Holmes, but he is... more than adequate. He actually calls his unit 'Mr. Twinkle' as in 'twinkle, twinkle, *little* star'."

The girls blushed and then giggled.

She took another sip of coffee and then continued. "What I meant is that he enjoys sex so much and is always ready to perform. It's amazing... and quite a change from my ex, Tommy."

"Okay, too much info now," Mel said, raising her hand in a stopping motion.

"Since you brought it up Stef," Paula said as breakfast arrived, "I had a rendezvous last night with a much younger man."

"Do tell."

"That's why you were so tired when I came in. I knew it," Mel said.

Paula grinned, took a sip of coffee and told her story. "I met him at a real estate party and we hit it off. By the end of the night we were slow dancing and I could tell—well, feel, actually—that he was ready for action. It was all I could do to keep his snake in his pants until we got home."

"Your place or his?" Stef asked.

"His. And what a mess! I don't know how guys can live like that."

"But it wasn't enough to turn you off?" said Mel.

"Girl, by the time I got to his place, a nuclear explosion couldn't turn me off! He was all over me. We must've done it three or four times last night and once again this morning."

"No way!" Mel said.

"You bet. And the best news is that I kept up with him, although I have to admit, I am kind of sore." She squirmed slightly in her seat and adjusted her skirt. "If you see me walking funny this morning, you'll know why."

AS THE FRIENDS finished their breakfast, and Bob Marley finished singing about 'Buffalo Soldiers coming to America', Mel asked Stef, "So what happened between you and Brad?"

"We had a minor disagreement over personnel."

"And?"

"And he suggested I work harder. I'm already doing the job of three people, and your husband wants me to work harder. He says John might be distracting me."

"He just doesn't understand all the pressure you're going through: The divorce and a new relationship. That's a lot for a girl to handle."

Stef nodded sadly, took a sip of her coffee and was about to say something when Mel continued. "And Brad's wigged-out all the time about our finances. I'm sure it's a more volatile time right now than normal.

And to top it off, a drunk husband showed up at the office yesterday. He claimed Brad caused his wife to jump off a bridge."

"Brad would never do that." Stef said, looking at the other women for validation. When they nodded, she asked, "Did Brad work it out?"

"He arranged for some grief counseling for the guy. But I can tell you, it really affected him. He was bummed all night long."

"Why didn't anyone call me?" Stef asked, suddenly looking very serious.

And slightly upset.

"I don't know. I guess we didn't think it was something he needed help with."

"Of course he needed help. You know as well as I do that he would never ask for help, but when he's upset, he always benefits from conversation."

Mel listened to the music playing in the background as she absorbed Stef's concern. This woman knows him as well as I do, she thought.

"Well, I think he's going to be just fine. You two should focus on getting back to work. Can't you two just kiss and make up?" Mel said.

"We will. I've just been overwhelmed with all the new compliance regulations. . .and John. And representing him and all," Stef replied. "Do you think I should call Brad?"

"Do what you feel is best. I know he needs you. I'm sure you'll figure it out." She took a final bite of her breakfast and then addressed Paula. "Now, how do we get to your incredible listing?"

"Follow me. I've got the key to the garage. I went by this morning before I came here. We can park on the premises. There is a painter working so watch out for his stuff."

And with that, the girls finished their remaining coffee, paid the check and exited Jeromes just as Bob Marley began to assure them that he 'shot the sheriff but did not shoot no deputy'.

The ride to the house took less than five minutes. They parked their car and entered the beautiful, ten million dollar, beachside home.

28

TED FLOWERS HAD HAD ARRIVED AT THE BEACH HOUSE SEVERAL HOURS BEFORE THE GIRLS.

He had figured that if she was going to make an appearance at her premier listing, Smith-Newhall would visit the home in the morning—make sure everything was in order just in case someone wanted a private showing. He smiled when he saw her park her car in front, run into the house and then hurry back outside.

'Bingo', he thought, hooked her on the first cast. His only regret was that she did not stay around long enough for the main attraction. He watched as she drove away and then focused his attention on the job at hand.

The painter was laying out his tarps and stirring his paints, clearly preparing for a long day of work. Flowers contemplated the most efficient way to neutralize the guy.

Should he kill him? Dump his body in the trash bin?

No, too messy and might scare the woman away if she didn't return this morning.

Noting the painter's name and phone number on the side of his parked truck, Flowers took out his throw-away cell phone and called the man.

"Hello, is this Sergio?" Flowers asked.

"*Si*. Who's this?" the painter said.

"My name is Johnson, Sam Johnson. I live in Santa Barbara and would like to meet with you to discuss painting my house. I was at a friend's house down by the beach and I saw your name and phone number on your truck. I figured you must be good if they trust you to paint such an expensive place."

He then added, "I have a very busy schedule this week. Today is the only day I can meet with you."

Excited by the prospect of more work, Sergio Godinez agreed to meet *Senor* Johnson at his home within the hour. The beach house could wait. That was a small job, anyway. Painting an entire house would take several weeks and could be extremely profitable. He'd have to remember to thank his wife, Gloria. She had demanded he put the phone number on the side of his truck. Now it was paying dividends.

The painter set up his ladder, spread his drop cloth and laid out various tools for the day and then departed the scene.

As he waited for the correct moment to take the painter's place, Flowers looked out to the sea. Again, dolphins frolicked, birds dive-bombed the water—searching for breakfast—and gentle waves caressed the shore.

What an ideal setting, he thought. Too bad I'm going to mess it up in a little while.

29

FLOWERS WATCHED AS SERGIO STARTED HIS ENGINE AND DROVE OFF.

He checked his watch. He knew it would take the painter at least forty minutes to reach the address he had given him. The house was on the other side of town.

Once there, the confused painter would linger. After a while he would realize he had been stood-up or had made a mistake with the address. He'd probably stop for lunch and then make the forty minute trek back to the beach house.

That should give the killer more than ample time, assuming Smith-Newhall was going to return.

The 'new' painter, dressed in coveralls, hat and gloves and wearing sunglasses walked across the driveway. He grabbed some paint, and climbed the ladder. He settled in, waiting for Paula Smith-Newhall to re-appear.

HE DIDN'T HAVE to wait long. Twenty minutes later, Flowers heard the sound of women talking. It was coming from the driveway. The sound grew louder as the women drew closer.

His target had company.

Shit.

He wasn't prepared to take out several people. It would be too messy. He decided to wait and see if the women would leave Smith-Newhall by herself. If not, he would have to regroup and form another plan. "Improvisation is sometimes necessary," his former military commander, Captain Howard would often say, "but it usually leads to unexpected consequences." In his line of work, Flowers could take no chances.

"Hello, Sergio, it's me Paula Smith-Newhall," the woman sang out as she entered the yard.

"*Si, hola*" came the response. Assuming that Smith-Newhall would be by herself and there would be no need for serious acting, Flowers had neglected to study the painter's mannerisms or dialect.

"Oh, there you are, Sergio" she said looking up the ladder, seeing his white painter coveralls—but not his face—high above the outside of the house.

"These are my friends, Melanie and Stefanie. They have come to inspect the house and make suggestions about minor improvements. If you're lucky, they might suggest some interior painting."

"*Bueno,*" Flowers said quietly, holding his head high and looking at the roof as if there was a spot up there he had missed.

If I'm lucky, they will leave quickly and allow me to kill you.

Mel and Stef followed Paula into the foyer and began examining the house. The kitchen was old but very functional. The deep blue cabinets and gray marble countertops went together well. After going through the kitchen, the trio inspected each bedroom and then returned to the living room.

"I wouldn't change a thing," Mel declared as the girls gathered around a large, picture window in the front room. "I know the kitchen and bathrooms are dated, but this *is* a beach house after all. The ocean view dominates." She swept her arm from side to side and fixed her view on the Pacific Ocean only fifty or sixty yards away.

"I agree," Stef added. "As long as the focal point is these large picture windows and this comfortable sitting area, the entire house works. Is there a good sound system?"

"Yes. I think so," Paula responded. "Do you think I should play some soothing music when showing the home?"

"Yes," Stef said. "Don't play it loud, though. You don't want to drown out the ocean entirely, just add to it. Try some Tony Bennett. He's sexy and he's smooth."

"And follow that with Van Morrison," Mel added. "That'll set the right tone."

"Good advice girls, that's why I brought you here, good ideas like that might just get you a free lunch later on." She winked at her friends. "Now did you bring your business cards?"

Both Stef and Mel reached into their purses and pulled out small rectangular cards. Stef's, of course, said "Assistant Loan Officer". Very official. Mel's just had her name and cell phone number. She wondered why she even carried the damn things. She hadn't had a job in years and she rarely was asked for a card, but Brad had insisted she get two hundred printed up by some cheap internet business and so she had. Right now, she was glad she had gone along with his suggestion.

"Good, now put them in this fishbowl. I want it to look like I've already had multiple, private showings."

While the girls did as they were told, Paula found the stereo. Surprisingly, a Tony Bennett CD was sitting on top of the CD player. She put the disk on the player and adjusted the volume.

"Perfect," said Mel.

OUTSIDE THE FRENCH doors, Flowers heard the girls talking and decided he would wait another few minutes. Maybe the other two would leave. They came to inspect the place, didn't they? Well, mission accomplished. You're done. Now, go home and leave Paula to lock-up.

It was wishful thinking.

He watched as Paula excused herself for a minute, went into the kitchen and came out with a bottle of ice-cold Dom Perignon.

So that is what she was doing earlier; putting the champagne on ice.

Nice touch.

Popping the cork, she looked at her friends and said, "I'd like to make two toasts. First, let's toast the eventual sale of this beautiful home." The friends clinked their glasses and took a sip.

"Secondly, I'd like to toast that young stud, Todd, who rocked my world last night. May his vines ripen and his grapes continue to gush forth," she giggled as they all chugged a second glass of the fine champagne.

Mel asked for a third.

What the hell, it *was* a social outing.

And, lord knew, she didn't get out much these days.

THE OTHER WOMEN aren't going to leave. Flowers thought. He would either have to take all three out right now or regroup and get Smith-Newhall later.

Fearing that Sergio might return earlier than planned, Flowers decided to discreetly make his exit. "Live to play another day," was another thing his former commander used to say.

He set the paint can on the ledge and began to descend the ladder.

Well, another day in Santa Barbara ain't too bad, is it?

INSIDE THE HOUSE, Mel faced Paula and made another toast. "You have been such a success. You are truly an inspiration to your friends." They clinked champagne flutes again while Mel, feeling the effects from too much champagne, stumbled towards the French doors.

"It's getting hot in here, don't you think?" Mel asked, fanning herself with her free hand.

"Not really. I think you might be 'flashing', but if you're hot, just open the patio door," Paula said.

Without hesitation, Mel pushed at the middle of the French doors, not sure which side would open. Neither budged. She pushed harder until both doors abruptly swung open.

30

FLOWERS HAD POSITIONED THE LADDER CLOSE ENOUGH TO THE DOORS TO MONITOR THE WOMEN'S MOVEMENTS—PERHAPS, TOO CLOSE.

It wasn't rational for both French doors to be opened simultaneously. He had felt safe placing the ladder in such a manner as to block the left side only.

Apparently, Mel wasn't thinking rationally.

She was seriously buzzed. It was mid morning and she was hot. As she swung both sides of the French doors open, the left side caught the painter's ladder and stuck. In her current state, she didn't realize the door was blocked by the ladder. She took a deep breath and pushed even harder.

"What the Hell?" she said out loud. "This damn thing just won't move..." She pushed again. Finally, the door gave way with Mel almost stumbling through it. She regained her balance and smiled at her companions. "There," she said proudly, taking in the fresh air.

A second later, Flowers came tumbling down with a startled, "Hey!" His body hit the ground with a thud. Mel watched in horror as the painter's head snapped back and then struck a small statue of a rabbit. He lay on the patio motionless.

"Oh, shit!" Mel said.

"Oh, shit!" Stef and Paula added simultaneously.

Mel approached the body but abruptly stopped when she saw a large butcher knife and a gleaming pistol lying on the ground next to the man.

Paula and Stef moved in closer to inspect.

"Mel! What have you done?" Paula screamed.

"I don't know. I was just opening the doors. It's so damn hot in here. I didn't see his ladder. I hope he's okay."

"Okay! Are you crazy?" Stef exclaimed. "What's he doing with a gun and knife?"

"We can ask him later," Paula offered.

"Bullshit," the street-wise Stefanie Ramirez shouted. "A painter doesn't come to a job armed with a knife and a gun. That guy was up to no good. Let's get the hell out of here before he comes to."

"Don't you think we should call the police and an ambulance?" Paula said.

"Yes I do, but not from here. We can call from our cell phones as we head back to *Jeromes*. Now get your things. Let's move." Stef began making herding movements with her hands and arms.

As Mel turned to go, she looked one last time at the crumpled man lying on the patio floor. Due to the angle of his fall, she couldn't quite see his face.

She wondered if she shouldn't sneak a quick peek. It might come in handy if the police had questions. The man groaned and began to move a little.

Mel suddenly froze like a mummy. She held her breath and tried to make her heart beat more quietly. After a moment, the man's movement stopped as well. She waited a beat, breathed again and then moved closer.

Sobering up by the second, she bent down to get a good look at the man. She saw dark skin, bushy eyebrows, a thin moustache and pock-marks on his face.

Either Hispanic or Persian she thought.

She saw big hands, big feet and blue eyes. The eyes looked out of place. Shouldn't they be brown, she thought. She made a mental note to ask the police about them.

She wasn't absolutely sure she'd recognize the man if she saw him again, but at least she could give a basic description to the authorities.

Just as she turned to join her friends, she noticed something peculiar on the man's leg. His overalls had slid up his right leg, exposing his shin and calf.

She saw that he had a small tattoo on his calf.

It didn't say "Momma" nor did it look like an L.A. gang engraving. It

was rather nice and very symmetrical. She made another mental note to research the design on Google when she got home. Maybe it would give the police a clue as to his identity?

The fallen man groaned again. That was the only signal she needed. Mel ran from the house like a bat out of hell.

31

THE THREE WOMEN *BURST INTO JEROMES AND BEGAN TELLING THE RESTAURANT OWNER THEIR STORY.*

"Excuse me ladies," Jerome, a squarely built guy in his mid-fifties with short gray hair and ample belly said. "Let's calm down. What did the police say?"

"They told us to stay put and someone would be here shortly," Stef said. "Frankly, I don't think they took us very seriously."

"Yeah, well, whatever." It was Paula speaking this time. "That guy was up to no good. And now that I think about it, I hope he didn't hurt poor Sergio."

"It gets stranger and stranger," Stef said, shaking her head slowly and wiping dirt off her designer shoes. She asked Jerome for a glass of water.

"Of course," Jerome said. He made a sweeping gesture and told the girls to sit down. "I'll get you all a glass of water." He strode towards the kitchen and then stopped. He turned around quickly as if startled by a thought. "You think he's gone? We're not in any danger here are we?"

The women looked at each other nervously. Paula shrugged. Stef shook her head. And Mel spread her arms wide. "Who knows? He was knocked out initially, but it seemed like he was coming to when we left," Mel said.

AFTER TAKING WHAT seemed like an eternity to the girls, an officer arrived at *Jeromes*.

Patrolman Kim Johnson, a tall, blonde guy in his mid-forties assured the ladies that they were lucky he had been in the area. Otherwise, it could've been forty-five minutes or more. They thanked him and urged him to inspect the beach house. After discussing it for a few minutes, he called for back-up.

"Knife and gun, you say," Johnson remarked. "Why would a painter carry both a knife and a gun?"

"That's just it, he isn't a painter," Stef said. "Duh!"

"He *was* up the ladder when this lady knocked him off, right?" the officer said, pointing his pencil towards Mel. "He was painting, wasn't he?"

"Yes he was. But I'm sure he was just biding his time," Paula interjected.

"Biding his time to do what?"

"To kill us or rape us or...whatever. Now are you going to go over to the house and arrest the guy, or what?"

"We'll go over just as soon as my back-up arrives."

"How long is that?"

"Could be twenty minutes, could be an hour. Our budget has been cut and there aren't many cars available. And, today is Annual Police Appreciation day. Most of the force is downtown."

"Twenty minutes to an hour! The guy hit his head hard. He could be dead by then," Mel exclaimed.

"Or, more likely, gone," Stef added.

"Yeah, we should go over there and keep an eye on the crime scene," Jerome said grabbing a baseball bat from behind the counter.

The group stared at him.

He stared back. "What, I can't protect my business? Those people who live up the beach are my clients you know."

"Now slow down there cowboy," Officer Johnson said. "Let's give it a few minutes. From what these ladies say, this guy is armed and could be dangerous. Your bat isn't going to stop a bullet."

Jerome replaced the bat, took a deep breath, and shook his head. "You're right. I don't know what I was thinking. It's just so frustrating sitting here when the guy could be halfway to Mexico by now."

Mel shook her head in agreement while thinking, *"I hope like hell he's on his way to Mexico. The further from us, the better."*

32

TED FLOWERS WASN'T WAITING AROUND FOR ANYBODY AND HE CERTAINLY WASN'T HALFWAY TO TIJUANA.

Rising to his feet, he rubbed the bump on the back of his head gently and tried to gain his equilibrium. Groggy at first and definitely sore, he grabbed his knife and gun and searched the premises. He remembered feeling this way once in Iraq. It had been an enemy land mine and it had been too close for comfort. He shook his head several times and surveyed the area around him.

No sign of the women.

How had this happened to him? He was a trained Special Ops soldier—a lean, mean, fighting machine. It was a simple operation. The real estate agent should be dead and he should be checking out of the hotel by now.

They were defenseless women, for God's sake!

Instead, he was rubbing the back of his head and staring at the empty house in disbelief. He'd have to alter his plans; that much was for sure. Should he stay and finish the job? Had they seen his face? Could they identify him? Who were the other women? Should he find out and take them out as well? Or should he move on to Pebble Beach?

No matter what he did, his employer would not be happy.

There had been no killing with 'maximum preju-dice'. Yet.

In the distance he could hear a police siren. It was time to make a swift exit. Searching for anything that might tie him to the scene, he took a quick look around the interior of the house. Convinced the place was clean, he walked through the kitchen towards the front door.

His eyes stopped on the goldfish bowl. He was pretty sure the bowl had been empty when he arrived.

He smiled.

He quickly grabbed the two cards sitting on the bottom of the bowl, tucked them in his back pocket and exited the house.

Gun held low by his side, his head on a swivel, he approached his car slowly. He scoured the area for any signs of the police. The neighborhood was quiet. And fortunately for him (and them), there were no neighbors walking the street. No witnesses to worry about. No collateral damage. The siren grew louder. He looked around once more and then got in his car.

He started the engine; hesitated before putting the Nova in gear. Shook his head and grimaced. He remembered falling off the ladder. He vaguely remembered hitting his head. A small bump was forming at the back of his skull. What he couldn't figure out was why the stupid woman continued opening the patio door, when clearly, his ladder was blocking it.

Perhaps he'd ask her before he killed her?

Staring into the rear-view mirror, he tore off the bushy eyebrows, removed the fake acne, discarded the thin moustache and, lastly, took out the blue contact lenses. It was a good thing he had donned a disguise. It had been a last minute decision.

Most likely one if not all of the women had seen the face of the fallen painter. It would do them no good of course if they described him to a police artist but perhaps it would point the police in the wrong direction.

At least *that* part of the plan had paid dividends.

He checked his watch and confirmed it was still before the eleven a.m. mandatory checkout time. He put the car in gear and headed back to his hotel.

AS HE PULLED into the hotel parking lot, Flowers made his decision about how to proceed. He would travel on to Pebble Beach and then north to Atherton. He would take care of business up there and then double back to Montecito. Loose ends.

The only question was: Would he only kill Smith-Newhall or take all three of the women out?

Easy decision. He'd kill them all.

He hoped Falicello would pay extra for the additional victims. Maybe, if Flowers were lucky, the 'Fridge' would view the triple murder as an adequate definition of 'maximum prejudice'?

Either way, it was a regretful necessity. Collateral damage.

He grabbed his bags from the room, paid his bill with cash and pointed the Nova north.

As he passed downtown Santa Barbara, he took the two business cards from his back pocket and stared at them. "You were lucky your friend—either Stefanie Ramirez or Melanie Stephens," he said quietly to himself as he read the names, phone numbers and addresses on the cards, "was such an idiot, Paula. I will catch you on the 'flip flop'. You will not be so fortunate next time."

His mind drifted to thoughts of how he would deal with his next victim, Roger Willowby of Pebble Beach.

"This one will be a clean, uneventful kill," he said to himself as he stepped on the gas.

No drama. Just the way he liked it.

33

LOS ANGELES IN THE MORNING IS, CONTRARY TO POPULAR EAST COAST OPINION, QUITE A BEAUTIFUL CITY—AS LONG AS YOU'RE NOT STUCK IN TRAFFIC.

The picturesque San Gabriel Mountains frame the city to the east, and the magnificent Pacific Ocean borders it to the west.

Brad and his 'posse' arrived at Parker Center—the main police headquarters in Los Angeles—a few minutes after eleven. The building was several stories tall with lots of chrome and glass. Busts cast in bronze of former police chiefs, adorned the exterior. Armed guards stood by the front door.

Another unfortunate consequence of 9/11—not even police stations were safe anymore.

The drive to L.A. had been decent. Stop and go in a few places and one minor fender-bender that slowed traffic by Van Nuys but other than that, nothing crazy.

Zindo had insisted on playing the USC Fight song as they passed the two cars involved in the accident.

Both drivers had raised their middle fingers in unison and flipped off the red Mustang as it passed.

"Must be Bruin fans," Zindo had yelled at them, while flipping them off in return.

Very classy.

AGENT JIM KRNICH greeted the group warmly at the entrance to the building and helped them pass immediately through security.

"This way boys; follow me. I've got a conference room reserved on the fourth floor," Krnich said.

"We really don't have much information," Espinoza said, walking briskly, attempting to keep up with the leaner Krnich.

"Let me be the judge of that," Krnich responded and then turned to Brad. "How's your wife and family, Brad?"

"They're doing just fine Jim. I think they're happy to still have their husband and father playing golf on this side of the grass."

"Yeah, Harbour Town was a close one," Krnich agreed. "We got lucky."

"It wasn't luck. It was your excellent work."

Nobody argued the point.

After a few moments of silence, Brad asked Krnich if the Secret Service was involved in the investigation.

"Nope. But I can understand your confusion. I don't work for the Service any longer."

"Really, what happened?"

"I couldn't stand those blowhards. Did you know that the Speaker actually sent a complaint to the

President about my performance that day at Harbour Town?"

Brad shook his head. There was nothing to say. Agent Krnich had acted with extreme competence. It wasn't his fault that a terrorist snuck into the famous candy-striped lighthouse at Harbour Town, became a sniper, slightly wounded the Speaker and almost killed Brad and John.

Krnich continued. "Well, that was it. That was the straw that broke the camel's back. Anyway, I like FBI work much better—it's challenging and it's... how do I say this... cleaner. I don't have to deal with the stench of career politicians anymore."

The group walked several yards further without talking. Officers in uniform and many in plain suits, walked quickly around them as if trying to catch a bus in New York, their eyes on the ground, papers or coffee cups in their hands and a sense of urgency in their tired and worn faces.

As they approached an office labeled Meeting Room 3, Krnich turned to the third member of Brad's party. "So this is the infamous Steven Zindo, entrepreneur and retailer of the decade in the eighties?" Krnich stated, pointing to the multi-millionaire.

"Yes I am. And I want to be on the record as saying that I don't function well in a bureaucratic, militaristic environment," Zindo said. "But I think you guys do a great job. Ours is a nation of laws. And you make it work."

"Good to know," Krnich said, shaking his head and furrowing his brow trying to figure out if he had been complimented or had just been called a fascist.

"Hopefully, we can get right to it," Espinoza said. "It's a long drive back to Santa Barbara and we'd like to beat the traffic."

"I hear you. This L.A. traffic is a bitch," Krnich agreed. "Took me two hours to get in from the airport the other day."

"Damn! That's a thirty minute drive on a good day," Espinoza said.

"I know," Krnich said. "Believe me I know." He walked a few steps further and then addressed Brad directly. "I'd still like to get up to your neck of the woods someday. I hear its beautiful and if I'm not mistaken, you still owe me a round of golf."

"Anytime," Brad said. "Mi casa, su casa."

As they approached the meeting room Krnich suddenly turned serious. "Here's the thing. We in the FBI don't know shit about real estate. Frankly, I don't even know why it exists as a business. But, apparently, in certain parts of the world, it's big business."

"Really big business," Zindo added.

"Yeah, okay, really big business," Krnich conceded. "We want to pick Brad's brain to see what else he might know about the mindset of the killer."

"I think you're drilling in a dry well," Brad said. "I've got no idea what's going on."

"Amuse me," Krnich said.

"Hey, it's your dime. I'm getting reimbursed for gas, aren't I?"

"Don't worry, Brad, it's my gas," Zindo quickly chimed in. "And I wouldn't take a penny from these guys. It would be anti-American."

"You'll get a few bucks," Krnich said. "Johnson over there will give you the forms to fill out." He pointed to a tall guy in a cheap brown suit standing in the corner. Brad waved. Johnson nodded.

Krnich opened the door and the group entered a large conference room. Uncomfortable looking metal chairs had been arranged so that the interrogators sat on one side and Brad, Espinoza and Zindo on the other. Large pots of coffee had been placed on the table, and of course, powdered donuts sat heaped upon a large platter in the middle.

Everyone sat down. Johnson came over and poured coffee for those who wanted it and before he returned to his post, grabbed a donut for himself.

A few minutes later, the official meeting began.

"Now, Brad, I want you to think about this first question," Krnich said as pictures of the victims appeared on a screen placed in the front of the room. "What do these victims have in common—other than representing expensive homes?"

Brad looked at Krnich, shot Espinoza a glance, stared some more at the pictures for a moment and then shrugged. "I've been thinking about it ever since Raoul told me about the killings," Brad began. "In real estate, the only way you can really piss somebody off is to either commit fraud or steal a competitor's client."

"How do you 'steal' a client?" Krnich asked.

"Well, it's very common actually. Buyers will go shopping for a property and along the way may talk to a listing agent when their own agent isn't with them. The listing agent will give them his or her business card and engage in conversation about the market. The listing agent then tries to represent both sides—effectively trying to steal the client from the other agent."

"And?"

"And...this never ends well. Real estate sales law provides for the concept of 'procuring cause'. Although there may be no formal contract engaging the sales agent, they will be deemed to be the procuring cause and deserving of the full sales commission. In extreme cases, it can become a real mess."

"Does this happen often?" Krnich asked.

"No, not as far as I know. But if it's going to happen, it will at the high-end. Lower priced properties are not very lucrative."

"Okay, so that might be one motivation. But it couldn't affect so many agents, could it?"

"I doubt it."

"So maybe it's fraud?"

"Maybe, but what kind of fraud would be so wide spread?" Espinoza asked.

They all looked to Brad for the answer. It amused him that these grown men—successful in their chosen professions—could be so naïve about an industry that had become a driving force in the U.S. economy. Brad had recently seen a statistic compiled by a conservative economist which estimated that real estate activity in the nation now accounted for up to twenty percent of the national gross domestic product.

Make no mistake about it; real estate had become *really* big business.

"I don't know what type of fraud would cause somebody to kill," Brad said. "Maybe these agents all met at one time or another and decided that they would list properties at twenty percent higher than their fair market price. Or conversely," he added with a grin, "listed them way below their market price."

Everybody but Zindo looked at him with a dull, dumbfounded stare.

"What Brad's saying is that the agents could've conspired to either juice the market or rip off the sellers," Zindo said. He unscrewed the top of a plastic water bottle, raised it to his lips and took a sip. "By the way," he said to nobody in particular, "plastic is poisonous. You should use glass bottles or paper cups." He put the bottle down, made a steeple out of his fingers and appeared deep in thought. Finally he said, "I don't think that's it, though, Brad."

"Why not?" Espinoza asked.

"The killings are too disjointed. And, if it was due to conspiracy, why not just shoot each one and get it over with? Why all the drama? And who would stand to gain by removing the agents?"

"The answer to your first question is easy. To throw us off," Espinoza said. "This is obviously a professional hit. The killer doesn't want to establish a pattern. That much is obvious. Now why, and who gains? I just don't know."

Zindo took another gulp of water and then said, "Exactly."

BEFORE ANY OF THE task force could comment on the Zindo's observations, Brad's cell phone rang. "Sorry guys; got to take this. It's Mel," he said, walking towards the hallway.

"Okay, but make it quick," Krnich said, appearing perturbed that his meeting was being interrupted by a domestic call.

"Hi Mel, I'm in a meeting. What's up?" Brad said.

Mel quickly told him about the events of that morning.

"No Shit? Is anyone hurt?"

She assured him that everyone was fine but they all were concerned that the painter could still be in the area. Conventional wisdom was that he was long gone by now, but Mel had her doubts.

"I'm taking the girls back to our house. Could you ask Raoul to send a policeman up to the house? I'd feel much better."

"I'll ask Raoul to do it immediately," he assured her. "Do the police know what the guy was up to? Was anything stolen from the property?"

"They haven't told us a thing. But, Brad, why would a painter have a knife and a gun on him? I think he was out to hurt us."

A sickening thought suddenly occurred to Brad. "Hold on for a sec, I'm going to put you on speaker," he said. He walked back into the room and motioned for everyone present to listen in.

"Was this the house that Paula has listed on the beach?" he asked.

"Yes."

"The ten million dollar house?"

"Yes, Brad. You know it's a high priced home. Why are you asking? Why am I on speaker?"

"I was just curious. And I wanted the other people in the room to hear me." He paused for a moment and looked around the room. Everyone—including Zindo—was listening intently.

They get it. Good.

Turning his attention back to the call, he said, "I think the protection is a good idea. In the meantime, you get the girls and yourself up to our house ASAP. I'll call Blake and Scott and tell them to hang out with you until the police arrive."

"Okay, that will make me feel better."

"Call me when you get home. Sit tight and I'll see you in a couple of hours." He began to hang up when he added, "And Mel..."

"Yes."

"Love ya."

"Love you too. Now get that police protection up to the house," she said and hung up.

Brad returned the cell phone to his pocket and glared at Krnich.

"Jim, I think you're going to get your wish. I think you should come up to Santa Barbara today." He looked around the room quickly and then bowed his head slightly and rubbed his chin. "You guys didn't hear the whole conversation, but you get the gist of it: The probable main target of this attack, Paula

Smith-Newhall, is a real estate agent. She specializes in high-end properties."

Krnich pursed his lips and frowned. "*This* isn't the way I wanted to visit Santa Barbara," he said under his breath.

34

"I'LL ORGANIZE THE TASK FORCE AND WE'LL BE UP IN SANTA BARBARA BY NIGHT-
FALL," KRNICH SAID. "THIS NEW CRIME SCENE COULD REVEAL SOME DESPERATELY
NEEDED DETAILS," HE TOLD THE GROUP.

"I hope so. Let's get this asshole," Espinoza said.
He pulled out his cell phone and hit speed dial. "I'll
let the chief know you're coming up."

Krnich paced back and forth like a racehorse
getting ready for the starting gate. "Sounds like our
guy," he said to no one in particular. He snorted a few
times and then continued. "We're lucky he didn't kill
the real estate agent. It would be nice to corral him in
a small area like Santa Barbara."

"He was unlucky my wife was there," Brad added,
watching Krnich closely, thinking the agent might
start kicking his hooves.

"Does she do this kind of thing often?" Krnich
asked.

"Well, she *does* have a nose for trouble," Brad admitted. "I'll give you an example. Before John and I went out to Harbour Town, she made a meatloaf loaded with olive oil and bran."

"Oh no!" Krnich said, apparently understanding the implications immediately.

Brad wondered if the special agent had had an embarrassing experience himself. He would inquire about that later. Hopefully, over a cold beer.

"Yep, gave Mr. Zindo over there and a few of our buddies the trots. But the good news is, she also gave these bad guys who were trying to kill me a few sandwiches—loaded with extra olive oil—and they were incapacitated the rest of the day. It gave Raoul enough time to prepare a sting operation."

"So, her screw-up became a positive?"

"That's the way I choose to look at it."

"And it appears she did it again," Espinoza added.

"From what you've told me, it sounds like if she hadn't knocked him off the ladder, the killer—if he's our guy, that is—would've struck. Who knows, he might have killed all three women." Krnich said.

Brad said nothing.

Zindo's ears had perked up when Brad mentioned the meatloaf. "I knew it! I knew it!" he exclaimed. "It wasn't our trip to Mexico the week before. It was something Mel fed us!"

"Yeah, I've been meaning to tell you," Brad said sheepishly. "Mel's meatloaf contained a bunch of olive oil and bran flakes. It gave you guys the trots. Sorry, buddy."

Instead of being mad, Zindo broke out in a broad smile. "Beautiful!" he said in a loud, deep voice. "You think she could show me the recipe? I'd love to have my cook prepare that dish for some of the blood- sucking leaches who come over to my house."

"You've got blood-sucking leaches for friends?" Espinoza asked.

"Not *my* friends; friends of my former wife. For some reason they feel fully entitled to still come by and stay at my home and eat my food."

"Well, you *do* have eight acres and four houses on your property," Brad said. "And you *do* always encourage people to visit and to treat your house as their house."

"I don't mean it for *them*. I mean it for you guys," Zindo replied. He opened his hands and nodded as if it were obvious.

"Good to know we're still welcome," Brad said.

"Always. My house is your home when you're in it; you know that. I only say those things to other people to be nice. I never want to see my ex again. Why would I want to see her friends? Lately, they've been asking me for money. But if I have my cook prepare food that will give them diarrhea, I bet they won't come back. It's brilliant!"

Brad laughed and patted his quirky friend on the back. "I'm sure Mel would love to show your cook the recipe. I'm sure it'll work. But for now, we need to get back up to Santa Barbara. Raoul, go fire up the Trojan Mobile; I'd like to make sure my wife isn't killed while we're dicking around down here in Los Angeles."

"Okay." Espinoza said. He turned towards special agent Krnich and gave a brief salute. "We'll see you in our neck of the woods tonight or tomorrow. Yes?"

"I'll call you later to confirm," Krnich said and left the room.

Zindo, Espinoza and Brad departed shortly thereafter.

When they got to the car, Raoul fired up the engine. Zindo sat in the back seat, a look of satisfaction filled his face and a sinister grin came to his lips. Apparently, he was still thinking about Mel's meatloaf and its future effects on his unwanted visitors.

Espinoza smiled as he put the car into gear. "Hi Hoe Silver, Away!" he shouted just before Zindo flipped on the USC fight song.

35

THE DAY HAD TURNED COLD AND GRAY.

Espinoza had dispatched a young officer named Murphy to watch Mel and the girls. With red hair and ruddy complexion, Murphy stood a mere five feet eight inches. His uniform fit him like a glove. His eyes were sharp and crisp. Although tidy and fit, he didn't look like the kind of cop who could stop a professional hit man.

Mel silently hoped that looks were deceiving.

She had brewed a pot of coffee and now the three would-be victims were gathered around the outdoor fireplace. The smoky smell of seasoned oak filled the air as the girls covered themselves with an old red blanket and huddled close to the burning wood. Overhead, a pair of crows chased a much larger hawk away from their nest. Across the canyon four or five deer chased each other amongst the avocado trees.

"I called John. He's coming right over," Stef said, breaking the silence.

"Does he have a gun?" Paula asked.

"No, I don't think so."

"Brad has a gun," Mel said in a very matter of fact tone.

"Since when?" Paula asked. "You hate guns."

"Well, I changed my mind," Mel admitted while blowing on and taking a sip of her coffee simultaneously. "Brad got a gun after that incident with IFPG. He's been taking shooting lessons with Raoul. I was against it at first, but now I see it might be necessary."

"Do you know where he keeps it?" Stef asked.

"I do, but I don't know how to shoot the damn thing." She stared into the fire and shook her head. Both Stef and Paula nodded and indicated that they didn't know how to shoot one either.

"Probably put my eye out," Paula said.

"Or, more likely, blow your foot off," Stef added.

"I've got to admit, I'd feel better if we had a gun and knew how to use it," Paula said. "I trust the officer Espinoza assigned, but he is kind of small. I'd feel better if we had some fire power of our own."

"Me too," Stef said.

"Me, three," Mel agreed.

THEY CONTINUED SIPPING coffee and making small talk while officer Murphy walked the perimeter of the property. The sky had darkened and a thin layer of fog blew through the valley below. Above them, the crows still chased the hawk as it flew in wide concentric circles.

"Look at that bird," Stef said, pointing at the hawk. "What a magnificent creature."

"It's only concern is where its next meal is coming from," Mel said.

Paula leaned forward and stared at the bird. "Must be nice," she said, sighing. "And he doesn't even seem concerned about those pesky crows."

"That's because they're not trying to kill him—just scare him," Stef said.

The group grew quiet and watched the birds make their way up and down the canyon. After a few minutes, Stef broke the silence. "Listen, I know you girls don't want to talk about it, but I'm just dying of curiosity. What do you think the painter wanted? What would he have done if Mel hadn't knocked him unconscious? And who the hell is he anyway?"

"I've got no idea," Paula said. "The normal painter, Sergio, is a nice little guy. I hope he's okay."

"The guy on the ladder was armed to the teeth," Mel said. "So we have to assume he was there to kill someone."

Stef and Mel both turned to look at Paula.

"What?" Paula said.

"I hate to say it, Paula, but I think he was there to kill *you*," Stef said.

"Why would anyone want to kill me? I haven't hurt a soul. I don't have any enemies—other than my former husband—that I know of."

Mel set her coffee cup down and looked her friend in the eye.

"I know this might be a sensitive subject...and I know it might not normally be any of my business, but do you think the guy might be a former client or a former colleague? I've heard from a few people who work with you that you're pretty tough to deal with."

"Former client?" Paula's eyes bugged out as if someone had hit her in the stomach. After a brief pause, she gathered her thoughts, smiled and said, "I doubt it. I treat all my clients very, very well."

"What about co-workers?" Stef asked.

She scrunched her face and thought about it for a few seconds and then assured the girls that she treated all of her colleagues with utmost respect. "As a matter of fact, I'd like to know who says I'm rough around the edges."

"No one in particular. It was just a passing comment I heard the other day," Mel said quickly, picking up her cup and taking a long drink.

"How about an ex-lover," Stef asked.

"Other than my ex, I don't have any former lovers. The guy last night is the first human I've had sex with in a long, long time."

"Could it have been him?" Stef asked.

"No, I don't think so," Paula said.

"What makes you so sure?"

"Well, Jerry, the guy I hooked up with last night, wears very strong cologne. I didn't smell any of that scent on the painter."

"And?" Mel prodded her.

"What do you mean...and? Can't that be reason enough?"

"No it can't. You said yourself that you wore him out last night. He probably showered extensively this morning. Maybe he didn't put on his cologne. And besides, we ran out of there so fast, you didn't see the painter's face."

Mel grimaced at the mention of the painter's face. Should she tell her friends that she had seen the man or should she wait for Brad and Espinoza? Fortunately, she didn't need to decide just then as Paula quickly responded to Stef's last comment.

"I guess you're right. But I just know it wasn't Jerry."

"How? How do you know that the guy you slept with last night is not a homicidal maniac who sleeps with beautiful women and then tries to kill them? Remember that guy down in La Conchita, the heir to the perfume fortune?" Stef said.

"That was different. He drugged his women and then raped them. Jerry didn't drug me. The sex was consensual."

"Okay then I ask you again: how do you know Jerry wasn't the guy on that ladder?" Stef prodded. Obviously, she wasn't going to drop the point.

Paula blushed and looked at her friends. "Jerry's a nice guy. I don't want to get him involved, so I'll tell you. The guy who fell off that ladder was at least six feet tall, right?"

Both girls agreed.

"Okay," Paula paused. "How do I say this?" Her blush reddened. She took a sip of coffee, stared at her friends and said, "Jerry is a... little fellow."

"Little. How little?" Stef asked.

"All right, I'll tell you. Jerry is about four foot three."

"He's a midget?" Mel said, trying as hard as she could to stifle a grin.

Paula immediately corrected her. "They don't like being called midgets. He's height challenged and prefers to be called a 'little person'."

"So you got your brains screwed out by a Munchkin?" Stef said.

"See, I knew you wouldn't understand. He's short, but very normal—in every way— and like I said earlier, he loves sex. It was thrilling, really."

Mel smiled, patted her friend on the thigh and said, "Okay, we'll rule out Jerry. The guy who fell was certainly no little person. And I'm glad you had such a good time with Jerry. I just hope I'm not going to see pictures of you two on the internet."

"Me too," Paula said quickly. "You don't think he'd post the movie we made, do you?"

"You filmed yourselves having sex?" Mel asked, spitting coffee from her mouth.

"I told you it was thrilling. It's really quite something to see one's self in the throes of passion."

"Oh, man. I hope that doesn't come back to bite you. But on the other hand, hey, good for you; I'm glad you're putting some spice in your life. Now, all we have to do is keep you alive," Mel said.

"So, who was it then?" Stef asked again.

THE FRONT GATE SWUNG OPEN before they could continue their discussion. John Linden strode through.

Apparently startled, Murphy, the cop, pulled his gun with a shaky hand. "Stop where you are sir," Murphy said. "And put your hands on top of your head."

Linden frowned.

The girls were forced to intervene.

"Officer Murphy, this is John Linden, he's a family friend," Mel explained as she approached the two men.

"You're John Linden? The U.S. Open Champ?" Murphy asked.

"Yes sir. That's me. Now let me pass so I can find out what happened."

"Not so fast. I've seen John Linden on TV. He's taller than you," Murphy said. He extended his free arm to block access. "If you're John Linden, what did you shoot to win the U.S. Open?"

"66, 71, 68, 67...the final round should've been a 64, though. I missed some easy putts. Here's my identification," Linden said, reaching for his driver's license.

"Slowly," Murphy said.

Linden kept his left hand up and carefully reached for his wallet with his right. He pulled it out of his back pocket using just his index finger and thumb. He handed it to the police officer.

Murphy examined the license carefully and then handed it back. "That's right. You did miss some easy putts. Okay, you can pass. Just one other thing..."

"Yeah, what?"

Murphy reached in his front pocket and pulled out a small note pad and pen. "Can I have your autograph?"

Suddenly proud, chest protruding, Linden took the pen and pad and scratched a quick, "To Murphy. May your drives be straight and your putts be true. Fairways and Greens. Your friend, John Linden."

True celebrity knows no bounds.

Handing him the autograph, Linden asked the young officer if he was a golfer, or just a fan?

"I'm an avid golfer, sir."

"What does 'avid' mean? What's your handicap?"

"It means I play once a week. I'm a twelve, sir," Murphy said while standing at attention.

Linden almost said "at ease, son", but instead, he offered the young man some advice. "Well, that's good. Playing once a week will keep you course-savvy, but you should practice once or twice a week as well. That's really the only way to lower your handicap."

And with that, Linden reached into his back pocket and pulled out a folded sheet of paper.

"Here you go Sean," Linden said. "Here's an invitation to join me at the driving range in Carpinteria on Saturday. I'm going to give a clinic on long irons and chip shots. There will be a raffle. The first prize is a round of golf with me and my caddie, Hank. And, for good measure, I have made arrangements for the newest, hottest, food truck in the area to be parked in the lot. I'll buy you lunch."

Officer Sean Murphy thanked Linden profusely, assured him that he would be at the range promptly at eleven—along with five or six of his buddies—and then resumed his vigil.

Linden put his arm around Mel, gave her a quick peck on the cheek and walked with her towards the other girls.

HE STOPPED IN front of Stef, threw his arms around her and gave her a deep, long kiss. "It's okay now. I'm here," he said.

"If it weren't for Mel, I don't think any of us would be sitting here," Stef said, squeezing Linden's hand tightly.

He turned towards the other women and said, "So girls, tell me the whole story. Don't leave anything out."

A half hour later, Linden took a long swig from a cold beer Mel had given him and said, "Okay, so forget the midget. He didn't do it." He stared at Paula, grinned and winked.

She didn't grin back.

He continued. "And thank goodness for Mel and the champagne. So the issues remain: Why might this guy want to kill Paula? And is he still in town?"

The girls looked at each other. None of them had an answer. The hawk they had been watching earlier reappeared—this time without the crows in tow. It suddenly dove towards the canyon floor. When it rose, a small snake dangled from its talons.

Wish the cops could do that with the painter, Mel thought.

36

LAS VEGAS.

IT HAD BEEN TWO FULL DAYS SINCE JIM STACK HAD SEEN THE PICTURES OF THE MUR-DERED REAL ESTATE AGENTS.

The positive and organized mind of the goal-setting guru was suddenly cluttered, his attitude not quite so optimistic. His conundrum: On the one hand he had a social, legal and moral obligation to contact the police if he thought he had information regarding a serious crime. On the other, he was extremely busy preparing for his next conference—a high-powered, blockbuster for experienced, successful real estate agents and their staff.

The conference was scheduled for the following week in Pebble Beach.

Maybe it was all a strange coincidence. Should he bother the police? He was at the apex of his career.

He really couldn't afford to get involved in this type of scandal.

Try as he might, he just couldn't stack the negative thoughts into their proper components on this one.

It nagged at him.

Finally, around mid-morning, he made a decision. He picked up the phone and made his first call.

"Can you please give me the phone number for the Federal Bureau of Investigation, Los Angeles," Stack asked the operator.

Having received the number, he immediately made the next call.

"Yes, I'd like to talk to whoever is taking tips for the special task force investigating the real estate agent murders in California."

He was placed on hold for several minutes. And then, much to his surprise, his call was answered by the agent in charge of the task force.

"Yes, hello, this is agent Jim Krnich. Do you have information for us, sir?"

"I think so. I'm not sure," Stack answered. "It might be nothing. I don't want to waste your time."

"Go ahead tell me what you've got. I'll decide whether it's a waste of time or not. But before we start, please give me a number I can call you back on in case we get disconnected. They transferred the call to my cell and I'm just beginning the drive north to Santa Barbara. I'm not sure about the cell service."

Encouraged by the agent's open mind, Stack gave him his number and then proceeded to tell his story.

"My name is Jim Stack," he began. "I run seminars for real estate agents and other professionals on positive thinking, organization of the mind, and goal setting. You may have heard of me?"

Krnich winced. Why would he have heard of this clown? Real Estate was a foreign enterprise to him. It was the province of the rich and the lazy as far as he was concerned. He did remember, however, there was a time when one of his comrades at the Secret Service, Richard Bly, bragged to his fellow agents about owning nineteen brownstones in the Bronx. This was probably 2003 or 2004—way before things went bad.

Bly, it turned out became a multi-millionaire—on paper—and quit the service. He invested all of his profits into condo projects in Florida. Krnich knew this because Bly had offered each of the other agents "the chance of a lifetime" to invest with him.

Last he heard Bly was bankrupt, unemployed and living off his pension and food stamps.

Once again, proof that greed knows no bounds.

Returning to the present, Krnich responded to the caller. "Mr. Stack, I'm sorry to say, I have never heard of you or your system. I'm sure you're very successful and well-known in your circle, but I'm just a low paid civil servant waiting to retire."

"That's a shame, agent Krnich. You sound like a very efficient and self-confident individual. I'm positive you would be very successful in sales—if you put your mind and positive energy into it."

"Thanks for the compliment. Now what new information do you have for us?"

Ever the salesman, Stack gave it one final effort. "Perhaps you'd like to attend my next regular seminar in Las Vegas? It will be held the week of July 7th."

"Sounds interesting," Krnich lied, realizing that it was best to play along with a reluctant informant. "I'll pencil it in and get back to you."

Satisfied with the agent's response and feeling a new sense of confidence, Stack launched into his story.

When he finished, he could almost feel the federal agent's excitement over the phone line. He had done his duty and now he could function with a clean conscience.

"That's great information, Mr. Stack. Not a waste of time at all. Please give me all of your contact information—including email address. I'll have one of my men follow up with you."

"You'll keep my name out of the press, won't you?"

"Certainly, if what you've told me leads to an arrest, you will be referred to as an anonymous source."

"Perfect! I think this is a win/win situation. Don't you agree agent Krnich?"

"You bet. I've got your phone number but go ahead and give me your other contact info." He wrote the snail-mail and e-mail addresses down on the same paper he had already put the phone number on and then thanked Stack. "We'll be in touch soon," he said and hung up.

A minute later, he turned to his assistant. "Zach old boy, I think we might have our first big break in this bizarre case."

37

AS THE RED AND GOLD MUSTANG PULLED UP BRAD'S LONG DRIVEWAY, ESPINOZA'S CELL PHONE BEGAN VIBRATING. FUMBLING TO PUSH THE RECEIVE BUTTON, HE GOT TO IT JUST BEFORE IT WENT TO VOICE-MAIL.

"Espinoza, here," he said while glancing at the caller ID and seeing it was the special agent calling. "What's up, Krnich? Using your personal cell phone I see."

"No, this is my official phone. The bureau instituted a policy recently that requires us to put our names on the caller ID; transparency and all that I guess," Krnich said. "Anyway, the reason I called is to tell you that I just got an interesting phone call. It seems that a famous motivational speaker may be involved in our killings. I want to meet with you and Stephens tonight. It can't wait until tomorrow." He paused and then added, "Don't bring that quirky Zindo guy. Okay?"

"Ten, four on that good buddy," Espinoza said with a smile. "Where do you want to meet?"

"How about Brad's house?"

"I'm sure that'll work. You want to give me any clue about what we'll be discussing?"

"Not now. I'm still processing the information. But I think we need the real estate input from Stephens more than ever."

"Okay. I'll arrange it. Do you know how to get to Brad's house?"

"Can't I just GPS it?"

"Nope. He's actually got three street names in the computer. It's a fluke of the sub-division. Nobody can correct it," Espinoza said.

"What if he has a fire or emergency?" Krnich asked. "How does the Fire Department know where to go?"

"That's a good question. I'll have to ask Brad. I just know that the last time I tried to use GPS or Google Search, it sent me to the wrong part of town." He grimaced at the memory. The damn thing had made them miss a tee-time in Ventura.

"Give me the directions, then. I'll get my guys set up this afternoon and meet with you at six. Does that work?"

"Should be fine," Espinoza said and then gave Krnich very specific directions. "See you at six."

Espinoza closed his cell phone and turned to Brad. "We've got a meeting scheduled with Krnich tonight at six," he said.

"Six!" Zindo exclaimed. "I've got a Board meeting tonight. I can't meet at six."

"Agent Krnich asked that only Brad and I attend."

"They don't want me? The fascist, police state is trying to exclude me?" Zindo said with mock disbelief. But then he straightened up. "Like it or not, I'm part of this investigation. You call Krnich back and tell him to kiss my ass. Some of my resources may come in handy. Go ahead, tell him Raoul."

"I can do that, Steve, but this meeting tonight is probably nothing. Why don't you just go to your dinner? Brad can fill you in later."

It was too late. Espinoza could hear Zindo calling his assistant.

"April, it's me Steve. Cancel my appearance tonight at the dinner," the millionaire began. "Yes, I know it will be controversial. Please, just do it. Tell them I got diphtheria or dysentery or something. Call Andria and ask her to fill in for me. She's a sucker for these meetings." He hung up and looked directly at Espinoza.

"Guess you're stuck with me," he said with a grin.

ESPINOZA PARKED THE car. Brad exited the passenger seat before the sergeant could set the parking brake. He ran into the house searching for Mel. Finding her sipping wine with Stef and Paula out on the patio, he ran forward and threw his arms around her. Before he could stop it, his eyes began to tear.

Joy? Or relief? Didn't matter.

Soon after, Mel followed his lead.

"God Brad! You wouldn't believe how scary it was," she sobbed. "At first I thought I killed the guy. And then when I saw the weapons..."

Actually, he knew how bad it was to have a stranger try to kill you. However, this wasn't the time to correct her or try to trump her. This situation was about her and her friends. He hugged her and looked at the other girls.

"I'm glad you're all okay," he said, wiping away a stray tear. He cleared his throat and then continued. "It sounds terrible. Lucky for you he was stupid enough to put his ladder so close to the French doors."

Stef stepped forward. "We *are* lucky. I guess it just wasn't our time to die," she said while glancing over her shoulder and staring at Linden.

"Women have a sixth sense about these things, Brad," Paula added. "It's true you could argue that Mel was drunk and didn't know she was causing the ladder to fall. But it's equally true that you could say that she sensed something weird was up and, without understanding her actions, decided to save us from harm."

Espinoza, Zindo, Brad and the others looked at the real estate agent with amusement. Raoul rolled his eyes and made the universal circling motion for Cuckoo with his right index finger.

"She was shit-faced drunk, looking for air, and she inadvertently decked the guy," Zindo said. "What about *that* scenario speaks to women's intuition?"

"Well, when you say it that way, it sounds like sheer dumb luck," Paula said. "I don't believe in dumb luck, however. I think everything happens for a reason. Mel was there for a reason. The ladder was too close to the door for a reason. We escaped for a reason."

"And that reason is...?" Zindo asked.

"Hell if I know," Paula said, extending her hand. "I don't believe we've met. I'm Paula Smith-Newhall"

"Steve Zindo."

They shook hands. She held his longer than normal.

"Mr. Zindo, such a pleasure. Brad has told me so much about you."

"Hopefully, just the good stuff," Zindo said with a slight blush.

"Only good things, I can assure you. And how is your eight acre, four residence, Tudor and California contemporary property doing?" the agent asked with a wink.

"It's a pain in the ass," Zindo replied, impressed she knew so much about his estate. He wondered what else she might know about him. What else had Brad told her? She was good looking. Maybe he'd take her out to dinner some time.

"If you ever get tired of the upkeep and expense, please give me a call," Paula said, handing him a business card. "I would think we could get thirty or forty million for your place."

"You think that much?"

"At least. Call me."

Brad watched the tango between the two capitalists until he could stand no more. "Okay, now listen everybody, the federal agents will be here at six. It will be the full task force and I think they will need room. So those of you who don't belong here should head home." He looked at Stef and John. He wasn't sure about Paula. She was in danger. Maybe she should stay with them tonight? What about her kids, he suddenly thought?

"Paula. Where's Luke and Ashley?" he asked. "Are the police protecting them?"

"Yes, they're supposed to be," Paula said.

Espinoza quickly joined in. "I've got police at her condo. The kids are fine."

Paula sighed and said thanks.

"What about tonight, Raoul. Should Paula and the kids stay at our house?" Brad asked.

"Let's play it by ear. There's a good chance that our guy is long gone by now. Let's wait until we meet with Krnich. He'll know what to do."

Mel's ears perked up and her expression changed from relief to curiosity. "Is this the same agent Krnich who had your back at Hilton Head?" she asked Brad.

"Yep, one and the same. It's a fluke. He no longer works for the Secret Service. He transferred to the FBI and now heads a special task force on major crimes."

"And he's coming to our house because I knocked this guy off the ladder?"

Brad cleared his throat and kicked at a small gopher mound in front of him. "Yeah, well there's something I didn't want to tell you earlier..."

"What is it?" Mel asked.

"Well, there's a chance—and it's only a chance, mind you—that your fake painter is the guy who's been killing high-end real estate agents up and down the state."

Mel's tan skin suddenly turned pale. "You're saying the painter was really a serial killer?"

"Maybe. They're not sure. They want to talk to you about it but it does sound like he might be the guy."

"And Krnich—our Krnich—is heading the investigation?"

"Yep. Strange isn't it?"

"Or, Kismet," Mel said slyly. "Don't you see what's going on here?" she addressed the whole group. "What are the odds that I could knock the painter off that ladder? What are the odds that we'd be reunited with agent Krnich?"

They stared at her blankly. Only Paula seemed to know what she was getting at.

Mel continued. "Today's events weren't just 'women's intuition', they were fate. For some strange reason, I was supposed to foil the attack. Agent Krnich has already saved you once," she said directly to Brad. "I think he's destined to save us again."

"Brilliant theory," Zindo commented. "The only flaw in it is that *you* saved the women. Krnich was two hundred miles away."

"I know that, Steve. But what if my actions were just the 'prologue'? And Krnich, because he knows John and Brad, pays extra attention to the clues and figures out who the killer is. And..." she was really on a roll now, "he kills the guy or arrests him before Paula can be harmed. Don't you guys see how this is a case of the 'universe' intervening in our lives?"

"What you're saying is that Krnich is our group's Guardian Angel?" Espinoza said.

"For lack of a better description, yes," Mel said. Then she added, "I think we're going to be all right. It's our destiny."

Glad for his wife's confidence and anxious to take a nap before the meeting at six, Brad adjourned the group, said good-bye to them all and went into his study. Before getting some much needed rest, he decided to check his email.

"Son-of-a-bitch!" he muttered. The fourth email on his screen had been sent by some kooky astrology website. Printed below the words "Greetings Sagittarian", was a simple horoscope:

You are full of life. Pay attention to past

relationships as they will

prove to be fruitful and life changing.

Someone you have known

will re-emerge and quite possibly allow you

to continue enjoying

the fruits of your labors.. Passion runs high.

Beware big business

decisions. Some confusion exists but things

will become clear soon.

Definitely not a believer in astrology, Brad shook his head, chuckled and lay down on the large brown couch in his study. "Taking a nap in the afternoon is how you 'continue enjoying the fruits of your labors' he thought just before he closed his eyes. As for the other stuff, I'll let the universe straighten it out.

He was snoring five minutes later.

38

"LIFE, REALLY, IS NOT FAIR," STEF SAID IN A MATTER-OF-FACT MANNER AS SHE AND JOHN RETURNED TO THEIR HOME SEVERAL MILES NORTH OF BRAD'S HOUSE.

The single-story four thousand square foot Craftsman home had been found by Brad when he was acting as Linden's real estate agent and mortgage broker. Linden's former fiancée, Fabiola, had wanted to buy a massive estate, but once she was out of the picture, John had settled for much less. He loved the simple home and once Stef had moved in he found himself anxious to make small repairs. What was that all about?

As Linden fumbled for his keys to unlock the front door, he responded to Stef's statement. "What makes you say that, babe?"

"Well, think about it. Here we are in the middle of this God-awful recession and Paula gets the biggest listing of her life. Then before she even gets a chance to sell it, some lunatic tries to kill her. Now she probably never wants to see that house again. I know I wouldn't."

"That's true. But look at the other side. She's still alive. And, because she is, you are too."

Linden grabbed Stef around the waist and drew her near. "You know, Ms. Stefanie Ramirez, I am very, very happy that nothing happened to you today."

"You just want someone around to do the cooking and pick up after you."

"And, don't forget the sex."

"You want to have sex with me?" she joked.

"All the time," he said as he pulled her even closer.

"Is this one of those special moments they advertise on TV for those boner pills? You know the one where the announcer says something like, 'you never know when it will happen but when you're ready to screw, make sure your ding-dong works'."

As he rubbed up against her, she could tell there was no problem with his ding-dong.

And with that, Linden planted a passionate kiss on her lips and lifted her like a newlywed into his arms.

"Don't need no pill," he answered as he carried her to the nearest couch and began to undress her slowly. "I just need you."

A HALF HOUR later, spent, her clothes rumpled on the floor and her hair a mess, Stef looked at Linden and asked the question that scared all men: "John, mi Amor. Is *this* going anywhere?"

He knew what she meant, but he had learned over the years that it was better to play dumb when women inferred something about relationships. It made the process of discussing emotions or personal habits much more casual and less intense. "What do you mean by *this*?" he asked in his best Eddie Haskell voice.

"You know. *This*. Our relationship. Us," she responded softly. "We've been living together for a while now. Are you happy with this arrangement?"

"Babe, I'm ecstatic," he said, hoping his answer would suffice and the conversation would end.

Nope.

"I know you've been burned in the past and you don't want to rush into a long term commitment. Lord knows Fabiola was a nightmare but, I need something to look forward to. We're not 'spring chickens' you know."

Shit.

Here comes the 'M' word.

"Are you talking marriage?" he asked, knowing full well that she was.

"Yes, I guess I am. I decided when I moved in that I wasn't going to have any major expectations. But I don't know, maybe the events today made me think about the future?"

"So a ring and a commitment from me will give you more hope about the future?"

"It will make me more comfortable. That's for sure. I love you, John. God help me, I do love you. You're a slob and you're self-centered, but you're a good man. I'd be proud to become Mrs. John Linden."

"Don't forget 'Mr. Twinkle' and my prowess on the golf course."

"What?"

"I'm a slob, a good man, a great golfer, and you've become very attached to 'Mr. Twinkle' is what I think you *meant* to say."

"Oh, yeah." She rolled her eyes. "Sorry I forgot the golf reference and the praise for your manhood. My bad."

"Completely understandable under the circumstances."

"Are you going to take this seriously?" she asked. "I was almost killed today. I need some security in my life. Don't you?"

The kidding around wasn't working. She wasn't going to drop the subject. Women loved to talk about emotions. Men like John, on the other hand, would pay good money to avoid such discussions.

It was earlier in the relationship than he had planned but he decided to address the subject head on. "I love you, Stefanie Ramirez. I think we'd make a great team. Will you marry me?" He looked around the room for something he could put on her finger. He saw a ring given to him for winning the U.S. Open sitting in a display case on the nearby mantle. It was several sizes too big, but it would do in a pinch.

He rose from the couch, naked as the day he was born and walked over to the display case and grabbed the ring. He returned to the couch, got down on one knee and slipped the large ring on her finger.

She stared him in the eye, moved her head down the length of his torso, stopping at his groin. She grinned. "It's a little hard to take you seriously with a limp 'Mr. Twinkle' staring at me like that."

He grabbed a nearby pillow and placed it in his lap. He grinned and then asked her the question again.

This time she said, "Why, Mr. Linden, I thought you'd never ask. The answer to such an unsolicited and surprising question is: Yes, I'd love to marry you."

They hugged, laughed, drank some champagne and made love again. Stef dozed off with visions of a fall wedding dancing in her head.

Linden, on the other hand, rested fitfully. "Damn," he thought, remembering the phone call he had received from a former girlfriend the other day. "I guess this is going to be the first big test of my new manager's career," he said to himself. And then looking down at his crotch, he thought of Laurel and Hardy and mused, "Well, this is *another* fine mess you've gotten me into."

39

SIX O'CLOCK CAME AROUND MUCH TOO QUICKLY FOR BRAD.

He had taken a fine nap but awoke a bit mush-headed. After splashing cold water on his face, he went into the kitchen. Made a pot of coffee. Poured a tall cup. Given the nature of the crimes and the new information to be discussed, it could be a long evening.

Mel was standing by the oven. "I've baked a wonderful casserole for our guests," she announced. "I hope they haven't eaten yet."

"Now Mel, remember the last time you baked for guests? You gave them diarrhea."

"That was because I improvised. I didn't have bread crumbs so I used bran flakes and flax seeds. This time I've followed the recipe to a tee," she declared. "Doesn't it smell divine?"

Brad had to admit it *did* smell good. He was experienced enough with Mel's cooking, however, to know that 'all that glittered was not gold'. He approached the next statement carefully.

"Mel, I love you. You've been my wife for thirty years. We've raised wonderful boys and built a nice—albeit recently financially strained—life together. But..."

"But what, Brad? What's your point?"

"My point is that you make great salads and decent desserts but your entrees are not so good. I think you overreach sometimes."

"You hate my cooking! Is that what you're saying?"

He cleared his throat. "I knew you were going to take this personally. It's why I've avoided discussing your cooking with you."

First Stef took our talk personally, now Mel. Damn!

Her eyes began to moisten. "You mean I've been cooking for you all these years and you've never really liked what I've made and you never said anything about it? What about the boys? Do they feel the same way?"

"Well, yes, they do. It's not your standard fare we dislike," he said, hoping to draw a distinction between basic steak and potato dinners as opposed to the more exotic concoctions she tried to copy from the *Cooking Channel*. "For the past several years, you have tried to duplicate every recipe presented by Emeril, Mario, Bobby and whoever else you've been watching on TV. They just don't turn out very well, dear. I think it's obvious that you don't mix the ingredients together properly."

Mel regained her composure and said, "I suppose I knew they weren't very good. But you and the boys ate the food so willingly. I figured it was just my palate."

"The boys love their mom. I love their mom. We didn't want to hurt your feelings. And it wouldn't be any big deal if the food just tasted bad. But your cooking can be dangerous too."

"Oh, come on, you're exaggerating."

"Am I? How about the time you used bad clams in the linguine vongole? I've never seen such gross projectile vomiting. And, more recently, how about how you poisoned my friends with that meatloaf'?"

"I just told you, the meatloaf was a bad decision on my part. I should've run to the store and got bread crumbs. The clams were the store's fault." She pursed her lips and fixed her gaze on him.

This isn't going well.

Can't give up, I've let the Genie out of the bottle. It ain't going back in.

"The clams were bad, that's true. Maybe there's no way to tell when clams go bad, I don't know, but the meatloaf... Well, any decent cook would know that bran, flax and olive oil combined in such large quantities would cause massive diarrhea."

"Okay. Okay. Okay. I see your point," she finally conceded. "I guess this is part of the destiny I was describing earlier. Had I died today, I would never have known that I was such an awful cook. Now I can do something about it. Let's save money so that I can go to that cooking school in Napa."

"Fair enough," Brad agreed, knowing he couldn't possibly afford to send her to the school anytime soon. "I'll try to put a few bucks aside."

He put a small serving on a fork, blew on it to cool it off, took a bite, and swallowed it. He cleared his throat and faced Mel.

"That bad, huh?" she said.

"Let's toss the casserole in the trash, we can send out for a pizza," he suggested.

"I can, at least, make a kick-ass salad, can't I?"

"You bet."

"And dessert? Can I make that apple crisp you seem to like so much? Or do you hate my desserts too?"

"We love your desserts," he said, making sure to emphasize the *we* in his statement. His boys would not be happy that he spilled the beans, but they'd be relieved to know that their mom wasn't going to inadvertently poison them again. Scott would be especially pleased. This would give him the ammunition he needed to reject his mother's continuous offers of cooking a 'special' dish for his food truck customers.

"Okay, that's settled. I'll make a nice Italian salad with pine nuts and sundried tomatoes. And for dessert, we'll have apple crisp."

"Sounds good. Right now, however, I need a cup of coffee," Brad said, yawning. "Then I'll get out of your way. Company should be here soon."

Phew! Turned that one around.

CHANGING THE SUBJECT from her cooking to the murders, Mel asked, "What new information do you think agent Krnich has?"

"I don't know, but it sounds intriguing. All he would say is that it has to do with some motivational speaker. Some guy named Stack. Jim Stack, I think"

Mel stopped what she was doing. She appeared visibly startled. She wiped her wet hands on a nearby towel and turned towards Brad. "I know you don't believe in my kismet theory, but this just can't be another coincidence," she said.

"What can't be a coincidence? You've heard of this guy?"

"Not only have I heard of him, but he's the guy Paula, Stef and I are going to see next week in Pebble Beach."

Brad looked at her quizzically. In all the recent fuss, he had forgotten that the women were scheduled to go on a four day trip. He hadn't really paid attention when Mel told him about the meeting—thinking it was something Paula's company sponsored and would be mostly recreational.

"I was going to tell you last night when we were discussing Paula and how organized she has become that she says she owes it all to her 'positive thinking guru', Jim Stack," Mel said.

She stared at the floor for a moment, and then seeing a stain probably left by the dog, grabbed a wet cloth. She wiped up the spot and then continued. "The conference is only for a select few 'super stars' in the real estate business. He encouraged the agents to bring their staff. Since Paula doesn't have a 'staff' right now per se, she invited us."

Brad knew real estate agents needed to be organized. And they needed confidence-building events. It wasn't easy begging a seller to represent them or to gain the trust of a new buyer. There was considerable rejection built into the business.

A good listing agent might actually sell only fifty percent of the properties they listed. That meant that they failed fifty percent of the time. And when they failed, an agent was bound to be criticized by the seller. However, he couldn't imagine his wife sitting through hours upon hours of goal setting drills and positive-thinking speeches.

Mel had the attention span of a hyper-active ten year old. This guy, Stack, better be entertaining.

Brad smiled, took the rag from Mel and knelt down to wipe the spot more thoroughly. "I don't know if it's a coincidence, or kismet, or divine intervention, or what," he said. "But Stack's got something to do with these killings and, if Krnich's big secret is that Stack is our killer, I just hope Paula can get a full refund."

They both chuckled and then Mel added, "You and John are coming on the trip too."

Surprised, Brad told her that they couldn't possibly afford a trip to Pebble Beach. "You and the girls go. Have a good time."

"Pish, posh. You're going. Stef already ran it by John. He's paying, but he says you two will win enough playing golf to pay for the whole trip. If not, he'll write it off his taxes. So, no worries."

Brad rolled his eyes and stared at where the spot had been. "Mel, you know we're doing better, but this trip will cost a couple thousand bucks. I'm not sure we both should go."

"Don't worry about it. You and John will have a great time. You'll figure out how to pay for anything John doesn't cover. You always do."

Oh, yeah. I always do.

Before Brad could put up a better argument, he heard a knock at the front door.

"Our guests are here," Mel announced.

"Showtime!" Brad said putting his coffee cup down and making his way towards the front door. He was ready to brain-storm with these guys but he couldn't quite take his mind off of the Pebble Beach excursion. Trips like this were common in the old days—the days before the Truckee fiasco and the recession. Now a four day trip to Pebble Beach not only would take a bite out of his meager savings, but seemed awfully ostentatious. Had he changed that much? Was he incapable of having fun anymore? Was he being cheap or thrifty?

Probably both.

He took a deep breath and opened the front door.

40

ESPINOZA WAS THE FIRST ONE TO ENTER THE HOUSE, FOLLOWED CLOSELY BY KRNICH AND CURLANDER AND THEN THE REST OF THE TASK FORCE.

Introductions were made and the group settled in the front room. Mel was especially glad to finally meet agent Jim Krnich in person.

She asked the assembled group if she could get anyone something to drink. And then she added, "I hope you're all hungry. We'll order a few pizzas later and I've made a nice salad and I made a dessert I think you'll like."

Brad breathed a sigh of relief.

They all requested coffee and assured her they were starving. Before they could begin their discussions about the serial killer, Mel pulled Krnich aside and thanked him for taking such good care of Brad at Hilton Head.

"Brad explained to me that he hired you to protect him and John as well as doing your normal duty in protecting the Speaker," she said.

It took agent Krnich a moment to remember the deal he had struck with Brad: Brad wouldn't tell the media that Krnich had initially rejected the information Brad had offered that the golfers at the Harbour Town event were in danger as long as Krnich assured Mel that he had been pulling double duty that day.

"It was my pleasure, ma'am," Krnich said. "When your husband told me he was contemplating hiring personal security for him and Linden, I assured them that I would cover their butts. I'm glad it worked out."

"Me too. I was certain that Brad would ignore my warnings, what with the recession and our personal financial difficulties and all."

"I'm sorry to hear about your reversals," Krnich assured her.

And he was.

He knew this recession was unlike any other in his lifetime. He didn't know anybody who hadn't been damaged. The various newspaper accounts following the assassination attempt had given substantial background on Brad Stephens. Most of them mentioned that he had suffered a serious financial reversal.

"I'm happy to see that things are going better for you both," Krnich said, looking around the spacious front room and sneaking a peak out the French doors at the setting sun over the Pacific Ocean.

"Between you and me, we're just barely holding on. This location is so special we don't want to part with it. We could never get it back." She shrugged as if to say, 'it is what it is'.

"You have a beautiful home. I'm sure Brad will bounce back."

Mel smiled. "If anybody can, that man can," she said, pointing to her husband.

He gave her a knowing wink. "I'm sure you're right." He took a deep breath, rubbed his hands together and concluded the conversation by saying, "Now, let's try to keep you and your friends alive."

KRNICH RETURNED TO the main table and began his presentation. "First, let's review things we know—or think we know," he said. "One: Based on his methods, this is a professional killer we're dealing with. Two: He has been killing real estate agents who apparently deal almost exclusively with expensive properties. Three: He probably tried to kill Paula Smith-Newhall today. Four: We don't know if he's still in the area waiting for another opportunity or if he has moved on. Therefore, we will be extra cautious with the intended target, Ms. Smith-Newhall. Where is she, by the way?"

"Paula went home to get her children," Mel said. "She has a police escort and is going to bring the kids up to our house for the night. She will stay here too."

"Good thinking," Krnich said. "This would be a difficult property to attack and it should also be easily defended if necessary. They should be safe here. That brings me to my next order of business..." Before he could finish, there was a noise at the front door.

"Sorry I'm late. I got caught up watching a very interesting documentary on Hitler's invasion of Poland," a smiling Steve Zindo announced as he entered the room.

Krnich looked at Espinoza, widened his eyes, tilted his head and frowned. "I told you *he* wasn't invited," he said under clenched teeth.

"You know, I think they should rename the *History Channel*, the *Hitler Channel*. If it weren't for that maniac, they wouldn't have anything cool to show the viewer," Zindo said as he walked into the house and began searching for a place to sit.

Brad welcomed him and offered coffee and a seat on the couch. "You haven't missed anything. Agent Krnich was just beginning his presentation. So far, he's outlined things we already know," Brad said.

Zindo sat on the couch and Rufus came over to lick his hands, legs and arms. "Hey Ruffie, how you doing boy," Zindo said. He looked around the room and told everyone how close he and Rufus were. "We just love each other—it's because I got animal magnetism. Now go ahead, please continue agent Krnich."

Shaken by Zindo's presence but quite sure he wouldn't be able to insist on the millionaire's removal from the meeting, Krnich sighed and was about to continue his presentation when Mel chimed in.

"Sorry to interrupt you, but there's something I think you all should know about the painter," she began. "I was so upset this morning that I forgot to tell anybody..."

"Tell them what?" Krnich asked.

"I saw his face."

They all stared at her in disbelief and then Krnich broke out a broad smile. "That's great! No harm done. We..."

"And he had a tattoo on his leg," Mel added quickly.

"You saw a tattoo?" Curlander asked. "Was it a big tattoo? Did it spell out a name? A place? A face?"

"No, nothing like that. It was an emblem and it was only about the size of a fifty-cent piece. It was on his lower, right calf. I was going to look it up on the internet when I got a chance but since you're here, and I just now remembered it, I guess we should add it to the list of things we know about this guy."

"No shit?" an astonished Krnich replied, feeling like he just received another big break in the case. "Mrs. Stephens, please take agent Curlander with you into the study and describe the man's face and the tattoo to him. Zach, you look up the tattoo on the internet and then contact an artist and get him or her up here pronto."

Brad had been pouring Zindo's coffee when Mel made her revelations. He put the pot down and said, "This is great. Maybe, if we're lucky, the guy wasn't wearing a disguise and the tattoo will be traceable."

"I'll bet the guy was wearing some type of disguise. Pros usually do," Krnich said. "But unless the tattoo was part of a disguise, we'll figure it out," he added.

Curlander and Mel departed for the study, but not before Mel reminded the group that there was coffee in the kitchen and pizza would be ordered soon.

Ever the hostess.

Brad turned to Krnich and asked him if the tattoo was important.

"Hell yes. Tattoos can be like fingerprints. If we can narrow down the symbol, we might learn a lot about our boy."

"I'm glad she remembered, then. What else do you have?" Brad asked.

———

IN SAN LUIS OBISPO, a hundred miles north of Santa Barbara, Ted Flowers sat down at an upscale, downtown Trattoria.

The restaurant was located a few blocks from the local university. Flowers had noticed an abundance of attractive young females milling about the area. Maybe a hook-up with one of them would help take his mind off of Mercedes?

He shook the notion from his head, wondered again what hold Falicello's granddaughter had over him and ordered dinner. He flashed back to the only time he had met her. The beautiful skin, the shiny white teeth, the soft oval of her face—there was no doubt about it, she was a beautiful girl. And she had gotten under his skin.

He was still thinking about her when a lovely, young blonde girl approached his table and asked if she could sit down.

"Of course," he said, making a welcoming gesture.

The girl adjusted her skirt as she sat. Flowers noticed a pair of long, tan legs highlighted by shapely calves. She wore a loose-fitting cotton blouse to go along with a very short blue skirt.

"To what do I owe the privilege of your company?" he asked, sipping wine while inspecting her upper half more closely. She had large breasts and a pretty, angular face. She wore little makeup and had green eyes.

The girl giggled. "I'm not usually this forward, but you're such a handsome man and you look so lonely and I thought to myself, Laura—that's my name, Laura—that handsome man could use some company tonight."

Flowers arched an eyebrow. "I see. And this company you would provide, how much would it cost me and what services could I expect in return?"

She bit her lip and hesitated. Obviously, she was not an experienced Hooker. A girl with more street smarts would immediately demand a high price and then negotiate it down. She, on the other hand, blushed and said, "I'm kind of new at this. I've got tuition payments due and I'm flat broke. I'll take whatever you think I'm worth."

He took another sip of wine, offered her a glass and stared at her for a long moment. "Well, I'd hate to take advantage of you Laura—you're very pretty by the way—let's say three hundred dollars."

"Three hundred..."

He raised his hand to stop her. "And you'll leave immediately when we're done."

She smiled and nodded her head enthusiastically. "You won't regret it," she said.

"We'll see about that. You happen to have caught me in a very vulnerable state. I was just thinking about a sexy woman I met recently."

"My good fortune," she said.

He gave her lazy eyes. "We'll see about that, too. And, by the way, for three hundred dollars, I expect nothing to be off-limits. Yes?"

She squirmed a little in her chair, took a deep breath and raised her glass to his. "For you, baby, nothing is off limits."

And for you darling, if you disappoint me, there will be no holds barred.

They finished the bottle of wine, paid the bill and strolled across the street to a nearby hotel. After checking in, Laura took him by the hand and led him upstairs.

When they entered the room, she immediately slipped out of her skirt, unbuttoned her blouse and began removing his clothes. When he was left with nothing but his boxers on, she kneeled before him and took his manhood in her mouth. He resisted for a moment, questioning his decision to hire this girl— he was on a job after all—but as he grew harder and her mouth and tongue faster, his thoughts drifted to Mercedes and he gave in to the pleasure of the moment.

An hour—and several uncomfortable positions for Laura—later, he paid her four hundred dollars, patted her on the fanny and asked her to leave. Fortunately for Laura, she had satisfied his needs.

He would rest comfortably now as he approached his next target and as he tried to figure out his feelings for Mercedes.

It had been a good decision after all.

41

THE SUN HAD SET OVER THE PACIFIC LEAVING A SHEET OF THIN FOG IN ITS WAKE. NO ONE NOTICED. THE GROUP SAT STILL, CAPTIVATED BY KRNICH'S PRESENTATION.

"As you know, this guy from Las Vegas named Jim Stack called me earlier today. He is some type of self-help guru." Krnich paused and looked around the room as if maybe everyone else would recognize Stack. Only Brad nodded.

After a moment, he chuckled and said, "I never heard of him either but trust me, he really thinks highly of himself."

"What does he do?" Espinoza asked.

Krnich rubbed his chin and thought about it before answering the sergeant. "I guess real estate agents sign up to have this guy teach them how to organize themselves and how to be more positive. Is that right Brad?"

"Yep, agents flock to guys like this. It takes a lot of confidence to stay optimistic in a down market and guys like Stack provide comfort."

Espinoza said nothing, just shook his head and sipped coffee.

Krnich continued. "Anyway, Stack said he might have some information about the killings. But, he cautioned, it might be nothing. He was very reluctant to share the information. I had to coerce him to finally spit it out."

"Why would he be reluctant?" Espinoza asked. "He called you, didn't he?"

"Yeah, I wondered the same thing myself, but I came to the conclusion that he just didn't want his name associated with the killings."

Espinoza and Brad nodded their heads as if the explanation made perfect sense and then beckoned Krnich to continue.

"Stack says he was contacted by a donor to his program who asked him to provide a list of the best real estate agents located along the coast of California. The donor indicated that he wanted his granddaughter to mentor under one or more of the agents."

"How many people were on the list?" Espinoza asked.

"Stack says he gave the donor eight or ten names. He wasn't sure. He knew it was less than fifteen."

"So we could have another three to seven victims waiting out there?" Brad stated in a matter-of-fact tone, as if he'd just solved a puzzle.

Mathematical genius in the making.

"Yes. I'm afraid so," Krnich said. And then added, "That is, if the information provided by Stack proves reliable."

"Have you looked into it yet?" Zindo asked.

Krnich frowned, stared daggers at Espinoza and then said calmly, "No, Mr. Zindo, we haven't had time to do that yet."

"Better get to it then," Zindo said, sipping his coffee and rubbing Rufus' ears.

Gee, wish I thought of that, Krnich thought.

Krnich gave Zindo a fake smile before continuing. "We *have* looked into Stack's background and I'll give you an overview of that in a minute. In the meantime, let me finish reviewing his call." Krnich paused and glanced at Zindo. "Is that okay with you?"

"Oh, please continue," Zindo said, looking bored and waving his hand like a Roman emperor bidding his servant to come forward.

"Okay. Anyway, Stack says he hadn't been following the news lately. He had been busy with his seminars and other various outside interests. Curlander did a little background research and discovered that Mr. Stack is dyslexic. He probably doesn't read the newspaper too often."

Krnich went on to describe the "stacking method of positive, organized, thinking" and gave a breakdown of the guru's current financial status.

"A dyslexic motivational expert! Beautiful!" Zindo exclaimed. "It actually makes a lot of sense. I'm slightly dyslexic, you know. We tend to create little ways to get around our reading deficiencies. In my case, I always asked for two reports written by different people. I would read each report the best I could and then hope to glean information from one report that I missed in the other."

"So you're saying that this "stacking" method of positive thinking might be the by-product of self-taught organizational training to help compensate for his inability to read?" Brad asked his rich friend.

"Sure. He probably figured out that holding on to negative thoughts disturbed his ability to read and/or to grasp new information," Zindo said proudly.

"Okay, well thanks for the education, Mr. Zindo," a slightly aggravated Krnich said. "Let's move on."

OUTSIDE THE WIND was beginning to blow and the air had turned ten degrees cooler. It wouldn't be long before much thicker fog would roll up the canyon. But for the humming of telephone wires below, and the chugging of a slow-moving train far off, the night was dead quiet. Inside, an uncomfortable silence fell over the group as Krnich studied his notes for a few minutes.

Finally, he broke the silence and continued. "So, it turns out that Mr. Stack is highly visual. When he sees the pictures in the newspaper, he recognizes all of the real estate agents as past participants in his various seminars. He can't remember their names but he immediately puts two and two together..."

"He gave his donor information on the dead agents, didn't he?" Brad said, butting in.

"Yes. All of the victims were among the names Stack provided."

"But what's the connection?" Espinoza asked. "I mean just because you tell somebody that John Smith sells the most real estate in San Francisco doesn't mean that John Smith should be killed. Why did the donor want the names again?"

"He said the guy wanted a list of potential mentors for his granddaughter. The grandfather paid Stack to provide individual guidance."

Krnich paused and looked around the room. It was obvious that everyone grasped the importance of this information. If someone was using the list to eradicate the agents, then the police could potentially protect the remaining intended victims while simultaneously attempting to set a trap for the killer.

"Unfortunately for us, Mr. Stack did not make a copy of the list he provided. He says he can't remember any of the other real estate agents he highlighted. He compiled the list last year. Since then, he has done over thirty seminars. He's seen thousands of faces; met thousands of aspiring agents. He says he might remember if we showed him pictures, but I don't know how we're going to narrow it down."

Krnich exhaled and turned to Brad. "Any ideas Brad?"

"Actually, yes, I have a few," Brad rose and walked to the other side of the room where a chalkboard had been set on an easel. Brad grabbed a piece of chalk and began. "We know that all the agents who have been killed so far represent high-end properties. . ."

"And attended Stack's seminars," Zindo added smugly.

Brad stared blankly at his friend as if to say, Duh! He waited a beat and then continued. "So, first of all we can narrow the field of participants to those agents who exclusively represent high-end homes in their respective communities." He jotted a few notes on the board. When he was finished, he turned back to group. "Then within that list, we can identify the twenty or thirty most affluent communities in California." He added this thought to the previous one written on the board. He stood back and admired his handwriting. "Can anybody read what I just wrote?" he asked.

"Nope," came the joint response.

"That's what I thought." He erased his chicken scratches and tossed the chalk to the side.

"Where do we get pictures of these agents?" Espinoza asked.

"That's the final piece of the puzzle, Raoul," Brad said. "We know that all of the agents I described will have attended Stack's seminars—at some point. Remember, real estate agents love this shit."

"So, we see if Stack has pictures of *all* his participants and then sort based on your criteria," Krnich interjected.

"That's what I think," Brad said. "Does he have pictures?"

"I didn't ask him," Krnich admitted. "I've got his cell number. I'm going to give him a call after dinner. Why doesn't everyone take a ten minute break?"

"Great, I'll check on Mel," Brad said.

"I'll order the pizza," Zindo offered. "And if you're nice to me, I'll pay for it too."

BRAD LEFT THE main room and walked to the back of the house where his study was located.

"Any luck?" he asked Mel and Curlander.

"I think so," the agent responded. "I've arranged for an artist to come by tomorrow and we're isolating the final details on the tattoo right now."

The computer screen in front of them went blank for a second and then a large graphic appeared on the screen. Mel's eyes widened.

"Yes, that's it. That's the symbol I saw tattooed on his calf," she said, pointing at the screen.

Taking a deep breath and wiping his brow, Curlander said "Oh Shit" under his breath and then turned to Brad. "Mr. Stephens, could you get agent Krnich for me, I think we've got a major problem on our hands."

42

"A SPECIAL OPS TATTOO! YOU'VE GOT TO BE SHITTING ME," KRNICH MUMBLED AS HE RAN HIS RIGHT HAND THROUGH HIS THINNING HAIR.

"That's the tattoo Mrs. Stephens saw. She's positive," Curlander said.

"I happen to know for a fact that you can only get one of those tattoos if you're badder than bad and have been honorably discharged from the service. The Special Ops don't want any of their active soldiers carrying identifying markings," Krnich said.

"Our guy is one bad hombre, then, sir," Curlander replied.

"Yes, I'm afraid he is. Let's take this back into the main room, Zach. I've got another bombshell to drop on the group. I was debating whether I'd do it tonight, but in light of this new discovery, I think we need to discuss it."

The pizza was scheduled to arrive shortly. Based on the looks of those gathered, everyone was hungry for information as well as pizza.

"With the help of Mrs. Stephens..."

"Mel" came a voice from the kitchen.

"Excuse me, what?"

"Call me Mel. 'Mrs. Stephens' is way too formal. We're all friends here," Mel said and then returned to her task.

"Very well. With *Mel's* help," Krnich began, "we've isolated the tattoo our unsub has on his right calf."

"Unsub? Since when did we start calling the killer an unsub?" Zindo asked.

"Technically, we should've been calling him that all along, but seeing as this is a joint effort, I've been using a civilian term. Now, I think we need to get a bit more technical. Some of the pieces are coming together and we might be able to start profiling this guy."

"Fair enough, just wondering. You probably can't tell but I'm a little sensitive to the over-reaching fascism that sometimes exists in our police forces in this country," Zindo said with a smile. "Please, continue."

Again Krnich stared at Zindo. "Excuse me for saying this, sir, but you must've had some bad experiences in your life. I'd like to talk to you about them when this investigation is over. In the meantime, please keep your opinions—unless they relate directly to our unsub—to yourself."

"Steve," came the millionaire's reply.

"No, my name's Jim."

"Not your name. My name," Zindo corrected the agent. "Since we're using first names, mine is not 'sir', its Steve."

Krnich shook his head. What type of loonies had he hooked up with? "Okay, Steve. Please refrain from expressing opinions until I call on you."

"Aye, aye, captain," the millionaire said as he saluted Krnich.

"Okay, as I was saying. The unsub has a distinctive tattoo on his right calf. The only person who can get this tattoo is a former Special Ops soldier who has been honorably discharged. There's good and bad to this information." Krnich bowed his head and rubbed his eyes. Clearly the bad part of this information was weighing heavily on him.

He took a deep breath and then continued. "The good is that we can search a specific data base for discharged Special Ops soldiers between the ages of 25 and 45. The bad news is very bad."

"I'll be damned, the guy is a trained assassin," Espinoza said to no one specifically. "He's not some low-life street punk who becomes a hit man. He's been trained by the finest killing machine on earth—the U.S. Special Ops unit."

"Holy shit!" Brad exclaimed.

"Exactly," Krnich concurred.

"And I've got some more bad news," Krnich confessed as the front door bell rang.

More bad news.

Oh good.

How much worse could it get?

Brad did a mental checklist: 1. Mel has pissed off a finely tuned, killing machine. 2. The guy was still on the loose. 3. They might be sitting ducks.

And then he turned his mind to the most pertinent questions: Who knew when or if the guy would strike again? Why? Why kill defenseless real estate agents? Before he could explore the questions with Krnich, he heard his wife enter the room.

"Pizza's here," Mel announced. "Everyone go wash their hands. I've got salad on the table along with paper plates and utensils. I'll put the pizzas out there too."

"The bad news can wait until after dinner," Krnich said, obviously trying to remain amiable, yet clearly deeply concerned.

The group proceeded to devour the food and wash it down with beer, wine, soda pop and, of course, a little Jack Daniels.

"Do you always drink Jack?" Krnich asked Brad. He had remembered that Brad had consumed his fair share at Harbour Town when the two first met.

"Sometimes I drink wine, but the older I get the more I get headaches from anything other than Jack. Don't know why; don't care why. I just know how my body works."

"How about Tequila?" Espinoza joked, obviously needling his buddy.

"Fuck you Raoul! You know I almost died on Tequila that time in the desert. And after watching Mr. Gonzales the other day—drunk as a skunk on the stuff—I've redoubled my vow to never consume the Devil's water again."

"What happened the other day?" Krnich asked.

"A despondent husband accosted Brad at his office," Zindo replied.

"Really, what did you do about it?"

"Like the well-trained executive he is, Brad diffused the situation," Zindo said with a smile, wiping the final remains of pepperoni pizza from his lips.

"How did you do that?"

"I offered to help him with grief counseling," Brad said, taking his first bite of pizza.

"That was good thinking," Curlander said, stringy cheese sticking to his chin. "Often times, people just need to talk to a professional." He took a big gulp from a bottle of Dr. Pepper and burped softly.

"It was obvious to me the guy was hurting. He thought I motivated his wife to jump off a bridge," Brad said.

"No shit!" Krnich said. "And how would you do that?"

"They got foreclosed on and she called me for some advice."

"She couldn't handle the truth?" Curlander said.

"Something like that."

"So what did the guy want?" Krnich asked.

"I don't really know. He was drunk and I think he wanted to take out his frustrations on somebody or something."

"So he was serious then?"

"Again, I don't know. Anyway, we talked and he's going to get some counseling."

Brad secretly wished he could arrange counseling for the millions of people wiped-out by the recession.

At least one guy will get professional help.

Krnich pounded Brad on the back. "You did good Brad, but let's see here, last time I saw you, you were almost killed by a right-wing extremist. This time you had a drunken widower come after you. Right now, your wife has foiled a trained Special Ops soldier from fulfilling his objective. Hell, you lead an awfully exciting life for a mortgage broker. Is it a requirement of the business?" Krnich joked. "If so, I'm glad I'm a career civil servant."

"It's an intense and sometimes, stupid occupation but no, death and destruction don't usually go hand in hand with interest rate issues and appraisal concerns. However," Brad continued, "if there was ever going to be consistent intrigue, it would be as a result of this economy. People are pissed-off and, contrary to popular media opinion, they're getting more pissed every day. I'm afraid this recession's got legs and things might turn really ugly before we get back to a stable economy."

"What do you mean by 'ugly'?" Krnich asked.

"I guess I mean... mild anarchy!" Brad responded. Obviously, he had thought about this issue before. "What I appreciate about America is that it is a nation of laws. People stop at stop signs. People generally don't speed. They don't park on the sidewalks. They honor their contracts." He took a bite of pizza, washed it down with some Jack and swallowed. When he could speak again, he said, "I see that gradually changing daily."

"What do you mean? I don't follow," Curlander said.

Brad looked at the lanky agent and said, "What I mean is that once a consumer decides to default on an obligation, it becomes easier the next time. We have a nation of consumers who can't or won't pay their rent, mortgage or car loan or...whatever. The middle class has been purged and deflated. Rightly or wrongly. These are people who had lived by the rules for forty or fifty years; done things the right way—the American way. Then they suddenly had to make decisions to try to retain their wealth, or save their home, or fight for their family..."

"I know what you mean," Curlander responded. "I've got a brother- in-law that just stopped paying his mortgage. He said that the bank wouldn't listen to him unless he was in default. So, he called me up and said, 'I'm going to become the biggest, stinkiest jerk they've ever seen'."

"I wish I had a dime for every time I've heard the same basic thing the past few years," Brad agreed ruefully. "It doesn't help when a guy like your brother-in-law sees a neighbor getting assistance and he's left hanging –like Mussolini—in the wind."

"He's a good guy; an average guy. He worked his whole life as a plumber. Always respectful. Always minded his own business. One day the plumbing company shuts down and his wife gets sick. He calls the bank for some help. They tell him to 'fuck off'. They only talk to people who are behind on their payments—not those who *think* they're going to fall behind," Curlander said shaking his head slowly.

"Now he's bitter, cynical, and pissed. I see what you mean about how things could turn even uglier."

"Well, you're in the proverbial 'eye of the storm'," Krnich said to Brad. "You'd know firsthand about all this. I just hope it doesn't lead to mass murders nationwide. They say the second kill is much easier than the first. I'm only a few years away from retirement. I don't need to spend the rest of my time on numerous cases. One every six months will do nicely."

AFTER DINNER, THE group re-assembled in the front room. Krnich got right to the point.

"The other bad news I was going to give you before dinner arrived is that the donor who asked for the list from Stack is a very bad man. His name is Gino Falicello. They call him 'the Fridge'. He's a former mobster from Chicago. Apparently, he has relocated to Las Vegas and is enjoying a quiet retirement."

"Sounds like 'the Fridge' may have come out of retirement," Zindo observed.

"Yep," Krnich agreed. "That's what I think."

Brad said what he was thinking out loud, "They say a leopard doesn't change its spots."

"The only problem with that analogy Brad, is that Gino 'the Fridge' Falicello is much, much more dangerous than a leopard," Krnich said.

"And now we have the pleasure of connecting him to these murders," Espinoza said, blowing out a deep breath and tossing his pizza down on his plate with a loud 'thunk'. "Perfect, just fucking perfect," he said. "So let me get this straight, what we're dealing with here is a highly-trained former Special Ops soldier—who can probably kill anyone with his thumb and forefinger, by the way—and a connected mobster who can hire a guy like that."

Krnich nodded slowly. "Yep Raoul, that just about sums it up, doesn't it."

A strange silence settled over the room. Krnich stared at Zindo as if waiting for him to make a snide remark. For once, the millionaire had nothing to say.

43

THE NEXT EVENING, TED FLOWERS ARRIVED IN MONTEREY, CALIFORNIA. AS WAS TYPICAL OF THE COASTAL HAVEN, THE FOG HAD ROLLED IN EARLY AND WAS NOW BLANKETING THE AREA.

He checked into his room. It was okay. Not the Ritz, but okay. He took a quick shower, decided to head out for a nice dinner. As he had in Carlsbad earlier in the week, he made a big deal out of revealing his plans for the evening to the hotel staff.

"Any action out there... Danny?" he asked the parking attendant while snatching a quick glimpse of the gawky teenager's name tag.

"I doubt it, sir."

"No worries, I'll check it out anyway." He tossed the kid a five spot and drove away.

It indeed was quiet in Monterey and Pebble Beach proper. Apparently, wealthy golfers didn't party during the week. That luxury must be reserved for the weekends, he thought. The rest of the time, they were boring, rich people, living boring, rich lives.

At least I'll spice things up around here.

The main decision Flowers had made on the drive north was to take his time on this Willowby job.

In retrospect, Coronado and Ventura had gone so smoothly that he had dropped his guard and rushed the job in Montecito. He went over the disaster with Smith-Newhall again in his head. Obviously, he was lazy with the ladder.

Less obvious was the other deadly sin he was guilty of: arrogance.

The house had been easy to find. The painter had been easy to neutralize. He had assumed the real estate agent would be alone. Big mistake. This time he would research his target, make sure that he isolated Roger Willowby. No friends or associates would interfere.

Flowers would park his ego at the door and do the job right.

He wondered what 'the Fridge' thought about his failure in Montecito. Had he heard about it? How much trouble was he in? Should he contact Falicello and discuss it with him?

No. Communication was to be one way. He had to honor his contract.

He would double-back to Santa Barbara in a few days. He could finish the job on Smith-Newhall—and her friends. It would give him an opportunity to visit his grandmother's grave one more time before he fled the country.

The thought made the killer smile. "You need to be flexible, Nino," his grandmother would say. "If life gives you a lemon, you gotta make lemonade." And his grandfather would add, "Yeah, Eduardo. If life throws you a curve, hit it out of the ball park."

Always with the baseball metaphors; that old man.

God he missed them both.

Maybe things would've turned out differently if they were still alive?

Maybe.

Doubt it.

Satisfied with his course of action, Flowers drove around Monterey for an hour getting acquainted with the area.

HE STOPPED ABRUPTLY in front of Cambridge Realty on Ocean Avenue. The building was a nondescript stucco and glass concoction with a large window facing the street. Tall Juniper bushes framed the entrance to the building and rose bushes lined the sidewalk.

Although it was foggy, Flowers could see his next target standing behind a large metal desk. Roger Willowby was staring at his computer screen, cigarette hanging from his lips.

Working late, eh, Mr. Willowby.

Better be careful, those cancer sticks will kill you.

A plain-looking man dressed in a gray suit with red tie, Willowby appeared to be alone. Flowers figured him to be about five foot ten, a hundred and sixty pounds. He had brown hair with graying temples and a neatly trimmed moustache. How easy it would be to take the real estate agent out right here, right now, Flowers thought.

No, take your time. Don't rush.

Mistakes happen when you rush.

Without warning, Willowby was joined by three people. The group stared at the computer screen and then Willowby gestured to his guests to be seated. From across the street, Flowers smiled, happy to have decided to use more caution this time around.

He put the car in gear and before he pulled out onto the street, he looked at the real estate office one more time. "No stupid friend of yours is going to trip me up, Mr. Willowby. There will be no ladder to knock over this time," he said quietly to himself. He discreetly made a fake gun out of his thumb and forefinger and pointed it at the unsuspecting agent. "Bang! You're dead," he said quietly and pulled away from the curb.

44

SCOTT STEPHENS WAS EXCITED YET CONCERNED AT THE SAME TIME.

Scott, the youngest son of Brad and Melanie Stephens had started his own unique restaurant several weeks earlier. Calling it simply, "Scott's", it was a traveling, specialty food truck.

Initially, he had intended to serve basic food to those fortunate enough to find his daily locations. However, after some rather creative experimentation, he had stumbled on to a real winner with his homemade, sizzling hot chili. Combined with his wonderful hamburgers, flavorful sausages, and healthy vegetable dishes, the chili was not only popular but profitable.

Soon word had spread through the internet. Scott's chili was a 'must eat' and had scored a nine on the ten point scale of gourmet food truck services on a local website that graded such things.

Although he enjoyed cooking, Scott still laughed at all the hoopla that surrounded his—and those of his competitor's—trucks. They were really just over-glorified lunch trucks after all. Like the ones you used to see around a construction site. Fortunately, web-based marketing, cleaner paint jobs, and, hopefully, healthier food had distinguished the gourmet trucks from the common lunch wagons.

Who was he to argue?

He would like to boast about the genius behind his truck, however, the truth was, it was a cheaper way to distribute food. Rent in downtown Santa Barbara was astronomical, reserved for established local eateries or national food chains.

When Scott had done the math with Brad it was obvious that the food truck was the way to go. Only problem at the time was money. His father couldn't help and Scott had only saved ten thousand of his own dollars over the years.

Bottom line: Not nearly enough capital to begin this enterprise.

Having written an extensive business plan, Scott was surprised when he couldn't secure financing from the local banks. Luckily for him, his two quasi "uncles", John Linden and Steve Zindo, loved him like a son. Not only that, they knew the former local football hero could develop a following. Without involving Brad, they partnered with Scott and helped make his dream a reality.

Now, several weeks into his new venture, Scott anticipated his biggest and, hopefully, most profitable, challenge.

John Linden was giving a golf clinic the next day, Saturday, at the local driving range. Hundreds, maybe thousands of golfers would attend. If he played his cards right, prepared his food properly and advertised his location on the internet, Scott should have his biggest pay day yet. The prospect excited him and made him nervous at the same time.

"Come on Scott," he said to himself, "view this like a football game. They've given you the ball. Go down and score."

Friday afternoon would be a dress rehearsal for handling volume. He had loaded the truck with all the proper ingredients, announced his location on the web, and added an advertising hook: "All Food Half Off Today Only".

It worked. By two o'clock, Scott had served three times the normal customer count and had gone through all of his provisions. He made a mental note to bulk up on buns, hamburger meat, cheese, onions, and cranberry sausages. He also noted that several customers inquired about salads.

He picked up his cell phone and called his mother.

"Hey, mom," he began, "would you be interested in making a few bowls of different types of salads for my truck tomorrow?"

Startled by the request, yet proud that he would ask, Mel quickly agreed. "Which salads do you think I should make?" She asked this rhetorically. She already knew she'd make the gorgonzola and pear mixed green salad and the bacon and spinach salad with pine nuts and cranberries.

"Whatever you make will be fine. You're a great salad maker," Scott assured her. "Now, please understand, I don't need any help in the truck. You don't have to come along. I don't need you to help with the entrees. I'll pick up the salads from your house tonight. Okay?" Visions of his mother cooking an absolutely awful casserole or mixing up the ingredients on an otherwise simple pasta dish danced in his head.

"It's all right, Scott. Your father talked to me about my crappy cooking. I'm honored that you want me to prepare some salads. I'm glad we can all agree I make a good salad. I won't get in your way. I love you and want you to be successful. Just let me know what I can do."

Scott breathed a deep sigh of relief. "Dad talked to you? What did he say?"

"He said that you all had been putting up with my lousy-tasting meals for years because you didn't want to hurt my feelings. We agreed that I could go to a cooking school up in Napa as soon as we could afford it. Want to come?"

"That might be cool."

"In the meantime, I'm willing to help however I can. I'll go shopping for the ingredients in a few hours and I'll have the salads ready to go by six o'clock. Does that work?"

"Perfect," Scott replied. "And, mom, be sure to keep the receipts. I insist on reimbursing you for the materials." And then as an afterthought, he said, "And I insist on compensating you for your time as well."

"Pssh-Posh," Mel said, swiping the air with her hand. "It's the least your father and I can contribute."

Changing the subject she asked, "Have you been taking care of yourself? These early hours can really wear you down. You sound a little congested."

"I feel fine, mom," Scott assured her. "I'm just a little tired from the lunch crowd today. And I'm excited about the golf exhibition tomorrow. I really think this could be my big break."

"From your lips to God's ears. I'll see you later." She hung up and began making her shopping list.

SCOTT CLOSED HIS cell phone and smiled. The day had been a big success. His mom was willing to help with the one thing she prepared very well and customers were guaranteed to be plentiful at the driving range. His throat was a little sore, but that was probably due to allergies and extensive talking.

Everything was coming together. Why did he feel so uneasy? Nerves, he assured himself. "I'll go home and take a nap. That'll fire me up," he thought as he drove the big truck out of the parking lot and merged into traffic. What could go wrong?

45

"I HATE TO ADD MORE DRAMA TO YOUR LIFE BUDDY, BUT YOU'RE MY AGENT NOW AND NOT JUST MY BEST FRIEND," JOHN LINDEN TOLD BRAD OVER THE PHONE.

"What's up?" Brad asked.

"Well I've got good news and bad news. Which do you want first?"

Oh, shit, more good news/bad news.

Now what?

"Give me the good news. I'm trying to be more positive these days."

"Is that because of that motivational speaker you guys are looking into?" Linden asked, clearly trying to delay the delivery of his news.

"He's got nothing to do with it. The guy's a 'tool' if you ask me. I just want to be more optimistic. Now, what's the good news?"

"I'm getting married."

"To who?"

"That's to whom if you're being grammatically correct."

Again, delaying.

"Okay, to whom?"

"To Stef, you idiot. Who else would I marry?"

"Hell, I don't know. Could be Fabiola came back in the picture or could be you found a new squeeze." Brad hesitated and then said, "I didn't realize you two had gotten *that* close."

"I know it's happening rather fast but, hey, what can I say? I asked her yesterday and she said yes."

"John, you sound like a sixteen year old who just asked the head cheerleader out to the dance. Are you sure Stef said yes? Not, maybe. Or, give me a few days. Or, we'll see..."

"Actually, if you must know, she asked me to marry her."

"I find that hard to believe. My Stef, got down on one knee and said, 'John Linden will you marry me?' I don't think so."

"Okay, well she didn't get down on one knee, I did. And she didn't ask me as much as she manipulated the conversation and convinced me it would be a good thing to do."

"So, you did it?"

"I did."

"Well, congratulations, then," Brad said, still somewhat in shock. John Linden had been married several times before. None of them had turned out well. He was paying many thousands in monthly alimony and his former wives hated him.

"Are you up to the challenge? You know, I think if Tiger had somebody like you around, he could've kept a lid on the whole mistress thing," Linden said.

"Do you really believe that? There were at least fifteen girls."

"See? Mine will be easier. There is only one girl and I'm sure she'll be reasonable. Here's her phone number. Call her immediately and then get back to me." He read off a long distance number and repeated it twice.

"Got it?" Linden asked.

"Yeah, I got it," Brad said. Then he asked, "What about Stef? Does she know?"

"No she doesn't. And, pards, if you do your job properly, she never will. Right?"

"I'm not sure I signed up for this duty, buddy."

"Sure you did. When it says professional manager, it doesn't just stop at golf and contracts and shit like that you know." Then he added, "Listen if you get me out of this, I promise you I'll meet with Nike. Okay?"

Despite himself, Brad had to agree. An endorsement from Nike would be huge. And it wasn't as if John had cheated. If this girl was pregnant with his child, conception had occurred before John had hooked up with Stef. Surely she would understand. Wouldn't she?

Oh, yeah. Sure.

He took a deep breath, exhaled, sat back and shook his head. What was he thinking? If there was one thing in the whole, stinking world that Stefanie Ramirez would not understand it was her fiancée fathering a child with an old girlfriend!

"Don't let them trash me in the press either," Linden half demanded, half pleaded.

"I'll do what I can," Brad said with absolutely zero confidence. What the hell did he know about keeping a jilted lover quiet? He was just getting the hang of booking tournaments and paying bills for Linden. And now this.

Damn!

Brad asked one final question. "Do I have your permission to negotiate on your behalf?"

"Yes. That's what I'm telling you. Make it go away and keep me out of the papers...please. I don't want to mess up my public reputation and I don't want to lose Stef." He was definitely pleading now.

"Okay, but realize this will probably cost you some money and even if I do manage to get her to sign a contract, there is always the chance she will breach it."

"Why would she do that if she's compensated and the baby is taken care of?"

"Hey buddy, you should know as well as anyone, 'Hell hath no fury like a woman scorned'. Think of all the politicians that thought they had their mistresses under control. And, then, whammo! To the press they ran; to the wives they confessed."

"What are you saying?"

"It happens. That's all I'm saying. I'll get an iron-clad contract written up once I work out the details—if I work out the details, I should say. But still be prepared that at some point—maybe when the kid turns

18—you could get a knock on the door or call from a reporter. Who knows?"

"Okay. I get it. By the time the kid turns 18, I'll be 68 and playing on the Champions Tour. My retirement will be intact and Stef and I will have had many wonderful years together. It won't matter so much then. Hell, I might even want to get to know the kid? Maybe he'll have a great golf swing."

Brad grinned. This whole thing was pure John Linden. "All right, I'll get to work on it immediately."

HE STARED AT the piece of scratch paper he had written notes on. How had Linden put them in this position? He took a deep breath and dialed the phone number.

"Hello, Mary? This is Brad Stephens. John Linden's manager," he began.

The response on the other end of the line was cold and perfunctory. "I know who you are. Where is that weasel? Where is Johnny? Is he going to come down here and marry me? Do the right thing by me and my baby? Or have you called me to try and buy my silence? I can tell you right now I am not getting an abortion!" She paused and then added, "And I don't come cheap!"

Oops!

She's really not going to be a good sport, is she?

46

Las Vegas

"I REMEMBER ALL THE NAMES I GAVE FALICELLO NOW THAT I'VE SEEN THE PICTURES YOU ISOLATED FOR ME," JIM STACK SAID IN A VOICE DRIPPING WITH PRIDE.

"That's wonderful," Zach Curlander responded as he put his cell phone down for a moment and grabbed a piece of paper and a pen. You'd think the guy found the Holy Grail, he thought. "Go ahead. Shoot," he said.

"You know," Stack began, "in addition to being a master motivator, I have a photographic memory for faces—not names. Seems strange, doesn't it? I'm brilliant in so many respects, but I obviously have a short term memory problem with names."

"Yes, strange," Curlander agreed wondering who in the world described themselves as being brilliant and why wouldn't the guy just cut to the chase. But Krnich had told him to be patient with the rich and famous. They loved to talk about themselves. Let them do that and gain their confidence.

Block them and they'd never trust you again.

"Perhaps I'll work on it, might even stumble on a new technique for name recall. Maybe I can tie it into my 'Stacking Method'."

"Sure, that would be a win/win," Curlander agreed. "Now how about those names."

Stack began listing the ten names he had given Falicello. When he was done, he added, "Of course, the first seven are already dead."

No shit! What does the guy think we do all day?

"Thanks Mr. Stack. I hope your short-term memory system works and you make a ton of dough from it," Curlander said.

"Thanks agent Curlander. But, rest assured, I don't do what I do merely for money. Wealth is a nice by-product, but my true motivation is to improve the lives of those around me." And then, just as he had done with Krnich the day before, the high-powered salesman added, "I'll tell you what, I'm going to send you and your whole task force tickets to my next conference. I'm sure it'll help you guys in your quest to rid the world of monsters and murderers."

And just like Krnich the day before, Curlander responded with apparent respect and admiration, "That would be great. I'm sure we would benefit from your teachings. Have a nice day, Mr. Stack and please keep your cell phone on in case we have further questions."

THE MOTIVATIONAL GURU hung up feeling relieved. The guilt that had plagued him earlier was gone and he was confident he had made several new converts. He dug through his pant pockets and found a slip of paper with the name and number of the girl he had so much fun with the other night.

"You, my dear, will be the first name I commit to memory," he said to himself. And then grinned and added, "That is, of course, if you're as much fun sober as I think you were when drunk."

47

"THE GUY REALLY DIDN'T THINK WE WOULD NOTICE THAT SEVEN OF THE NAMES HAD ALREADY BEEN KILLED?" KRNICH REPLIED WHEN CURLANDER BRIEFED HIM.

"That guy is so full of his own bullshit, I think he would declare, in that pompous voice of his, that we obviously don't know the sky is blue," Curlander said.

"Well, it doesn't matter what he thinks—unless he's our killer—I guess. And it sounds like you did a good job of placating him. We got the list, that's all that matters."

Curlander smiled. "Yep, I did, didn't I?"

"Let's take a look at it," Krnich said.

Curlander had taken the time to put the list of names on a power-point slide. He clicked on the computer and all ten names appeared on the screen. Next to each name was a listing of the area in which each agent sold real estate, a notation as to whether the agent was dead or alive and a recent photo of the salesperson.

The second name on the list was Paula Smith-Newhall. A very bold **ALIVE** was written after the word, Montecito, and in parenthesis (Santa Barbara).

Two other names were treated in similar fashion: Roger Willowby, (Carmel/Pebble Beach) and Susan Ornstein, (Atherton. Palo Alto area, by Stanford University).

"We've got surveillance on Smith-Newhall already," Krnich said. "I think we should send Simmons and Johnson up to Atherton to watch Ornstein. And you should head up to Pebble Beach to watch Willowby."

Curlander took notes while Krnich spoke. He stopped for a minute and asked about Smith-Newhall.

"As luck would have it, she and Melanie Stephens and Stefanie Ramierz are heading up to Pebble Beach on Sunday for Stack's superstar conference. I'm going to head out to Las Vegas this afternoon and confront Gino Falicello. I want to find out what the Fridge was really doing with that list.

"Good idea, boss."

Krnich stared at Curlander for a moment with a look that said he knew it was a good idea. When Curlander shrugged, Krnich continued. "Then, I'll accompany the ladies on Sunday and make sure they are protected. You find Willowby and stick to him like 'white on rice'."

"Should I call him first and set up a meeting?" Curlander asked.

"No, I don't want to alert him. It might scare off the killer," Krnich said with more confidence than he actually felt.

It had been a few days. Who was to say that the killer wasn't already in Carmel...or Atherton for that matter? Perhaps he planned to strike today? Didn't Krnich owe the potential victims adequate warning? Wasn't he using these unsuspecting people as bait in a very deadly game? Without reversing himself entirely, he instructed Curlander to call the local police chiefs in both Atherton and Carmel and fill them in accordingly.

"Brief them only on the threat to Willowby and Ornstein. Suggest they have a man discreetly shadow each real estate agent until we get there. If the officer notices anything suspicious, I want to know about it. Immediately."

"Will do, boss."

"Oh, and Zach," Krnich added. "Be sure to tell them our killer is highly trained and very dangerous. If spotted, do not attempt to take him down. Wait for backup." He paused and then looked his second in command directly in the eye. "That goes for you too. Don't try to take him out by yourself, okay?"

"Got it, chief. I'll call when I get to Carmel." Curlander rose, gathered his things and started to say something but thought better of it and strode towards the door.

"What's on your mind, Zach?" Krnich asked.

"Nothing. See you Sunday."

"Bullshit. You were about to say something. What is it?"

"It's just... do you think it's a good idea for Smith-Newhall and the women to travel—especially to an area where one of our next potential victims lives?"

"I don't like it," Krnich said. "In a perfect world, I would demand they remain under protection here in Santa Barbara but the women insisted and, the more I think about it, it might be convenient to have all the potential victims in one spot so we can throw a blanket over them."

"Hope you're right."

"Me too."

The two shook hands, exchanged good-byes and Curlander exited the room. Krnich focused on the photos of Smith-Newhall and Willowby. What were the odds that the killer knew that both 'superstar' agents would be in Pebble Beach Sunday through Wednesday? Was he planning on taking them both out at the same time? He hated the thought, but in a strange way, it might make things easier. Odds were they'd catch him before he could harm the real estate agents.

Krnich called two of his men and told them to be prepared to go up to Carmel to join Curlander. He finished the coffee he was drinking, turned out the lights and walked out the office door.

As he strolled down the hall he experienced one recurring thought: We're ready for you, you son-of-a-bitch.

AS HE ROUNDED the final corner before the elevator, Krnich pulled out his cell phone and called Jim Stack. The call was answered on the fourth ring.

"Mr. Stack, sorry to bother you, sir. This is special agent Jim Krnich."

"Yes agent Krnich. I just talked to agent Curlander a few hours ago. Seems like a very bright fellow. He's going to round up your team and bring them to my next major conference in Las Vegas. I hope you will consider my offer and join them."

Over my dead body.

"I just might. Thanks for inviting us. Listen, I have a question for you.

"Yes, what is it?"

"Can you look at your list of participants for this upcoming 'superstar' seminar in Pebble Beach?"

"Sure. I got it right here. What do you want to know?"

"I know that Paula Smith-Newhall will be there. How about Roger Willowby and Susan Ornstein?"

"Are those the only three remaining agents alive on the list I gave to Falicello?" Stack asked.

Damn! Krnich didn't want anyone outside his immediate circle to know details, but this guy was so pushy and it really was important to get this information. After wrestling with his conscience for a minute, he decided to answer the question. "Yes. We have narrowed it down to those three. Ms. Smith-Newhall, of course, knows that she's in danger. The other two don't and I want to keep it that way. Please do not contact them."

"Understood. I have no reason to contact them in advance. Now, let me check the list of confirmed attendees. I believe there are over two hundred confirmed. It might take me a few minutes."

While Stack went through the list, Krnich contacted the hangar where the Special Task Force jet was parked. He spoke to the pilot and made arrangements to depart for Las Vegas at one thirty that afternoon.

Great perk of the new job, he thought. Not even the Secret Service offered access to air transport spur of the moment.

Stack came back on the line. "Okay, I've reviewed the list. Both Willowby and Ornstein have confirmed." He paused for a moment, cleared his throat and added, "You know, it's going to be the biggest and best conference ever!"

"I didn't know that, but I'm happy for you," Krnich said, thinking perhaps he should provide more protection for the potential targets. Then another thought came to him. "Does anyone else have access to that list?"

"Just my assistant, Joyce. Do you want to talk to her?"

"Maybe. Is she there?"

Stack looked at the naked blonde now lying next to him, her large breasts covered only by the gray silk sheet. He smiled, thinking of all the kinky fun they were going to have that afternoon. Most assuredly, she was not Joyce.

"No, agent Krnich. Joyce is not here. I'm at home. She should be at my office." He gave Krnich the number and then asked semi-seriously, "Do you think I should cancel the conference? Are there other 'superstar' agents in jeopardy?"

The guru was relieved when Krnich told him to go ahead as planned. He and his men would be at the conference. Nobody should be in danger.

"Good. Thanks for the call. I've got to get back to work," he said as the blonde reached across the bed and ran her fingers up his thigh.

HEY SAID THEIR good-byes and Stack put the phone back in its cradle. He looked at the blonde and said, "Sheila, you've got me ready, willing and horny. Let's get busy."

The blonde bent forward and was about to use her mouth to further arouse him when she stopped. She stared him the eye for a moment and then shook her head softly. "For such a smart guy, you really do have a bad memory. My name is Laurie, not Sheila. I don't know who Sheila is, but can she do this?" she asked as she mounted him.

Stack grinned and shook his head. "I'm working on my short term memory, Laurie. I've got a theory that if I associate a person's name with a very positive, enjoyable event, and tie the first letter of their name to another word that starts with the same letter, I will remember their name."

"Let's start now," she moaned. "My name is Laurie and I assure you, you're going to have fun. And you can associate the 'L' in my name with lust."

Stack made a mental note and then got down to business.

48

THE FLIGHT FROM SANTA BARBARA TO LAS VEGAS TOOK LESS THAN AN HOUR.

Krnich had called in advance and had been told that Falicello would be glad to meet with him. It wasn't the response he expected. If the 'Fridge' was responsible for all of this recent carnage, wouldn't he be concerned by a visit from the commander of a Federal task force? Suddenly, it didn't add up.

Krnich began to wonder if he'd gain any meaningful information from this trip or if it was just a waste of time. He only hoped he wouldn't tip his hand and inadvertently send Gino Falicello underground.

He couldn't worry about that now. He was in Vegas. It was hot. The landing had been rough and he had a job to do.

His rental car was waiting for him on the tarmac. It was a non-descript Ford Taurus with all the new amenities: Bluetooth, GPS, MP3 Player. Why the hell would he need an MP3 Player? Whatever happened to listening to the radio? Get a little local flavor. He shook his head in disgust, threw his briefcase in the backseat, got in the vehicle, cranked-up the air conditioning and set the GPS for Falicello's address.

He turned on the radio. Wayne Newton was belting-out Danka Shan.

Now that's what I'm talking about.

In normal Vegas traffic, it should only be a forty minute ride. Krnich could tell the moment he exited the airport, this was not a normal traffic day. A man dressed like Elvis held what was obviously a squirt gun to a woman's head near the entrance to McCarron; police, fire trucks and ambulances blocked all vehicles from leaving. Krnich slammed his hand on the steering wheel and then chuckled lightly to himself, "I guess it's really true. What happens in Vegas stays in Vegas."

A FULL HOUR and a half later Krnich pulled into the Falicello compound. "Agent Krnich, a pleasure to meet you," Gino Falicello said as Krnich approached the front door of the mansion.

"Mr. Falicello," Krnich said, taking in the opulence that surrounded him. Nobody had told him that Falicello lived in a palace. The exterior boasted large marble pillars, beautifully crafted stained-glass windows and a huge wooden entry. The front room alone was as big as Krnich's entire condo.

So crime does pay after all.

"Please follow me. We can talk out on the patio," Falicello said, pointing towards a large flagstone-covered area adjacent to an Olympic-size swimming pool.

"Can I get you a drink? You've traveled a long way, you must be parched," Falicello said with all the charm and grace of a politician entertaining a major financial contributor.

Remembering the advice he had given Curlander about dealing with the rich and famous—be gracious, get them talking about themselves—Krnich smiled and asked for an iced tea. Falicello signaled to his butler (or man servant?) to grab two iced teas.

"I guess we could exchange pleasantries, you know, talk about the weather, discuss current politics, bemoan the state of Tiger's golf game, but you haven't come here for that," Falicello began. "I can see you are a man of action."

Krnich gave him an appraising glance and raised his left eyebrow. He said nothing.

Let the guy talk. Feed him some rope.

"I took the liberty of researching your background, agent Krnich. Twenty years with the Secret Service. Less than one year with the FBI. You have a sterling record. You now run a special task force which deals with serial crimes." He stopped and smiled at Krnich.

"You do your homework, Mr. Falicello. That is all correct," Krnich said.

Be careful, this guy is good.

"You've killed several men in the line of duty. So I know you're not just a paper-pushing bureaucrat. Is this not true?"

"I hate paperwork and yes, I've been forced to defend myself a few times."

"So, let's cut to the chase then, shall we. To what do I owe the honor of a visit from a man such as you?"

"I'm investigating some murders in California. I have reason to believe that Las Vegas is connected to these killings," Krnich said, choosing his words carefully. He didn't want to insult the old man, however, he wanted to make it known that the Feds might have something linking Falicello to these killings. This visit wasn't just a 'fishing expedition'.

The old man leaned back, crossed his left leg over the right and took a long sip of his iced-tea. "California is a long distance from here," he said. "As you can plainly see, I now live full time in Las Vegas. Why would I want to harm anyone in California?"

"I don't know. That's what I'm here to find out."

"This is quite unusual. Do I need my attorney? Or are we just going to have a nice chat?"

"It's your call, Mr. Falicello. I'm going to ask you a few questions. I haven't read you your Miranda rights and I don't yet consider you an official suspect. If that status changes, you'll be the first to know."

"Fair enough, go ahead and ask your questions. I have nothing to hide."

From the corner of his eye, Krnich saw a woman's figure staring at the patio from a second story window. Falicello caught his eye, followed it to the bedroom window, turned and waved.

Having been spotted, Mercedes Falicello opened the window and shouted down to her grandfather. "Would you like me to join you, Papa?"

"No darling, not now. Perhaps in a few minutes. We have work to discuss. It would just bore you." He winked at Krnich.

"My granddaughter, Mercedes. I have raised her since her parents died," Falicello explained. "She had a very rough time with their deaths and has presented me many challenges. In her youth, she was known for being very rebellious. Now, look at her, she's an angel. In fact, she is the love of my life, my reason for living... my everything." He sighed almost like a lover fawning over his mate. For a moment he seemed to drift off and then, just as suddenly, returned to the present. "Now go ahead, let's get this distasteful matter behind us."

Krnich pulled a well-worn note pad from his jacket and flipped it open. He produced a pen from his front shirt pocket and swirled the tip around on the paper to get the ink flowing. After a moment he was ready to begin. "Mr. Falicello did you ask for a list of real estate agents from Mr. Jim Stack of the 'Stacking Method School of Positive Thinking'?"

"As I'm sure you're aware—or you wouldn't be here—yes, I did ask for a list of successful real estate agents from him. Mercedes trained with him and I thought he would be a good resource to provide some names and locations of people she might be interested in mentoring with."

Falicello paused for a second, took a large gulp of iced tea, rearranged his square frame in the patio chair, and then continued. "You see, Mercedes is about to enter the business world." Again he winked and lowered his voice as if he and Krnich shared some deep, dark secret. "Or at least the business world suited for women."

"What world is that?"

"She isn't sure yet, but it will be something initially in California. She loves the weather out there. If this is what she truly wants to do, I thought it might help if she mentored with other successful people."

"Sounds like you don't fully support her decision?"

"I guess California is a nice place, but I would prefer she stay here and study to become a lawyer or doctor. She is very bright and the world is her oyster." He spread his arms wide in a grand gesture. "However, she has made up her mind. Maybe she will meet a nice doctor, get married and forget the business world?"

Krnich nodded as if agreeing. He made a mental note to talk to the girl if things continued to progress. He began to jot down her name when the pen ran dry. Looking embarrassed, he asked Falicello if he could borrow a pen. The 'Fridge' snapped his fingers and his servant quickly appeared with a brand new Monte Blanc.

"Please feel free to keep the pen, agent Krnich. It is my little gift to you for making such a long journey," Falicello said.

Krnich said thank-you and quickly wrote a few things on the paper in front of him. Outside, the day had turned at least ten degrees warmer and a mild wind began swirling within the complex.

How do people live in this heat?

Krnich took out a handkerchief, wiped his brow and then continued with his questions. "Okay, getting back to the list, you say you asked for the names as possible mentors. Is that right?"

"That is correct."

"Have you had occasion to contact any of the real estate agents?"

"No, I haven't. I gave the list to Mercedes and I instructed her to begin calling them this summer. I suggested she arrange interviews with them." He made this last statement with a self-satisfied grin, as if he were Andrew Carnegie sharing the secrets of success.

It was obvious from his body language that Gino Falicello felt absolutely confident in his rendition. Krnich had done hundreds of interviews in the past. He could tell when a witness, victim or perpetrator was being truthful. So far, Falicello was telling the truth. Krnich decided to broaden the scope of inquiry.

"The reason I'm asking these questions is that seven of the ten people on that list have been killed recently," Krnich said, staring directly into the old man's eyes, searching for a reaction. When he didn't get one, he cleared his throat and continued. "I know it makes no sense that a man in your position would be involved in such a horrible matter, however, it is either the biggest coincidence in the world, or..."

"Or what, agent Krnich?" The 'Fridge's' voice turned colder. "Or, Gino Falicello, the businessman from Chicago with reputed connections to certain unsavory characters, suddenly takes a disliking to innocent real estate agents in California? Come on, agent Krnich, you really don't believe that do you?"

Confused, Krnich stumbled for the correct response. "I don't know what to believe, to tell you the truth. It seems far-fetched to me that you, a retired businessman, never convicted of a major crime, would waste time or resources on this matter. That much is true. But, on the other hand, it is too much of a coincidence to let it lie. That list figures in this mess, I'm sure of it."

"Perhaps I can help," Falicello offered, now the gracious host once again. "Here are a few much more plausible alternatives: Theory number one," he said, raising his right index finger: "Somebody else got their hands on that list from Mr. Stack before he gave it to me and that person has a financial motive for these killings."

Krnich said nothing as he wrote down this suggestion.

Falicello held up his second finger. "Theory number two: The creator of the list, Mr. Jim Stack, is killing these agents. He may be shrewd enough to know that I would become the number one suspect once the list was discovered. Why? I don't know. But it seems to me that you should be concentrating your efforts on him. Wouldn't you agree?"

Krnich sat back in his chair and raised the forefinger on his left hand to the tip of his nose while cupping his chin with his thumb. It was the look of a deep, confused thinker. "I'll tell you the truth, Gino.

May I call you Gino?" Krnich hoped to keep the old man talking. Intimacy and familiarity might motivate him to continue.

"Hey, it's better than 'the Fridge'. Please call me Gino."

"I hate this case, Gino. I hate everything about it. I can't find rhyme nor reason for these killings. There is absolutely no evidence these real estate agents harmed anyone, stole any money or committed any type of offense that would result in their deaths. The only thing they had in common is that they sold high-end real estate."

Falicello looked at him blankly, took a sip of tea and wiped his mouth with a napkin.

Man is he smooth.

"And the damndest thing about it, Gino," Krnich continued, "is that I'm positive the killings are being done by a trained hit man." He let the last sentence hang in the air for a few seconds, hoping he'd see a dramatic response to this new revelation.

Still no obvious 'tell'.

Like a Rottweiler coming out of the water, Falicello shook his massive head and readily agreed with the federal agent. "It don't make sense, does it?"

But something had changed in Gino Falicello's demeanor. It was slight. Only a trained inquisitor such as Krnich would notice it. The big man took another gulp of his tea, his once steady hand shaking slightly as he put the glass down. Eyes that earlier had been so clear, so focused, so steady, began to blink intermittently.

The true "tell" came a few moments later when Falicello suddenly rose from his seat and extended his pudgy right hand once again. "It has been a pleasure meeting you, agent Krnich. I hope we meet again someday... under different circumstances. I believe our business here is done. I am an old man and I find it necessary to take afternoon naps. It is now an hour past my normal time," he said, glancing at the Rolex on his wrist.

Krnich rose, extended his hand. He recognized a rushed, forced departure when he saw it. He decided to take one more stab at it. "I appreciate the hospitality, Gino. I'm sorry I've kept you up." And then without missing a beat, he looked the incredibly tan man directly in the eye and asked, "Are you sure there's nothing you can tell me about that list? Some little thing you may have thought of while we were talking?"

The Fridge shook his head. "Other than recommending you investigate Mr. Stack, there is nothing more I can add to your investigation. If you feel I have been less than honest with you and you want to question me further, please contact my attorney. Here is his card." Falicello reached into his front pocket and produced a standard business card. "I wish you a safe flight home. Good day, Agent Krnich." He turned to his butler. "Dwayne, please show our guest out."

And with that, Gino 'the Fridge' Falicello abruptly shook Krnich's hand one more time, turned and walked into the house, closing the door behind him.

Krnich looked at Dwayne—who had overheard most of the conversation— and asked, "So Dwayne, you got any ideas?" The six foot five two hundred and sixty pound assistant just shook his head and made a gracious gesture to escort Krnich out of the house. "This way, sir," was all he said.

As Krnich opened the door to his rental car, his eyes drifted up the steep face of the mansion. Standing in the middle of a large upstairs window was the grand-daughter, Mercedes. Her presence seemed strange. Either she had the biggest bedroom in the world or she had left her bedroom when the agent started to depart and walked across the house to another room with a window facing the driveway. Had she been watching him the whole time?

In one hand she held what looked like a doll with no head, in the other, a cell phone. He understood the cell phone, but a doll? She was, what, twenty years old? And why no head on the damn thing? He shook his own head, felt to make sure it was still attached, got in the car, put it in gear and drove off.

AS SOON AS it was obvious from security cameras that Krnich had cleared the front gate, Gino Falicello, walked to the bottom of the stairs and shouted in a loud, yet loving voice, "Mercedes, dear. Please come down here. We have some important family business to discuss."

49

AGENT ZACH CURLANDER SMILED AS HE WATCHED ROGER WILLOWBY MEET WITH PEOPLE HE ASSUMED WERE CLIENTS.

At least he's still alive, Curlander thought. *We're not too late.*

Sitting in his government issued Crown Victoria Friday afternoon, sipping on a cup of coffee he had purchased from a nearby Starbucks, Curlander was parked across the street from Willowby's real estate office. The fog had lifted about an hour earlier and now bright sunlight filtered by large trees made visual contact remarkably easy. He pulled his cell phone from his pocket and called Krnich.

"Jim, I've got Willowby under surveillance. I relieved the local officer and told his chief that I'd keep him in the loop."

"Okay, that sounds good. Keep that guy under tight observation. I have a feeling our killer is up there."

"Why?" Curlander asked. "Did Falicello tell you something?"

"Nope. He's one cool customer, that guy. But, I did find out from Stack that all three remaining real estate agents are scheduled to attend the 'superstar' conference in Pebble Beach. I think the killer might be going for a 'turkey'."

"What's a turkey?"

"Don't you bowl?" Krnich said. Didn't everybody in law enforcement bowl? "A 'turkey' is three strikes in a row, Zach. I think our boy might be trying to get all three targets at the same time."

"It certainly would be easier."

"It would."

"Anything else you want me to do?" Curlander asked.

"Just keep an eye on Willowby. I'll have Simmons and Johnson check in regularly with the movements of Ornstein. Maybe we'll get lucky and find everybody at one time and in one place."

"Hey boss, the other thing I promised to the locals is that you'd meet with the Chief of Police when you got into town."

"All right, I should be there Sunday afternoon. I'll meet with him then."

"Cool," Curlander said and signed off, telling Krnich he'd see him Sunday.

———◆———

FLOWERS VIEWED THE entire conversation through military-issued binoculars. Part of his training had been learning to read lips—a talent the military downplayed.

It seemed awfully important right now.

The young agent shadowing Willowby made reference to Falicello and then asked what a 'turkey' was. That much was clear. How did they know about Falicello? And what did a turkey have to do with anything?

He had been concerned earlier in the day when, suddenly, a local unmarked police car parked across the street from Willowby's office. His surprise turned to shock when the local policeman was replaced by someone in a Crown Victoria. It had to be a federal agent. Who else would have the clout to trump the local police? His mind raced. The Feds obviously knew Willowby was a target. What else did they know? He could tell that the agent mentioned Ornstein in the conversation. Were they watching her in Atherton too? What about Smith-Newhall in Santa Barbara?

He should call Falicello.

Nope. Communication would flow one way.

Damn.

It was time to improvise again. And again, he hated it. Unintended consequences and all that.

Have to be careful; don't get too creative.

The obvious first step was to neutralize the most immediate threat—the federal agent. Flowers went through a checklist in his head. By the time he finished, he knew just what to do.

A few minutes later, he watched as Willowby exited his office, got into a brand new Mercedes and

headed north on Seventeen Mile Drive. Shortly thereafter, the Crown Victoria fell in behind him. Thirty
seconds later, Flowers joined the caravan.

FLOWERS FOLLOWED CURLANDER and Willowby
for several miles to a house located next to the Inn at
Spanish Bay. The house, a modern, slightly contemporary two story was surrounded by pine trees and coastal scrub. It looked out of place in its current setting,
he thought.

Wonder if it's worth ten million too?

He watched as Willowby met three clients in front
of the house; handshakes and smiles all around. The
real estate agent pointed to the yard, made a quick
comment, smiled broadly and slapped one of the men
on the back.

Sell it today, baby, Flowers thought.

It will be your last.

Flowers parked a discreet distance away, exited
his car and walked along the road trying to look like
a middle aged man out for his afternoon stroll. He
waited for the federal agent to leave the Crown Vic
and then approached the vehicle slowly from behind.
When the agent disappeared around the north side of
the house, he took a crescent wrench out of his back
pocket and slipped under the rear of the vehicle.

A few minutes later, with mission accomplished,
Flowers returned to his Nova. He got in the car,
tossed the wrench on the passenger's seat and picked
up his binoculars. Now it was time to watch and wait.
He had loosened the agent's hydraulic brake line. The

brakes would go out at some point as the agent followed Willowby. If all went according to plan, the
agent would have to call for a tow truck. That's when
Flowers would take out Willowby.

At least, that was the plan.

———

WILLOWBY AND HIS clients emerged from the
house all smiles. Curlander returned to the Crown
Vic, started the engine and prepared to pull out from
his parking spot. He watched as Willowby shook the
client's hands once more and then got back into the
Mercedes. After talking on his cell phone for a few
minutes, Willowby fired-up the engine and pulled
away from the residence. He was on the move.
Curlander settled in behind him.

It soon became obvious that Willowby was not
going back to his office. The route he chose took him
further north instead of south.

This was the part of the job Curlander hated most.
He was following the guy in order to protect him, but
in the process, he might uncover personal activities
that nobody needed to know about.

Please be going to the market.

Or to get your haircut, or something.

No such luck.

Fifteen minutes later, Roger Willowby pulled into
a condominium complex, turned off his engine and
strolled confidently towards the front door of unit
number three. He stopped for a brief moment and

fussed with his hair and then, apparently pleased with the way he looked, knocked on the door.

Curlander watched as a scantily clad redhead opened the door and planted a big kiss on the realtor's lips. The two giggled like school children and closed the door behind them. Curlander pulled around the corner, parked and waited.

Unknown to the federal agent, a small puddle of brake fluid was beginning to form under the rear of the Crown Vic.

A full hour later, Willowby emerged from unit number three with wet hair and a grin as big as the eighteenth green at Pebble. He gave the redhead one final peck on the cheek, slapped her on the bottom and made his way down the sidewalk to his car. "Definitely not a haircut," Curlander said quietly to himself. He watched as Willowby hopped into his car and sped away. Curlander put the Crown Vic into gear and followed.

Unknown to Curlander, a Gray Nova trailed him by several hundred yards.

Willowby's eight-cylinder, 500 horsepower, black Mercedes suddenly accelerated. Curlander saw a long stretch of country road ahead of them. Probably 'letting the big dog eat' Curlander thought as Willowby sped up.

Startled by the sudden acceleration and then understanding that the real estate agent was just letting his hundred thousand dollar engine breathe, Curlander punched the accelerator on the Crown Vic and advanced.

———

THE FEDERAL AGENT was going way too fast. Flowers bit his lip and mumbled, "Slow down asshole." He rubbed his forehead as he watched both cars accelerate.

He didn't mind if Willowby crashed and killed himself. That would be very convenient, actually. But the fed... that would be a bad deal. His death would bring unwanted scrutiny and would probably flood the area with other agents.

"Slow down buddy," Flowers mumbled again.

The cell phone in his pocket suddenly vibrated.

A call?

Who has this number?

He viewed the screen. No caller ID, but it did show a Las Vegas area code. Falicello? No, he wouldn't call, he'd text.

Mercedes?

Not now, dammit.

50

HE KEPT HIS EYES FOCUSED ON THE TWO SPEEDING CARS WHILE DEBATING WHETHER TO ANSWER THE CALL.

Finally, and for reasons he didn't fully understand, he answered it on the fourth ring.

"I thought we agreed you wouldn't call me until I was finished with this business," he said abruptly, not giving the caller a chance to speak.

"Well hello to you, too, lover."

Flowers pursed his lips, told himself to calm down.

Lover?

She doesn't even know me.

Where did this come from?

"I'm sorry. It's just that I'm in the middle of something," he said.

"You're job?" Her voice grew more excited. "Right now?" she asked.

"Yes. I can't talk about it. Can I call you back?"

Before the girl could answer, Flowers said loudly, "Jesus, slow down, you idiot!"

"What's going on Ted? Is someone driving too fast? Tell me; I want to know."

"No, you don't. A beautiful woman like you has no reason to be involved in this business."

"So you *do* think I'm beautiful?"

Somewhat flustered, he quickly answered, "Of course."

The girl sighed and then asked about the 'idiot'. "Is he going to die?"

Again, Flowers shook his head. What was it with this girl and death? "It's too early to tell. I really have to go."

"Ted, do you love me?"

He paused. Did he? He wasn't sure. He *had* enjoyed meeting her. And he *did* regret hanging up on her the other night. And he *did* find her fascinating. She *was* beautiful and...sensual. But, love?

"I can't talk right now. Can we discuss this later?"

"No, I want an answer. Now!" she demanded in a firm, yet calm voice.

"I don't know."

"You don't know? Well, fuck you, Ted Flowers."

The line suddenly went dead. He could almost envision her slamming the phone down on a table as she hung up.

He slammed the steering wheel with his free hand. He would never understand women.

Was it over?

Before it really began.

Shit.

A half mile in front of him, the Crown Vic looked as if it was picking up speed again. He punched the Nova's accelerator. Maybe there was some way he could slow down the federal agent?

———•———

OUTSIDE THE GIRL'S bedroom, Dwayne, watched as Mercedes did indeed slam the phone on her bedside table and then collapse into a ball of tears and fury on her king-size bed.

The door had been slightly ajar and, as he passed, he had stopped to hear most of her conversation.

She's in touch with Ted Flowers, the assassin?

And not just 'in touch', but in love with him?

Gently, he closed her door and continued down the hall. He hated to wake him from his afternoon nap, but Mr. Falicello needed to know this startling information.

The 'Fridge', he was certain, wouldn't like it one bit.

51

AS HIS SPEEDOMETER HIT EIGHTY-FIVE, CURLANDER'S CELL PHONE RANG.

Seeing Krnich's name displayed on the screen, he answered the call. "What's up boss?"

"Just checking in," Krnich said. "I know we said we'd see each other Sunday, but I just had a feeling I should call you. You know, see how things are going?"

"Glad you did. I'm following Willowby now. Apparently, he likes to take the back roads home. I bet it gives him a chance to test his car; really open her up. The guy must be going a hundred. Hell, I'm pushing ninety."

Krnich smiled. He knew how much Zach loved to drive. They both had attended the FBI speed track earlier that year. He still remembered the wide-eyed Curlander zipping around the track at over two hundred miles an hour. He was probably frustrated that the Crown Vic couldn't keep up with the Mercedes. "Just be careful. You aren't in an expensive European car. You can't keep up with a hundred thousand dollar Mercedes."

"Oh, yeah. Watch me."

Curlander smiled, tapped the brake slightly as he took a turn and then accelerated again. He noticed immediately that the brakes felt sluggish but shrugged it off as normal on an American-made car. The Mercedes was now half a mile in front of him. He sped up.

"Hey Jim," he said. "You think the agency would pay for us to play a round of golf at Pebble Beach when this whole thing is wrapped up?"

"I got bad news for you Zach. The last time the FBI paid for any recreational activity was when J. Edgar Hoover was forty years old. That was about 1935."

Curlander chuckled. "I didn't think so, but I was hoping...hold on, I'm approaching a fairly sharp turn. I've got to pay attention."

Curlander laid the phone on the seat and tapped the brakes again but this time the response was even more sluggish. He frowned. "Stinking American car," he mumbled.

He pushed the brake pedal harder.

The car wasn't slowing as it should. He contemplated down-shifting from Drive to third gear, but at this speed, the transmission might freeze or the engine might blow.

He depressed the brake pedal again. This time he pumped it gently. Still no significant response.

Damn.

I'm going way too fast for the upcoming turn, he thought.

He gave the pedal one last try and then, in an act of desperation, down-shifted and engaged the parking brake.

On the other end of the line, Krnich heard his friend scream a wild, animal-like curse.

"Zach, you there buddy?" Krnich yelled into the phone. There was no answer just the sound of tires on the road and commotion coming from the inside of the car. "Zach talk to me. Are you okay?"

No response.

"Shit," Krnich cursed as he heard the car begin some type of skid.

"Fucking American car. Fucking brakes. Goddammit!" Krnich heard his agent scream in frustration.

"Zach, what's going on? Zach talk to me. Zach!"

There was no response.

A moment later, he heard the sound of metal scraping against metal, and then suddenly the sound of thumping and heavy cursing filled the line. It was the most god-awful sound Krnich had ever heard. And then just as quickly has the noises had begun, there was dead silence. Krnich glanced at his cell. The call was still connected but there was no sound.

And in that instant, the silence was deafening.

Krnich would learn later that Zach Curlander, his special task force lieutenant, had died from 'probable vehicular mal-function'. It appeared that the hydraulic brake lines had given way under the stress of such extreme speeds. The findings were preliminary, how-ever, and the inspector cautioned that it would take several days to fully examine the burned car.

———

TED FLOWERS WATCHED the action from several hundred yards away. He had come to an abrupt stop when he recognized the driver was in distress.

At least the agent probably never knew what hit him, Flowers surmised. The car had gone into a spin and then smashed through the barrier and had flown down the side of the hill, resting two hundred feet below the paved road.

"Damn it!" Flowers exclaimed, looking down the canyon. "You shouldn't have been driving so fast buddy. Now I got to change my plans."

Shaken by the knowledge that more agents would be forthcoming but confident that it would take the FBI several days to determine the actual cause of the accident, he put the Nova in gear and drove back towards town.

Welcome to unintended consequences.

52

SCOTT STEPHENS ARRIVED AT HIS PARENT'S HOUSE FRIDAY EVENING FEELING FEVER-
ISH AND COUGHING SLIGHTLY.

Walking through the front door, he cleared his throat and forced a smile. Tomorrow would be the biggest day of his young business life. He was going to serve the best food he possibly could, come hell or high water.

But, man, was he ever tired.

"Oh, Scott," Mel said when she saw him standing in the kitchen. "I didn't hear you come in. The dog didn't even bark." She paused and took a close look at her obviously ill son. "Are you feeling okay, honey? Don't take this the wrong way, but you look like shit!"

He coughed. "Thanks, mom. I'll try not to take it personally." They both smiled.

"I'm a little tired, that's all," Scott lied. "I just want to pick up those salads and then I've got some organizing to do in the truck and I'll be set for the lunch crowd at the driving range tomorrow."

"You sure?"

"Mom, I'm not a little kid." He coughed some more. "Believe it or not I take vitamins daily and yes, I wash my hands twenty times a day. My stream is strong and my bowel movements are regular, too." As he finished the last statement he went into a prolonged coughing fit.

Mel grabbed a glass of water and offered it to her son. She had raised him from birth, changed his diapers, nursed him through the chickenpox, and watched him puke his way through his first hangover. She knew he had a cold or flu—it was just a matter of severity.

Scott and Blake were troopers, very little got them down. Brad, on the other hand, was a big baby. A slight sniffle and it was directly to bed; a splinter and you'd think he needed surgery; and god forbid if he drank too much alcohol. His vomiting could be heard twenty miles away.

"All right, then, but get some rest." And then she added, "Call me if you need anything."

Scott grabbed the salads and left. Mel went back to reading her book.

————

THE NEXT MORNING, the phone rang early. Mel, still half asleep, answered it in her typical fashion. "What? Who's calling at such an ungodly hour?"

"Mom," Scott mumbled with a scratchy voice. "I'm really sick. I don't think I can even get out of bed."

Mel cleared her throat and gained her focus. Without hesitating, she suggested that she take his truck to the driving range, prepare and serve the food.

Against his better judgment, Scott quickly agreed and gave her basic instructions on the food preparations. They agreed that she would limit the menu to Scott's Sizzling Hot Chili, Salad, and Hamburgers.

Nothing exotic.

Nothing difficult.

"Okay, this should work," Scott said. "My truck is parked at the house. You'll need to get over here by ten so that you can do the prep work. You need to get to the driving range by eleven."

"I'll go shower right now. I'll be at your house before ten," an excited Mel assured him.

Relieved, Scott was about to say goodbye and hang up when he added, "Mom, please be careful driving the truck. It's brand new, doesn't even have a scratch on it."

How roles have changed, Mel thought. It used to be me pleading for him to drive safely. She shook her head and assured him that she would use extra care.

"And, Mom, the truck has a manual transmission. Do you remember how to use a clutch?" Scott asked, suddenly thinking this might not be a good idea after all.

"Of course I do. Don't you remember the car I drove when you were little boys? It was stick shift and we got around just fine."

"Just fine!" Scott exclaimed and then coughed some more. "Mom, I think you've got selective memory. You nearly gave Blake and me whiplash in that car."

"You're exaggerating. It's true I burned out a few clutches, but your Dad says it was partly the car's fault. It was a turbo and it was hard to drive. You guys were never in any real danger."

Yeah, sure.

Too tired to argue, Scott conceded the point and asked her, once again, to be extra careful and then hung up. Within minutes he was back asleep, disturbing dreams of popped-clutches and fatal crashes filling his feverish head.

On the other end of the line, Mel thought, "This is just what I need to take my mind off of Paula and the painter."

This will be fun.

53

THE DEATH OF ONE OF HIS MEN—WHETHER ACCIDENTAL OR INTENTIONAL—DIDN'T SIT WELL WITH JIM KRNICH.

Groggy from lack of sleep, confused by the events of the previous day, the special agent arrived in Carmel early Saturday morning. Along the way, he had placed three phone calls.

The first had been to agent Randall Simmons in Atherton informing him and his partner Horatio Johnson about Curlander's death. It looked like an accident, he said, but in their line of work, one could never be too sure. He commanded them to be on a heightened state of alert.

The second call had been to headquarters requesting a forensic investigation into Curlander's death. It included a request for a special team to inspect the burned Crown Victoria. Krnich knew by talking to Curlander just before the crash that he was traveling at a high rate of speed. Still, Zach had been a skilled driver. Something about the crash bothered Krnich.

The final call had been the toughest.

Curlander had mentioned several times that the reason he joined the FBI was because he wanted to make sure that rapists and murderers didn't walk free. His mother, father and brother had been killed during an aborted robbery at the family business when Zach was young. As luck would have it, he had been home, sick with a stomach virus. As a result, the only person for Krnich to contact regarding his death was Julie Burnette, Zach's fiancée who lived in St. Louis.

Zach had told Krnich about her recently. He said she was his 'five foot six, ball-o-fire'. He had described her as having short, pixie blonde hair, green eyes, and a smile that filled up the whole state of Missouri.

This wasn't going to be easy.

"Hello, Julie? This is special agent Jim Krnich of the FBI special task force," he began.

"Yes, agent Krnich, Zach has spoken of you many times," she replied.

He cleared his throat and continued. "Julie, there is no good way to tell you this, so I'm just going to come out and say it." He paused and cleared his throat again.

"What is it, agent Krnich?"

"Zach was involved in a car crash."

"Is he okay?"

"No, he didn't survive. I'm so sorry."

There was a long moment of silence on the other end and then Julie's shaky voice came back on the line.

"When, where, how? Oh, no. No, no, no," she moaned, shock and grief replacing inquisitiveness.

Trying to make sense of the senseless.

"He was killed in the line of duty. His car apparently malfunctioned and he crashed. I'm so sorry. He was a good man. The FBI is launching a full investigation. We'll know within a few days if this was an accident or if someone tampered with his car."

He could hear her trying to compose herself in the background. A moment later, she came back on the phone. "I can't believe it. I just talked to him yesterday." Her voice drifted.

"I know this is a shock. I'm so sorry, Julie." There was silence and then he could hear the woman break down on the other end of the line. He asked softly if she had anyone to stay with—a relative maybe or a close friend.

The line went silent. Finally Julie came back on. Through sobs, she said, "Yes. I've got relatives. I'll be okay." And then she broke down once again.

Krnich gave her all the time she needed. He knew death wasn't easy to process. One day the person you love is here, the next they're gone. Wasn't fair and wasn't right. Unfortunately, it happened all the time.

You just didn't want it to happen to you or to those you loved.

Julie composed herself and came back on the line. "I'm sure you'll do everything you can, agent Krnich. This is such a shock." Her voice began to tremble, "As you know, we were going to be married in six weeks."

Krnich cut her off, he couldn't take anymore of her sorrow. There was nothing to be gained by commiserating at this juncture. That time would come. "Listen Julie, I'd like to come out there soon and go over the details of his death, give you his belongings and get to know you. Zach was an important member of my team."

"That's very kind of you. I just don't know. I need some time," she said.

Krnich could hear her wiping away tears. She paused and then said in a voice devoid of emotion or life, "We were going to surprise everybody, but now I guess it doesn't matter."

"Surprise? With what?" Krnich asked.

"I'm pregnant." Sobs and moans filled the line. "What am I going to do now? How am I going to raise our baby? Oh, Zach."

Shit!

Pregnant!

That was the proverbial straw that broke the camel's back. Krnich cleared his throat, composed himself, and said something stupid like "I'm sure he'd be proud of the way you're handling this" and then signed off.

A minute later, he pulled over to the side of the road, pounded the steering wheel, dropped his face into his hands and for the first time in a very long time actually shed a few tears.

54

"PERFECT TIMING," MEL SAID AS SHE LOOKED AHEAD AND SAW JOHN AND BRAD PULL-ING INTO THE DRIVING RANGE SATURDAY MORNING.

"They're going to love Scott's chili," Mel said to Stef.

"It's such a nice day, I hope Scott makes a ton of money," Stef said.

After pulling their clubs out of the trunk, Brad and Linden headed towards the range to set up for the exhibition.

The day was full of brilliant sunshine—not a cloud in the sky. The driving range faced towards the Pacific and a slight breeze blew from the water. Several golfers were already working on their long-games, checking their aim and making all sorts of downward motions with their arms and hands. Most of them didn't even notice the former U.S. Champ as he pulled out his sand wedge, hit a few shots and then leaned the club against his bag.

"You going to leave your clubs on the range?" Brad asked.

"Just for a few minutes. Besides, I hired Jessie, here, to watch them for me," Linden said with a wink, putting his arm around the shoulder of a young man standing next to him. "Let's go see what the girls are doing."

"At least we get first crack at this world-famous chili I've been hearing so much about," Brad said, rubbing his hands together in hungry anticipation.

AS THEY STROLLED over to the food truck, Brad's cell phone rang its familiar tone: The Mexican Mariachi song, *Volver, Volver*. Come back, Come back. Damn, he loved that song. He answered it on the third *Volver*.

"Hello, this is Brad Stephens," he said.

"Brad, its Jim Krnich. You got a minute?"

"Sure, what's up?"

There was a crackling over the phone and then the line went dead. Brad stared at his phone, wondering if the lack of signal occurred on his end or Krnich's. A second later the phone rang again.

"Krnich?"

"Yeah, sorry about that. I'm driving. Must've hit a bad patch."

"Happens to me all the time," Brad said.

"You'd think with all the money these goddamned phone companies make they'd cover this whole state," Krnich said in an angry voice.

The tone wasn't lost on Brad. "You doing okay? You sound angry. What's up?"

"I went up north earlier than I had intended."

"Pebble Beach?"

"Yes."

"Why?"

Krnich went on to tell Brad about Curlander's death. "It doesn't feel right to me," he concluded.

"You think our painter is behind the accident?" Brad asked, as if reading the agent's mind.

"You're getting good at this. Ever consider changing professions?"

"Actually, I'm in transition right now," Brad said, glancing over at Linden who was now busy signing autographs for a few of the early bird golfers who did recognize him.

"That's right, I forgot about managing Linden. I hope that works out for you."

"Me too. Now what can I do to help."

"Oh, yeah, the reason I called is that if our boy did kill Zach, it means he's still in California and he's still active. I want you to keep an eye on your wife and Paula until I can get someone else over to your house."

"No problem. Mel is here right now and Paula is due to be at our house later today."

"Good. I'll let you know when I think we can back off."

They were about to sign off when Brad caught himself. "Hey, I know Curlander was a friend of yours. I'm really sorry about his death."

"Thanks." Krnich paused for a moment and then said in a soft voice, "And to make matters worse, I just found out his fiancée is pregnant."

"Ouch!"

"Yeah, ouch."

Brad could hear the pain in Krnich's voice. He wished he could find the words.

But what do you say?

"Sorry, Buddy," was the best he could come up with.

The two made small talk for a few minutes longer and then said goodbye.

Brad grabbed Linden by the arm and escorted him towards the food truck. His appetite, however, had been severely reduced by the call.

55

It was Saturday morning and the killer had assumed Willowby would be at his desk just like every other weekend warrior in the real estate business. He was surprised, but not upset to find out differently. Plan "B" had been to take the real estate agent today and then head straight to Atherton.

It's starting to get messy. . .

"Yes sir. Mr. Willowby will be attending a very intense—*very* real estate specific—motivational conference led by the internationally famous speaker, Jim Stack. He's the founder of the 'Stacking Method' you know," she said enthusiastically sounding as if she were reading from a script. "It's being held at the Inn at Spanish Bay. That is why Mr. Willowby can't personally show you properties tomorrow."

"How about Monday?" he asked.

"I'll check his schedule, but I believe he's in the conference until Wednesday. All of the top agents from around the country will attend. It's quite exciting, really. Can one of his assistants help you?"

"No thanks. I only deal with the head honcho on these types of things." He paused and then asked, "Did you say ALL of the top agents in the country?" Since his Plan B wasn't working, it suddenly dawned on him that he might need a Plan C.

"Yes. As I understand it, agents from New York, Florida, Nevada, and, of course, California will be there. It's by special invitation, you know."

Again, no, he didn't know, but his mind was now functioning in overdrive. What other agents might be at this conference? He'd have to get a list of attendees.

Was this making lemonade from a lemon just like grandmother had suggested?

"Why don't I take your name and phone number and I'll see if Mr. Willowby can call you back later today," the receptionist said.

Flowers said, "That won't be necessary. I'll try him after Wednesday. I don't plan on buying before then. Thanks for the help and have a nice day." He closed his cell phone and watched from across the street as the pretty redhead got up from her desk and dropped the message on Roger Willowby's desk.

Recognizing the girl immediately, Flowers said under his breath, "Messing around with the secretary, eh, Mr. Willowby."

Well at least I know where her condo is located if we need to take this show on the road.

Willowby was now being shadowed by local police officers. The feds wouldn't be far behind. The agent's death had thrown a wrench in the works. How to isolate his target now? Flowers would think about it as he researched the list of attendees for the upcoming conference.

IN THE MEANTIME, his next stop would be the costume shop he noticed back in Salinas, twenty miles east. And if he had time, he might double-back down to Santa Barbara and take care of Smith-Newhall and her pesky friends.

He pulled the two business cards from his pocket and stared at the pictures again. Did he really want to kill such nice-looking women? Even if they saw him, what the hell, he was wearing a disguise.

But, then again...

Santa Barbara was only a few hours south. In reality, he could easily drive back down there, finish that job and return by late afternoon.

The final thought made him smile and cringe at the same time.

56

"HOLY CRAP MEL, YOU TRYING TO KILL US?" LINDEN AND BRAD SAID NEARLY IN UNI-SON AS THEY EACH SWALLOWED THEIR FIRST BITES OF CHILI LATER THAT MORNING.

Sweat poured from their foreheads as they feverishly wiped their lips and tongues with their hands and napkins. Like hikers in the Mojave Desert on an exceptionally hot afternoon, each grabbed cold water bottles from a nearby ice chest and gulped quickly.

"What are you guys talking about?" Mel asked. "Can't you babies take Scott's chili? Is it too hot for you?"

"I've had Scott's chili before; his isn't *this* hot," Linden replied. "What did you do to it?"

"Nothing."

"Mel," Brad said sternly. "What did you do? Have you been experimenting with recipes again?"

"No. I didn't do anything, I swear. I just followed Scott's directions. Stef was there. Isn't that right Stef?"

"She's right, guys," Stef confirmed. "As far as I know she didn't have time to do anything creative. We just followed his directions. You know: a pinch of this, a tablespoon of that." Her eyes wandered to the spice rack as she continued her explanation. She stopped cold when she saw the empty space where the cayenne pepper had been stored.

"Hey, Mel, where did you put that super-hot cayenne pepper?" Stef asked.

"It's up there on the ..." Mel didn't finish. She froze when she saw the empty rack. She looked at Stef. Stef looked back at her and raised her hands as if to say, "Beats Me".

Linden and Brad both continued to dance around like they'd been attacked by a swarm of bees, hands fanning lips, faces turning deeper red. They continued to gulp water and curse. Fortunately, no other golfers had ventured over to the truck yet.

"Here, drink these cold glasses of milk," Mel instructed, handing them each a frosty glass. "And eat these raw corn tortillas. They'll neutralize the heat. It takes a few minutes, so be patient."

Stef took a big stirring spoon and began to work it through the chili pot. She stopped when she hit something solid. Carefully, she positioned the spoon to push the object against the side of the pot and work it up out of the sauce. She knew what she'd find. She wasn't surprised when the cayenne pepper container emerged.

"How the hell did that get in the chili?" Mel whispered to Stef.

"Must've fallen in when we hit a bump or something," Stef whispered back.

"Damn! That's a helluva lot of pepper."

"Yeah, must be hotter than snot," Stef concurred, stating the obvious.

Turning towards the men who were now breathing deeply and blowing air through their mouths, Mel announced, "We found the problem. The whole bottle of cayenne pepper fell in the pot by accident. Sorry guys. I didn't do it on purpose, it was a freak accident." She paused and then added, "I take it back. You are not big babies."

"I'm going to start calling you 'Calamity Mel'," Linden proclaimed. "It's a good thing you didn't serve this to the general public. Scott would be run out of town."

"Ha, ha, very funny. It was an accident. Give the girl a break," Stef demanded.

"Hey, John, here comes some of your fans," Brad said as he looked past the putting green to see three young guys hurrying towards the truck.

"Quick, pour this crap out," Linden said hurriedly to Stef. "And give us new bowls with the regular chili."

Fortunately, they had another pot so she did as instructed and by the time the young golfers made it to the truck both John and Brad were slurping away. "Man this is the best chili I've ever tasted," Linden said loudly. Truth be told, his taste buds had been ravished—his mouth was as numb as a coke addict's nostrils.

All three guys ordered a bowl of Scott's Sizzling Chili. Mel, feeling terrible about what had happened to John and Brad, was determined to make sure the chili she served was the best it could be. She added sour cream, avocado, and shredded cheese to the top of every bowl she served.

Everyone seemed to love it.

Brad exhaled a sigh of relief and slurped some more water.

A FEW MINUTES later, feeling much better, Linden and Brad walked away shaking their heads. Somehow, Mel had turned a negative into a positive with her cooking.

Amazing.

They were about to continue the exhibition when Brad noticed John's attire for the first time.

"Dude, you're not wearing any of your sponsor's stuff," Brad whispered in Linden's ear.

"I only got one sponsor. Do you think it's a big deal?"

"Yes. You've got to get used to wearing their shit. How do you expect to get any others?"

"I'm not sure I need others. What do you think?" Linden said with a wink. He knew full well Brad was chomping at the bit to acquire new sponsors.

"I think I better go back to your house and get you a shirt and hat. Sit tight, try not to be photographed while I'm gone."

"Okay, but you better hurry up, looks like there's going to be a big crowd." He pointed towards the parking lot where cars were lined-up, waiting to park.

"Good turn out," Brad agreed. "Direct them to the food truck. Maybe we can delay your exhibition for a while. I'll be right back." He started to make his way to his parked car, when he turned to address Linden again.

"Oh, I almost forgot." He narrowed the distance between the two. "I think we've come to an equitable solution to your problem with Mary."

"Fantastic. I knew you could do it. Did it cost me much?"

"A new house in Orlando, a million dollar endowment for the child and three grand a month support for her."

"Did you put a limit on the price of the house?"

"Of course I did. Five hundred thousand."

"And she went for it?"

"Her lawyer did."

Linden threw his arm around Brad and slapped him on the back. "Way to go, dude."

This was all brand new to Brad Stephens. Unchartered waters. The settlement seemed fair, but it wasn't cheap. John was acting like he just hit the lottery.

"What gives? This isn't a great deal, you know."

"Compared to what my friends have gone through, this is dirt cheap. You did a fantastic job!"

"You mean compared to Tiger?"

"Oh, don't be so innocent. You think Tiger's the only guy who screws around on the tour?" Linden asked. "I could tell you stories, past and present."

"No. Don't. It's okay. I want to maintain my idols. Let's just deal with your situation. Okay?"

"You got it. How do we pay so that Stef never sees the money going out?"

"I hadn't thought about that. She's my assistant. In theory, she should see everything."

"Well, figure out this last detail and we'll be on my jet next week to Portland, talking to Nike."

"I thought you said you hate their golf ball?"

"I do. That will be your next challenge. You've got to convince them to sponsor me without making me use their ball."

"Seriously, what's wrong with it?"

"Nothing really, it's just that I grew up in the era of the balata golf ball. Most of these modern balls feel funny to me. They're too hard. I finally found one I like. The manufacturer won't sponsor me, but I like their ball. How's that for a nice 'how do you do'?"

"Okay, let's secure Nike with the condition you don't have to use their ball. Are you okay with their irons and woods?"

"Sure. Tiger uses them, doesn't he? They work fine. I just don't like their ball."

"I'll make the call. I'll push for a meeting next week. You want to play Pumpkin Ridge and Bandon Dunes while we're up there?" Brad asked.

"Sounds good," Linden said and then quickly added, "Make it so, Commander Stephens."

———

HAVING CAUGHT A glimpse of her husband moving towards their car, Mel asked Stef to watch things for a few minutes and ran after him. She needed a few items from the house. Perhaps he could pick them up for her?

Brad rolled down the window as Mel advanced. "What's up?" he asked.

She approached the car quickly, wiping her hands on her apron and blowing the hair out of her eyes. She bent forward, gave Brad a quick peck on the cheek and handed him a slip of paper. "Could you pick up these things from the house for me?" she asked. "And I'm not sure if I have any extra avocados. If I do, please bring them; if not, stop at the store and get a few ripe ones."

"Okay. "I'll be back in thirty minutes. Save some chili for me."

As Brad pulled on to the main road, a voice came from the back of the car. "*Ju* keep driving and keep quiet," a man said in a slight Hispanic accent. It sounded like the guy was lying on the floor.

"What the fuck?" Brad exclaimed, barely missing a fire hydrant to his right.

"Stay calm. Focus on *tee* road," the man said angrily.

Now what?

Brad glanced in his rearview mirror. The man was sitting fully erect now, his face obscured by a hoody and a pair of large, round sunglasses. A thought suddenly swept thru Brad's brain: Is this Mel's painter coming back to finish the job? And if so, why is he coming after *me*?

Brad didn't feel any better when his uninvited passenger discreetly raised a small handgun and pushed it into the back of his neck.

57

"WHY ARE YOU DOING THIS?" BRAD EVENTUALLY MANAGED TO SAY. "IS THIS BECAUSE MY WIFE KNOCKED YOU OFF THE LADDER?"

"Shut up and drive," was all the man said.

"Where to?"

"*Ju'll* see. Now, keep *goin* north *til* I *tel ju* to turn."

They hopped on the freeway and headed north.

Does he know where we live?

Five minutes later, they passed Brad's turn-off and continued north. The man in the backseat still held the gun firmly but said nothing.

Not going to the house. Phew!

But where then?

As they approached the next off-ramp, the man spoke. "Take *dis* one. Turn left at *dee* bottom."

Did the painter speak with broken English? He suddenly wished he could call Mel and ask her.

Funny the things you think about in times like these.

"Turn here," the man said.

Brad stared in amazement as he viewed the writing on the stone pillars straight ahead: St. Bernard's Cemetery.

What are we doing at a cemetery?

———◆———

"RAOUL, MEL AND I think something's wrong," Stef said loudly and quickly into her cell phone.

"Calm down, Stef, you don't have to yell," Espinoza replied. "Just tell me what's up?"

"Mel asked me to call you and tell you she's concerned about Brad."

"What did he do now?"

"Maybe nothing, but he said he'd be back in thirty minutes and it's been almost an hour and Mel can't reach him on his cell phone."

"Where did he go?"

"To get John a hat and shirt with his sponsor's logos. And to get Mel some supplies," she said.

"Where's Mel?"

"She's here with me; we've got dozens of people to feed. It's crazy down here."

"Okay, sit tight, I'll look into it. Anything else I should know?"

Stef hesitated for a moment and took a few more steps away from the food truck. She cupped her hand over the phone and whispered. "I haven't said anything to Mel because I don't want her to worry, but I caught site of Brad's car as he pulled onto the frontage road. I was out back washing a pot..."

"Yeah, yeah, yeah. Get to the point."

"Okay. Well anyway, I could swear I saw a dark figure in the back seat of his car. It looked like it kind of rose to a sitting position as he pulled down the frontage road."

"What kind of figure? Man or woman?"

"I couldn't tell from my angle. But it just didn't look right. I thought it might be the shadows, so I didn't give it a second thought. But now I'm beginning to wonder."

"Have you and Mel called the house or just his cell phone?"

Stef rolled her eyes. "Both of course; we're not idiots."

"And..."

"All went to voice mail."

"Okay. Let me put out an A.P.B. on Brad's car and then I'll collect my things and come right down. I was planning on catching some of the exhibition anyway." He paused for a moment and then asked, "What's John doing?"

Stef glanced over her shoulder and found Linden in the crowd. "He's signing a few autographs and making golfer talk."

"I think you should tell him about your suspicions. Maybe he can keep an eye on you and Mel until we locate Brad. Hell, maybe he can help you cook."

"Oh, yeah, he'll be a *big* help around this kitchen. The guy can barely boil water."

Despite himself, Espinoza chuckled. Then he turned serious and told her he'd be there in ten minutes. He hung up wondering where Brad was.

———◆———

"WHY A CEMETARY? And why me? What's this all about?" Brad asked, his mind racing, his heart beating rapidly. "I haven't seen your face. You can still get out of here and I won't say a word. My wife is no threat to you."

"Hmm," the man softly snortled. "Look. Here's my face," he said, pulling the hood back and removing his sunglasses. "Now *ju've* seen it."

Fearing that viewing it would be like staring at the Medusa, Brad at first refused to turn around and look at his captor. The man pressed the gun deeper into Brad's neck. "Look at me," the man yelled.

Reluctantly, Brad did as he was told.

"Oh no," Brad said, exhaling and staring straight into the cold, hard eyes of the bereaved widower, Jose Gonzales.

58

TWO HUNDRED MILES NORTH, A TALL, GRAY-HAIRED BUSINESSMAN IN A BLUE SUIT, ORANGE TIE AND THICK GLASSES WITH BLACK FRAMES, WALKED INTO THE BUSINESS OFFICE AT THE INN AT SPANISH BAY.

"Excuse me, Miss. . ." The man glanced at the receptionist's name plate. "Miss Knudeson. My name is Richard Santiago." He handed her his phony business card.

Amazing what you can get printed quickly these days.

"Yes, Mr. Santiago, what can I do for you?" she inquired. She was the dowdy type, mid-forties, heavyset, thick horn-rimmed glasses; nothing like the perky redhead at Willowby's office.

"I am planning on attending the Jim Stack seminar for 'superstars'. You can see from my card, I am a realtor of some renown in my home town of Santa Fe, New Mexico," he said with an arrogant attitude that he assumed a 'superstar' would possess. He stared at her and smiled doing his best Ricardo Montelban.

"The conference starts tomorrow. It will be held in the Monterey room, down the corridor to your left," she said in a bored voice.

Laying on the charm, Flowers explained that he thought his secretary had failed to file the proper paperwork with Stack. Could he take a quick look at the guests scheduled to attend and see if his name was on the list?

"Sure, why not?" she said in the same bored manner. "I'm sure it's public information. Knowing that guy Stack, he's probably already taken out an add in the Wall Street Journal advertising what a success the conference was—even though it hasn't even been held yet—and I'm sure he would include a list of the 'superstars'."

"Sounds like you don't like the man very much," Flowers said.

She fidgeted with some papers, sighed and continued. "I've had to coordinate the whole thing for him. He's such a control freak. He has seating charts, timelines for breaks and very specific requirements for the food and beverages served. I don't know who died and made him King."

"I know what you mean," he lied. "I've known about Jim for many years and that's his reputation. I think he's gotten worse since he gained so much fame." He winked and took the list she handed him.

He turned to leave. "Hey, Mr. Santiago," Knudeson said. "You can't take that list with you. That's my master list. Search for your name and if it's not there, you can make arrangements with me to pay for the conference."

"My mistake, I'm sorry. I thought it was a copy," he said. His eyes skimmed the list quickly. The third name beginning with 'O' jumped out at him. Ornstein, Susan, Atherton, and staff. He smiled. He already knew Willowby would be attending, so no big deal. He decided he had better make a good show for Knudeson. He scoured the 'S's' and scrunched his face, deep in concentration.

He almost missed the fifth name beginning with 'S': Smith-Newhall, Paula, Montecito. It was followed by the same notation: 'and staff'.

Bingo!

He was glad he had decided to stay in Pebble Beach rather than rush down to Santa Barbara. This scouting expedition was paying off in spades.

All three final targets will be here.

It'll be like shooting fish in a barrel.

He handed the list back to Knudeson, made arrangements to pay. She assured him that several people had paid late. No worries. Stack only charged fifty additional dollars for late registration.

"But I can't get you a room at the Inn. We're all sold out." She apologized as she handed him a receipt and a full packet containing the activity list.

"That's okay. I assumed that to be the case and have taken a room in Monterey."

"The one thing I want you to notice is the mandatory orientation and cocktail party," she said, pointing to the first event on the schedule. "Mr. Stack wants this to be very informal and friendly. He insisted that the theme be a Hawaiian Luau. He's such a pain in the ass." She rolled her eyes.

"What's wrong with a luau?"

"This is northern California. We drink wine and eat cheese at these things. I had to really hustle to find the appropriate food and décor."

"Sounds like fun to me."

"Yeah, I guess. Just be sure to wear shorts and a Hawaiian shirt. The women are to wear Hawaiian sun dresses. Mr. Stack was very insistent."

"You seem flustered by all this," he said, hoping to get additional information out of her.

"The theme just doesn't seem right to me. We're going to have over two hundred people standing around in Hawaiian attire, drinking Mai Tais or Rum or whatever, and at 5:30 sharp, our bagpipe guy is supposed to stop outside the cocktail area and play a few special songs. Can you imagine; Hawaiian food and Scottish music combined!"

Flowers took her hand and said softly, "I'm sure it will be perfect, just perfect. Don't worry about it anymore." She seemed relieved, smiled and told him she would see him tomorrow.

His spirits lifted considerably, Flowers opened the door to the Nova, slid in and took off the thick glasses. Almost giddy, his mind beginning to form a plan, he started the engine, put the car in gear and drove away slowly.

He suddenly understood the reference to 'turkey' he had lip-read earlier.

It was a bowling term.

Come 5:30 tomorrow I'm going to get three strikes in a row.

59

"GRIEF COUNSELING, MY ASS," JOSE GONZALES SAID, ALMOST SPITTING THE WORDS OUT.

Brad had made the mistake of asking Mr. Gonzales how his counseling was going.

"When I sober up, I know *wha ju doin. Ju* trying to get rid *ub* Jose," he said, raising his chin proudly as if he had just solved a difficult problem.

"Get rid of you! I was trying to help you."

"Yeah, well, I *don* need *jur* fucking help." He did spit this time. A small amount sprayed onto Brad's shoulder.

"What *do* you need then?" Brad asked.

The man's eyes softened. "I need my Lupe."

"She's gone Jose, she's not coming back. I'm so sorry for your loss, but this isn't the answer."

Gonzales nodded slowly. For a moment Brad thought he may have convinced the man to calm down but Gonzales pursed his lips and pointed towards a parking spot close to several headstones. "Park *ober tere*," he said.

Brad pulled the car into the spot and turned the engine off. "Listen Jose, I know you're hurting. I'm sorry if I said or did anything that contributed to Lupe jumping off that bridge." He took a deep breath and asked again what he could do to help.

"Oh I *tink ju* done *'nough* already."

"I would do anything to take back whatever I said to her when she called."

"*Ju tell* my Lupe to kill herself."

"That's not true," Brad said calmly. "I suggested she short-sell the house. That's all. I mean I understand this is a difficult time for you and I've already said I feel awful if she misinterpreted my advice. I'll have to live with that the rest of my life..." his voice drifted with the last statement. He composed himself and added, "Let me help you, I'll go to the grief counseling sessions with you if you want."

Gonzales rubbed his chin with his free hand as if contemplating what Brad had said. Finally, he shrugged and raised the gun higher. "I *don tink* so. *Ju* get out of *tee* car. No funny *bidness*."

They exited the vehicle and Gonzales motioned Brad to move straight ahead. After a brief walk, he told him to stop. Brad looked down at the headstone marker in front of him: Lupe Gonzales.

Oh, damn!

A fresh bouquet of roses had been placed lovingly around the base of the tombstone. To the side, a shovel sat near a clump of dirt. Large rocks encircled the gravesite. Brad stared at the rocks for a long moment.

Weapons?

"Okay, I get it," Brad began, moving a little closer to the rocks. "You brought me here to show me your wife's plot. I'm sorry she's dead Jose. But I didn't kill her."

"Maybe not but guy's like *ju kill* her. The system *kill* her. And now *ju goin* to die right next to my Lupe." He pointed the gun at Brad's head.

"Don't do it!" a lady dressed in a long black dress screamed from behind a nearby tombstone.

Gonzales turned towards the woman slowly. Flashed her an eerie smile.

60

AS IF WAKING FROM A DAZE, GONZALES PUSHED BRAD TO THE GROUND AND RAISED THE PISTOL TO HIS OWN HEAD.

"The woman *ees* right, I no shoot *ju*," he mumbled. "I *gonna* join my Lupe, but *ju* got to watch. *Ju* gotta see what *ju* cause."

Brad sat in stunned silence. Was Jose Gonzales going kill himself while standing on Lupe's grave? Or, was he bluffing—just trying to get attention?

And scare the hell out of Brad.

There was no time to find out.

Timing it as well as he could under the circumstances, Brad rolled to his left and reached for a rock he could throw. He knew it was lame, but he needed to do *something*. He found one about the size of a grapefruit.

Across from him, not more than five yards away, Gonzales looked as if he was doing the final self-talk of suicide. He mumbled softly, small tears lined his cheeks and he began rocking slowly back and forth. All the while, the gun stayed firmly pressed against his temple and his finger twitched on the trigger.

Shit, this might be the real deal.

Guilt can ravage a man's soul. Brad knew that all too well. And now Jose Gonzales had let that guilt drive him to a dark place—a place where you can check-in, but very few ever leave.

Panicking for a moment when he couldn't get a firm grip on the rock, Brad abandoned his first plan and instead dove to his right and grabbed the shovel. He swung it towards Gonzales's knees. Instantly, he felt a contact jolt shoot through his hands. It was like a golfer who had just hit a perfect shot. Gonzales lost the grip on his pistol and yelped in pain.

"What the...*pinche puto*," Gonzales shouted as he reached for his injured thigh.

In a flash, Brad was on top of him. He pinned Gonzales to the ground and searched for an appropriate way to apply a head lock with one arm while feeling for the gun with the other.

Finding the weapon, he let Gonzales go and then rose quickly. "Don't move Jose," Brad said. "I won't kill you but I'm a good enough shot to put one in your other thigh."

From the corner of his eye, Brad caught a glimpse of the woman in black running towards the parking lot. "Thanks for the help," he yelled after her. She did not stop.

Brad dusted himself off and stared at Gonzales who by now was lying on the ground. "This was a stupid plan, Jose. What did you hope to gain? I mean, I was trying to help you."

The man's face filled with sorrow. "I *jus* trying to help Lupe," he said, shaking his head slowly and wiping tears from his eyes. "It was my fault. I forced her to take out *tee* stupid loan. *Tole* her 'eeb Trump can do it', why *can* we?"

"You bought a second house with the subprime loan didn't you?"

Gonzales held up two fingers.

"You bought two other houses?"

"*Si*. And we lose *tem* all. And now I lose Lupe."

There was really nothing else to say. Brad knew that Jose Gonzales was not alone. So many people had reached for the gold ring with their real estate—only to be slapped down by the realities of the recession. Preaching to any of them at this stage wasn't going to do any good. Hell, he'd even been stupid about his own investment up in Truckee. And his dark cloud had been forming when Mel, Zindo and his boys had saved him.

Now it was his turn to help Jose Gonzales.

Karma?

Righteous retribution?

Social responsibility?

Whatever...

Brad exhaled deeply. He took the ammunition clip out of the pistol, put it in his pocket and threw the gun into some nearby bushes. He sat on the ground next to Jose Gonzales and put his arm around the distraught man's shoulders. "I know you're hurting Jose.

Believe me, I get it. But killing me—or actually, killing yourself—isn't the answer. Like I said last time, I don't think Lupe would want you dead."

Gonzales said nothing. He wiped his nose with the sleeve of the hoody and stared at the ground.

———

FROM THE LEFT side of the parking lot, Raoul Espinoza came running towards the tombstone, gun pulled, breath heavy.

"Did I miss all the fun again?" he asked.

Brad smiled. "Yep."

"Damn," was all Espinoza said, bending over and gasping for air like a miner who had been buried for days.

"You are not in good shape Raoul," Brad said.

"Me? I'm not the one everybody keeps trying to kill."

Brad shrugged as if conceding a point well made.

When it became clear Espinoza didn't want to talk about his personal health, Brad asked, "How did you find us anyway?"

"GPS in your cell phone."

Surprised and impressed at the same time, Brad handed Espinoza the ammunition clip while patting his buddy on the back. "Here take this. I'm glad I didn't have to shoot the guy." He glanced one last time at Jose Gonzales sitting by the grave and then walked towards his parked car.

"You're going to have to file a statement you know," Espinoza called after him. "I'm pretty sure I know what happened here but I need you to put it in writing."

Brad shook his head. "I won't be pressing charges."

"What? The guy tried to kill you."

"I don't think so. I think Jose just needed to make sure someone acknowledged his wife. The best thing would be to give Jose a ride home and make sure he begins attending those counseling sessions." He paused for a second and then added, "I already paid for them. Let's make sure he goes this time. Right now, I need to see Mel and let her know I'm okay."

It was Espinoza's turn to shrug. "Sometimes I don't understand you, amigo, but I'll do what you ask. Come on Jose," he said, grabbing the man by the arm and leading him towards his car. "Mr. Stephens just gave you a breakfast ball, don't fuck it up."

As he started the engine, Brad heard Espinoza call after him. "Hey, give Mel my love. Tell her I'm sure glad *she* won't be needing grief counseling of her own."

Not yet, at least.

But if this shit continues. . .

61

"MAYBE I SHOULD SKIP PEBBLE BEACH," BRAD SUGGESTED AFTER HE HAD GIVEN MEL A FULL RUNDOWN OF THE EVENTS FROM THE TIME HE LEFT THE DRIVING RANGE.

"No way," she said. "After what we've been through lately, a quiet, relaxing week is just what the doctor ordered. Besides, Jim is already up there with his men. I'm sure we'll have adequate protection. And, need I remind you, there should be lots of hotel sex."

Nice.

"We really can't afford it, you know," he said rather meekly.

"John is paying for most of it. You'll figure out the rest."

Sure.

"Right now, though, I need to help Stef pack up the truck," she said. "And you should get back to the house and rest."

"Okay, you're the boss," Brad said. He had a bad feeling about the Pebble Beach trip, but maybe that

324

was just the adrenaline in his system. Or maybe it was his wallet talking?

Oh what the hell, Mel's always right. It will be great to relax.

And he really could use some of that hotel sex.

62

"FUNNY HOW THINGS TURN OUT," Flowers thought as he made plans for his evening dinner.

Falicello should be proud of the killer's efficiency; getting three at a time would make the old man happy. And, perhaps, his new... what was she? His love? His girl? His friend? Well, whatever she was, maybe Mercedes would be inspired too.

If all went well tomorrow at 5:30, he'd be eating steak, lobster and caviar the rest of his life. Why not start now? He decided to shave and shower and go out to the best restaurant he could find in Monterey.

His cell phone vibrated. It was Mercedes again.

"Hello, my love," she said before he could formally answer.

Flowers stared at the phone for a moment before responding. "Last time I talked to you, you told me to 'fuck off' and hung up on me. Now you're calling me your love. What gives?" he said.

"Oh that. Well, I was a little upset with you. We women do that you know. But I'm better now," she said, purring like a kitten.

What a change.

There was silence on the other end of the line. Flowers said, "Mercedes are you there?"

"Yes I am, my love. I was just wondering if I should tell Papa about us. Where are you now?"

Tell Papa?

Tell him what? There was no 'us'.

Yet.

As for his location, should he tell this lovely creature where he was and what he planned to do? It wouldn't be prudent to spill too much information—especially over the phone, but what could it hurt? He waited a beat and then said, "I'm in Monterey."

"Okay, I'll tell Papa, he'd want to know. And I'm sure he'll be quite happy to hear things are going well. Now, for more important matters, have you missed me?"

He said nothing.

Silently, he imagined her radiant smile, her dark hair falling on her shoulders and her perfect breasts heaving with delight. Whoa! He had to slow down. He had a job to do. And besides, who was she really? Was she the spoiled brat that hung up on him yesterday or was she the purring sweetheart he was now speaking to?

Stay focused.

Bad things happen when you deviate.

"Listen, thanks for the call. I'll contact you very soon."

"Aren't you going to ask me what I'm wearing?"

Phone sex?

Now?

While he was driving?

While he was getting ready to kill three innocent people?

Actually, he liked the idea, but, no. The job came first. He had to focus on the job.

"Next call maybe. Let's do that after tomorrow, okay?"

"After tomorrow we will see each other in person." She sighed and then in a husky voice she said, "I'll make sure to make it worth your while. Goodnight, my love." She hung up.

What was that all about?

———

DURING HIS SECOND glass of wine at dinner, Flowers refined the details on his plan of attack. He had seen the guest list and the list of activities. He had also seen enough of the layout at the Inn at Spanish Bay. Things would come to a head tomorrow at sunset, at the cocktail party. He knew just what to do. He smiled to himself and enjoyed the Kellner Buoni*Anni* Sangiovese in front of him.

Soon, he would have money to eat this way every night. And maybe even a beautiful woman to share his life with.

Funny how things turn out...

63

KRNICH HAD BEEN IN CARMEL ALL DAY SATURDAY. HE PLANNED TO STAY UNTIL EI-
THER HE CAUGHT THE KILLER OR, AT LEAST FIGURED OUT WHAT REALLY HAPPENED TO
ZACH CURLANDER.

His investigation team was working the site. And his mechanical team was inspecting the car.

He, as usual, was fretting.

Frankly, he didn't have much to do except dwell on the death of his friend and ponder the existence of God. The local police chief had been no help and the task force agents in Atherton—Simmons and Johnson—had seen no suspicious activity.

Things appeared to be at a standstill.

Still, his gut told him this was the calm before the storm. Whatever was going to happen in this crazy case—whatever the outcome—it was going to come to a head here in Pebble Beach.

The killer is here.

Shortly after six p.m., his cell phone rang.

"Agent Krnich?" the caller asked.

"Yes, who's this?"

"This is Dwayne, Mr. Falicello's assistant. Are we being recorded?"

Intrigued, Krnich assured him the call was off the record and asked him to continue.

"Mr. Falicello has asked me to call you to invite you back out to his home. He said to tell you that, after making some discreet inquiries, he might have additional information to help you on your quest."

"What kind of information?"

"That, I do not know," Dwayne said. "He would like to meet with you personally."

"And we can't talk about this over the phone?"

"Oh no, Mr. Falicello never talks business over the phone. You know that, agent Krnich."

Krnich could almost see the big man-servant flash him a patronizing grin. "I'm tied up in Carmel right now. I lost one of my men last night and I have to stick around for the investigative findings. Please ask Gino if it would be all right for me to send one of my colleagues. It would be a man I trust. His name is Raoul Espinoza."

Dwayne asked Krnich to hold and came back to the phone three minutes later. "Mr. Falicello says he would prefer you, but under the circumstances, he understands and will accept your surrogate—as long as you will vouch for his competence and agree to keep the source of the information Mr. Falicello provides confidential."

Knowing full well that he didn't have the authority to grant immunity, but wanting to arrest the killer before the son-of-a-bitch struck again, Krnich made a split second decision. "Okay. I'll tell Espinoza that any information he gets comes from an anonymous source. I'll call Raoul and make arrangements for him to be there tomorrow before noon. Is that acceptable?"

Dwayne put him on hold again, returned a few moments later. "Mr. Falicello agrees. He thanks you for your professionalism." The call disconnected.

Krnich hoped he hadn't made a mistake.

How bizarre...but definitely more interesting than guarding politicians and bureaucrats. He called Espinoza. "I need you to fly to Las Vegas tomorrow morning."

Startled by the request, but pleased to be needed, Espinoza replied, "Sure, what's going on?"

Krnich explained the deal and urged the sergeant to call him the minute his meeting with Falicello ended. Raoul quickly agreed. They were about to say goodbye when Krnich added, "Hey Raoul, you be careful out there. I already lost Curlander, I don't think I could take another one."

"No problemo," Espinoza said and then hung up.

64

THEY SAY RECOVERING ALCOHOLICS OFTEN SUFFER 'DRUNK' DREAMS.

For Brad it was the 'Debt Nightmare'.

Unlike nightmares in which you fear for your safety, the debt nightmare preys on your ego and your sense of self-worth. It threatens your confidence, making you feel stupid, frail and impotent.

It didn't take much to set it off in Brad Stephens these days.

The property tax collector, the poor, grieving, Jose Gonzales, the upcoming expenses of Pebble Beach and John Linden's reluctance to accept additional sponsors—they all played havoc with his psyche.

Tonight, the dream was very vivid:

Brad stands in front of a celestial looking judge whose bench floats on a cloud fifteen feet above the floor. The judge, a huge man in a white robe, white beard with grizzled hands and a booming voice says, "How did you ever think you were going to repay the two and a half million dollars you borrowed?" Brad clears his throat and says in a quiet voice, "I had exit strategies."

"What's that? Speak up. I can't hear you," the judge bellows.

"I had exit strategies, your honor," Brad says louder.

"Exit strategies? What type of 'exit' strategies did an idiot like you have?"

"Well..."

"Silence!"

Brad stiffens. He's dying to explain his actions. "But..."

"I said, Silence!" The judge bangs his gavel, looks down his long nose, over the top of his reading glasses and declares, "Guilty! You will serve time in debtor's prison."

Before the judge can render final punishment, John Linden comes running down the aisle dressed in loud green pants, a bright yellow golf shirt and black golf shoes. "Brad, buddy, I'll save you. Let's sign that deal with Nike. You can make some decent money from that."

Brad begs the court's permission to speak, "Your honor, this is, perhaps, my last chance at financial solvency. My friend, John Linden, has changed his mind and will consider sponsorship from Nike. I should be able to continue to pay my bills!"

The judge looks at John and barks, "Is this true?"

John hesitates and then says, "Well, actually, on second thought, no." He turns to Brad and says, "Sorry, pards, I don't like their ball."

Brad's jaw drops. He sighs and holds his wrists out for the manacles he knows are coming.

"To debtor's prison!" the judge shouts while waving his hands in the air.

From somewhere deep inside the building, the Rolling Stones blast "Sympathy for the Devil."

Brad is led off as Linden signs autographs to his right and Jose Gonzales and the tax collector smirk to his left.

The dream ends when Mel shakes him awake. "Brad, you were tossing and turning. Is everything okay?"

How does he tell her that, no, everything is not okay? It's going to take a miracle to get through this economic downturn without losing everything they've built together.

"Get up now, it's time to pack. We have to be on the road to Pebble Beach in an hour."

Oh, swell.

Hopefully the golf with Linden at Spanish Bay, Pebble Beach and Cypress will be good. It will be a good warm-up for Linden before the Players' Championship and maybe he, personally, can win a few skins and pay for his share on this trip. Then again, maybe he'll lose?

Stay positive; stack those positive thoughts.

Ugh!

65

RAOUL ESPINOZA DEPARTED HIS COMMERCIAL FLIGHT IN VEGAS STILL WONDERING WHY THE MOBSTER WANTED TO MEET. DID HE HAVE MORE NEWS ABOUT JIM STACK? HAD HE REMEMBERED THE REASON HE WANTED TO KILL REAL ESTATE AGENTS? OR DID HE JUST WANT TO CHEW THE FAT?

Krnich had briefed him extensively about Falicello's background and told him what to expect upon arrival. "You'll be frisked," he had warned and then went on to describe the man servant, Dwayne. "He's a big guy, but seems okay." Finally he had been told that 'the Fridge' would make some type of ceremonial entrance.

The police sergeant who came from humble roots and who led a simple life was intrigued.

He rented a car from the first available vendor and followed the map to Falicello's compound. He was amazed a house like this could sit, basically, in the middle of nowhere. He guessed if a person wanted to build a fortress, the desert was as good a place as any.

The day was hot and dry. A strong wind blew from the east and he watched in amazement as tumbleweeds raced past his car. He stopped at Falicello's gate, announced his arrival and prepared for the opening ceremonies. True to form, Dwayne met him and escorted him into the main room. Shortly thereafter, Falicello sauntered in.

"Sergeant Espinoza," the old man sang out. "What a pleasure to meet you."

Krnich had warned him about the false humility and insincere generosity. His advice: Play along.

"Mr. Falicello, the pleasure is all mine," Espinoza said as he extended his hand.

This was quickly turning into a scene from the Godfather XV, Espinoza thought.

"Dwayne, please get our guest something cold to drink."

The butler, or whatever he was—man servant, maybe—suddenly appeared and asked Raoul what he would like to drink.

"Iced Tea would be fine. Thanks."

Dwayne disappeared and Falicello motioned to Espinoza to follow. At various intervals, 'the Fridge' stopped and pointed out something interesting about the design of the house or discussed a specific piece of artwork. It was clear he took great pride in his accomplishments—legalities notwithstanding.

"Mr. Falicello, your home is beautiful," Espinoza said. "Agent Krnich sends his regrets. He would have preferred to attend this meeting, believe me."

The 'Fridge' pursed his lips and nodded his head several times. "I understand he must attend to some very regretful business. Please express my sympathies for the loss of his man." He paused as if in serious reflective thought. "I know what it is to lose someone close to you in a car accident. My son and daughter-in- law were both killed several years ago. The heart bleeds," Falicello said, pounding softly on his chest.

What a piece of work.

"That's awful. I didn't know. How old was your son?"

"Only thirty-three, the same age as Jesus when he died."

Now he's comparing his mobbed-up son to Jesus. Wow!

Dwayne arrived with their iced teas and the two took a seat in what appeared to be the living room. In a house this big and this ornate, it was hard to tell one room from the next.

"Agent Krnich has indicated that you have some information concerning our recent slate of murders in California."

"Yes I do; ugly, awful business, these murders. I note that you're a Sergeant in Santa Barbara. Has any-one been killed in your jurisdiction?"

"No, not yet but we believe there was an attempt on a local realtor."

"I believe I can help you there," Falicello said. "You see, a friend of a friend of mine contacted me just yesterday." The former mob boss paused for emphasis. He raised his eyebrows a few times as if prompting Espinoza to acknowledge the sharing of a secret. When Espinoza didn't respond, the old man continued. "My friend said he had a problem. A man with whom he trained in the military had become a professional assassin. This friend of mine indicated that the man had gone rogue and was trying to make a name for himself. My friend believes this man is your serial killer." The 'Fridge' sat back and smiled, apparently quite satisfied with his own bullshit.

Espinoza stared at him intensely. He reminded himself to 'play along'; don't question the man's sincerity. "Very interesting, does your *friend* have the name of the former military guy?"

"If he's correct, your killer's name is Ted Flowers. He stands slightly over six feet tall, is of Hispanic origins, weighs approximately one hundred ninety pounds and is very, very dangerous."

Raoul took notes furiously.

This guy knows more. Play along.

The obvious, yet most insulting question left his lips before he could retract it: "Why did your friend come to you for assistance? What did he hope to gain?" The asking of this question challenged the false foundation upon which this meeting was based.

Falicello smiled. Everything about him said: I'm an old, retired businessman. I have no knowledge of illegal activities. I wasn't 'connected'. Rather, just an ordinary citizen performing my civic duty.

Espinoza waited for a formal response.

The old man took a sip of his iced tea. Several moments passed before he spoke again. "I have seen many things in my life, Sergeant Espinoza. Some of them pleasant, some of them not so. Because of my experience and obvious financial success," he waved his arm around the room, "friends solicit my advice. Do you understand?"

"Yes, sir," Espinoza lied.

"Good. I don't always know what motivates my friends, but I listen and I help when I can. In this case, I believe my friend was conflicted. He wanted to report his thoughts to the authorities but he didn't want to see an innocent man unduly harassed—if he was wrong."

"And you have no misgivings?"

"None. I have done some additional research and I can confirm with absolute confidence that your killer is Ted Flowers." Falicello snapped his fingers and Dwayne appeared out of nowhere again. Dwayne handed Falicello a manila envelope. Falicello turned it in his hands a few times and then handed it to Espinoza.

"This is the only recent photograph I could find of Mr. Flowers. My friend tells me he is a master of disguise and that he takes his work very seriously. Who knows what he looks like now?"

Heart racing, Espinoza took the photo. It had been taken by a security camera. It was grainy but clear enough for facial recognition. The background looked surprisingly similar to Falicello's driveway. Should he say something? No, let it lie. He said, "Thank you, Mr.

Falicello. Your help in this matter is greatly appreciated. I hope you will thank your friend for me and assure him that he has done the right thing."

"I'm sure he knows. Now if you will excuse me, I have a very strict exercise regimen to attend to. When you get to be my age, you have to take good care of yourself. Otherwise, you can't keep up with the ladies when the time comes, if you catch my drift." Again, he raised the eyebrows on his pudgy face.

Espinoza had been exposed to so much bullshit the past thirty minutes he didn't know what to believe any longer. He smiled and rose to shake the old man's hand. "I know what you mean, gotta be able to perform when the time's right. Thank you for your hospitality. I'm sure Agent Krnich will call you when we bring Flowers in."

"That would be nice. I will sleep better knowing that there is one less violent criminal running around out there. Good day, Sergeant."

Dwayne appeared for the final time and escorted Espinoza out to his car.

"Dwayne. Man to man. I couldn't see you, but I know you heard our entire conversation. What do you think really happened in there?" Espinoza asked pointing back into the house.

"Man to man, I think Mr. Falicello just solved the case for you," he said with a broad smile. "Have a safe journey home Sergeant."

ONCE HE CLEARED the gates, Espinoza couldn't pull his cell phone out fast enough.

"Jim, I can't believe it. Falicello gave up the name of the killer."

"The name. Incredible. What's his name?"

"Ted Flowers, he's a former Special Ops soldier."

"That makes sense, based on the tattoo Mrs. Stephens saw on his calf. Anything else?"

Espinoza cleared his throat. "Oh yeah, a friend of a friend of a friend, or some bullshit, provided him with a fairly recent picture of our man. I'll scan it and send it to you from the first Kinko's I see."

"A picture too? Hmm...interesting," Krnich mumbled. He caught himself and continued. "Thanks for going out there. I knew the old man would talk to you." Krnich paused for a long moment and then asked in a very serious tone, "Why do you think he gave us Flowers?"

"Civic Duty," Espinoza said.

"Oh, yeah, civic duty, I should've known."

"That's what he said, but of course that's bullshit. Everything the guy said was bullshit. It just doesn't make sense. He gets the list of real estate agents from Stack. He hires Flowers to kill them. They start dying. There's still at least three to go. He gives us the killer. What gives?"

"Maybe cutting his losses. Maybe he knows we're on to him and he decides the best thing to do to deflect attention is to throw his boy under the bus."

"Well, I still don't get it. Why not just call the other hits off and stay mum? By talking to us, he's admitting he knew what was going on."

"Maybe we'll find out later. For now, I don't care why. Falicello is a very complicated man."

"And rich; did you see that spread?"

"Yep, he rubbed my nose in it when I was there. Did you see his beautiful granddaughter?"

"No I didn't. All I saw was ugly, Dwayne," Espinoza joked.

"Well, your loss, she's really a looker. In the meantime, good job, now get your ass back to Santa Barbara in case our guy decides to make a return appearance. And when you get there, put Flowers' name in the database for hotels in San Diego, San Francisco and Ventura. Let's see if we can really nail him to the cross."

"Will do. You think he's headed my way?"

"My gut tells me he's up here in Pebble Beach. This is just too ripe of a killing ground for him—assuming he knows that Ornstein and Smith-Newhall will be attending the Stack seminar."

"All right, look for the picture in an hour. I think I remember seeing a Kinko's over by UNLV." They said their goodbyes and disconnected.

Whistling softly, Krnich looked to the sky and said, "Zach, buddy, we got a name. We got a picture. Now we just got to find this asshole before he kills again. And I'll tell you what, if we can prove he had anything to do with your death, I will personally put the mother fucker down."

66

Pebble Beach

LOCATED IN THE NORTHERNMOST SECTION OF SEVENTEEN MILE DRIVE, *The Inn at Spanish Bay* **IS KNOWN FOR MANY THINGS: SCENIC VIEWS, WONDERFUL FOOD, FANTASTIC ROOMS, GREAT SERVICE AND LUSH COASTAL VEGETATION.**

It is also associated with championship golf—eighteen challenging and scenic holes along the Pacific and up into thick woods. Of course, there is also the Scottish bagpipe player who strolls up the eighteenth fairway towards the Inn each evening while the sound of rich music drifts through the air.

The beginning of the music signifies the official start to the cocktail hour; the conclusion, dinner time.

In better times, Mel and Brad visited the Inn often. Lately, not so much. Perhaps this would be a special trip, signifying the rebirth of better economic times, Brad thought.

Then again, it could be a financial disaster.

—◆—

"HURRY UP, BRAD. Drive faster. You're driving like a little old lady. The introductory cocktail party starts at five thirty. I want to get checked in and take a shower before we go to it," Mel said as they passed acre after acre of newly planted wine vines along Highway 101 north of San Luis Obispo. Gone were the fields of asparagus, cauliflower, and lettuce replaced by miles upon miles of chardonnay, cabernet and merlot. Apparently, the world's appetite for fine wine trumped its need for dietary fiber.

They had left Santa Barbara at ten a.m. Sunday morning. The drive would take only a few hours. Barring a major accident, they should be there in plenty of time.

"Calm down," Brad said. "Unless we run into traffic, we'll be there no later than three. You don't expect me to go to that stupid 'Stacking Method' orientation do you?"

"You can come if you want. If not, no big deal. I'll be back by seven. Perhaps we can have a nice quiet dinner before the conference gets crazy."

"Sounds good to me."

"Okay. I'm just so excited. It seems like forever since we've gone any place special. And you know how much I love Spanish Bay. The bagpipe player at sunset is magical. I could listen to that guy every night for the rest of my life."

"Oh yeah? Maybe I should get a kilt and walk around the house while I play bagpipe on the stereo;

might get lucky more often." He pinched her bare thigh lightly.

She grinned. "I doubt it, but one never knows."

Brad rolled his eyes and changed the subject. "I'm glad we can do this. Maybe it'll be the first of many special trips."

"I hope so."

"Me too." He let his answer linger for a few moments while he focused on the road. After he navigated a particularly tricky turn, he added, "John is talking about the four of us going out to Palm Springs in the fall, before his wedding."

"That would be wonderful," Mel said. "I love Palm Springs in the fall."

There goes another few thousand...

She moved her left hand to his shoulder, rubbed it gently. "I know you have to constantly worry about money these days, but this will be a good break."

Ever the optimist.

"You can clear your head and focus on how to make money going forward," she said. "What about managing John's career? Are you making any money from that yet?"

"He's not playing much golf. He seems content playing house with Stef," Brad said. He suddenly accelerated to pass a slow-moving old, beat-up Ford pickup. As he passed, he could see that the truck was filled to the brim with rusty tools in the back and packed with Hispanic workers in the front. "That truck shouldn't even be on the road," he said softly.

"It looks dangerous," Mel agreed, "but you know they got to do what they got to do." She smiled as if the common sense of her statement was beyond reproach.

Focusing on his management of Linden once again, he continued. "I've got a meeting scheduled with Nike next week. Maybe something will come from that."

"We'll be okay. You'll figure it out. You always do." She threw him a warm, knowing smile, gave him a quick peck on the cheek.

Sure, I always do.

Uh, huh.

THEY CONTINUED DRIVING in silence for several miles. After they passed another slow-moving truck, he turned his head to the side and faced Mel directly. "I guess the other thing that's bugging me is the fact that you were almost killed by that painter."

"No I wasn't. The painter didn't actually pull his gun. What about you and Mr. Gonzales," she said, hoping to turn the tables.

"I think Jose was bluffing. He was just very confused."

"Bluffing! The guy put a gun to your head."

"I know and believe me it scared the crap out of me. But I don't think he would've pulled the trigger. I think he just wanted to scare me and get some attention for Lupe. He's very distraught."

"Maybe; I guess we'll never know," Mel said.

"And that fake painter could be anywhere," Brad said.

"It'll be okay. I don't think the painter would dare make a move against us in Pebble Beach; too many people around. I bet he's in Mexico by now, licking his wounds."

"I hope so. But I've got a bad feeling in my gut," Brad said. He appreciated Mel's optimistic conclusion but he wasn't buying it. Too many weird things had happened lately.

"Well not me. I think we dodged a few bullets. I think we'll be fine and now it's time to relax."

"Woman's intuition?"

"That and the presence of Jim Krnich and his agents."

She stretched across the middle counsel and planted another kiss on his cheek. This one lasted much longer. "Who knows, maybe we'll have a few quiet nights to ourselves." She gave him an inquisitive raising of the eyebrows and a sexy smile.

Brad accepted the reference to hotel sex without commenting. Of course that was always welcome, but he couldn't shake the feeling that the killer was still out there.

And Mel, Stef and Paula might still be in his crosshairs.

He shrugged it off, put a book on CD in the player, sat back and enjoyed the rest of the ride to Pebble Beach.

———

AS THEY ENTERED Salinas, thirty minutes outside of Spanish Bay, Brad's cell phone rang. It was Linden.

"Hey Brad. I pulled some strings and got us a game at Spanish Bay. We tee off at three thirty today. Are you going to make it?"

Brad's mood brightened instantly. Nothing like a competitive golf match to pick up the spirits.

"We'll be there. Who are our opponents?"

"The 'pigeons', you mean?" Linden said with a chuckle. "A local businessman named Dennis Starling and a local teaching pro named Ralph Cassill. Everyone will stroke off of me as a +5 and they have agreed to a hundred dollar Nassau."

A hundred dollar Nassau was a bit steep for their first match of the week, Brad thought and he told Linden so.

A Nassau bet was broken down into three parts: winner of front nine, winner of back nine, and over-all winner. It meant that minimum exposure for each player was three hundred dollars. A Nassau, however, frequently includes additional bets. The most common of these, the 'press'.

If pressed, Brad could lose six, twelve, or maybe twenty-four hundred dollars.

It was a sobering thought to a guy in his current financial position.

He couldn't afford to be on the wrong end of the bet.

Lee Trevino, the famous professional golfer had even coined a joke about this particular situation: When asked about the pressure of playing professional golf, Trevino quickly replied, "Pressure? This ain't pressure. This is fun. Pressure is when you play for five dollars a hole and only got two in your pocket."

Brad had fifty bucks cash and a bunch of credit cards. He was beginning to feel the pressure.

He took a cleansing breath, vowed to remain positive—he was playing with one of the best golfers in the world, after all—and told Linden he'd see him on the putting green before three thirty.

"All right, bring your 'A' game," Linden said.

"Sounds like John is going to round up some fun games for you guys the next few days," Mel said.

Yeah, fun.

Hope I don't have to borrow money from my 'client'.

A half hour later, the sun shining brilliantly, the weather a comfortable sixty-five degrees, he and Mel pulled into the majestic *Inn at Spanish Bay*.

67

TED FLOWERS WAS NERVOUS. SOMETHING WASN'T RIGHT.

Maybe it was the death of Curlander. Maybe it was the failed attempt on Smith-Newhall. Maybe it was because he was so close to getting paid. Maybe it was the fact that this conference seemed too convenient.

Maybe it was Mercedes?

Whatever the reason, Flowers was definitely uncomfortable. He despised discomfort.

Whenever he had felt nerves in the military, he focused on the mission at hand. That usually brought his mind back into the present and relieved some, if not all, of the anxiety. He had concocted a solid plan for this final kill. Focus on it and he'd be all right.

Dressed in a dark suit with thick glasses and a gray wig, Flowers once again donned the persona of Richard Santiago. He left his hotel shortly after two p.m. and drove directly to Spanish Bay.

The only target he had yet to make visual contact with was Susan Ornstein, the agent from Atherton. He'd rectify that shortly. He'd hang out by the front desk and catch her when she registered.

Fortunately for Flowers, the front desk was located very close to a large cocktail area. He sat down, ordered tea and pretended to read the newspaper. His seat gave him a perfect view of the front desk.

AT TWO THIRTY, a tall woman in her late thirties or early forties with short brown hair, deep tan, wearing a blue and white Armani pant suit, pushed her way through the front doors. She berated the doorman for not opening the door sooner and, aggressively, approached the front desk. She was followed by three younger females. Dressed in similar apparel, they appeared to be her younger clones.

"Susan Ornstein," she declared to the clerk loudly as she flopped her purse on the front desk. "I'm here for the Jim Stack seminar. I have one room and these are my assistants, Audrey, Sheila, and Chris. They all should have rooms reserved under my name."

While the flustered clerk quickly looked up the reservations, Ornstein turned and surveyed the room. Obviously disappointed that nobody recognized her as the 'superstar' from Atherton, she sighed and then returned her attention to the check-in process.

Sipping his tea, and glancing over the top of the newspaper he was pretending to read, Richard Santiago made a mental note of Ornstein's look and mannerisms.

Bingo!

Flowers now knew all of his next victims: Smith-Newhall, Willowby and Ornstein. He paid his bill and prepared to leave the lobby when he noticed a man and a woman come through the large glass front doors. He had seen this woman before. Who was she? Suddenly it hit him. She was one of the faces on the business cards he had taken from the Santa Barbara beach house. Was she Melanie Stephens or Stefanie Ramirez? When he heard the man refer to her as Mel it confirmed that she was in fact Melanie Stephens. What was she doing here? Would she recognize him? He smiled, confident that his disguise would protect him.

Professional planning.

For fun, he rose and walked close to the Stephens woman and purposely bumped her arm. Her purse fell to the ground.

"I'm so sorry," Flowers said in his Ricardo Montelban accent as he reached down to pick it up.

"That's okay," Mel said. "It's crowded in here. No harm done." She bent down at the same time and the two almost bumped heads.

For a brief moment they made direct eye contact. She smiled. He smiled. Flowers apologized once again and walked slowly towards the front door.

No sign of recognition on the woman's face.
Good.

As he left the lobby, the final surprise of the afternoon occurred. From the corner opposite the front desk, a woman came running towards Melanie Stephens, arms outstretched.

"Mel isn't this wonderful," Flowers heard her say as he watched Stefanie Ramirez hug her friend.

He paused long enough to hear the women's full conversation. "It's beautiful. Just the way I remember it," one of them said.

"The boring men are going to play golf. Let's go get ready for the cocktail party. I can't wait to show you my Hawaiian skirt. I hope it's not too skimpy," the other replied.

Flowers grinned. What a great opportunity to clean the slate before leaving the country. His plan grew in dimension but remained relatively unchanged. He left the premises, planning to return at four forty five.

This is going to be one great cocktail party, he thought.

I wonder if they have a term in bowling for FIVE strikes in a row?

68

"WE PRESS," THE BUSINESSMAN, DENNIS STARLING, DRESSED IMMACULATELY IN GRAY SLACKS, ECCO GOLF SHOES, AND A BLACK TURTLENECK ANNOUNCED ON THE FIFTH HOLE—WHICH WAS REALLY THE 14TH, SEEING AS THE GROUP TEED OFF ON THE BACK NINE.

"And I think you should adjust your handicap to a +10 the rest of the way in," he added, staring daggers at Linden. "And I want to start playing barkies, sandies, greenies and snakes," he declared, sounding like that spoiled brat in the original *Caddyshak* movie.

Presses, barkies, sandies, greenies and snakes are common side bets made during a recreational round of golf. Obviously, golfers can be very creative—or just plain goofy.

Way too much time on their hands.

John smiled and winked at Brad before responding. "I'm just getting lucky, Mr. Starling. The putts keep rolling in. Even a blind hog finds an acorn every now and then. I tell you what. I'll give you a breakfast ball on the back nine. You can use it whenever you want. How's that?"

The teaching pro, Ralph Cassill, a tall guy with a small moustache and a long, looping swing had been preparing to hit his tee ball. He paused and then made a reasonable suggestion. "How 'bout we keep the handicaps the same for the next four holes and adjust at the turn?"

"And I still get a breakfast ball on the back nine?" Starling almost begged.

Cassill turned and looked quizzically at Linden. John nodded and then deferred to his playing partner. "What do you think pards; we got enough game for these 'hustlers'?"

Brad did the math in his head. Most he could lose—everything taken into consideration—was a few hundred bucks. He liked the odds. He quickly agreed but with one caveat. "Let's increase the overall bet. Let's make it worth two hundred dollars."

They all agreed and proceeded to hit their tee balls. Cassill, Linden and Brad piped their drives down the middle of the fairway. Starling, still angry at how badly he and Cassill were being trounced, pushed his ball fifty yards to the right. Given the ten inch eel grass bordering the fairway, it would be difficult, if not impossible, to find his ball.

Sounding like Judge Smails in the original *Caddyshack*, Starling slammed his club on the ground and cursed loudly. "Shit! I never slice the ball!" He then added, "That grass is so thick I'll never find the damn thing!"

Acting as if he had no clue as to the ruling on his particular shot, Starling turned to the group and asked, "What are my options? That area isn't red staked and I don't think it's out of bounds."

"Let's look for it and if we don't find it in a few minutes, I say we call it a red stake hazard, take a stroke and a drop at where you think it crossed." Linden winked at Brad knowing full well the guy should have taken a stroke and distance penalty for lost ball.

"Okay, that's fair," Starling replied somewhat grudgingly, as if he were giving in. "Maybe we'll find it."

The foursome, accompanied by two local caddies, walked off the tee and down the fairway.

———————

"WHAT DO YOU think the girls are doing?" Linden asked Brad as the group approached the spot where Starling's ball had disappeared.

"You know women. They're primping and poofing and getting ready for that stupid cocktail party."

Linden looked at his watch. In the distance, he could hear the bagpipe player warming up his reeds. "It's almost five. I bet we'll hit the eighteenth hole which is right around the corner from the girls about the same time as the bagpipe player. Maybe we can sneak over and grab a beer?"

"Okay, but only one beer. I don't want you playing the back nine drunk. You're smoking the ball and I've never seen you putt better."

"The claw, babe, it's all about the claw," Linden said, referring to his new, unorthodox putting grip.

"Hey, I'm a believer. Just keep it going."

Starling emerged from the grass to their right and declared his ball lost. Linden allowed him to take a drop much closer to the hole than was permitted by the rules and encouraged him to hit his next shot well—which, to everyone's surprise, he did. Now laying three and putting for par, Starling smiled and strode confidently towards the green.

"I hope you didn't let the 'genie out of the bottle' pards," Brad said semi-seriously.

"I'm not worried about him; it's Cassill I'm concerned about. That guy can play. I figure he knows I cut his partner a break and he'll be embarrassed about it for a few holes." He winked again. "Might throw his game off."

"You've always got an angle, don't you?"

"Always."

The match progressed nicely with Brad winning the next two holes. By the time they got to the final hole of their front nine, the 18th, he and Linden sported a healthy five shot lead.

Starling was the last to hit his tee ball. It was a decent shot. He looked proud of his accomplishment. His face sank on the second shot, however as he hooked it into some green bushes lining the fairway. Contrary to his caddy's advice, Starling tried to retrieve his ball from a very thick, prickly gorse bush. He came out with a two inch thorn stuck in his left hand and no golf ball.

The caddy extracted the thorn, warned him again about the gorse needles, poured some water on a towel and wiped the blood off Starling's hand. Declaring himself good to go, Starling dropped another ball and hit it squarely to the middle of the green. "Lying three or four?" he asked Linden.

"Well, buddy, since you've lost a little blood—and I know that wound is going to start itching pretty soon, gorse needles always do—let's say you're lying three."

"Sounds fair; I appreciate your understanding."

Brad glowered at his partner. "You going to give him every break? Why don't you concede his putt for birdie?" he said through clenched teeth.

"Don't worry about it. I know what I'm doing. You know pards, you get more bees with honey than vinegar. Don't be such a sour puss." Linden took his putter from the caddie and punched Brad in the shoulder. "I'm thirsty. You thirsty? Let's make our putts and go steal a beer from the cocktail party."

69

THE REEDY, MECHANICAL TUNE GREW LOUDER AND MORE DISTINCT AS THE LARGE MAN DRESSED IN A PLAID SCOTTISH KILT WALKED UP THE EIGHTEENTH FAIRWAY.

Beyond the wandering minstrel, waves crashed on the beach, seagulls soared to new heights, deer grazed amongst the gorse and small bonfires on the beach gave off smoke and that wonderful aromatic smell you can only get from sandy driftwood. On the golf course, players lined up their putts, completed their shots, and fist-bumped a job well done.

It was a glorious afternoon in a glorious location.

Wearing khaki shorts and a green Hawaiian shirt, Richard Santiago entered the cocktail party at 5:30 sharp. He mingled with the crowd, kept an eye on his targets. As the bagpipe player drew close, Jim Stack asked the ukulele player to take a break and then tapped his glass with a fork.

"People, please. Your attention for a few moments," Stack began. "I want to welcome you all to the fabulous *Inn at Spanish Bay.*" He paused and smiled like a cat that just cornered a mouse. Satisfied. Pompous. A king amongst peasants. The attendees clapped. "Over the next few days, I'm going to help you unlock personal tools you never knew you possessed," he began. "Together, we're going to enhance your productivity, strengthen your confidence, and position you to make more money during a recession than you ever thought possible." The group broke into another round of enthusiastic applause.

He was getting filthy rich from this bullshit and he loved it.

He raised his hands to quiet the crowd. "You're all 'superstars' in your respective communities. I know you have been successful in the past. I'm not trying to trivialize your success—I'm trying to maximize it!" Two hundred slightly inebriated disciples clapped and cheered-on their hero.

"Before we begin the grueling process of 'Stacking' your hidden talents," he shouted to the group, "I want you all to enjoy this social gathering. Get to know one another. Share stories of family, business and success. Don't be afraid to confide in each other. For the next few days, you are not competitors, you are allies."

Stack paused a beat. He surveyed the patio. Which one of the unsuspecting females would he attempt to seduce? So many choices, so little time. The beautiful Latina in the short Hawaiian skirt caught his eye.

Hmmm...

"Please make sure you have checked in with my assistant, Charles. He's the big guy in the pink shirt sitting at the table over there." Stack pointed to the back of the room.

The noise from the bagpipe had grown louder as Stack began his speech. It suddenly came to an abrupt halt. The Scottish musician stood in the middle of the fairway, twenty yards from the gathering.

"Ladies and gentlemen, it is my distinct honor to present Lawrence McMichael," Stack said sweeping his arm in a grand gesture towards the bagpipe player. "Mr. McMichael has agreed to play several of his favorite songs for our little group. I hope you find him as inspiring as I do." The party-goers clapped and moved closer to the wall separating the fairway from the patio.

———

THIS WAS THE opening Flowers had been waiting for. Everyone's attention was either on Stack or McMichael. If he acted swiftly, he could accomplish his task in a few minutes.

The poison he had in his pocket was quick—but not immediate—acting.

It would take five minutes to paralyze the nervous system, another five to cause the person respiratory failure. That should be plenty of time to put a few drops in Ornstein's drink, move to his left a few yards and slip it into whatever Willowby was drinking and finally, on his way out of the party, hit Smith-Newhall and her stupid friends.

Fish in a barrel.

Pulling a small vile from his back pocket, he unscrewed the cap and approached Susan Ornstein and her entourage. The pushy agent from Atherton and her group had somehow managed to capture the front row just behind a five foot retaining wall. Right where a true superstar belonged.

The bagpipe music began. *Amazing Grace* filled the night air.

———

KRNICH ARRIVED AT the cocktail party late. He found Mel, Stef and Paula in the crowd and asked what he had missed.

"Nothing so far," Stef said while sipping on some type of tropical drink. "Just a bunch of realtors standing around talking about how great they are."

"Hey, we don't just talk about how great we are. We also talk about how great we *want to be*," Paula joked. Then turning serious she said, "These gatherings are very helpful for high-end realtors. You never know when you're going to run into another agent who has the perfect buyer for one of your listings."

Stef acknowledged her point, apologized and turned her attention to the musical performance. The bagpipe player was working effortlessly through the song, the goat bladder expanding and contracting as he blew in the pipe. After a few moments, Mel declared that she was thirsty and asked if anyone wanted something to drink. She took their orders and headed for the bar.

To her right, she saw John and Brad sneaking through the ropes, grins as wide as the fairway on both of their faces. Brad noticed her stare and made the internationally recognized gesture for drinking a beer: right hand in a rounded, open fist with wrist bending towards mouth.

Little boys, trying to steal candy, she thought.

She was about to wave to them when her attention drifted to her left. A man in a green Hawaiian shirt was moving quickly through the crowd, towards the front row. A large woman wearing a blue Mumu that fit her like mismatched drapes and drinking what looked like a Blue Hawaiian cocktail bumped him, spilling her drink on the man.

Mel immediately noticed it was the same guy who had knocked her purse to the ground at the registration desk. "The bumpee, this time," she thought, chuckling to herself. She started towards the bar once again but stopped to glance at the scene one last time. She wanted all the details so she could tell her friends.

She noticed that the front of the man's shirt was drenched with blue goo. A good amount of the drink ran down his right leg.

"I'm so sorry," the woman in the Mumu said loudly. "I didn't see you there. Let me help, hon." She grabbed a towel off the bar and moved towards the man.

Mel watched as the man brushed her away. "No that's okay," she heard him say. The man grabbed the towel from the woman and wiped the goop off his shirt. She was about to turn away and complete her journey to the bar when Mel noticed the man bend down to replace a patch on his lower right leg. Apparently, the liquid had loosened a medium-sized square bandage. What she saw next took her breath away.

70

"Be back in a minute; just grabbing a beer," Linden replied. "Want one?"

"Sure, make it a Heineken."

"Make it two," Cassill added. "The damn things cost twelve bucks on the course."

Grabbing their drivers so that they'd be ready to tee off on the next hole, Brad and Linden jumped the small wall separating the pavilion from the course and tiptoed towards the nearest bucket of beer.

"Very tricky, gentlemen," a female voice called to them.

They turned to face the event organizer, Ms. Knudeson glaring at them as if she had just caught two teenage boys trying to steal a Playboy from the local liquor store.

"It's not what it looks like," Brad said.

"Oh, I know what you guys are doing. Trying to save a few bucks and steal beer from our gathering," Knudeson said sternly.

Linden flashed a toothy grin. "Guilty as charged. But you don't really understand..."

"Oh, yeah, educate me," she said, giving no quarter.

"I'm John Linden," he said, hoping to elicit recognition. When she didn't respond, he continued. "Perhaps you know me as the U.S. Open Champ?"

No reaction.

Was this woman brain dead?

Doesn't follow golf. Damn. Need a new angle.

Linden gave Brad a slight nudge. "This is my buddy and manager, Brad Stephens."

Brad gave a little wave.

"We have wives attending your conference," Linden said.

"We were supposed to attend as well," Brad quickly added.

"And?"

"Don't you see?" It was Linden talking this time. "If we had gone to the cocktail party, believe me, we would've downed several beers each."

"Yeah, we're just claiming what is rightly ours," Brad said defiantly, as if their argument made as much sense as two plus two equals four.

Clearly not buying their logic but perhaps tiring of the conversation, Ms. Knudeson was about to have the final word when she heard a commotion behind her.

"Mr. Santiago, are you okay?" she said, moving hastily towards Flowers.

As he bent to replace the slightly dangling bandage, Flowers looked up to see Ms. Knudeson coming towards him. He held up his free hand. "I'm okay, Ms. Knudeson, just a little spill. No problem."

BRAD AND JOHN continued forward, grabbed four beers and prepared to descend back down to the next tee.

Ms. Knudeson returned her attention to them for a moment. "Hold it right there... Oh what the hell, help yourself. Stack is paying for them." She turned and disappeared back into the crowd.

"Phew, that was close," Brad said.

"Yeah, dodged a bullet on that one pards. Come on, let's get back to our match."

Brad shot one last glance towards the gathering, searching for Mel. He wanted to show off his catch and gloat about his victory over the ruthless Ms. Knudeson, but his wife was nowhere in sight.

"Wish I could see Mel," he told Linden. "She was over there by the bar when we approached the wall. Wonder where she is?"

"Probably 'stacking up' some good food," Linden said. "Come on, let's get back to our meal tickets."

71

HER MIND RACING, HER PULSE QUICKENING, MEL PUT DOWN HER DRINK AND
RETURNED TO HER GROUP.

"Hey, where's my pina colada?" Stef asked.

Flustered, Mel grabbed Krnich's arm and drew him close. "I don't want to be an alarmist," she whispered in his left ear. "And it might be a coincidence. After all, I'm sure there are lots of them in the world, but I just saw a guy walking through the group with the exact same tattoo on his calf as I saw on the painter in Montecito."

"The Special Ops tattoo? Are you sure?"

"Absolutely, there's no doubt in my mind. It's very distinctive you know. Please tell me it's just a strange coincidence."

"Could be a successful realtor who was once in the military," Krnich suggested, trying to keep Mel calm while inside he knew—just knew—this was their guy. What were the chances of another Special Ops Tattoo at this party?

In a soothing voice he said, "However, since it's the only identifying mark we have on the killer, I should probably find him and ask him a few questions. Did you see his face? Does he look familiar?"

Mel shook her head and then changed her mind. "Well, actually, I do recognize him."

"Really? Is he our guy?"

"I don't know. I don't recognize him from Montecito, but rather from the front desk earlier today. He bumped into me."

Immediately understanding what the killer had done—testing Mel to see if she recognized him—Krnich raised his voice slightly. "Come with me. Point him out to me." He took Mel by the arm and had her lead him through the cluster of bodies.

Krnich discreetly contacted Simmons and Johnson with a hidden microphone attached to the inside of his shirt collar. He instructed them to take positions fore and aft.

It took a few moments to reach the front section of the patio but once the plump woman in the Mumu moved to the side, Mel could clearly see the guy's leg with the tattoo on it. He was standing directly behind a very attractive middle-aged woman. The woman—along with three younger girls who could have been her clones—stood close to the stone wall.

Krnich recognized the woman from Curlander's slide show: Susan Ornstein from Atherton. He quickened his pace.

Krnich could see that the guy with the tattoo was holding something in his hand. Was it a small gun? A knife? From this distance, he couldn't tell. He pushed past Ornstein and grabbed the man's arm.

———

FLOWERS FELT THE pressure on his left arm and turned gently.

Don't panic.

Act natural.

Probably a waiter wanting to serve him a drink or pupu. Or maybe that fat woman wants to wipe off more of the blue drink? As he turned, he was surprised to see a man's face directly behind him. Not a waiter. A cop? No, more likely a federal agent or a local detective. Either way, this wasn't good.

"Yes, what can I do for you?" Flowers asked over the music, moving the vile he had been holding behind his back and pouring the contents on the tile floor behind him.

"Just need a few words with you sir," Krnich said in a flat voice.

Before returning his hand to his side, Flowers felt for the small Walther PPK he had tucked into the back of his waistband.

Glad I decided to carry back-up, he thought.

"What was that behind your back?" Krnich asked.

"Nothing, just scratching," Flowers said.

Apparently, the cop had noticed the vile but not the gun. Bending close to speak directly into Flower's ear, the cop said, "I need a few minutes of your time.

I'm a federal agent and I've got a few questions." He showed Flowers his badge.

"Certainly, agent Krnich," Flowers said. His eyes darted left and right like a caged rat. To his left, he could see another agent standing on the perimeter. He assumed there would be at least one more agent to his right. Clearly, there was only one way to go: straight ahead, over the wall.

"Sir, can we go someplace quieter? The lobby, perhaps," Krnich suggested.

The federal agent's grip was like a vice on his arm, but Flowers knew he could break it with one quick move if he wanted to. The question was should he run or should he stay and play the game?

He loved this shit. It made his blood flow and his senses grow acute. He remembered one especially hairy incident in Iraq when his platoon was pinned-down in a small town. Deciding at the time that there was no logical way out, he had grabbed his commander's machine gun and had single-handedly gone on the offensive. When he was done, twenty of the enemy lay dead, dying, or wounded. He had been given a medal—and a lecture—for that maneuver.

Now, his back was up against the wall once again. Time to go on the offensive. He briefly wondered if Falicello would pay if he failed to take out the last three real estate agents. Then he thought, "He'll pay. This whole operation has been one big clusterfuck because he wanted it done so quickly. He'll pay."

Satisfied with his internal dialogue, Flowers shrugged and nodded his head in agreement with Krnich's request. He made as if to follow the federal agent. When Krnich loosened his grip, Flowers pushed the Ornstein group aside and jumped over the wall.

Startled at the swiftness of the man's moves, Krnich gathered himself, jumped over the wall and gave chase.

72

Brad and Linden had returned to their golf cart, ice cold beers in each hand. "What's going on over there?" Linden asked, pointing towards the patio.

Before Brad could respond, a well-built guy in khaki shorts and green Hawaiian shirt appeared and grabbed Linden by the shoulders. He threw him from the cart and on to the grass. The guy got in the golf cart with Brad in the passenger seat, took control of the vehicle and punched the accelerator. Brad tried to jump out, but the man grabbed him by the arm.

"You're not going anywhere, muchacho. You're my insurance policy."

"Who the fuck are you? What's going on?" Brad stammered.

Two shots were fired and the golf cart began to wobble. Krnich or one of his agents had punctured the rear tires. Flowers cursed, hit the brakes, did a full one hundred eighty degree slide and turned to face the federal agents who were now thirty yards away.

"I got me a hostage, you fuckers," Flowers yelled. "This is the way it's going to go." He pulled the gun from his waistband and pressed it to Brad's temple. "You rush me or make one stupid move, this man is dead. Do you hear me? Dead!"

Not another gun to the head, Brad thought.

73

KRNICH KEPT HIS WEAPON AIMED SQUARELY AT THE KILLER.

He warned Simmons to stay put, took several steps forward. He stopped ten yards short of the golf cart. He caught his breath and said, "Let Brad go and put your gun down Flowers. Give it up. You will not escape."

Flowers? How did they know his real name? He had been so careful. No clues. No prints. Nothing but the mild set-back in Montecito. In retrospect, he should have stayed and finished that job.

Shit! Stupid women.

But certainly—even if they had seen the face of the painter—those women couldn't recognize him. He hardly recognized himself when he looked in the mirror earlier in the day. His disguise was the total opposite of the one he had donned at the beach.

"How...how do you know my name?"

"I'll tell you once you surrender. Now put the weapon down and move away from the golf cart."

Like a caged animal, Flowers knew his options were limited. He would not surrender his hostage. He might need to barter for his life. But he needed a distraction if he was going to escape.

In one impossibly fast motion, Flowers removed the gun from Brad's head, swiveled and shot Lawrence McMichael, the bagpipe player. The big man fell to the ground instantly.

Returning the gun to Brad's temple, Flowers yelled, "I never could stand that fucking music!" He grabbed Brad and turned to run. As he took his first step, a section of gorse tore through the skin on his left leg. Obviously, he hadn't noticed how close to the prickly bush the golf cart had settled.

"Damn," the killer yelled in pain, his gun hand instinctively dropping to rub the wound.

Thinking quickly, and remembering his self-defense lessons—and suddenly wishing he had attended all of the sessions—Brad stomped on his attacker's foot, turned and kneed him in the groin. Flowers yelped in pain and loosened his grip. Remembering the main lesson, Brad broke free and ran like a bat out of hell. The instructor would be proud.

Flowers fell to the ground, rolled and came up with the gun aimed at Brad's back. He was about to pull the trigger when a bullet tore through the front of the golf cart. Startled, Flowers shifted his attention away from his fleeing hostage.

Jim Krnich now stood a mere twenty feet away from the cart, smoking gun in his hand. "That was just a warning shot, Flowers. I'll put the next one between your eyes. Now drop the gun," Krnich demanded as he began to inch closer.

Flowers let go a low chuckle and then spit at the federal agent. He kept his gun aimed squarely at Krnich. "You're in charge, I assume," he said. He ripped off his fake moustache and discarded the coke bottle glasses. "I guess it was always going to come down to you and me wasn't it—especially after I killed your agent the other night—a regrettable accident, really. He was driving much too fast and that brake line just couldn't hold the load."

So he did tamper with Curlander's brakes.

Krnich's blood began to boil. He wanted to take this guy alive. He wanted to make this piece of trash pay for Curlander's death. Life in prison would be hell for this guy.

"Fuck you, Flowers. You don't deserve to comment on his death. He was a true American. You. . . you were a fake Special Ops soldier."

They knew about his military record too? What the fuck? These guys were good, Flowers thought.

Too bad they weren't good enough.

"I see you've done your homework. Well, what we have here, agent Krnich, is a Mexican stand-off. Who's going to blink first?" Flowers said, slowly backing away, being careful to avoid the gorse this time. He scanned the area with one roaming eye for possible exit scenarios while staying focused on Krnich with the other.

"Not me," Krnich said.

"I think I got the advantage, seeing as I'm Mexican," Flowers said with a nervous chuckle.

"I'm telling you, stop or I'll shoot," Krnich shouted.

"Then I'll shoot you and we'll both be dead. Just like two scorpions in a bottle."

Flowers continued to back away. He was suddenly struck in the leg by a very hard object. A bullet? Nope, no bang, no searing pain, no immediate blood. "What the fuck?" he mumbled as he watched a white golf ball come to rest on the ground beside him.

Krnich wasted no time. This was his opening. He sprinted forward, covering the remaining distance like a defensive back closing in on a receiver. And just like the defensive back making a tackle, he pounced on Flowers shoulder first and drove him to the ground. He tried to wrestle the gun from the killer's grip.

Initially, Krnich gained the upper hand, but then, in the blink of an eye, the much younger Flowers quickly reversed positions. He slammed an elbow into Krnich's face, disarmed the him and pointed his gun directly at the agent's forehead.

"Before I kill you, tell me, how did you find me? Was it one of the women? Did she recognize my face?"

Krnich laughed. "For such a smart guy, you really made a bonehead mistake."

"What mistake? I don't make mistakes," Flowers screamed.

"She didn't recognize your face, she recognized your tattoo, you idiot."

Shaking his head as if he didn't understand and then suddenly remembering the brief moment the tattoo had been exposed, Flowers said under his breath, "I should've killed the bitches when I was in Santa Barbara. I knew it!"

He raised the gun and took dead aim at Krnich. His finger tightened on the trigger. Krnich closed his eyes. This was it, this was the end of the road he thought. "Sorry Zach," he said to himself.

A loud shot rang out.

An eerie, cold smile came to the killer's lips.

74

ALMOST IMMEDIATELY, BLOOD BEGAN TO POUR FROM THE ASSASSIN'S LIPS. WITHOUT A WORD, FLOWERS COLLAPSED TO THE GROUND LANDING NEXT TO THE STARTLED KRNICH.

Opening his eyes and realizing he hadn't been the one shot, Krnich jumped to his feet, grabbed the bleeding man and applied pressure to Flower's wound.

"No you don't asshole," Krnich shouted. "Death is too good for you." He applied more pressure to the quarter-sized hole in the killer's chest.

Flowers stared at him, his eyes stale and cold.

"Why Flowers? Why kill innocent real estate agents you son-of-a-bitch? Who hired you?" Krnich asked, shaking the dying man.

What about Curlander? You piece of shit.

With his last dying breath, Flowers said, "Why he wanted them dead, I don't know. You will have to ask him. Why I killed them? For money, of course and...because I could." He coughed one last time, mumbled "I'm sorry mama." And then, with the pained expression of a jilted lover, he grabbed Krnich and said, "Tell the girl..."

He exhaled and then went still. Krnich shook Flowers and felt for a pulse. There was none.

Ted Flowers would not retire a wealthy man. He would not ride off into the sunset with the love of his life. All that was left for him was the same fate he had brought upon his victims: cold, violent death.

———•———

JIM KRNICH TURNED to thank either Simmons or Johnson—or whoever fired the shot—for saving his life. Neither agent was within twenty yards. Apparently, they had stopped advancing when Flowers obtained the upper hand. He looked at them as if to ask who shot Flowers. Both agents raised their hands and shrugged.

If neither agent had pulled the trigger, then who killed Flowers?

Krnich spun around, surveyed the golf course. Brad and Linden were standing to the side with Drivers in hand and goofy smiles on their faces. Neither held a gun.

He moved past them and continued his survey.

He stopped when his eye caught site of a large man standing on the cliff above the fairway several hundred yards away. The man was putting something that looked like a rifle back into a case.

It took Krnich a moment to put two and two together. Then it hit him. Dwayne! Falicello's Man Friday.

The two stared at each other for a long moment. Confused, Krnich didn't know whether to hug the guy or arrest him. Instinctively, he gave a slight wave. The man waved back and then saluted. He got into his car and drove off.

Coming to his senses—he was a federal law enforcement officer after all—Krnich quickly signaled for Simmons to go after the man.

"I don't know what make of car he's driving, but if it's who I think it is, he's about six foot, four, dark-complexioned and should be considered dangerous," Krnich told his agent.

Simmons raced off. Krnich took a deep breath, felt his body again for bullet holes. Finding none, he began to coordinate the scene.

———

"NICE SHOT PARDS," Brad said with a grin.

"I'll bet that ball hurt like hell."

"Probably, seeing as you swing that club a hundred and twenty miles an hour."

Linden nodded. "But dammit, I must be getting old. I meant to hit him in the chest. I guess I needed more loft," he said, staring at his seven-degree Driver.

Remembering Espinoza's joke from the other day, Brad patted Linden on the back and said, "Nope, buddy, you've got lots of fucking talent." He would explain the joke later.

As things settled down on the fairway, Starling approached them from behind. "Hey guys, there's still some light left. I bet, if we hustle, we can get three or four more holes in. I'm willing to go double or nothing—as long as I still get my breakfast ball."

Brad and John looked at each other, shook their heads and grinned. "Fucking golfers," they said in unison.

75

JIM KRNCIH EXPLAINED THE SEQUENCE OF EVENTS TO HIS TEAM AND THE GROUP FROM SANTA BARBARA AS THEY SAT AROUND THE OUTDOOR FIREPLACE A FEW HOURS LATER.
At least, as much as he had pieced together so far.

"We believe Flowers was hired by a retired gangster, Gino Falicello, to kill various real estate agents," he began, watching the look of disbelief on everyone's faces. "Flowers was to be paid handsomely for this job," he added as if he needed to provide motivation for the killer's actions.

"Why real estate agents?" Brad asked. He sipped a Jack Daniels while resting his feet on a nearby stool. The evening had turned cool and crisp, only a slight amount of fog had rolled in. The fire burned brightly and smelled wonderful.

"I'll get to that in a minute. Let me rehash what we know," Krnich said over his shoulder as he threw another log on the raging fire. "Flowers was discharged from the military a few years ago. Apparently, he took his skills private; worked for the highest bidder. Falicello must've found out about him from one of his mafia buddies. Anyway, the guy was good. Never left fingerprints, didn't repeat his method of killing, was very meticulous. Even Curlander's death, if you can believe the psycho, was an accident. He knew killing a federal officer would bring the heat down on him. He meant to incapacitate, not kill. The guy was so good, if Mel hadn't seen the tattoo, we probably wouldn't have caught him."

The group exchanged glances. Brad hugged his wife. "Good job, old lady," he joked.

She elbowed him in the ribs. "I've got woman's intuition and I've got good eyes, what can I say?"

"Not only would we not have caught him, we'd be dead," Stef said quietly, looking from Mel to Paula and then back again.

The group looked at each other and nodded their heads slowly. There really was nothing to say.

After a brief pause, Krnich continued. "The list Stack provided showed several agents who were scheduled to attend this conference. We decided to increase security, and still, the son-of-a-bitch might've succeeded if not for the Hawaiian theme party. Mel saw the tattoo because the guy was forced to wear shorts."

"And that woman spilled on his leg," Mel said.

Krnich shook his head slowly and smiled. "Sometimes, it's the damndest things."

Linden raised his glass in toast and said, "Here's to the damndest things."

Everyone, including the other guests sitting nearby, raised their glasses and said, "Here, here."

Looking a little uncomfortable with the inclusion of the outsiders, Krnich moved closer to the group and continued in a softer voice. "Our crime scene guys have confirmed that the thing I saw Flowers holding behind his back was a vile which contained a homemade poison. Flowers probably learned how to make it in the military. I talked to the local military commander. He won't confirm nor deny that Special Ops are trained in chemical combat."

"Of course not," Smith-Newhall said, rolling her eyes.

Linden stretched his long legs, threw an arm around Stef and pulled her tight. "Why didn't he stay in Santa Barbara and finish the job?"

Stef, Mel and Paula glared at him. "You would have preferred he attack us again?" Stef asked.

"No, I'm not saying that," Linden said. Backpedaling. "I'm just saying if it was me and I thought my cover had been blown, I would try to erase the witnesses before moving on."

"The guy was a master of disguise and very disciplined. I'm sure he felt he could travel around Santa Barbara incognito if he had to. I think he was planning on back-tracking to Montecito though," Krnich said. "But we can't know for sure. I'll bet he had no idea that so many of his targets would be here in Pebble Beach. We're pretty sure he came here exclusively for Ralph Willowby, but once he figured it out, he devised a plan to infiltrate the group and poison all of his targets."

"Like shooting ducks in a barrel," Linden said.

"Yep," Krnich agreed.

"So, the guy was cocky," Brad said. "I still don't see why he did this? What was there to gain from killing a bunch of harmless real estate agents?"

"You know, Brad," Krnich said, shaking his head and pursing his lips, "I have a theory, but the truth is, we may never know."

"Sounds like this mob guy, Falicello, will know. Are you going to arrest him?" Linden asked.

"I'm not sure. The thing I haven't told you is that I'm pretty sure it was his body guard, Dwayne, who shot and killed Flowers."

"And saved your life," Mel said.

"And saved my life."

"Wait a minute! Let me get this straight. The guy hires a trained killer at considerable expense, gives Raoul the assassin's name and then, before the killer has completed his task, has his right-hand man shoot him? That doesn't make any sense," Brad said.

"I know. I know," Krnich said shaking his head. "I have a theory, but I have no proof so it would not be wise to share it with you. Let me just say that there are now two things in this world I may never understand: The mind of an older gangster and, of course, the mind of a woman. When you guys figure either one of those out, let me know." He smiled for the first time, took a long swig of the ice cold beer he was holding and threw another log on the fire.

"Well, *I've* got two pieces of good news," Paula Smith-Newhall interjected. "Jim Stack has arranged for the Inn to extend our stay and comp our rooms and the bagpipe player is going to be okay. Apparently, the bullet was slowed down by one of his sheep bladders. He'll be sore, but he'll be back playing the pipes in a week or two."

"That is good news," Brad agreed.   "Stack is so slick, he's putting a positive spin on the whole thing. Without acknowledging who might've been targets, he just sent an email to all the 'superstars'." He grabbed Paula's smart phone and read the message: **"You should be proud to have been a target of this mass murderer. It proves you really are a 'superstar'."**

"Well, you know, it takes all types," Krnich said. And then in an act of friendship and relief, he raised his beer high in the air. "I'd like to raise my glass in a toast to all of you. Mel, your powers of observation saved the day. Brad, those self-defense classes are obviously working. John, your well-placed drive disabled and wounded our man. You are all 'superstars' in my book." They clinked glasses and took a sip.

Brad cleared his throat and raised his glass anew. "I have three toasts tomake."

Linden rolled up his napkin and threw it at Brad. "Make'em short. You tend to get long winded and I still haven't eaten dinner."

The group laughed. "Okay, boss. My first toast is to agent Krnich. Once again he has performed above and beyond the call of duty." They touched glasses.

"My second toast, surprisingly, is to Dwayne. I really don't care why he did it but the guy saved Jim's life and probably many other lives by taking Flowers down."

"To Dwayne," everyone but the federal agents said.

"And finally, I'd like us all to raise our glasses to a really good guy," Brad's voice choked. He cleared his throat. "To special agent Zach Curlander. May he rest in peace."

"Curlander," they all said in unison.

"Amen," Krnich said, raising his glass and his eyes to the sky. "I told you I'd get the asshole, buddy."

A waiter appeared holding a bottle of Dom Perignon in one hand, a note in the other. "Your champagne sir," the waiter said to Brad. "Would you like me to pour it now?"

Brad stared at the expensive bottle and then glanced at his friends. "Did any of you order this?" he asked. They all shook their heads.

"Maybe this will explain it," the waiter said, handing Brad the note.

Brad read it quickly and then his face broke into a big smile. "It's from Steve Zindo. He says he's sorry he missed all the fun; he's glad we're all alive and he asked me to ask Paula if she'll have dinner with him next week."

"Next week?" Paula said. "I'll have to get my hair done and my nails polished when I get back. I'm not sure I can do that by next week."

"Oh sure you can," Mel said, punching her friend lightly on the shoulder. "And if you can't, so what, no big deal. I bet Steve would still like to go out with you."

"You think so?"

"I know so. I've known him a long time and I can tell he's interested in you."

Paula smiled. "Well, he does have a nice house... and he is a multi-millionaire." She asked Brad to call Zindo and confirm her acceptance.

"Good, all settled then. Please pour the champagne," Brad told the waiter. "I think we'll need another bottle, put it on my tab."

To a person, the group turned and stared at Brad. He stared back. "What? I know I've been bitching about money this whole trip, but I got a feeling that John and I are going to win enough to cover several bottles of bubbly. Call it Men's intuition," he said, wrapping his arm around Mel's shoulder.

76

THE NEXT DAY, KRNICH SAID HIS GOOD-BYES, TOLD BRAD HE'D STOP BY SANTA BARBARA SOON AND DEPARTED PEBBLE BEACH.

Brad, Linden, Stef, Paula and Mel enjoyed a quiet breakfast and then the girls went to the Jim Stack conference. Brad and Linden prepared to tee it up against some local members at Cypress. Now that the room was paid for and all the meals were on the house, Brad felt confident and relaxed. He suggested they play for higher stake wagers.

"They threw out a two hundred dollar Nassau from the get-go," Linden said.

"I'm good with that. Let them win a few holes so they'll press us and then we can really take it to 'em."

"I like your attitude, pards."

"Hey, John, not to mix business with pleasure, but I made an appointment with Nike for next week. You still up for talking to them?"

"You bet I am," Linden said. "You probably didn't notice, but the ball I hit at Flowers was a Nike One. If I can hit the ball that straight, I don't care how it feels when I chip and putt."

Relieved, Brad said, "Right on. Let's go win a few bucks."

THEY DROVE TWENTY minutes to the course, announced themselves to the front gate and proceeded to the club house.

Before they parked, Linden looked at Brad, his demeanor suddenly very serious. "Are you sure my 'special problem' with Mary is all taken care of?" he asked, making quote marks with his fingers.

Brad nodded. "They're sending the contract over next week. I explained what happened up here to her attorney. He was sympathetic. He swears the terms will be as we discussed."

"Okay, I feel better about it. I wonder what the kid will look like."

"Probably goofy like you."

"No, really. I wonder if I'm doing the right thing. Maybe I should break it off with Stef and go down to Orlando and help raise the child?"

"She doesn't want you, John. She wants the money. Her lawyer told me she has a very steady boyfriend. A tennis player named Sven."

"Tennis player! You know Brad, in this fucked up world, there's just no accounting for taste."

"None," Brad agreed.

"But what about the other thing? You know... Stef? Should I tell her?"

"Eventually, I think you should. Right now, though, I need to make things right with her at the office. You need to practice for the upcoming tournament. We need to sign with Nike and..." Brad paused, smiled and continued, "Mel needs to learn how to cook. Right this minute, however, we need to go kick some Cypress butt."

And they did, winning over fifteen hundred dollars a piece by the time all the presses, sandies, barkies and snakes were added up.

77

SPECIAL AGENT KRNICH DID NOT GO STRAIGHT BACK TO LOS ANGELES.

It was a nice day for a drive. Feeling the need for some form of closure, Krnich put the car in cruise control, set the GPS for Vegas and drove east across the great state of California.

Arriving in Las Vegas shortly after three p.m., Krnich pulled to the side of the road and made the call he knew he had to make.

"Mr. Falicello's residence," the voice on the other end answered.

"Agent Jim Krnich, FBI special task force, calling for Mr. Falicello," Krnich barked into the phone.

"Mr. Falicello is taking a nap and cannot be disturbed," the guard said.

"Get me Dwayne, then."

The call was put on hold and a minute later, the deep, masculine voice of Falicello's right-hand man came on the line.

"Yes, agent Krnich, what can I do for you?"

"I want to see 'the Fridge', Dwayne."

"I believe your business with Mr. Falicello has been concluded—hopefully, satisfactorily on both sides."

"Well, that's the thing. I still have a few questions. I really need to see him. I'm not leaving until I speak to him. I would rather keep it off the record."

Silence.

"Dwayne. You still there?"

"Agent Krnich, Mr. Falicello is an old man. He needs his rest. But more than that, he needs his privacy. I can't allow the FBI to storm in here and disturb him. If you have proof of wrong-doing, then I suggest you get a warrant and contact Mr. Falicello's attorney."

"Dwayne," Krnich said as if the bodyguard were his best friend, "you and I both know I don't have any concrete evidence. Hell, I can't even swear it was you on the knoll. I just want to talk to him—clear a few things up."

"Off the record?"

"Off the record."

"Complete immunity for Mr. Falicello?"

"Complete."

"You'll sign a waiver to this affect?"

He knew he shouldn't but he also knew he'd never stand a chance in court. The pieces didn't tie together. The facts didn't add up. He had a theory. That's all it was as far as the law was concerned—just a theory and nothing more. "I'll sign a waiver and give you my blood oath."

Dwayne paused to consider the answer. "I will talk to Mr. Falicello when he wakes up. Can I call you at this number?"

"Yes, any time. I'll be staying at the Stardust."

"Oh, you're in town already?" Dwayne said with a deep chuckle. "You're a confident man, agent Krnich."

"I was hoping."

"Don't stay at the Stardust. You can do much better than that. Mr. Falicello maintains several rooms at the Bellaqua for his out of town guests. Please feel free to check-in and wait for my call."

Krnich processed the offer. "I can't stay there on his dime. How would it look?"

"The meeting is off the record, is it not?"

"Yes, but..."

"Well, then, you were never here. It should not be an issue. Mr. Falicello would reprimand me if I did not make you more comfortable. Please do not insult him or me."

Krnich paused, but only for a second. "Okay. Yes. Thank you. I will check in at the Bellaqua and will wait for your call."

"Very well. Until later, then," Dwayne said.

Before hanging up, Krnich said quickly and sincerely, "And, Dwayne. I know you did it. You're good; my man Simmons couldn't find you." He paused and then added, "Thanks...I think."

Dwayne said nothing.

———•———

THE CALL CAME a few long minutes later.

"Mr. Falicello will see you tonight at eight p.m.," Dwayne said. "Please dress for a formal dinner."

Formal dinner? Krnich didn't have any clothes for a formal dinner. All he had was his traveling bag and one rumpled brown suit. "Dwayne, I didn't come prepared for a formal dinner."

"Not to worry. Go down to the men's shop on the first floor and buy the necessary clothes. Put them on Mr. Falicello's account."

"No offense, but I'm not an Armani type of guy."

Dwayne sighed. "Krnich just do as I say. I know that Armani is higher than your pay grade but there are no Men's Warehouses or J.C. Penney's near you. Now, please indulge Mr. Falicello. We will see you at eight p.m. Please be prompt."

Krnich thought he got it. If Falicello could pay for his room, buy him a new suit, and wine and dine him then he could use these 'gifts' to bribe the agent somewhere down the line. What the hell. He had already disregarded policy on at least five occasions during this case—what was one more? He really didn't intend to prosecute Falicello. Why not give the old man his minor victory? But again, 'the Fridge' didn't get his nickname by letting people butt into his business. He was old, but he was—and probably always would be—dangerous.

And besides, Krnich knew he personally could not be bribed.

He put the car in gear and headed towards the Bellaqua. A half hour later he settled into his room on the thirtieth floor. He had an unobstructed view of the lake below and the strip to the side. "The guy doesn't fuck around," Krnich mumbled as he collected his wallet and keys from the nightstand and headed down to get a new suit—a suit he'd never be able to show to another living person.

And if things went well, it wouldn't turn into his burial outfit. If they went bad, at least he'd go out in style.

———

THE DRIVE TO the mansion from the hotel took only forty five minutes this time. Krnich was fifteen minutes early. As he pulled through the front gate, the guards gave him a slight wave.

Old friends?

Dwayne met his car at the front of the house and escorted him into the foyer.

"The suit looks good. It fits you like a glove," Dwayne said.

"Remarkable they could alter it so quickly," Krnich said tugging at the lapels, looking uneasy. "You really think it looks okay?"

"Tonight, you look like a million bucks. Mr. Falicello is finishing a phone call. He will be with you shortly. What can I get you to drink?"

"I'm okay."

"Agent Krnich, this is a formal dinner. You must have a cocktail, champagne or wine. No beer. Now what will it be?"

"Geez, Dwayne. I didn't realize I was going to cotillion tonight. If I must, I'll take a Jack Daniels on the rocks."

Brad would appreciate his selection, Krnich thought.

"Very good choice. I'll be right back. Make yourself comfortable."

And with that the large man disappeared into one of the many nooks and crannies of the mansion. Five minutes later, he reappeared with a silver serving tray. A liter bottle of Jack Daniels and a glass full of ice sat comfortably upon the tray.

A whole bottle?

Hope I don't need it.

Then again, if his theory was correct...

78

"AGENT KRNICH, WHAT A PLEASANT SURPRISE, I DIDN'T THINK I WOULD SEE YOU AGAIN—AT LEAST, NOT SOCIALLY. WELCOME TO MY HOME ONCE AGAIN," FALICELLO SAID WITH ARMS OPEN WIDE AS HE STRODE INTO THE ROOM.

The former mobster was impeccably dressed. Wearing a dark brown suit, blue silk shirt, perfectly shined Ferragamos, and bright red tie, his look screamed power and money. Krnich suddenly felt very meek in his own thousand dollar ensemble.

"The cook has made a wonderful Oso Bucco for us. And I have chosen the perfect Brunello wine. It should be a fabulous dinner," Falicello assured him.

The guy really did know how to eat, dress and entertain. Seeing these guys later in life could be a real head fake, Krnich thought. He forced himself to remember that his host had been a notorious killer in a younger life.

Quite possibly, still was.

"Thank you for seeing me, Gino. I'm sorry to impose. I just have a few questions and then my business with you will be done."

The old man looked him in the eye, raised an eyebrow in a knowing gesture and smiled. "We will have time to talk business. Please, enjoy your cocktail. Tell me how you are? I understand you suffered a harrowing experience."

Playing along with the subtle reference, Krnich said, "Yes. I was lucky. The gentleman you so kindly identified for us was shot before he could blow my head off."

The 'Fridge' smiled. "That is very fortunate indeed. So, Mr. Flowers is dead?"

You know he's dead.

What game are you playing?

Krnich took a sip of his drink and said, "Yes and unfortunately, he died before he could confess all his sins."

"I'm sure he had many."

"Probably, but the only sin I'm concerned with is the recent murders. I asked him why he did it. He said, and I quote, 'You'll have to ask *him*'." Krnich took another sip of his drink and stared at the old man over the brim of his cocktail glass.

There was no reaction. Once again, no 'tell'.

A moment later, Falicello asked, "So, you have come to me to find out who the man Flowers referenced is?"

"Perhaps. But more importantly, I want to know why," Krnich said. "Why the murders of seven successful real estate agents? Why the death of my assistant, Zach Curlander? Why the near death of many more people? To what end?"

Falicello put his drink down, rubbed his chin and looked sympathetically at his guest. "I am truly sorry about your friend. I have lost many in my time. They always hurt." He paused, as if searching for his next words. "Dwayne has assured me our meeting is completely off the books. Yes?"

"Yes. Nobody knows about it and I will not, under any circumstances, acknowledge it."

"You are a smart man, agent Krnich. In my prime, I could've used a man like you. Now, I am an old man and all I can do is admire your sensibilities."

"Thank you... I think."

"Let me tell you a story I heard recently from a friend," Falicello began.

"The same *friend* who knew about Flowers?" Krnich asked.

"Yes, as a matter of fact, the very same. This friend of mine has certain very delicate business needs. From time to time, he finds it necessary to engage the services of a man like Flowers."

"I thought you told Espinoza that your *friend* was a former Special Ops guy and he was concerned about Flowers going rogue," Krnich said.

"Ah, yes. You must forgive an old man for taking poetic license. At the time I spoke to Sergeant Espinoza, I wished to conceal the nature of my friend's interest in Mr. Flowers. Now, you and I—with our understanding—can speak more freely. Yes?"

"We can."

"As I was saying, my friend has the need for a man like Flowers from time to time. There are many enemies in his world, agent Krnich. Jealousy and greed surround him. You understand this, yes?"

"Wrath, Greed, Sloth, Pride, Lust, Envy, and Gluttony. The seven deadly sins. Yes, Gino, I understand they exist in the human experience."

"You know your bible. That is good, agent Krnich. I am impressed." Falicello paused, took another sip of scotch and then continued. "My friend tells me that he hired Mr. Flowers to transact some minor business. My friend had been swindled out of several million dollars—a crime laden with disrespect. Flowers performed admirably. My friend had instructed Mr. Flowers to expect other business orders in the future. I'm sure Flowers was excited by the prospect. In the meantime, something very regretful occurred."

Here it comes.

Easy; wait for it. Hold your enthusiasm.

Let the old man tell his story.

79

OUTSIDE, A SUBTLE YET STEADY WIND BLEW THROUGH THE SURROUNDING DESERT. FALICELLO SNAPPED HIS FINGERS TWICE. DWAYNE APPEARED. "PLEASE SHUT THE BALCONY DOOR, DWAYNE," HE TOLD HIS SERVANT.

Dwayne said nothing, turned on his heels did as his master asked.

"A fine servant," Falicello said.

Krnich nodded. Said nothing.

"Now where were we?" Falicello said. "Ah, yes, I remember. It seems Mr. Flowers received orders to carry out several more business transactions."

"More business?"

"Yes, apparently he believed the orders had come from my friend. You see, agent Krnich, my friend has a wonderful family. His son is a handsome boy—quite precocious, a graduate of a fine college who is trying to make his way in the world. This economy is so bad. Young people; they don't have many opportunities. Wouldn't you agree?"

"That's what I read in the papers."

"Quite. But what is your actual experience?"

"I don't know to tell you the truth. I have worked for the federal government my entire adult life. First it was the Secret Service and now, the FBI. My job has been secure for many years. I don't have kids."

"I'm sure you would have been a wonderful father."

Krnich said nothing.

"You would agree, however, that there are not many opportunities for the young. Yes?"

"Again, I defer to the media. This is a fucked-up economy and I think anyone—young or old—looking for a job is shit out of luck." The Jack Daniels was kicking in. His tongue was loosening. He didn't care.

At this stage, he just wanted answers.

Falicello smiled. He seemed to recognize the agent's anguish over Curlander's death. He also seemed to perceive his frustrations. "Well, to make a long story short, it seems that my friend's son decided to hire Mr. Flowers independently. Somehow he knew about Flowers and he provided him with the names of several potential future competitors. This was all done anonymously you understand, but like I said before, Mr. Flowers had reason to believe the instructions were coming from my friend." Again Falicello winked as if what he was saying was now a shared secret.

Leaning forward and beckoning Krnich to do likewise, Falicello continued in a much quieter voice. "Apparently, the boy decided that he already knew enough about the business and wished to succeed quickly. He contacted Flowers and instructed him to eliminate these competitors so that he could be assured of success in his new profession. It is very sad and very regrettable." The 'Fridge's' face actually drooped and his overall body language was that of true sorrow.

"What profession is the boy going into Gino?" Krnich asked as Dwayne poured him another Jack.

"Why, I believe it is the sale of real estate," the old man answered coyly.

"So you're telling me that your friend's son is going into real estate sales along the coast of California and, because that business is so competitive, he decided to hire Flowers to kill his future competition?"

"Yes, agent Krnich, that is what happened. My friend's son still doesn't know what city he will end up in, so. . ." He spread his arms wide.

"So he had Flowers kill in various cities," Krnich said.

Again, the old man spread his arms and nodded. "May I continue?"

"Sure what the fuck," Krnich said. He gulped the remainder of his Jack.

Falicello didn't look the least bit insulted. He continued. "You see, agent Krnich, Mr. Flowers received his instructions anonymously via text messaging. My friend doesn't even know how to text. The son jumped in—and quite ingeniously I might add—and provided Mr. Flowers with instructions which he obviously thought were coming from my friend."

"And these instructions were to kill all of these agents?"

"Apparently, yes."

"This is amazing, Gino," Krnich said, fighting the urge to express righteous indignation. "Your friend's '*son*' brought forward all of this pain –all of this suffering—for very minor economic advancement?"

Falicello sighed. "Yes. It is a pity. The boy doesn't know it, but he is already wealthy beyond his wildest dreams, yet he feels the need to gain this advantage in his chosen profession. I believe he thought his success would make his father proud."

"Wow!" Krnich shook his head. "That's it? Curlander dies. Seven real estate agents die. Families are devastated. For what, a kid who wants to be the next 'superstar' of the real estate business?"

"You can doubt it. You can dismiss it. But that is what I have been led to believe."

Krnich stared at the priceless paintings hanging on the wall. His eyes moved to the statues and the various busts displayed prominently throughout the house. This is monetary wealth. This isn't ethical wealth. This is what cheating, conniving, and, yes, killing might get you, he thought.

He shook his head for about the hundredth time since Falicello began telling his story. Hell, they could have it. He couldn't wait to escape this house with its phony graciousness; its over the top ostentatiousness and its murderous secrets. He'd burn his Armani outfit as soon as left the property. Better yet, maybe he'd give it to a panhandler on the Strip.

He recovered and focused on the conversation. "So, your friend, what does he do now? Is he proud?"

"He loves his son. What would you do agent Krnich?"

"I don't know, Gino." The booze was obviously continuing to loosen his tongue. "If I found out, I would put a stop to it. Immediately." He pounded the table in front of him with the palm of his hand. "And I'd make it right," he added a bit more calmly.

"Exactly," Falicello said with a smile, seemingly hoping his response said it all. He took an envelope from his breast pocket and handed it to Krnich.

"What's this?"

"My friend asked me to send this to the family of your fallen agent," Falicello said. "Dwayne was going to mail it to you but since you're here..."

Somewhat reluctantly, Krnich reached for the envelope. His initial thought was to throw the damn thing back into the old man's face. But then, as it often does, reason took over. Zach's fiancée and unborn baby needed the money. Krnich could always say it was a special insurance policy pay-out. "I don't like it, but I'll make sure his family gets it."

"Good. Let's have dinner, shall we?"

SLIGHTLY INEBRIATED, KRNICH rose and followed Falicello into the dining room. He almost stumbled into a marble bust.

"Augustus Caesar," Falicello said, grabbing him by the arm to steady him. "Very expensive. We wouldn't want to smash that beauty."

"Sorry about that."

They headed into the dining room where a beautiful table had been laid out, full of breads, cheeses, wines and salads.

Three places had been set at the table.

Was Dwayne going to join them? Krnich wondered.

A moment later, a figure emerged from the patio. Several pounds lighter and several degrees paler than the last time Krnich had seen her, Mercedes Falicello approached. She extended her hand.

"Agent Krnich, what a pleasure to see you again. Grandfather didn't tell me we were having company tonight. I would've worn something more appropriate," she said waving her hand, palm up at what Krnich considered one of the most beautiful dresses he had ever seen. Her handshake was not as firm as the last time and he detected a subtle quiver in her fingers.

"I surprised him," Krnich said. "I get the feeling he's had many surprises recently."

"Yes, even though he's retired, life continues to throw him curves, I'm sorry to say," she said. She waited a beat, looked chagrin and then added, "To what do we owe the honor of your visit?"

"Just trying to close a case. Your grandfather has been very helpful. I have an agent who died recently. His pregnant fiancée would like to know why? I have some friends who were almost killed. They would like to know what they did to deserve such a fate. And," he added almost as an afterthought, "there are several people dead in California whose families and friends would like some answers."

"And has he been able to answer your questions?"

"I believe so, Mercedes."

"Do you feel relieved?"

"More than anything else, I feel pity for your grandfather's *'friend'*. And I feel sorrow for my friends and their families."

She accepted his answer with a courteous smile and asked the gentlemen to be seated. The formal dinner was served. In a strange way, Krnich tried to block-out the negative thoughts he had formed. After all, Curlander was dead. He wasn't coming back. Smith-Newhall, Mel and Stef were still alive. Shouldn't he just stack the positives and enjoy the fine meal?

Fuck no!

I'm not going to allow that idiot, Stack, to influence me.

His mind still raced as he desperately tried to tie all the ends together. He struggled to follow the table's conversation. He had given his word that this meeting was unofficial, however, based on what the 'Fridge' had told him, shouldn't he be arresting somebody?

Every fiber in his law-enforcement body said yes. But, sadly, he had no evidence—just the twisted story of an old man. Besides, he had given his word that the meeting was off the record. The evidence would be considered here say. It would never hold up.

And, of course, there was Dwayne.

The guy had saved his life but still it didn't sit well with Krnich.

As the three began coffee and dessert, Krnich looked at Mercedes and said, "Mercedes, I remember we discussed this before, but where did you go to college?"

"The University of California, Santa Barbara."

"That's right. It's a beautiful area isn't it?" Krnich had decided to play Falicello's game: false humility, false interest and double-entendres. No need to confront her directly.

"I love it there. I want to make it my home. And grandfather likes it too, don't you papa?" Mercedes said.

Falicello grunted an acknowledgment as he took another bite of white cake. The 'Fridge' tilted his head slightly and stared at Krnich as if to say, "Let it go."

Maybe it was the alcohol. Maybe it was his sense of duty. Krnich wasn't sure. But he wasn't going to let it go without getting someone to verbalize the final elements of this strange event.

"What line of work did you say you are you going into?"

Mercedes produced a fake, half-smile. "I didn't say, but I'm leaning towards real estate sales."

"Do you have any contacts to help you get started?"

"I had one. I interned for her when I was in school. Turns out she's a real bitch."

"How so?"

Mercedes actually smiled at this question. "Well, I'll tell you. She stole a marketing idea I came up with and never gave me credit."

That was it? That was the extent of the crime Paula Smith-Newhall had committed: stole an idea. What bullshit, Krnich thought.

The girl seemed to read the agent's mind. "There were other things too," she said. "Anyway, I don't think she'll help me. I'm just going to have to roll up my sleeves and earn the business the old fashioned way." She took a bite of her cake and chased it with a sip of coffee.

"Have you decided what type of real estate you're going to sell: commercial, residential or apartment buildings?"

Again, Falicello stared daggers at him. Krnich could feel the old man's rage at this line of inquiry. He'd probably be dead by now if the 'Fridge' were forty years younger, Krnich thought.

"Oh, I'm going to specialize in high-end sales. Major estates along the coast," she said pleasantly.

"I'm sure you'll be a 'superstar' in no time."

"I would assume so. I've already put extensive time into preparations." She straightened and stared at him coldly.

"Are you going to focus on Santa Barbara?" Krnich asked.

Mercedes gave him a tight, little smile. "There and San Diego and Los Angeles and, maybe, San Francisco. All those areas have high-end homes you know."

Suddenly, it all made sense. It was as if a light had gone off in his head. His original theory was that Gino Falicello had killed for his granddaughter, but now the reality of the situation hit him like a cold brick: the girl had orchestrated the hits. Somehow, she had convinced Flowers to do her dirty work.

When had Falicello figured it out? Was it near the end of their first meeting? Yes, it had to be. Krnich closed his eyes momentarily and remembered how Falicello's face had changed when he was told the murderer was a professional hit man.

And Flowers had said before he died, "Tell the girl. . ." Krnich had assumed it was gibberish at the time, but now it made sense. He had meant Mercedes. She had used him and Flowers had never known it.

Krnich looked at Gino 'the Fridge' Falicello. The old man shrugged, raised his cup of coffee to his lips and took a sip. He wasn't going to kill Krnich today. Instead, he spread his hands, palms facing skyward. "Kids, eh?" was all he said.

Krnich shook his head, leaned over towards the old man and said quietly the words he knew would injure the mobster the most, "I guess the acorn doesn't fall far from the tree, does it Gino?"

Falicello raised a bushy eyebrow. "Sadly, my friend, often, despite the best efforts of those who can influence the young, it is true."

The three of them ate the rest of their dessert in silence. Immediately upon finishing his last bite of cake, Krnich was startled to feel a tap on his shoulder.

"I would be happy to show you out, agent Krnich," Dwayne's deep voice cut through the silence.

"That's not necessary, Dwayne, I know the way." Krnich rose, placed his napkin on the table and said to neither Falicello nor Mercedes in particular,

"Goodnight and thank you for such an enlightening evening."

His host said nothing.

"I insist," Dwayne said, grabbing him gently by the arm.

AS HE GOT into his car, Krnich grudgingly thanked Dwayne for saving his life. "But I'm telling you right now, if I can prove it was you, I will prosecute."

The big man said nothing.

"What will happen now?" Krnich asked. "According to Gino, his 'friend' possibly had more assignments for a man like Flowers in the future."

"There are many mysteries in this world, agent Krnich. I assume business will proceed as usual." He paused and added, "By the way, you *are* welcome. Please travel safe. I trust you will not be returning."

"Nope, my job is done. I know what happened here. No need to harass the 'Fridge' any further. I think he's suffering enough from her actions," Krnich said.

"Yes, agent Krnich, I agree. It will be his cross to bear. He really tried hard to shield her from his business life you know."

"Yeah, well, sins of the fathers, and all that," Krnich said. He turned on the radio, put the car in gear and drove off.

STANDING IN THE driveway, watching Krnich drive away, Dwayne nodded his head slowly and thought about his life so far serving the needs of Gino Falicello, the man who was his biological father—the result of a long term relationship with Dwayne's mother—and said quietly as he turned to re-enter the mansion, "Yes, agent Krnich, sins of the fathers, indeed."   He chuckled softly, "If you only knew my friend, if you only knew."

80

Santa Barbara

A WEEK LATER, Brad, Linden, Espinoza and Scott stood on the first tee of the local muni, preparing to hit their first shots of the day.

The match was to be a five dollar Nassau. The Stephens Boys versus the 'ringers'. Automatic presses when two down, sandies, greenies, barkies, and snakes were added for one dollar each. After much discussion, Linden agreed to play to a plus six and the match was ready to commence.

Things had been hectic since returning to Santa Barbara. Brad had contracts to sign with Nike; Linden had to transfer funds to what they were now calling the 'special' (Mary) account; Espinoza had been required to file extensive paperwork regarding his involvement in discovering the killer; and Scott had been busy perfecting his chili recipe.

416

This morning's golf outing was the first chance they all had to chat face to face.

"You really are like the Lone Ranger," Espinoza said to Brad as they walked down the first fairway.

Brad knew what his friend meant. There had been a lot of drama circling the Stephens family lately. "Hey, unlike the Lone Ranger, I don't go courting trouble, it just seems to find me," Brad told Espinoza.

"Well whatever. It's found you a lot lately and you're lucky to be alive. My advice is to not make a habit out of it."

"Good advice. I'll try to keep it in mind. And you know Raoul I'm really not like the Lone Ranger. You want to know why?"

"Okay, I'll bite. Why?"

"Because the Lone Ranger always traveled with his trusted companion, Tonto, and, you, Tonto, were not there when that bastard tried to kill me. Ergo: No Lone Ranger."

"*Si, Kimo Sabe*. You make a good point. I stand corrected. I'll change my analogy to a cat with nine lives. You've already used up two or three. Again, don't make a habit of it."

THE ROUND PROGRESSED nicely until the group reached the thirteenth hole—a long par three that always caused delays. True to form, there were two groups waiting on the tee box. It would be at least twenty minutes before Brad's group could play the hole.

"Shit, Brad," Linden began. "I told you we should play the country club. But, nooooo, you had to insist on the public course. Now see what you got us into."

"I know, I know. I always make bad decisions. Just ask Mel but let me remind you, Mr.'Let's Hurry Up', Scott and I are now three up on the match, one up on the press, and one up on the back nine. Seems to me that you and your partner might want to use this break to regroup."

"I'd rather use it to discuss the call you got from Krnich this morning," Linden said.

"How'd you know about the call?" Brad inquired, and then answered his own question. "Stef took the call and then overheard me talking to him, didn't she?"

Linden shrugged.

"So, what did our favorite federal agent want?" Linden asked.

Brad paused for a moment, sorted out his thoughts—he hadn't told Scott or Blake about how close he had come to death—and so he responded cautiously. "Agent Krnich called to thank us again for helping catch the killer. He told me that he went out to Las Vegas and confronted the mafia guy who probably hired Flowers."

"Gino the 'Fridge' Falicello," Espinosa quickly added. "I met him. He's polite and all, but you definitely do *not* want to cross the guy. He's got a compound in Vegas that would make Oprah green with envy."

"Let the man finish his story, Raoul," Linden implored.

Brad watched his two friends quarrel like an old, married couple, grinned and continued. "Falicello refused to admit he had anything to do with the killings. Instead he used round about, mafia-speak, to confess that his granddaughter, Mercedes, had commissioned the hits."

"Why?" both Linden and Espinoza asked at the same time. Scott remained quiet during the presentation.

"This is where it gets really, really bizarre. She is going to go into real estate sales in California. Not sure where—maybe Santa Barbara; maybe L.A.; maybe San Diego. Apparently, she decided to hire Flowers to kill off some of the competition in the markets she aspires to sell high-end real estate in."

"No shit!" Scott finally spoke up. "How old is this chick?"

"Your age."

"And she hired a hit man to kill the competition? That's cold."

"And stupid," Espinoza said. "How dumb does she think we are? Eventually, we would've connected Flowers with Falicello and her plan would've been uncovered."

"Would it, Raoul?" Brad asked. "If Mel hadn't noticed the tattoo on the guy's leg when he fell from the ladder, I think he would've gotten away with it. According to Krnich, the guy was good."

Scott stopped taking his practice swing and looked at his dad. "Were you and mom in jeopardy?"

Linden and Brad exchanged knowing glances. John grabbed Scott by the shoulder and took a few steps away from the tee box. "You know how your dad likes to exaggerate. When he's got a headache, he tells everyone he survived a brain tumor."

Scott nodded in agreement and smiled.

"Same thing. Your 'pops' was there, but never in any real danger. He just likes to think he was." Linden winked at Brad. "And your mom was always protected."

Linden's answer didn't seem to satisfy Scott, but before he could follow up, and before anyone could say anything about the Jose Gonzales affair, Brad said, "Okay, enough of this bullshit. The green is clear. Do you losers want to press?"

LINDEN AND ESPINOZA did press and then proceeded to win the back nine and the entire match.

"Fucking pro!" was all Brad could say as he paid out the winnings to Linden.

"Yeah, that's right, the 'fucking pro' who's now sponsored by Nike!" Linden added.

"That's true. I guess I owe you for finally talking to the biggest company in the world and graciously accepting their multi-million dollar sponsorship."

"Damn right. I still don't like to putt their balls, but my 'claw' grip is so good, I could hit a rock and it would go in. When's my first commercial?"

"Right after the next major tournament and don't screw it up. It means big bucks to me," Brad said, happy that Linden had finally signed the contract and had, just that day, received his first advance endorsement fee. It wasn't a fortune, but Brad's ten percent would pay the bills for another few months and would give him some breathing space to manage both his mortgage business and Linden's golfing career.

The group moved into the nineteenth hole and ordered a round of drinks. As he finished his first beer of the evening, Linden turned to Brad and asked him about his working relationship with Stef.

"We're good," Brad replied. "She apologized. I apologized. We hugged. We compromised."

"Oh, yeah? What's the compromise?" Linden asked.

"She won't dote on you so much and I'll work a little harder on the paperwork details. And, Blake will come in to work three days a week."

"Blake!" Scott said, almost spitting out his beer. "He doesn't know shit about your business. He's never worked in that environment."

"Stef says she can train him and, if he's like his younger brother, he will be a quick learner. I'm confident it'll work out."

"What about Mel," Espinoza chimed in. "Is she doing okay?"

"Mel's a trooper. She's already looking forward to that cooking class I promised her and she's pushing Scott for another chance in the food wagon."

"I'm going to give her another chance. But, dammit, pops, you've got to tell her to confine her cooking to the salads."

"You tell her. I'm not her boss."

The group shared a good laugh and prepared to depart the bar. Scott pulled his father aside. "Pops. Man to man. Did that guy almost kill you?"

"Let me put it this way, son. He was a very disturbed person. He had been trained as a Special Ops soldier. Those guys don't fool around. I'm sure the military screens these guys as well as they can, but if a bad seed gets through, watch out." Brad put his arm over Scott's shoulder, walked towards the exit with him.

"And?"

"This guy, Flowers, was trained to kill in a hundred different ways. Do you see what I'm saying, Scott?" Brad asked.

Scott shook his head. "No, I don't get your point."

"The point is we were all at risk. If he wanted to, Flowers could've killed any of us at any time."

"You're avoiding the question," Scott prodded.

"Okay. The answer is, yes, the son-of-a-bitch, almost killed me. . .and Krnich. . .and the bagpipe player. But he didn't and life goes on."

"All for the sake of some rich-ass, spoiled, mafia daughter," Scott said shaking his head.

"Granddaughter," Brad corrected.

"Whatever."

"You know, son. If there's one thing I've learned the past few years it's this: The U.S. economy is one stubborn bastard. Life will never again be what my generation thought it would be. And this little episode just reinforces it."

"How so, Pops?"

"Well, the wealthy have issues too. Just because they appear to be skating by, doesn't mean that life is easy for them. Those who've been hurt by this recession or those who want a job tend to blame the wealthy for creating this mess. And, maybe they're right. I don't know."

Brad paused.

He scratched his chin and continued. "But I also know that those who want to get ahead immediately without working their way up the totem pole—whether born of wealth, or modest means—are cheating. This country was founded on hard work and a conviction to get ahead. For a few years there in the early two thousands', it appeared that every Indian could become a chief without working too hard. Well, the past few years have debunked that myth!"

"You really think so? Isn't it human nature to try and take the short cut?" Scott said.

"Those, like Mercedes, who try to circumvent the process, deserve to fail. And, in her case, she deserves to go to jail. But, sadly, she won't. All I can say is keep doing what you're doing. If your food service is good and your prices fair, you will succeed. Americans—especially Santa Barbarans—always reward quality."

Scott stared at his father for several moments. Finally, he hugged him and said, "I'm sorry we lost to those guys today, but I'm sure glad you're still here to play golf with."

"We'll get 'em next time, buddy," Brad said with a smile. "Just remember, payback is a bitch."

Brad slapped his son on the back as the two got into his car. "Come on, let's go home and see what your mom's made for dinner."

Scott just rolled his eyes.

Enjoy an excerpt from the next Brad Stephens' Novel:

<u>SUBPRIME INDISCRETIONS</u>

Hole #3

Available, Summer of 2014

PROLOGUE

A SLIGHT SLIVER OF LIGHT SHONE THROUGH THE BOTTOM OF THE CLOSED DOOR.
Dazed and groggy from whatever drug he had ingested, Brad Stephens tried to stand up only to find his ankles were wrapped by duct tape. He reached down to loosen the tape but discovered both of his wrists were bound together in a similar fashion. He felt confined, as if stuffed inside a closet.

How long had he been unconscious? Where, exactly, was he? Who had bound his feet and hands?

Shaking the cobwebs from his head and adjusting his eyes to the minimal light, he looked around and confirmed that he was, indeed, sitting inside a closet. Clothes hung casually above him and his right hip sat squarely on something hard and angular. From the feel of the long, pointed, objects, he deduced it was either a women's high heel shoe or a stick of some kind. He suddenly realized that his lips were covered with tape as well. Thankfully, whoever placed the tape over his mouth had avoided his facial hair. There was no pulling on his beard.

He heard voices—no not 'voices', just one voice—outside the door. It was a female speaking into a phone.

"When will you be here?" he heard her say.

Brad couldn't hear the response on the other end of the line, but based on the girl's next statement, "Hurry Up. They're unconscious. Let's just get this done," he guessed that the person on the other end was running late and that the person's presence was needed to complete whatever they had in store for him. But she had said 'they're' unconscious. Not 'he's' unconscious. Who else was in the closet with him?

He rocked from side to side trying to dislodge the thing poking him in the hip. If he was lucky, the motion might loosen his bonds. The tape held firm but he got away from the sharp object. As his body came to rest in its new position, he felt something solid pressing against his left shoulder.

He turned his head as far to left as he could and squinted. Was that another body? Yes it was. And from the slight scent of perfume and the overall shape of the form, it was obviously a female body. Next question: dead or alive?

Gotta check before I do anything else, he thought.

He rolled over the top of the woman and brought his taped hands forward. Stretching his arms as far as he could, he reached for her left wrist. He felt a pulse. She was alive. He breathed a sigh of relief.

Now, how about *his* immediate problem?

Before he could begin processing what had happened to him, he heard a door open, then shut and then a man's voice.

"Where is he?" the man asked.

"In the closet," the girl said. "I drugged him, taped his mouth shut and wrapped his hands and feet in duct tape. He isn't going anywhere."

"What about the woman?"

"She's in there with him. They both should be unconscious for several more hours. I used enough sedative on her to knock out an elephant. I went light on him. I thought he should be semi-conscious when we kill him."

"That was a good idea. It might throw the police off."

Brad could hear one of them take a deep breath—probably the man, he thought—and then the male voice continued, "I'll pull them out of the closet and you unwrap their hands and feet. Okay?"

"Then what?" the female voice asked.

"Then, you open the window and I'll throw them both out. It will look like he pushed her first and then jumped himself. The perfect murder/suicide."

The girl giggled.

She actually giggled.

He was about to die at the hands of unknown assailants and one of them had the audacity to giggle. Maybe he heard her wrong; his head was still full of cobwebs.

She giggled again.

What the hell?

As he prepared for the inevitable, Brad was astonished to hear the girl ask her male companion if he
"wanted to do it on the couch right now?"

More astonishingly, he heard the sound of buttons being unsnapped, zippers repelling and clothes
hitting the floor. He saw shadows moving from side
to side and then up and down. Brad heard the two
strangers fall on to the couch. The squeaks of flesh
against leather filled the air.

What the fu...?

"You know killing always gets me fired up!" the
girl exclaimed, her voice raising an octave.

"I know; I've been with you right after. This
is the first time I've been with you during, though."
He paused and then after a few minutes of relative
silence, he said, "Wow, that was fantastic."

"My turn," Brad heard her say somewhat aggressively. A moment later, he heard the two fall back on
the couch. Again, the leather made a squeaking sound.

Brad listened to their moans for a few minutes.
He tried desperately to remove the tape from his
ankles while simultaneously avoiding any form of
unintended voyeurism. His brain told him to focus on
the duct tape. If the guy was a real stud, perhaps he
would have five or ten minutes before they finished
and came for him. He had to act fast.

Sadly, the guy was no sexual athlete.

Three minutes later, the closet door opened.
Full light flooded into the confined space like a crisp
morning sunrise. Brad Stephens, mortgage broker,

professional golf manager, husband and father, said a silent prayer and prepared for the worst.

He suddenly remembered coming up to the office earlier in the day. It was on the twenty-seventh floor.

It would be a long, long drop.